"Certain things are best left unspoken..."

Aiden whispered, backing her against the wall. For the love of God, she had to be the bonniest creature he'd ever seen. Aye, he'd dreamed of kissing her while enduring endless nights at sea.

How could a man resist such temptation? His hands slipped to her waist, so small he could nearly touch his fingertips together.

Maddie inhaled sharply. "M'lord?"

"Aye?" he growled, his tongue slipping across his lips as he enjoyed watching the rise and fall of her breasts with her quick breaths.

"Y-y-you think me bonny?"

Holy Christ, had she only just realized what he'd said when they'd started down the passageway? "Any man who isn't blinded by your radiance the moment he walks into a room is utterly blind."

When she parted her lips to speak, he silenced her. With a slight dip of his chin, he captured her mouth and plundered it with reckless abandon. He slid his hands up her spine and drew her body into his. Oh yes, this was exactly what he'd been craving...

ALSO BY AMY JARECKI

Lords of the Highlands series

The Highland Duke

THE
HIGHLAND
COMMANDER

A Lords of the Highlands Novel

AMY JARECKI

FOREVER

NEW YORK   BOSTON

Copyright © 2017 by Amy Jarecki
Preview of *The Highland Guardian* copyright © 2017 by Amy Jarecki
Cover design by Elizabeth Turner
Cover illustration by Craig White
Cover copyright © 2017 by Hachette Book Group, Inc.

Forever
Hachette Book Group
1290 Avenue of the Americas, New York, NY 10104
forever-romance.com
twitter.com/foreverromance

First Edition: June 2017

Forever is an imprint of Grand Central Publishing. The Forever name and logo are trademarks of Hachette Book Group, Inc.

The publisher is not responsible for websites (or their content) that are not owned by the publisher.

The Hachette Speakers Bureau provides a wide range of authors for speaking events. To find out more, go to www.hachettespeakersbureau.com or call (866) 376-6591.

ISBNs: 978-1-4555-9785-7 (mass market), 978-1-4555-9783-3 (ebook)

Printed in the United States of America

OPM

10 9 8 7 6 5 4 3 2 1

To the wonderful staff at Grand Central Publishing and Forever, especially my editor, Leah Hultenschmidt. Thank you for believing in me. I also want to thank Elizabeth Turner and the brilliant designers at GCP who have worked diligently to develop ideal covers for the Lords of the Highlands series. I give them general notes on my character's description and they come up with something amazing.

Chapter One

Stonehaven, Scotland, 31 December 1707

*N*ight made darker by dense clouds drew attention to the fireballs. They rolled down Allardice Street, illuminating men dressed in black who levered iron rods to push barrels of blazing tar toward the harbor. Lit only by flickering fires, the players' faces took on hollow shadows akin to the grim reaper.

Ghostly and cadaverous.

Atop the hill on the edge of Dunnottar Parish, Lady Magdalen Keith watched the spectacle below. She shuddered while her teeth chattered. During any Hogmanay celebration, Highland players were meant to look like Death, representing the old year's passing to give rise to the new. Maddie never cared to think about morbid endings. She preferred to look to the future.

Though she clutched her hands together inside a sealskin muff, the icy cold of winter made her shiver all the more.

Over the fur-lined collar of her cloak, she glanced at her father. "What do you wish for in the year of our Lord 1708?"

Dressed in dashing finery, the earl smiled, his eyes glistening from the light of the brazier burning beside them. "Perhaps 'tis time to bring the true king back from exile and boot his half sister off the throne?"

Maddie laughed. She could have predicted such a response. A consummate Jacobite, William Keith, Earl Marischal of Scotland, wasn't one to hide his true allegiance from his illegitimate daughter, though he did represent Aberdeenshire in the *new* British Parliament.

Regardless of his predictability, Maddie harbored her own reasons to agree with him. "I wish the queen would remove the vile dragoons patrolling the north. Two more women arrived at the hospital this morn—set upon by those beasts." Rape and pillage weren't new to the northeastern village of Stonehaven, but the miscreants had changed through the ages. Red-coated dragoons infesting the Highlands believed they had the right to take anything they pleased, including local women. Since before she was born, the entire island of Britain had been embroiled in war and unrest. And the present state of affairs had spurred Maddie to open a hospital as soon as she reached her majority two years past.

Da placed a firm hand on her shoulder and squeezed. "You're providing an honorable service. Of that you can be proud."

She pursed her lips. "I'd rather see our women safe than be prideful."

"That is why we must continue to fight for *the cause*." He gestured toward the dark outlines of two frigates moored in the harbor. "We shall think on that no more. Tonight we celebrate the new year. Have you your mask?"

"'Tis in the coach." Maddie glanced over her shoulder at the waiting team of horses. "Thank you for inviting me."

"Thank you for attending." His nostrils flared officiously. "I do wish we could spend more time together."

Rarely did Da ever make such a comment. Unaccustomed to words of affection, Maddie blinked to push away the sudden sting at the backs of her eyes. She'd been on her own since the age of seven, and though her father rarely denied her anything, he was a capricious presence in her life. Due to his station, he was oft away in London. Otherwise he spent his time with his new wife and children. Regrettably, the countess, Lady Mary, refused to include Magdalen as part of the family.

Thoroughly snubbed, Maddie had pledged her life to proving her value to society—not to the aristocracy, but to the people who comprised Scotland's backbone. True, she'd maintained the title of Lady Magdalen Keith, but she didn't feel very ladylike. Nor did she feel aristocratic. In fact, she communed far better with those who frequented her small hospital than she did with her father. Regardless, she appreciated the time Da spared for her, and his unfaltering maintenance, which supported her cause of the care of battered women.

Moon glow shone through a break in the clouds over the harbor. She pointed to bobbing skiffs ferrying men from the ships to shore. "It looks like they'll catch the end of the fireball parade."

"Are you excited for the dancing?" Da asked.

"*Mortified* is more apt." She cringed. "I've only ever danced with Tristan."

"You'll be fine. As a matter of fact, I recall the old guard was quite light on his feet in his day."

"Aye? So says Agnes."

Da always gave Maddie a sideways look when she mentioned her lady's maid, though Agnes had been Magdalen's companion since birth. He tweaked his daughter's hood. "A masque is a delightful way to flirt with society incognito. I know you to be a lady of sober character. However, you can be as unabashed as you please on the dance floor this eve and none will be the wiser." He offered his elbow. "I suggest you dance with the officers. They'll be wanting to kick up their heels. I daresay an officer in the Royal Navy would be a good catch for you, my dear—something to think on for certain."

Placing her hand in the crook of Da's arm, Maddie sighed. "Mayhap, as long as he's a Scot and doesn't mind living in Stonehaven." Which she doubted would be the case. Sailors were renowned for being adventuresome. Elsewise who on earth would be able to tolerate such deplorable conditions while living aboard a ship, constantly at the mercy of the sea?

* * *

After riding from Stonehaven Harbour to Dunnottar Castle, First Lieutenant Aiden Murray stepped out of the coach and stretched. Dear Lord, it felt good to be off the ship.

"Bloody oath, 'tis so cold my cods are about to freeze," Second Lieutenant MacBride said. He must have received top marks in complaining at university, for he never ceased to have something unpleasant to say.

"Then you'd best keep moving, else someone else will be plowing your wife's roses," said Captain Thomas Polwarth. God love the man, he could be counted on for a stern retort to any complaint.

As Aiden turned, his jaw dropped. Aye, he'd heard tales of the magnificence of Dunnottar, but even beneath the cover of darkness, he was awestruck as he beheld the dramatic fortress dominating the expansive peninsula ahead. A steep path led down to the shore, and from there torches illuminated hundreds of steps climbing to the arched gateway, looking like something straight out of medieval folklore. On the wall-walk above, sentries stood guard, their forms lit by braziers with flames leaping high on this chilly eve.

"This way." Aiden beckoned, leading the men down the steep path.

"Would you have a look at that," said Third Lieutenant MacPherson, Aiden's wayward cabinmate. "Christ. How in God's name did Cromwell take this fortress? I reckon our cannons would miss her curtain walls by a hundred feet from the *Royal Mary*, even with all guns cranked to the timbers."

"She has stood the test of time for certain," Aiden called over his shoulder, speeding the pace. "Quit your gawking and make haste. I'm starved." He was, too. He'd been on duty until the ship anchored and missed his meal to catch one of the last skiffs to shore. With the promise of something tastier than the *Royal Mary*'s pickled herring, there was no bloody chance he'd miss the fare the Earl Marischal would serve this Hogmanay eve.

"Have you been here afore, Your Lordship?" Aiden's superior officer, the captain, used his formal address only to be an arse.

"Never, sir."

"I would have thought the duke and the earl would have been kissing cousins."

Aiden looked skyward with a shake of his head. "I beg your pardon, sir. My da's a Whig and the earl sides with the Tory party."

"Bloody Whigs," said MacPherson.

Aiden chose not to respond. Since the Act of Union one year past forced England's merger with Scotland's navy, he'd grown more sympathetic with the Tories as well. Though he'd rather not let his loyalties become common knowledge at the moment. He'd be the one to break the news to his father in due course.

As they started the steep climb up to the gates, Polwarth slipped and crashed into Aiden's back. "God's teeth, 'tis slicker than an icy deck."

Steadying the captain with his elbow, Aiden chuckled under his breath. Fit as a stag, he could sprint up the steep slope to the gate even with ice making the stone steps slippery. And it was all he could do to suppress his urge to run. Officers didn't race through castle gates like wee lads. But by the saints, he'd been aboard the *Royal Mary* for the past month without setting foot ashore. Bloody oath, he intended to kick up his heels this eve—swill ale, swing the lassies in a reel—mayhap he'd even find a bonny lass he fancied.

Damn the cold.

Damn political posturing.

Damn the war.

And whilst I'm at it, damn the queen.

This was Hogmanay—a pagan Scottish holiday—and he would enjoy the piss out of it for once in his miserable high-born life.

Before he reached the gate, he stopped and looked to his companions, thirty paces behind and looking like a gaggle of old men. "Put on your bloody masks."

"What?" sniggered MacPherson. "Do you not want to hear your name boomed throughout the hall?"

MacBride laughed. "The Right Royal and Very Miserable—"

"Don't forget *Honorable*," piped Captain Polwarth.

True, Aiden could tolerate a ribbing from his mates, but the captain? Good God, he was sunk.

"Aye, the Miserable yet Honorable Lord Aiden Murray," MacBride finished.

"Shut it." Aiden tied his bandit's mask in place just beneath his tricorn hat. The officers had received masks from groomsmen once they'd reached the shore—compliments of the earl, as were the coaches that had ferried them to the castle. "Last I checked I was First Lieutenant Murray, division officer of the watch."

Stepping beside him, Captain Polwarth clapped his shoulder. "Nay, tonight you're a courtier behind a mask, m'lord."

"A rogue," said MacBride.

MacPherson snorted. "A rake."

"I'm a bloody maker of merriment." Aiden gave him a shove. "Give me a meal and a tankard of ale and I'll be in heaven."

"Not me. I'm looking for a woman to ignite my fire." MacPherson secured his long-beaked mask in place. At least Aiden didn't have to put up with a crook on his face that looked like a phallus.

MacBride pushed to the lead. "Ye ken what you need, Murray?"

Aiden followed beneath the sharp-spiked portcullis. "I ken I bloody well do not need you to tell me."

"Och aye?" MacBride snorted. "'Tis on account of you're too embarrassed."

"You're full of shite." Aiden threw his shoulders back and clenched his fists. He could best every one of them, and showing an iota of fear now would only serve to illicit a month of jibes in the officers' quarters—but he knew what was coming, and the twist in his gut only served to increase his dread.

"I agree with MacBride." MacPherson jabbed him in the shoulder. "Young Aiden here needs to dip his wick."

"Ye miserable, ox-brained maggot." Aiden could have slammed his fist into the papier mâché beak on the bastard's mask. They'd all guessed he was a virgin, though he'd *never* admitted it to a soul. How was he supposed to sample the offerings of the finer sex? He'd gone to university at the age of seventeen, spent three years with his nose in volumes of books, and from there joined the Scottish navy, where he'd scarcely had a chance to step ashore. Aye, the whores in port always tempted him, rubbing their buxom breasts against his chest, but it took only one peek at a flesh ulcer to turn his gut inside out.

At the age of two and twenty, the last thing he needed was to contract the bloody pox.

Regardless of his experience or lack thereof, Aiden refused to allow MacPherson's remark to pass. Oh no. There wasn't a self-respecting sailor in all of Christendom who wasn't man enough to come back with a retort. "And whilst we're ashore, make certain you go shag your mother."

Take that, ye bastard.

Before the braggart could take a swing and start a brawl on the icy gateway steps, a yeoman stepped between them. "Welcome the Royal Scots Navy."

Aiden shot a look to Captain Polwarth and grinned. "It seems news of the Act of Union hasn't reached this far north."

"Beg your pardon, sir," said the yeoman. "Only the *Royal Mary* and the *Caledonia* are moored in our harbor. Mark me. No bleeding English warships would be welcomed to a Hogmanay gathering at Dunnottar."

"I would think no less from the Earl Marischal," said the captain.

"Indeed." The yeoman gestured to the gatehouse. "Gentlemen, if you'll check your weapons, we shall escort you to the gallery."

Chapter Two

Once they were inside the enormous fortress grounds, a sentry ushered Aiden and the other officers past the old keep to the north range, where stood the more modern buildings of the castle. Luck rained down upon him when he found the dining hall spread with platters piled with meats and slices of fine white bread to fill his gullet. Aiden continually ate like a glutton, yet never managed to put on an ounce of fat.

Tankards of ale in hand, he and Lieutenant Fraser MacPherson headed from the dining hall to the long gallery, where the music had already grown jaunty. Though constantly at odds with him, Aiden always stepped ashore with the stout Highlander, the son of the MacPherson laird. They quarreled like brothers, though if Aiden had to choose anyone from the crew to watch his back, it would be Fraser MacPherson...or the captain.

Aiden jabbed his mate in the ribs. "Why did you choose a beaked mask? You look like a charlatan."

"Isn't that what a masquerade is about?" MacPherson's

grin stretched under the ugly black nose. "Besides, the lassies like charlatans."

Aiden rather doubted such wisdom. "Do they now?"

"Aye, but you wouldn't ken anything about that, young pup."

"Two years my senior and you're so much wiser in the ways of the world, aye?" Pushing through the crowd toward a gathering of more masked gentlemen, Aiden took a healthy swallow of ale.

"Too right." MacPherson slapped him on the back, making froth slop down Aiden's doublet.

He brushed away the mess. "Well then, why is it I outrank you?"

"That's easy. Your father's a duke."

Nothing like a cutting slight to make Aiden's gut clench—most every officer in the navy was the second son of a noble lord. "You ken as well as I my da has nothing to do with my rank." Holy Christ, how many times must he prove himself? Being the second son of a duke should have made his lot easier, but thus far his birthright had only brought a heavier burden. Aiden had learned early on that he had to be better skilled with a sword, have better aim with a musket, be wittier at the captain's table, and sing like a lark while doing it all.

His biggest problem?

Aiden hadn't yet perfected the art of being a rake.

According to every officer he knew, Aiden should have established his reputation in every port in Britain. Unfortunately, thus far he'd failed miserably. Of course he blamed the *Royal Mary*'s ridiculously long stints at sea. How in God's name was a sailor supposed to gain experience in the boudoir when aboard a ship full of foulmouthed, smelly men?

"Jesus, I've died and have gone to heaven." MacPherson's jaw dropped like a simpleton's while he gaped at the dancers.

Aiden followed his friend's line of sight. He inhaled sharply, and his fist tightened around his tankard's handle. The woman dancing a reel smiled as if a dozen torches formed an archway around her. She wore a shimmering blue gown, and her fair tresses curled down the back of a slender neck, secured by a plume of feathers. Though a bejeweled mask hid part of her face, by the smile on her rosy lips, Aiden could tell the lass was bonny—possibly the bonniest woman in the gallery. In an instant his breathing turned ragged, his curiosity sizzled. If only he could slip behind her and untie the mask's bow and reveal all of her face. Was her porcelain skin completely flawless?

She skipped and twirled like a nymph. Above the drum and fiddle, Aiden caught her laughter. Not high-pitched like a silly gel's, but sultry, stirring a base desire that had become familiar.

His heart practically leaped out of his chest.

MacPherson gave him a nudge. "I saw her first."

Aiden arched an eyebrow. "Stand down. That's an order." Being a senior officer did have its merits, and before the braggart could make a move, Aiden strode straight to the line of dancers. He tapped the lady's partner on the shoulder. "Cutting in."

The man gave a haughty cough. "I beg your pardon? Have you officers forgotten your manners whilst at sea?"

"Forgive me, sir. I meant no impertinence, 'tis just that the ship sets sail at dawn and I haven't much time." Perhaps the rake in him had finally come to call. Aiden handed the man his tankard of ale, then stared directly at the lady, who stood aghast with her hands on her hips while the other dancers skipped in a circle. He bowed slowly and politely. The last thing he needed was to ruin his chances before he even kent the lassie's name. "Forgive me, m'lady. Regrettably, poor sailors must make merry when the opportunity arises. Have mercy on a young lieutenant. On the morrow I'll be back at sea for months on end, leagues away from civilization." *And such sweet visions as this lass.*

Gripping the tankard with white knuckles, the man didn't budge. "Do you approve, my dear?"

The beauty gave Aiden a look from head to toe. "Very well. After all, you told me to ensure the officers enjoy the merriment this eve."

Aiden sized up the man. Far older, he was nearly as tall and broad shouldered as Aiden. He wore finely tailored velvet and sported a periwig that had not a hair out of place. Recognizing nobility, Aiden again bowed. "I thank you, m'lord."

The lass resumed the reel, regarding Aiden with an enormous pair of blue eyes peeping through her mask—blues as enchanting as shimmering crystals.

He quickly joined the men's line, thanking his mother for her interminable enforced hours of dreary dancing lessons.

"You're light on your feet for a sailor," the lass said as they moved together and joined elbows. Heavens, her voice sounded alluring, like nothing he'd before heard.

"Thank you." A subtle grin played across his lips. "But my polish is nothing compared to your grace."

She actually laughed out loud—quite audacious for a lady. Nonetheless her laughter tickled him on the inside. "Do not tell a soul, but this is the first time I've danced with anyone besides my frumpy old guard."

He threw his thumb over his shoulder. "That man was your guard?"

"Nay." A delightful laugh pealed through her lips. "He doesn't count."

Aiden liked that even better—it sounded as if she had even less experience than he. At least he'd stolen a kiss or two in his youth. Perhaps he'd steal another this night. He grasped her hands and sashayed through the two lines, a line of men facing a line of women. "Then I am even more impressed."

"Which is your ship?" she asked, her fair eyebrows arching above her mask.

"The *Royal Mary*."

"It must be exciting to see exotic places."

A frigate, the *Royal Mary* mainly patrolled the waters of Scotland, and now England. Not exactly exotic. "Aye, but 'tisn't much fun when you're under cannon fire."

Those blues grew rounder beneath her mask. "Cannons?"

"Aye, we are at war, miss." His shoulders fell when the dance commanded he take a place in the men's line and wait for the next couple to sashay through. Across the aisle the young lady seemed enlivened by their separation, smiling and clapping. Though poised like a queen, she had a warmer, more common quality about her. Possibly it was that she actually looked as if she was having a good time rather than donning aristocratic airs and pretending she merely endured the dance.

The tune ended and Aiden dipped into a bow.

"Mind if I step in?" asked Fraser MacPherson from behind.

"Yes, I do mind," Aiden said in a strained whisper, careful of his language given the present company.

The lovely masked lady across the aisle clasped her hands together. "My father said there wouldn't be enough partners for the officers and encouraged me to dance with any gentleman who asked."

The only problem was that MacPherson was no gentleman. He'd spirit her to some dingy cellar and seduce her with charm until he had her skirts hiked up around her thighs.

The innocent lass would succumb to the rogue's wiles before she realized what was happening.

Aiden groaned. Throwing a fist was out of the question.

She wanted to take a turn with the beak-masked ugly varlet? Holy crosses, MacPherson was shorter than she by a half inch at least. But Aiden bowed. No use causing a stir over a silly reel—though he'd be watching his cabinmate closely. "As you wish, m'lady."

When he turned, slender fingers wrapped around his wrist. Cool fingers softer than brushed doe leather. "Thank you, sir." Oh yes, and a voice smoother than melted butter.

Heaven help him, Aiden couldn't stay irritated when a smile as radiant as hers lit up the entire hall. "Perhaps another turn anon?" he asked.

"I'd be honored," the lass said as the piper launched into another country dance.

Fraser nudged him out of the line. "Go on and assuage your thirst."

"And you watch your manners." A little lighter on his feet, Aiden took a goblet of wine from a passing servant and surveyed the hall. Indeed, the men outnumbered the women by at least two to one. But what could a sailor expect so far north, with two ships in port? True, several other lassies danced gaily, though there was only one from whom Aiden could not pull his gaze.

Sipping, he watched the nymph from behind his goblet. Though her eyes were shadowed behind her mask, he thought she glanced his way.

His heart thrummed when she met his stare a second time—a direct meeting of the eyes for certain.

He straightened his neckerchief, wishing he'd spent a bit more time in front of the dingy looking glass he shared with MacPherson—the same toad with whom the lady still danced.

With his next blink, Aiden's gut clamped hard as a rock. Heat flared across his nape as he took a step toward the dancers.

Had Fraser's hand nearly skimmed her breast? It happened so fast he couldn't be sure, but those thick fingers came awfully close.

Grumbling under his breath, Aiden took a healthy swig of wine. If the lieutenant made *any* move aside from kicking up his heels for a sashay, Aiden would bury his fist in the bastard's beak, and not the one on his mask.

Aboard ship the braggart had gloated plenty about his conquests. That might be acceptable talk around dockyards and at sea, but MacPherson had best keep his kilt hanging down around his knees when it came to courting ladies. Besides, the man was merely a chieftain's third son.

"The maid is quite lovely, is she not?" The gentleman who had been dancing with the lass earlier stood beside Aiden. His black mask appeared menacing under the curl of his periwig, and he maintained a tilt to his chin as if he held a position of great importance.

Given the present company, Aiden didn't doubt the man's exalted rank, though he was starting to abhor masquerade balls. He preferred to know to whom he spoke. By the lines etched around the nobleman's mouth, he appeared older, but before another word was said, a question had to be asked. "Have you spoken for her?"

"Hardly." The lord laughed, relaxing his stance. "Let us just say I have a vested interest in the maid's welfare."

Hell, that could mean anything. Worse, the words *vested interest* added layers of complexity to Aiden's simple desire to dance with the lass and prevent his mate from raising her skirts. "Forgive me, m'lord, but may I ask your name?"

A wry grin played across the man's lips. "Och, this is a masque, son."

"Right—perhaps it is not the best of ideas to invite a parcel of naval officers to a masquerade. Mind you, these officers have been a month at sea without setting eyes on a woman." Aiden leaned in. "And I can tell you right now the beaked mask dancing with your *vested interest* is looking for more than a wee turn on the dance floor this eve."

Periwig-Nobleman stroked his fingers down his aristocratic chin. "You are outspoken for such a young fellow."

Aiden raised his goblet. "I was brought up to speak my mind."

"Well then, if you must ken, I am your host."

Good God, he'd just launched into a war of words with an earl, telling him his gathering was a bad idea? Could he jam his shoe any farther into his throat? Lord knew the square toe was about to end up in his own arse. Aiden bowed. "Forgive me, m'lord. I spoke out of turn."

"Honestly, I've thought the same myself. I was young once and I'd recognize a licentious pup from a hundred paces. Why, that fellow Maddie is dancing with had best slip his tongue back in his mouth and pay a mind to his footwork."

Aiden swiped his hand across his lips to ensure his tongue was in its proper place.

Maddie? Is she a Matilda? Madeline? Mary?

"'Tis why I'm watching him, m'lord...ah, to ensure his hands and his tongue remain where they belong." Aiden wouldn't tell the earl that when it came to women, he didn't trust Fraser MacPherson any further than his nose, but he certainly could pledge to keep an eye on the rake.

The earl's gaze narrowed. "Pray, what is your name... ah...Lieutenant, is it?"

"Aye, first lieutenant and master of the watch, Lord Aiden Murray." Sliding his foot forward, he bowed.

"Atholl's son?"

"Second son, m'lord."

"And the man dancing with my ... um ... *vested interest*?"

"Third Lieutenant Fraser MacPherson. His da's a chieftain."

"Is he the heir?"

"Third son, m'lord."

"Hmm." The earl clapped Aiden on the shoulder. "I do believe the maid looks a tad flushed. Might I suggest you offer her refreshment?"

An awkward flurry spread through Aiden's stomach. "It would be an honor ... if I can pull her away from the dance floor?"

"Leave that to me." The earl started off, then turned. "And keep her away from that MacPherson fellow. If his choice in masks is any indication, I'd prefer it if the lass had no more interaction with him."

* * *

No sooner had the music stopped than the crowd all but swallowed up the officer in the beaked mask. Maddie breathed a sigh of relief. The man had gripped her waist with a heavy hand and tugged her much too close during the promenade. He reminded her of an overly anxious, drooling deerhound.

"Would you care for a refreshment?" a deep voice asked. Though low, it was clearly audible, as if a man had come up from behind and pressed his lips to her ear. Maddie turned. Gooseflesh pebbled over her skin. Goodness, the tall, slender officer with a bandit's mask grinned as he held out a goblet. "'Tis watered wine."

"My thanks." She took the offering and sipped, happy he hadn't tried to give her something more potent.

He stared at her for a moment, as if watching her drink

was a most interesting occupation. Then his teeth grazed his bottom lip—such a slight gesture, but one that made her breath catch.

A flutter tickled her insides.

Was he feeling as awkward as she?

At least when dancing, she had something to keep her mind occupied.

Heavens, there were so many masked people and she did feel out of sorts. Maddie hadn't ever been invited to a large gathering—at least not since her father had married Lady Mary so very long ago.

The dashing tall man grinned. White teeth. Dimples. Perhaps the dimples made him a wee bit boyish—but endearingly so. Maddie looked closer. Goodness, his eyes were the most expressive shade of moss.

"This is my first masquerade." He rolled his *r*'s with a Highland burr for certain, but there was something more precise in his enunciation. In fact, he spoke similarly to her da.

And he looks to be young—not wrinkled and crusty like many of the other gentlemen here.

"Mine, too," she admitted.

"Are you having a good time?"

"Of sorts." She sipped. "'Tis fun to dance, but I would prefer to see people's faces."

"I'd prefer to see *your* face, m'lady." Though his words were cheeky, his expression remained quite sober.

Gracious, her face burned. "You are brash, sir."

"Forgive me." He dipped his chin in apology. "I meant that I would be blessed to gaze upon your entire countenance, for I am quite convinced it is bonnier than your lovely mask."

She snapped open her fan and fanned her face. "Now I'm quite certain you've made me blush right to my toes."

"Such color would become you, m'lady." He again bowed

his head. "Now I've experienced one, I'd say a masque is a wee bit sinister."

She laughed. In fact, she'd thought the very same thing, especially when dancing with Beak-Mask. "Aye—it seems hiding one's face allows for more groping."

Those vivid green eyes narrowed with flash of ire. "Has someone touched you inappropriately?" His tone had a growl to it, as if he might fight for her virtue right then and there.

Maddie quickly shook her head. "'Twas nothing I shouldn't allow to pass." She glanced around the hall. People congregated in groups, and her father stood by the hearth, apparently talking to the beak-masked officer, Da's man-at-arms in tow. That didn't bode well for her former dance partner.

She again regarded the officer who'd offered her refreshment. He stood at a respectable distance while he sipped his wine. A pleasant countenance—what she could see of it. His lips were thinnish, though the bottom lip fuller, and beneath the black cloth his nose suited his face—straight and angular, somewhat like his sturdy jaw. Her fingers twitched. What would he look like if she removed the mask?

Wigless, he wore his walnut-colored locks pulled back and tied with a bow at his nape. The torchlight flickered, bringing out auburn highlights. If only she could finger a lock and hold it to a candle. "What color is your hair?" she asked, leaning in.

"Brown." He flicked one of her curls with the tip of his finger. "Dull compared to yours." He took a step closer and eyed her intently. "I'd call your coloring burnt honey."

"Oh, would you now?" As a matter of fact, her serving maid, Agnes, oft used that very term.

"'Tis lovely." He lifted a lock to his nose. "And bears the scent of lilacs in spring."

She leaned back far enough for her tresses to slip from his fingers. "How much wine have you consumed, sir?"

He grinned—an infectious smile that made her want to laugh. "Not enough by far."

Maddie strolled toward the wall so they wouldn't appear as conspicuous as when standing in the center of the gallery. "Forgive me for not asking earlier, but have you found the masque to be a pleasant diversion from your shipboard duties?" She tapped her lips. "Ah, regardless of the clandestine nature of these affairs."

He chuckled—a deep roll, sounding a wee bit devilish. "I would attend a masque every night if it meant avoiding my mundane life aboard ship. Though I do prefer smaller gatherings than this."

"As do I."

The officer leaned against the wall and finished his goblet before placing it on a passing servant's tray. "Would you be missed if we took a stroll atop the wall-walk?"

Honestly, that sounded like the best idea she'd heard in sennights. "In the cold?" What would Da say if she allowed a strange masked man to accompany her on a turn around the battlements? At least there was a guard posted at every corner, so this sailor couldn't try to take advantage—could he? Jitters flitted about her skin. She'd seen many a woman who had been abused by a savage redcoat, but this gentleman had the manners of an earl and wore neither red nor a saber in his belt.

"Forgive me." He cringed while deep dimples formed at the corners of his mouth. "At sea it seems there's always a cold wind blowing a gale with rain spitting in your face. If a man doesn't grow impervious to it, he's in for a miserable cruise."

How could she resist such a grin—and those expressive

green eyes? Aye, he seemed delightfully chivalrous. "Perhaps if I donned my cloak." She glanced to her father, who was still talking to Beak-Mask. "Mayhap we need a guard to chaperone?"

Mr. Moss-Green Eyes bowed. "I could perform as both chaperone and companion. Besides, I'm the officer of the watch aboard the *Royal Mary*, skilled in all manner of defense."

Her gaze trailed to his arm. Though at first she'd considered him lean, the tall man's muscles stretched taut his woolen doublet sleeve. Indeed, such a man was hewn from solid Highland stock. "Then I shall trust you to uphold a code of chivalry, sir."

Chapter Three

*H*e could have been walking on air when Aiden took the lady's elbow to assist her to step out onto the blustery wall-walk. But no mere wind could cut through Aiden's armor—not when the thrill of anticipation fired across his skin. The lass, however, nestled her hands in a sealskin muff and shivered.

"Is it too cold for you, m'lady?" he asked, silently cursing propriety for not allowing him to slide his arm across her shoulders and impart a wee bit of his warmth. Hell, the way his heart hammered, he might have just run a footrace. He couldn't feel the cold now even if he wanted to.

She bunched her shoulders together. "No, no. 'Tis all right for a time."

Aiden thumped his forehead with the heel of his hand, unfastened his cloak, and swung it around her shoulders. "Perhaps this will help stave off the frigid air a wee bit longer."

She grasped the collar as if she planned to give it back. "Oh no, sir. I couldn't."

He held up his palm. "Please. It gives me much pleasure to see to your comfort." Oh Lord in heaven, the smile playing on her lips was worth spending an entire night in the freezing snow without a cloak.

She paused at a crenel notch and gazed out over the sea. "Goodness, we're up so high."

Such a statement further increased Aiden's curiosity. She was a person in whom the earl held a great interest, yet she was unfamiliar with the wall-walk at the most illustrious of the Earl Marischal's castles. "You haven't been up here before?"

"Not since I was a wee lassie. Last I remember I couldn't even peek through a crenel and my father had to lift me up to see. I suppose I mustn't have been afraid at the time because Da had ahold of me."

Aiden strengthened his grip on her elbow and moved to the outside position to help her feel more secure. "And who is your father?"

"Och, is that not why we are wearing masks...so our identities will remain in question?"

"I suppose, though I'd like to ken your name regardless." Aiden hadn't let on that he'd caught her moniker, Maddie. She'd probably be mortified if she were aware he'd garnered such a tidbit without knowing her title.

Bloody titles. Contrary to popular belief, they do not define a man. But it would be nice to know the full name of this lass, title or nay.

They proceeded slowly while the icy chill practically froze his nose, though the rest of him remained warm as a brazier—two years aboard ship had a way of hardening a man. Standing at the helm of the *Royal Mary*, Aiden had endured worse. And presently he had more important matters to ponder than the weather.

"What if we exchanged familiar names?" he asked, hedging. "Then it would be our secret."

The lady's brow arched above her mask. "Ooo, a slip of confidence known only to us."

"Aye." When they rounded a corner that blocked the wind a bit, he pulled her to a stop.

A delightful smile played upon her lips. "Can I trust you to keep such incriminating information silent? After all, my reputation might be in peril if anyone kent it was I strolling atop the wall-walk with a lieutenant who claimed to be both my companion and my chaperone."

The lass certainly did have a sharp wit. Aiden chuckled. "Your secret is safe with me, m'lady." He leaned against the wall, allowing his gaze to sweep from the top of her head down to her diminutive satin slippers. She was a bit more than a head shorter, and her height suited him ideally. "My name is Aiden." He tucked a wisp of hair into her hood. "See, that wasn't all that difficult."

Cocking her head, she eyed him. "I'm Magdalen."

He drew in a sharp breath. Of all the *M* names he could think of, he'd never considered Magdalen, a name associated with a woman reputed to be—

"Does my name surprise you?" she asked with a wee edge to her voice.

"Uh...of course not. I think it is lovely." After all, Magdalen had an air of mystery to it.

Intriguing.

He moved his hand to her waist. Lord only knew what had prompted him to do that, other than the moist glow of her lips, pursed and looking incredibly delicious.

A kiss on Hogmanay just might bring him the luck he needed.

He knew he was staring, being forward and a bit unmannerly, but he was stunned, as if frozen in place, unable to avert his eyes. Had a woman's mouth ever looked so inviting? Aiden doubted he'd ever been so charged to be near a woman. Well dressed, well spoken. And oh, his mind ran amok when the wind changed, showering him with the intoxicating scent of lilacs.

Maintaining his gaze on Maddie's mouth, he lightly brushed his lips across hers—a wee testing of the waters. Aiden's heart beat erratically. Nothing cold existed in all of Scotland as their lips made the slightest of contact—not quite a kiss, though it was a firm promise of more to come.

He gazed into her eyes—eyes he wanted to see entirely unshaded by a mask. "Why is it you are so captivating, Lady Magdalen?" He'd spent far too much time at sea. Was this what he'd been missing? What the sailors endlessly dreamed about? Stealing kisses? Raising skirts? He brushed his fingers over her...his...woolen cloak while his knees practically turned to boneless mollusks. Could he chance a wee tryst? Create a memory to fill his mind while he spent countless hours at watch on the navigation deck?

She chuckled, a deep, womanly laugh that made his chest swell. "And you are dark and mysterious, Lord Aiden."

Me? Nay, nay. It must be the mask. But I reckon I like her words—dark and mysterious.

Indeed, the lass played this masquerade ruse to perfection. There was no way she could possibly know he was a lord, and she wasn't about to correct him on his use of *lady*. But that was the last thing on his mind.

His other hand slid to her waist.

"May I kiss you, m'lady?" Och aye, his voice had grown gravelly, and deeper than he'd ever heard it before.

"But you have already kissed me." She batted those feathery eyelashes.

He chuckled. "That was no kiss, lass." He dipped his chin and lowered his mouth until he was but a finger's breadth away, daring her to close the gap.

A new surge of tingles coursed over his skin while the lady's gaze shifted to his lips after a moment's hesitation.

A wee sigh slipped through her mouth while she moistened them. No more beguiling invitation had ever been made. Cupping her cheek, he plied her mouth, soft and unhurried at first. When the lady didn't pull away, he teased her lips with his tongue.

Back and forth he swept his tongue until the lady parted her lips and allowed him inside. Mercy, his knees weakened with the warmth and rush of sweet ambrosia. His hand slipped up her spine as he fought to maintain control of his hardening cock. Backing her against the wall, swirling his hips into her, would be complete heaven. A kiss from an angel? Indeed, he would remember this moment for the rest of his days.

"You there," called a menacing voice as footsteps slapped the stone battlements. "Why are you up here in the blustering snow? You'd best hasten back to the hall afore you pair freeze in that embrace."

With a squeak Magdalen jumped so high, Aiden clamped his hands to prevent her from falling off the walk. Easing his grip, he pulled her behind him to ensure no one would recognize her and therefore tarnish her reputation. Looking down, he noticed the layer of white snow covering his doublet. How long had it been snowing?

What in God's name have I been thinking? 'Tis blizzarding up here, for Christ's sake.

He cleared his throat and addressed the sentry. "You are right, sir. We shall return to the hall forthwith."

Aiden quickly ducked into the stairwell and led the lady down the many winding steps.

"You handled that well," she whispered, though her words echoed like a gong.

"Oh?"

"Firstly, you protected my identity just as you said you would."

"As any true gentleman should. And secondly?"

"I'm surprised you didn't try to stand up to the guard. After all, you're an officer—and you're twice as big as that man."

"Aye, but you could have been hurt and the guard would certainly have caused a stir. I wouldn't have wanted that to happen in the presence of a lady." Aiden stopped and faced her. Though she stood on the stair above, she was still shorter than he. "Especially a nymph who can kiss like an angel."

She giggled, her smile radiant even in the dark. "You've kissed many angels, have you?"

His fingers grew a mind of their own and slid to the back of her neck. "Nary a one, but I daresay I ken an angel when I kiss one."

This time when their mouths joined, the timid woman from the wall-walk proved more adventuresome. Magdalen matched him swirl for swirl as they kissed in the dark stairwell with no one the wiser. His mind completely blanked. She consumed him wholly. The stone stairwell spun like a wheel while a driving need hit him low and rendered him a slave to lust. Trembling fingers sank into her skirts and clenched them in his fists. If only this were a loose woman on the wharf or a courtier with a world of experience—a woman who could usher him through the world of passion.

If only.

With a heavy sigh, she pulled away and rested her forehead against his. "Och, dear Aiden. You kiss like a prince, though your ship will set sail on the morrow and I shan't lay eyes on you again."

A melancholy void swelled through his chest. "Must you remind me?"

"Aye, I must. I've seen too many women ruined by tinkers and sailors, and I've no mind to be one of them." She smoothed soft fingers over his cheek. "But I'll not forget my first kiss given by a gallant officer ashore for the Hogmanay festival—ashore for only one night. I shall cherish this moment in my heart and never tell a soul."

* * *

Humming, Maddie held out her arms while Agnes unlaced her stays.

"Given the hour, I'm surprised you're still on your feet, m'lady, but you sound as if you could continue dancing until the sun rises." Matronly and caring, Agnes Dixon meant the world to Maddie. As far back as she could remember, the gently aging lady's maid with kind and shiny blue eyes had posed as mother as well as servant.

"If the fiddler was still playing, I reckon I'd still be sashaying through Da's gallery."

"Oh?" Agnes pulled away the constricting stays and set them on the dressing table. "But I thought you didn't care overmuch for dancing."

Maddie watched herself in the looking glass and swayed. "'Tis different with an orchestra of minstrels, especially when there are so many gentlemen with whom to dance."

Agnes smiled in the mirror, looking pleased. "I'm happy you had a good time."

"'Twas perfect."

"Perfect?" Agnes let out a snort and urged Maddie down

to the stool, where the maid set to pulling out hairpins as if she were plucking a chicken. "I cannot for the life of me understand why the earl chose that drafty old castle for the Hogmanay celebration."

"Ow." Maddie rubbed her head where strands of hair had come out with a rather resistant pin. "I think it was an ideal location. Besides, it was nice to see the old place filled with masked merrymakers."

"Och, and a masquerade of all things." Agnes picked up the brush and set to making quick work of brushing out Maddie's curls. "Your da is shameless. I do hope no one behaved poorly. I've heard such gatherings can be scandalous."

Maddie smiled on the inside. She had partaken in a wee scandalous act herself, though she'd promised utmost secrecy. "I wouldn't ken about that. I danced every set." *Except perhaps one or two—but I cannot account for those since I was strolling on the wall-walk with Aiden.*

Maddie suppressed her urge to laugh.

How delightfully scandalous to call a perfect stranger by the familiar... and kiss him.

"Well, I worried the entire time you were gone." Agnes set down the brush and headed for the garderobe.

"Oh please. Surely after caring for me for twenty years, you ken I'd never act irresponsibly." *For the most part.* Maddie sneezed.

Agnes pulled out a woolen dressing gown with a look of alarm stretching down her careworn features. "Oh my heavens, you see what I mean? That old castle is so drafty I imagine a gale was blowing through the gallery and chilling you to the bone."

"Nay, it was toasty warm." Maddie slipped her arms inside and tied the sash.

Turning to the hearth, the lady's maid picked up the tongs

and stirred the fire. "Mayhap you didn't notice the cold whilst you were dancing."

"It was only chilly when Da and I watched the Hogmanay fireball celebration from Dunnottar Hill."

The stirring stopped. "You did what?"

Maddie plucked the tongs from the maid's fingers and hung them back on the mantel hearth. "Goodness, Agnes, sometimes you speak to me as if you're my mother."

"Forgive me, m'lady. I only worry after your health."

"Well, I have never felt better." Maddie ambled toward the bed.

Wringing her hands, Agnes followed. "Nonetheless, I shall bring you a cup of chamomile tea."

"I'd like that." She retrieved her book from the bedside table. "Not because I have a sniffle, but because a warm drink will soothe my thumping heart."

The lady's maid clapped her palms atop her coif. "Oh Lord in heaven, do tell me the earl ensured you were well chaperoned every moment."

"Of course." Maddie twirled in place. "Besides, dancing is quite invigorating. It makes one's heart beat ever so fast."

Agnes pursed her lips with a pointed stare. "That had best be the only reason for your outbreak of merriment."

"Oh please. Listening to you carry on, you would have me believe happiness is an affliction of the head."

"It is." Agnes picked up Maddie's petticoats from the floor. "I can attest to that a hundred times over."

She stopped dancing and planted her fists on her hips. "My heavens, Agnes. You've alluded to having a miserable life a number of times of late. Tell me true, if being my lady's maid is so disagreeable, why not seek other employment?"

The woman smiled, though with a touch of sadness in her blue eyes. "Och, child." Moving forward, Agnes smoothed her palm over Maddie's cheek. "The only happiness in this old woman's life is you. I'd wilt like a vine without water if I ever lost you."

"Well, you have nothing to worry about there." She clutched her book to her chest. "On the morrow Hogmanay will be forgotten and we will be back at the hospital, caring for those who need us most."

"We will." Agnes headed for the door. "I'll fetch you that tea."

Maddie sighed. If only she could tell Agnes about kissing Aiden. But that could never be. Da had entrusted her to the old serving maid's care, and any slip of her tongue might be hastily reported to the earl. Everything would be ruined if Da discovered she'd been kissed by a masked gentleman. If word got out, her reputation would be ruined, and poor Aiden might be tracked down and forced into a betrothal.

Maddie's breath caught.

Was the young man already betrothed?

He certainly kissed as if he might be... as if, perhaps, he was well experienced in such endeavors.

Her lips quivered with delight.

Closing her eyes, she imagined Lord Aiden kissing her once more. His big hands sliding around her waist scandalously. Oh, heaven, if only she could kiss him again and again. But one fleeting moment on the eve of a new year absolutely must last her a lifetime.

Well, perhaps Da might find her a husband before she became a confirmed spinster. He'd alluded to the fact that an officer would make a good match—though who knew if he'd remember his words on the morrow? Most likely the countess would have something far more important to bend Da's ear, and that was the last Maddie would hear about any foolish ideas of finding her a husband.

Besides, what could he possibly have meant by telling me an officer would make a good match? We were all wearing masks, for heaven's sake. For all I know, Lord Aiden with the moss-green eyes could have had a hideous wart in the center of his forehead.

Chapter Four

Stonehaven, Scotland, 30 March 1708

*T*hree months had passed and Hogmanay was a distant memory as Maddie plucked her harp strings, sending resonant and soothing music through the tiny hospital's passageways. As benefactor for the facility, she saw to the comfort of the women who came to them for help at all hours. She employed a physician to visit two times per week. Otherwise the Seaside Hospital for the Welfare of Women maintained a staff of three local women and a cook who tended to the patients' needs.

Most of their patients needed healing of the heart, which was something the physician could not provide. Maddie trusted her music and daily readings provided solace for those in her care.

Da had given her a Celtic harp on her ninth saint's day, and she'd received lessons thereafter until she reached her majority. For the past two years she had practiced daily, given an audience or nay. For it was said, "It is a sin not to put God-given talent to use."

The clatter of horse and coach rose outside. Across the hall Agnes stopped folding linens and peered out the window. "What on earth is *she* doing here?"

Maddie stood her instrument straight and moved beside the maid. "'Tis the countess." She quickly patted her hair to hide any fly-aways. Since her father had married Lady Mary it had been made eminently clear that the woman held her illegitimate stepdaughter in low esteem.

Staring out the window, Maddie took a calming breath. Never had her stepmother paid her a visit. "I wonder what she wants."

Agnes turned on her heel and started for the kitchens. "I've no idea, but it mustn't be good."

"Where are you off to?"

"Into hiding." Agnes threw a grimace over her shoulder. "Else I might do something I ought not. After all, bopping a countess on the nose would sorely affect my employment prospects."

Left standing alone in the entrance vestibule, Maddie squared her shoulders and opened the door to the woman responsible for exiling her from the family. Her sweaty palm slid on the latch, though she painted on a bright smile. "M'lady, to what do I owe the honor of your visit?"

Heavy with child, the countess swept inside, catching her breath as if the effort caused much consternation. "'Tis your father."

A lump caught in Maddie's throat. She gestured to a chair. "Please sit. Tell me what's happened."

Dear God, the news cannot be bad.

Flicking open a fan, Lady Mary took the seat and cooled herself. "I still cannot believe it."

"What?" Maddie asked, wringing her hands.

"They've taken him."

"Da?"

"Yes, your father." The countess straightened her back, her gaze sharp like a buzzard's. "Why else would I be here if it weren't for your father?"

Heat spread across Maddie's face, but she squeezed her fingernails into her palms. This was no time to allow the years of rejection to claw at her insides. She met her stepmother's gaze. "Who has taken him and where?"

"'Tis all because of the missive from His Majesty, James Francis Edward Stuart."

"Da received a missive from the king?"

Lady Mary fanned herself faster. "Aye. The French agreed to support a new rising. Granted our exiled king five thousand men and a fleet of ships. It all seemed so perfect."

Merciful mercy, Da had prayed for the day when James would set foot in Scotland. But something must have gone awry. "What happened? You have received news, have you not?"

"A messenger arrived today." Leaning forward, the countess touched the back of her hand to her forehead. "Oh, dear Lord, I can hardly bring myself to say it."

Reaching out, Magdalen nearly placed a consoling hand on the countess's shoulder, but snapped her fingers away. "But you must." She clenched her fist. Not knowing had to be worse than knowing. "Where is my father?"

With a shake of her head, Lady Mary sniffed. "They captured him in Edinburgh. And now the queen's men are taking him to the Tower of London to stand trial for treaaaaaasooooon." Tears streamed down the woman's face while she shook her head. "I have no idea what to do. This bairn is due to come in a month. And I cannot imagine my husband sitting in a cell in London with no family there to care for him."

Maddie pulled a clean kerchief from her sleeve and offered it to her stepmother. "Of course you cannot travel in your condition."

"He loves you." Lady Mary snatched the kerchief, wiped her eyes, and blew her nose like a blast from a trumpet. "I've tried to keep you away, but though you're his bastard, you still hold a place in his heart."

Maddie chewed her lip, willing herself to resist the urge to burst forth with a litany detailing exactly how horribly her father's wife had treated her illegitimate stepchild.

This is not the time.

It took a deep breath to calm her ire enough for her to speak without shrieking. "I would imagine any good man wouldn't forget his children, bastard or nay."

"That's what I reasoned." Lady Mary wielded her fan pointedly. "You must go to him at once."

Looking up, Maddie caught Agnes poking her head out the kitchen door and shaking it so rapidly 'twas amazing the woman's coif remained in place. The lady's maid could be unduly opinionated, and this was one time Magdalen did not agree with Agnes in the slightest. Her father was in prison and there was no one else who could help him. She would swim to London if forced. "No question. I must be the one to go, especially since you are great with child."

"Thank heavens. I kent you would be useful for something one day." Heaving a sigh, Stepmother pushed herself to a stand with great effort.

Normally Maddie would hasten to help a woman in Lady Mary's condition, but it took a moment for her to choke down her hurt feelings and offer a hand. "I'll do what I can to ensure he receives a pardon."

"Demand an audience with the queen. Remind Anne how useful your father has been in Parliament—he's supported her many a time." The countess glanced away. "When it made sense, of course."

"Of course. What else do you suggest I do?"

"Stay in his suite at Whitehall. Find an advocate." The woman swooned on her feet. "Oh dear. What am I to do? If your father is beheaded, I'll be ruined for the rest of my days."

Maddie caught Lady Mary's elbow while grinding her teeth.

You selfish woman. What about Da? What if he loses his life for showing support for the queen's brother?

"Come." She ushered the countess toward the door. "They will not behead my father, I'll see to it, and I'll swear to his innocence on a stack of Bibles."

"Thank you." The countess patted Maddie's cheek. "I'm afraid the future of the earldom rests on your shoulders."

"Yes, m'lady." Maddie opened the door.

"God save us," the countess said, doom filling her voice as if all were lost.

Waiting while her pregnant stepmother flounced outside, Maddie's mind raced. How fast could she travel to London? A transport from the Stonehaven Bay would be quickest by far.

After the countess climbed into her coach, Maddie waved, closed the door, and turned.

"London?" asked Agnes from the kitchen.

"Quickly, we must pack our things and book passage." She grabbed her cloak from the peg and swung it around her shoulders.

Agnes didn't budge. "But what of the hospital?"

"I'll ask Mrs. Boyd to take over. She's been with us the longest and I trust her implicitly."

Chapter Five

The Royal Mary, *moored off the port of Blackwall, 14 April 1708*

*A*iden rapped on the captain's door before opening it. "You wanted to see me, sir?"

"Aye, Lord Aiden, come in and take a seat." The captain gestured to the chair opposite his desk, where Aiden often sat to discuss shipboard business—though the captain rarely referred to him as *lord*. "Are you looking forward to your leave?"

Dear God, his stomach squeezed. Never in his naval career had Aiden been so ready to step ashore, and for a fortnight. He could already taste the fare at Whitehall. "Indeed, sir. It's been so long since I walked on land, I'm ready to leap over the hull and swim for the wharf."

"Och, youth. I remember having that kind of verve once."

"Are you not stepping ashore, sir?"

"Nay. I'll be overseeing a few repairs to be carried out

by Her Majesty's carpenters whilst you and the officers are kicking up your heels."

Aiden bit his lip. He'd offer to stay under most circumstances, but he'd go mad if he didn't step ashore soon, and he'd been looking forward to this leave for months. "Anything you need help with, sir?"

"Nothing at all." Polwarth drummed his fingers on the desk as if he was nervous about something. Then he pulled a missive out of his drawer. "To be honest, I'm a bit taken aback."

"Oh? Does that have anything to do with the officer of yards' visit after our mooring?" Even Aiden had been surprised to see a skiff approach as soon as they'd dropped anchor. He'd been minding the watch while the men paid a hasty call.

"In fact, their business concerned you."

"Me, sir?"

Captain Polwarth ran his hand down his face and heaved a long sigh. "More things we need to comply with as a ship in Her Majesty's Royal Navy, I'm afraid."

Aiden rolled his eyes to the rafters. He would have liked to spew a number of expletives stressing his opinion of merging Scotland's navy with England's, but the captain already knew his opinion. He tapped his foot. The sooner this meeting ended, the sooner he could start his leave. "You said they singled me out, sir?"

"Aye. Fortunately, they consented to allow me to present the news to you myself, rather than making a spectacle." He shoved the missive across the desk. "It seems I'm not quite up to snuff for the likes of Queen Anne."

"I beg your pardon?" Aiden picked up the missive, sealed with the lord high admiral's stamp. "You're the best bloody captain in the fleet."

A rueful chuckle rumbled from the captain's belly. "That may be, but I'm not a member of the gentry."

Aiden dropped his jaw. "I thought all Scottish posts were being grandfathered in."

"They are." Polwarth combed his fingers through his thick gray hair. "I'm still the captain of this ship, but that missive in your hands is your advancement to commander of the *Royal Mary*."

"Commander?" Aiden ran his thumb under the seal and unfolded the document. "Does such a posting exist?"

"Only on this ship. I was duly informed that since I am not of gentle birth, the position of commander has been created to ensure all commissioned officers aboard Her Majesty's *Royal Mary* behave as proper gentlemen whilst in the service of the queen."

Aiden guffawed hard enough to spit out his teeth. "This is about pompous posturing? You must be jesting." He didn't mind being recognized for a promotion, but advancement on the grounds of his noble birth didn't feel right. At times the captain seemed more of a gentleman to Aiden than his own father.

"I'm dead serious."

"That's absurd. You've been captain of this ship for what, fifteen years?"

"Sixteen."

Aiden slapped the missive on the desk. "I do not accept this. It's just another mindless edict passed down by Whitehall that makes no sense whatsoever."

"Och, the promotion is yours and well deserved, and it doesn't do anything to me but ruffle my feathers a wee bit." The captain sat back and folded his arms. "At least they were right about you. If they'd tried to advance MacPherson or MacBride, I would have been enraged."

He still didn't like it, just as he didn't care for dozens of other edicts that had come down from the admiral's office. If only the *Royal Mary* could have remained a Scottish ship. "So what does it mean, sir? Will anything change?"

Polwarth shrugged. "You were already my second in command. But since you'll be receiving an extra shilling or two in pay, I'll have you start assuming more of my duties. Comes as a surprise, though, especially since they tend to promote English officers over Scots."

Aiden smirked. "Well then, I say thank God there are no Sassenach bastards aboard this ship."

"Well said, lad." The captain waved his hand through the air. "Go on, enjoy your fortnight of leave, then we'll break the news to the crew upon your return."

Aiden shoved his chair back and stood. "Aye, sir. Thank you, sir."

* * *

"I need an entire keg of ale," Aiden said, slinging his satchel over his shoulder and heading across the wharf with Fraser MacPherson. He wasn't about to spill the news to his cabinmate. Hell, he didn't even know if Fraser would still be sharing a berth with him once they set sail a fortnight hence. In fact, Aiden didn't want to think about his conversation with Captain Polwarth. Aside from baffling him and bouncing him between elation and irritation, it changed nothing regarding his leave. And for the next fortnight, he intended to do everything in his power to forget he'd ever joined the navy.

"I need something stronger than ale." As usual, MacPherson stayed close on Aiden's heels, bragging as he always did. "And then I aim to find a woman and spend a sennight in her bed."

"A sennight?" He snorted. "How much will that cost you?"

"I don't care. My cock's been hard for ninety days."

Aiden couldn't argue. On the odd occasion when he'd actually been able to head for his cot, he'd tried everything from counting sheep to calculating sums in his futile attempt to think of anything but wrapping a sweet-smelling lassie like Magdalen in his arms and kissing her. It seemed like ages ago that his wee tryst upon the wall-walk at Dunnottar Castle had served to incite his untapped lust and make him more curious—not to mention on edge. With luck, during his fortnight of leave he'd find an experienced, wholesome widow to show him the ropes.

Dear God, 'tis about time.

And he had a plan. His father held apartments at White-hall Palace where Da stayed when Parliament was in session—otherwise the rooms remained empty. Fortunately, Parliament was not in session, and as the son of the Duke of Atholl, Aiden planned to enjoy an entire fortnight flirting with the courtiers of the female persuasion. With luck there might be a suitable widow with whom he could arrange a discreet tête-à-tête.

A woman who would be more than willing to take a young protégé under her wing.

"Where's the nearest alehouse?" MacPherson stepped beside him on the Blackwall Pier on the Thames and took in a deep breath, which was followed by a cough. "Och, the stench of humanity and rotting fish."

In truth, things didn't smell much better aboard the *Royal Mary* after the past three months chasing French ships. Damn it all. If Aiden had known the Scottish navy was to be combined with the English, he never would have taken a commission.

The French had *always* been allies with Scotland. He

wouldn't have been able to live with himself if the *Royal Mary* had been forced to fire her cannons at King James's fleet. What if they'd killed the true king? For the love of God, James was a Stuart, not to mention Queen Anne's half brother. What was the queen thinking?

And now Aiden had been advanced up the ranks, to serve none other than the queen herself. *A bloody commander.* He looked to the skies. At least aboard the ship he could remain aloof from politics for the most part.

"Yoo-hoo!" a high-pitched voice called. Above the busy wharf, a scantily clad woman hung out a second-floor window above a sign that read "The Boar's Head Alehouse." "Are you looking for a bit o' fun?"

"I'll be right up." Grinning, MacPherson waved at the tart, then gave Aiden a nudge. "Everything we need is right here, mate."

The harlot looked tempting—enormous breasts, a welcoming grin. Perhaps she lacked wholesomeness, but Aiden had only a fortnight.

Aye, if there's no merry widow at court, I might just come back here.

"Don't stand there with your mouth agape when there are women to shag." Fraser started across the road.

Aiden already regretted having stepped ashore with his cabinmate. Who could compete with a licentious shark? "A pitcher of ale, then I'm on my way."

MacPherson gave him a nudge. "Still planning to try your luck at Whitehall?"

"And why not?" Dodging a cart loaded with hides, Aiden followed. "My brother says there are courtiers by the dozens."

Fraser reached for the door handle. "Aye, but loose women are more fun."

"How would you ken? You never make it past the whores on the waterfront."

"Perhaps not, but I'll wager I've been luckier than you. In fact, I still reckon you're a virgin, even if you do out-rank me."

If you only knew by how much.

Though his hackles stood on end, Aiden wasn't about to take MacPherson's bait. Damnation, he aimed to lose his virginity within the next fortnight. Och, he'd prove his mates wrong, and then all their jibes would be thrown out with the slops.

As Aiden pushed inside the Boar's Head, it was clear the *Royal Mary* wasn't the only ship in port. As a matter of fact, three of Her Majesty's fleet had dropped anchor in the Thames. Aiden muscled his way to the bar at the back with his friend in his wake. Fraser might be good at flapping his mouth, but Aiden was bigger and stronger.

"Bloody hell, they cannot fit another man in this alehouse," MacPherson mumbled from behind, barely audible for the noise.

"Stay with me, mate." Aiden led with his elbow while the pall of stale beer bit his nostrils. "I can plow through the lot of them." A benefit of being tall and sturdy was that not many people stood in his way, even in an alehouse packed full of thirsty sailors.

He took off his tricorn hat and slapped four pence on the bar. "Give us a quart pitcher and two glasses."

"And send over a woman," added MacPherson with a snort.

The barman glanced up from tapping a barrel. "Bloody hell. Do not tell me the Scots are in port as well as all these rutting tars?"

"You're from the bleedin' *Royal Mary*, are you?" asked

a sailor with a missing tooth. From his mangled nose, he looked as if he'd been in one too many brawls, and he smelled as if he'd been cleaning the bilges. "You bastards could have sunk the French schooner and sent the Pretender to hell."

Aiden's gut twisted into a knot along with his fists.

Another scraggly-looking tar sneered, "Yeah, I reckon you're a yellow-bellied Jacobite just like the rest of the back-stabbers up in *Snot-land*."

Without a word, Aiden moved closer to the sailor, towering over him with a scowl. Shrinking away, the little tar suddenly took a fixed interest in his ale.

The barman snatched Aiden's coin and placed a pitcher on the bar with two tin tankards. "We're out of glasses."

With a backward glance, Aiden took quick inventory. Everyone he saw was drinking from glass—and they were all dressed in scruffy breeches and dingy linen shirts; not a well-dressed officer among them. Though not appointed with uniforms, only officers could afford well-tailored garb. But he didn't care. He needed a damned beer.

He poured, eyeing the loudmouthed cur beside him while his starched cravat prickled his throat. "Orders were to ensure the queen's brother didn't set foot in Britain, not to sink his ship."

"Well, I think you're yellow."

Carefully setting the ewer down, he took a long pull of his ale. Aye, his gut clamped harder than a vise, but he wasn't about to let the Sassenach varlet know he would soon regret those words.

The nice thing about being six foot two inches tall was that few people bothered him, unless they wanted to see if they could take on a man of his size. Definitely not smart.

Once he'd placed his half-empty tankard on the bar, he faced the jackass. "You will apologize to me now."

"I beg your pardon?" The man pinched Aiden's velvet doublet and rubbed it between his fingers. "A bloody sheep reiver dressed in gentlemen's garb."

Aiden watched the tar's fingers. "Remove your hand from my person, sir, else I'll have no recourse but to remove it for you."

The noise in the alehouse ebbed to a hum. Aiden swept his gaze across the faces gaping at him as if he were the aggressor. They looked like wolves ready to side with the Sassenach in an all-out brawl.

That would be right. Show up at Whitehall with two blackened eyes.

He waggled his eyebrows and grinned at the lot of them. "After this pig-nosed codpiece removes his hand from my doublet, I'll buy the house a round," Aiden bellowed loud enough for everyone to hear.

"You'll bloody what?" MacPherson whispered from behind.

A cheer boomed clear to the rafters.

The insulting maggot with his grip on Aiden's doublet looked up with bloodshot eyes. "Why I ought to—"

Aiden caught the man's fist midair, bent the bastard's wrist down until the cur dropped to his knees. "You want to throw another punch," he growled, baring his teeth, "or forget you ever called me yellow and enjoy a brandy?"

The man's face turned scarlet as his eyes nearly bugged out of his head. "Brandy," he agreed in a strained croak.

"That's what I thought." Aiden yanked him up and gave him a shove. "Barman, you heard me, ale for all."

MacPherson leaned in, moving his lips toward Aiden's ear. "What, throwing your coin around on a mob of turn-coats? I would have asked the blackguard to step outside if it were me."

Aiden pretended to wipe his mouth, holding his fingers up to muffle his words. "Good thing it wasn't you, 'cause three-quarters of the buggers in this establishment would have followed." He picked up his tankard, downed the rest of his ale, then motioned for the barman. "Three drams of brandy here as well. Let us drink to our success, shall we? After all, we sent James back to France with his tail between his legs." Blast it, the words burned like bile in his mouth. Not a single cheer had been heard aboard the *Royal Mary* when the true king's ship changed course and headed back across the Channel.

The yellow-bellied cad licked his lips and squinted. "Why would you offer me a brandy?"

"To show there are no hard feelings, mate." Aiden thwacked the man on the shoulder, sinking his fingers into fleshy meat to test the man's strength. The tar would have been an easy mark—as long as fifty other sailors didn't join him in the brawl.

He glanced back over his shoulder.

Correction. If I buried my fist in this maggot's face, there'd be a hundred lining up to do the same to me.

Fortunately, the barman poured the shots in quick order. Aiden plucked up his glass. "To your health."

"Health," the man said.

"Agreed," said MacPherson, throwing back his tot. With a snort the third lieutenant looked to the stairway and elbowed Aiden in the ribs. "Have a look at that."

Leaning on the banister, the woman from the window waved. Given a closer look, except for breasts the size of cannonballs, there wasn't much enticing about her. She had crooked teeth and three black "beauty" patches covering only God knew what. Thankfully, she ogled MacPherson, though Aiden couldn't fathom what she saw in the swine, other than his velvet doublet and lace cravat. Officers' clothing oozed wealth unobtainable by most folk. He toasted his friend. "Looks like you've been given an invitation."

After setting his glass on the bar, MacPherson started off. "I've business to attend to."

Aiden chuckled. "Just don't show up in a fortnight with the pox."

The young Scot shuddered. "You ken how to wring the fun out of everything."

Aiden poured another tankard of ale for himself, then pushed the pitcher to his new English *friend*. "Here. Looks like I've been passed over for more entertaining fare."

"You heading out alone?" The man was a dog. Buy him a couple of drinks and he'd become a fast friend.

"Reckon I'll hire a coach to take me to Whitehall."

Where I aim to find a pretty widow.

The tar gave Aiden a once-over. "What business have you at the palace?"

"My da keeps apartments there."

"Dear God, don't tell me you're a bleeding duke or something."

"Nay, my da's the duke."

The sailor swilled his ale. "What the hell are you doing in an establishment like this?"

"I needed a wee drink to quell my thirst." Aiden guzzled the rest of his.

The man snorted. "You could have ended up dead."

"I doubt that." He picked up his tricorn hat and shoved it atop his head. "Though I'd best be off. I prefer whisky to brandy, and I ken where I can find the best spirit in London."

The sun hung low in the western sky when Aiden pushed out into the street. He opened his pocket watch—half past six. Plenty of time to make his way to Whitehall and have a good meal in the Banqueting House. He smacked his lips at the thought of a juicy cut of beef. He didn't care if he ever looked at another serving of pickled herring again in his life.

A clerk with his arms full of papers nearly walked over him. The entire yard was a flurry of activity, with warships being loaded and merchant ships unloaded. If anything, the activity along the wharf had picked up, as if everyone was in a hurry to end the day.

"Sir, you cannot leave us here without transport." A woman's voice carried from across the road. A Scottish woman's voice at that. Though exasperation filled her tone, the voice sounded enticingly sultry.

Tingles spread over Aiden's shoulders as if there was something familiar about that voice. He peered through the crisscrossing traffic of horses, ox-drawn carts, and wagons pushed by laborers. A young lady and her maidservant stood beside a coach missing one wheel. And the coachman had unharnessed the horse. "Beg your pardon, my lady, but I've naught but to take this wheel to the smithy and have it repaired. I'm sorry, I will not be able to take you into London until the morrow."

"The morrow? What are we to do until then?" The woman grasped her companion's arm, glancing up and down the avenue, clearly unaccustomed to being amid so much enterprise. "This is unheard of. You are leaving us stranded in a most unscrupulous part of town."

Clenching his fists, Aiden huffed. The last thing he needed was to become embroiled in the plight of a damsel and her serving maid. His nostrils flared. Damn it all, he only had two bloody weeks' leave. But by the saints, his breeding could not allow a woman to be treated with such disdain.

"'Haps you might hail another driver. He'll help you."

The discourteous coachman climbed aboard the horse. "If I do not have this wheel to the smithy before dark, I'll be forced to go another day without a fare."

The lovely lady drew a hand over her heart. "But—"

Ballocks.

Casting aside his agenda, Aiden groaned as he hastened to cross the busy road, dodging horses, wagons, and a pile of manure. If he hailed a coach for the lassie, it ought to set him back only a few minutes at the most. Hopping onto the curb, he tipped his hat. "Can I be of assistance to you ladies?"

The woman's enormous azure eyes regarded him, and a rapt O played on her lips as if he were the deliverer of salvation. "Sir, how gracious and kind of you to ask." She thrust her finger at the immobile carriage. "The coach we hired has lost a wheel and we are *stranded* in this ghastly place."

Aiden stood frozen for a moment and stared. Flushed and flustered, the lass was adorable, yet something about those eyes was familiar. A woman with such expressive blues could twist a man around her finger simply by batting her eyelashes.

"Aye, we ken nothing of London," said the maidservant. "What are we to do?"

Shifting his gaze to the older woman, Aiden remembered his purpose—and he wasn't about to be taken in by a wee lassie's bonny eyes, especially one accompanied by such a dour matron. "Please allow me to hail another coach for you. Where are you headed?"

"Whitehall," said the lady, blinking rapidly. Damnation, those eyes were distracting.

"Ah...I am off to the palace as well." Aiden stepped into the street and flagged a driver with his handkerchief. "May I ask what you ladies are doing alongside a naval dockyard?"

The woman watched the approaching carriage as it cut

off riders and wagons while veering to the curb. "Our passenger ship moored up the way. There were drivers waiting, and after I agreed to payment the crew loaded my effects."

The maidservant wrung her hands. "We hardly traveled a quarter mile when we were nearly thrown from the coach."

"Indeed." Lady Bright-Eyes scraped her lovely white teeth over her bottom lip—a gesture far too alluring to ignore. "The wheel fell off."

Pulling his rig to the curb, the hailed coachman leaned down from his perch. "Where to, gov?"

"Whitehall." Aiden gestured to the luggage. "Please load the ladies' effects."

"Straightaway, my lord." The man's demeanor immediately became more respectful with the mention of Whitehall.

Aiden returned his attention to the ladies and his brow furrowed with a sigh of resignation. There was no reason not to be friendly. After all, there were presently no merry widows in sight. "You must be out of sorts."

The young lady hid her face in her palms. "Can nothing go right? I cannot believe my miserable luck."

He opened the door to the coach and offered his hand. "Ladies, if you wouldn't mind sharing with me, I trust we should arrive in one piece as long as no other disasters befall us."

When the lady placed her fingers in his palm, a crackle of energy zinged across his skin. Taking in a sharp breath, he met her gaze—nearer now. Dear God, those eyes were blue as the summer sky.

She gasped and blinked. "Thank you . . . sir, is it?"

Aiden bowed his head. "Lord Aiden Murray, ah"—hell, he had to use the title sometime—"naval commander, at your service, m'lady."

Something flashed across her face—as if she recognized his name. Her lips parted. He'd seen lips like hers before—a bow-shaped mouth, rosy, feminine, *incredibly inviting*. In fact, he'd never forget seeing such kissably shaped lips.

Before he could comment, the maidservant grasped his hand. "Imagine this, we sail all the way to London and 'tis a Scotsman who stops to help us. I thank you for coming to our aid, m'lord."

He again bowed. "It is my pleasure."

Situating herself inside, the lassie grinned. Why in God's name did she have to look so bonny?

Dammit, Aiden, share the coach, arrive at Whitehall, and leave them to their affairs. A wee lassie and her maidservant? Not for a fortnight's leave. You need to find a widow...or a courtesan...or anyone but a winsome Scottish lassie with enormous blue eyes who has a guardian dragon following in her shadow.

After climbing inside, he sat opposite the two women. That needling prickled the back of his neck again. Was it because he missed home, or did this Scottish lass truly remind him of someone he knew? *But who?* "I beg your pardon, miss, but have we met?"

She leaned forward, her brow furrowed with a contemplative expression. "Ah...I rather doubt it, unless you've been to the Seaside Hospital for the Welfare of Women in Stonehaven."

"Stonehaven?" His stomach flipped upside down. "My ship docked in her harbor on Hogmanay."

Gasping, the lass drew her fingers over her mouth. Her gaze shifted to the window just as they rolled past a clear view of Aiden's ship. "The *Royal Mary*?" she asked.

His stomach continued to jump. Was it the same woman? "Pray tell, what is your name?"

The maidservant cleared her throat. "My lady is Lady Magdalen Keith, and I am Miss Agnes Dixon."

His tongue went completely dry. In all his life he'd met only one woman named Magdalen—a woman whose memory had occupied his every thought for the past three months.

He clenched his fists against the ridiculous gooseflesh rising across his skin.

What about the Earl Marischal and his vested interest?

Aiden rolled his eyes to the black ceiling. He had his own agenda, dammit. And it had to be with someone unattached.

Find a bloody widow and stay out of trouble.

Could this be she?

Could there be more than one Magdalen from Stonehaven? Dear God, he hoped not.

No, you dolt, you'd best hope it isn't she.

"I am ever so pleased to make your acquaintance." He chewed the corner of his mouth as his gaze met hers. Those vivid blue eyes assessed him as if with anticipation, but there was a great deal of worry behind them as well.

Should he mention the masque?

Certainly it would be the right thing to do.

After all, the maidservant needn't know they'd strolled atop the wall-walk, or that he'd taken the liberty of placing his hands on the lassie's waist. Ah yes, he could still feel the narrow arc of her form beneath his fingers...and then he'd kissed the softest, most delectable lips in all of Christendom.

"You did not, perchance, attend the Hogmanay masquerade given by the Earl Marischal of Scotland?" he asked.

"Why, yes." She smiled, but sadly.

Aiden's fists relaxed. "I was there as well."

"Hmm." It was not a questioning but a knowing hum.

"I wore a Spanish bandit's mask."

A pink tongue slipped out and moistened her lips. Lord in heaven, he'd like to kiss them again.

"I remember," she said almost in a whisper. "But were you not a lieutenant?"

"I've received an advancement." He sat straighter, the earlier crackle of energy now more like a bolt of lightning. "May I ask what has brought you to London?"

* * *

Tears welled in Maddie's eyes when Lord Aiden asked the reason for her visit. Unable to help herself, she covered her gasp with her hand. How on earth could she say it? Her father in good faith had shown his support for James Francis Edward Stuart, and had been rewarded by being arrested for treason. Heaven help her, she knew what happened to noblemen who were actually convicted of treason. And she aimed to do everything in her power to see it didn't happen to her father.

But the handsome broad-shouldered man sitting across from her was a naval officer. Regardless of his kindness, the Royal Navy had blocked the port. Had Lord Aiden been in Edinburgh to witness her father's arrest? Was he a Jacobite, or did he side with the government? He wore a dark-blue gold-trimmed doublet with a fashionably matching kilt.

Of course he's a government supporter. He's an officer in Her Majesty's Royal Navy.

She shifted her gaze to Agnes. The serving maid shook her head with a frown.

Whom could Magdalen trust? On the morrow she must hasten to the Tower and request an audience with her father. This man ought to be able to advise her on how to proceed.

However, she and Agnes had to first make it to Whitehall in one piece.

Would Lord Aiden drop her at the curb as soon as she

told him the true reason for her visit? Surely he must have a suspicion, if he hadn't already guessed why he'd found her on the wharf.

How can I word it to draw suspicion away from Da?

She gulped. "My father received a missive from *Prince* James in France. Ah...are you aware of James's attempted visit to Scotland?"

"I am." Lord Aiden made no show of surprise. As a matter of fact, aside from his eyes' growing a wee bit darker, he could have passed for a statue.

Agnes squeezed Maddie's arm, but she ignored the warning. Allies were few and far between, and she needed every one she could reap, especially in deplorable London. Dear Lord, her father hated it here—said he had more enemies in the royal court than in hell. "Were you involved in the maneuvers to prevent his ship from landing?" she asked, trying to look curious rather than accusing.

His Lordship's moss-green eyes narrowed as he tapped a finger to his lips. "Prince James's *ships*, you mean—carrying five thousand men," he corrected. "Regrettably, m'lady, as an officer in the queen's navy, the *Royal Mary* was one of the warships ordered to guard the Firth of Forth and prevent James's armada from dropping anchor."

Regrettably?

Maddie's heart skipped a beat. These were such dubious times, but the man's use of *regrettably* ignited a light of hope.

Can I trust him?

He is a Scot.

But his father, the Duke of Atholl, is a Whig for certain.

What about the duke's son?

Furrowing her brow, Maddie watched the man intently. Then she grazed her teeth over her bottom lip—something she'd done several times since Lord Aiden crossed the busy road to hasten to her rescue.

Who else could help her? Since the age of seven she'd lived apart from her father. She knew nothing of politics.

Nothing of London.

Nothing of this whole sordid mess.

She drew in a quick breath. "Da was arrested in Edinburgh and taken to the Tower."

Agnes tightened her grip. "Magdalen!"

Maddie huffed. "I'm sure it is no secret."

Lord Aiden's mouth dropped open. "Your father…is he the Earl Marischal of Scotland?"

"Aye."

"Odd."

"Why?"

"He spoke to me at the masque." The commander held up his palms and shook his head. "Forgive me. My place is not to question. You were saying your father's welcoming party was intercepted in Edinburgh?"

Welcoming party?

Maddie looked to Agnes and arched her eyebrows. Why hadn't she thought of that? "Aye, and now he is to be tried for treason."

The officer glanced away, as if he had a great many thoughts. "This is grave news indeed."

"Indeed," echoed Agnes.

"So you've come to provide support?" he asked, regarding her with such intensity it made gooseflesh rise on her arms.

Maddie nodded. "My stepmother is with child. She implored me to come in her stead."

Lord Aiden's eyes widened with deep intelligence—or cunning. "I see."

"Whitehall, m'lord," the coachman called from above.

Maddie looked out the window as the coach rolled to a stop. A stately redbrick gatehouse loomed above a walkway lined with statues of lions, unicorns, and eagles, and guarded by yeomen in red and black. She shuddered.

Why does it look like a prison?

Plucking up her courage, she allowed Lord Aiden to pay the driver and call upon a host of servants to take charge of her portmanteaus.

An official-looking gatekeeper wearing a periwig approached from the tower. "Where to, my lady?"

Maddie threw back her shoulders and tried to look aristocratic. "The Earl Marischal of Scotland's apartments, please."

The man dropped his hands to his sides. "I beg your pardon? The earl has been convicted of treason and his suite has been seized."

"Convicted?" Maddie's heart dropped all the way to her toes. "Do you mean to say I've missed the trial?"

"No, but mark me, he's as guilty as Judas," the man said, puffing out his chest like a peacock. Never in her life had Maddie wanted to issue a slap, but this heartless cur instantly piqued her ire.

"How can you be so sure?" Lord Aiden addressed the man, towering over him by a good eight inches. "As a member of the queen's navy, I had an excellent view of the pier, and I saw naught but a peaceful welcoming party waiting to greet the prince."

Perhaps the commander should have considered becoming an advocate rather than a naval officer. But Maddie couldn't think about that at a time like this. The sun had set and she had no place to sleep for the night. Worse, if she was forced to pay for accommodations, the small sum of coin she'd brought would not go far.

As the coach pulled away, she looked to her luggage. "Good heavens, what are we to do now?"

"Perhaps there is a lady with whom you can stay?" asked Lord Aiden.

Maddie regarded the well-meaning officer. He had no idea that she hardly knew her stepmother, Lady Mary, let alone any of the gentry. Because her father recognized her as his child, she had been granted the privilege of the address *lady*. Maddie might have been a bastard, but she was the daughter of an earl all the same.

She shook her head, her skin growing hot. Holy crosses, was she to become a guttersnipe in London? Dropping her head, she cupped her hand over her forehead. "There is no one."

Lord Aiden passed the guardsman a coin. "Please see to it Lady Magdalen's things are promptly delivered to the Duke of Atholl's lodging."

"The *duke*, m'lord?" Though he sounded aghast, the sentry's fingers closed around the shilling.

With a flicker of hope, Maddie slid her fingers from her forehead to her lips.

Looking ever so official, Lord Aiden tugged on his lapels. "That is what I said, and I shall see to it that the duke is informed of his houseguests myself."

The man hastily slipped his hand into his pocket. "Very well, my lord."

As he offered his elbow, Lord Aiden's noble countenance didn't even crack a smile. "This way, m'lady."

Once out of the gatekeeper's earshot, Maddie turned her lips up toward His Lordship's ear. "I cannot possibly accept your father's hospitality. It would be scandalous."

Green eyes met hers while a single eyebrow arched. "No one would dare. Besides, your maidservant is employed to ensure your virtue remains intact, is she not?"

"But I—"

"Do not even think about placing a single finger on my lady's person," Agnes said loud enough to heard by the dead. "I shall sleep at her door with a dirk in my lap."

"I would have thought no less, matron." Lord Aiden chuckled, then lowered his voice. "Trust me and there will be no scandal."

Maddie wanted to believe him.

The only problem?

Her entire life had been a scandal.

Chapter Six

*A*iden paced the passageway outside Magdalen's door while his heart hammered a fierce rhythm. He'd played right into the lady's plight like a daft fool.

Jesus Christ, Lady Magdalen was not an experienced courtier. On Hogmanay she'd admitted his was her first kiss. She was as virginal as a bairn.

Och aye, he remembered kissing her...all too well. Though it had been unbelievably thrilling, she'd proved *far* less experienced than he. He couldn't take advantage of a novice. And what would that be like—a novice fumbling with a novice—even if she did show the remotest interest in him, which she did not? For all his rotten luck, Lady Magdalen was grief stricken by her father's plight. She was worried and distraught and a million leagues out of her element. He could see it now. The vultures at court would eat her alive, especially since her father was in more trouble than a pirate on a sinking ship.

Damnation, Aiden had only a fortnight to find a widow— or any healthy woman willing to lead him through the wiles of the boudoir. He wasn't looking for an attachment. The last thing on this earth a navy man needed was attachment—or a woman in dire need. Besides, what good could he accomplish in a mere fortnight?

Christ, he'd had it all planned. Hide out in Da's suite and turn it into a love nest of debauchery. Return to the ship with an entire year's worth of tales that would make MacPherson's and MacBride's pursuits pale in comparison.

On the morrow I must help Lady Magdalen find more suitable accommodations.

But she is darling.

He stopped pacing for a moment.

What if I allowed her to stay on a few days?

Absolutely not.

He slammed his fist into his palm.

No bloody chance.

He never should have crossed the road. Damn his chivalrous streak. Before he joined the navy, he would have been elated to have the lady stay with him for an entire fortnight. If he were in the market for a wife, he might even enjoy her company despite the circumstances.

But not now.

And her father was in more hot water than King Charles I, who'd been beheaded right inside Whitehall's courtyard.

Dear God, Aiden never should have joined the navy.

Crossing his arms, he stared at the door; then he pushed his fist against his chin.

I cannot allow myself to grow affectionate. I cannot allow myself to be overly compassionate, either.

He threw up his hands.

But the poor lass is distraught.

She needs comfort and an advocate to help her negotiate the political waters in London.

And that person cannot possibly be me.

I'd be crucified by MacPherson, not to mention my father. Damnation, Maddie's da is a flag-waving Jacobite.

Hell, I may as well slip my head onto a chopping block alongside the earl.

He resumed his pacing, clasping his hands behind his back.

However, mayhap I can make a few inquiries on her behalf.

The poor lass. Here all alone, a wee flounder swimming amongst the sharks in London.

Lord knew it was difficult enough for Aiden's father to keep his nose clean—that's why Da stayed as far away from this city as possible and only paid a visit when commanded by the queen.

Aiden wrung his hands. No, he couldn't shake the thought that he ought to have kept walking when he'd seen Lady Magdalen's crippled coach stalled right across from the alehouse. Now he'd be lumbered with worrying about the lassie's plight for the duration of his leave.

Damn, damn, damn.

Sucking in a deep breath, he faced Her Ladyship's door and raised his fist to knock. When he swung forward, the blasted thing opened, nearly sending him stumbling into Miss Agnes. "P-pardon me, miss." Aiden quickly regained his composure and straightened his cravat. "I was…ah… stopping by to inquire as to your comfort."

"Everything is lovely, thank you." She shifted her gaze down the corridor. "But could you please tell us where we might find the evening meal?"

"I ordered a tray of meats and bread to be sent up from the Banqueting House." Was this his opportunity to speak with the lass alone? He stepped back and gestured toward the apartment door. "Would you be so kind as to find the chief steward and ask him to make haste? He should be easy to spot—out the door, at the end of the passageway turn right, take the stairwell down two flights, and the hall is halfway along the south passage."

The maidservant held up a finger as if to object.

"It really is quite easy." Aiden led her toward the door. "And if you're not certain, anyone along the way can point you in the right direction."

"Down two flights and then—"

He flicked his fingers impatiently. "Follow the rumble of the crowd. There is always quite a gathering at this hour of the evening."

After ushering Agnes through the corridor and practically shoving her out the door, Aiden turned to find Maddie standing with her arms crossed. "Do you think she'll be able to find her way back?"

"Of course."

Eventually, anyway.

He sauntered toward the lass. "Are your accommodations acceptable?"

"Very comfortable, thank you."

"And Miss Agnes has quarters above stairs."

"Aye, the valet showed us."

"Good."

A wee blush spread in her cheeks. "But I cannot continue to impose upon you and your father."

True.

Standing at a respectable distance, he liked how she had to crane her neck to meet his gaze. His tongue slid across his bottom lip while the tension in his shoulders melted away. "Oh no, it is no imposition whatsoever. 'Tis just me, really. Da only resides here when Parliament is in session."

"I see, and when is the next session?"

"Not certain." Aiden's fingers twitched, itching to brush a stray curl away from her cheek.

"Then I am not imposing?"

"Not at all." He leaned on the doorjamb and grinned like a simpleton. "Not in the slightest."

Had he just heard himself?

Dear God, I'm daft.

She leaned against the jamb on the other side. "And you? How long will your ship be in port?"

"As of today I've been granted an entire fortnight's leave."

She smiled sadly, but her grin still looked as radiant as it had when he'd first seen her at the masque. "You sound happy about it."

"Overjoyed."

He should be, though the present company stifled his plans—for now.

"I'm so sorry to be such a bother. I imagine you must need solace after chasing James Francis back to France."

"Not at all." Aiden sighed. At least the present company was incredibly lovely to gaze upon, and smelled like a simmering vat of lilacs. "I needed time away from the ship altogether. This is the first leave I've had in over a year."

"My, that sounds dreadful." Her gaze slid from his face and settled on his chest. Her tongue slipped out of the corner of her mouth. Did she have any idea how tempting she looked? If he wasn't a gentleman, he'd have her pinned up against the wall with his tongue halfway down her throat—mayhap working her skirts up her long, slender thighs. He'd heard enough from MacPherson to have a fair idea of how it all worked.

She met his gaze with a wee exhalation, making that damned errant lock of hair flutter. "After visiting my father on the morrow, I shall endeavor to find more suitable accommodations."

His gut twisted. "I thought you said that you were comfortable here. Is your chamber not large enough? Would you prefer a better view?"

Aiden looked to the ceiling.

Good God, stop encouraging her to stay, damn you.

"No, no." She cringed shyly. "I'm just afraid of what people will say."

Blast it, his hands could remain still no longer. The flippant thing was just too damned enticing. He brushed the wayward curl away. "Because you are a guest of the Duke of Atholl?"

"No, silly, because I'm staying here...ah...with *you*."

A fire hit him low and churned through his aching cods. "But you have the companionship of your maidservant," he choked out with a rasp.

"I do."

"I could bring in a sentry to guard your door." Again Aiden looked skyward.

Jesus Christ, do I need to gag myself?

"Do you think it necessary?"

"Not really." He took her hand and ran his thumb over the petal-soft skin. "Have you a plan to help your father?"

"Aside from visiting him in the Tower on the morrow and asking his advice, no." Drawing her hand away, she pressed her knuckle against her lips. "I feel like a fish out of water. London. Whitehall. Court. It is all so foreign to me."

Honestly, though Aiden had visited court now and again, he didn't quite know what to expect this visit—aside from...

He shook his head. "You are right, Whitehall is nothing like Stonehaven. Every nook and cranny has a spy, the walls have ears—"

She looked into her chamber. "Even these walls?"

"Mayhap the only place in all of London where you can speak freely is within these walls."

"All right then. Tell me, why is it that *you* have been so kind? Is your father not a Whig?"

Aiden made it his habit not to reveal his true politics. Doing so would put him in the center of an unmitigated mess. "Och, m'lady. 'Tis well known the Duke of Atholl sides with the Whig Party, as does his firstborn son. But I am merely a second son. I am free to choose any party I wish."

"But as an officer of the Royal Navy, are you not forced to carry out the queen's bidding?"

"That is correct, though it doesn't mean I must leave my mind on the shore. Besides, I joined the Scottish navy. It wasn't until the Act of Union was passed last year that we merged with the English."

"You don't sound very happy about it."

"Can you keep a secret?"

"Aye." She looked at him with eyes that could enthrall with a glance.

His heart fluttered like a moth to light. "I'm not at all happy about the merger, nor is any sailor aboard the *Royal Mary*."

"But you were part of the armada that prevented James Francis from stepping ashore in Edinburgh."

"Even officers must obey orders." Still leaning on the doorjamb, Aiden crossed his ankles. "Though you speak true, my crew was also able to ensure none of the English ships grew overly enthusiastic and tried to sink *King* James's ship."

"King?"

"Aye, you ken as well as I he's the man who should be on the throne of Britain. It is his birthright, Catholic or nay."

She smiled. "Well then, I do hope you can help me wade

through the mire of naysayers here." She stepped closer, almost close enough to touch him, her gaze practically boring a hole through his heart. "Will you be my champion, Lord Aiden?"

Hell's fire, who could resist a pair of blues as round and trusting as Lady Magdalen Keith's? Perhaps he could make some inquiries, steer her in the right direction.

Mayhap steal a wee kiss afore my next great adventure? After all, what is a day or two out of a fortnight?

"I am at your service, m'lady." Standing straight, he again reached for her hand, and before she had a chance to draw away, he bowed over it. As he caught the fragrance of lilacs and something a bit more exotic, his heart stuttered. Time slowed while he closed his eyes and inhaled deeply before he pressed his lips to her silken flesh. Sweet feminine flesh thrumming with heat.

Och, if only a lass like Lady Magdalen could lead him through the maze of a lover's tryst. But alas, it could never be. She was the daughter of the Earl Marischal of Scotland, not some harpy from the waterfront. Nor was she an experienced courtier looking for a brief liaison.

As his lips plied her hand, the lady's breath caught with a wee gasp.

The sound made Aiden's heart hammer all the more.

He straightened and smiled.

Magdalen's moist lips pursed. "I thank you for your chivalry and kindness, Lord Aiden."

Blast.

He needn't ask to know that was her way of telling him a kiss on the back of the hand was most likely as far as she would let him go.

* * *

The Tower of London was every bit as cold and menacing as its reputation. Looming above the Thames, the immense stone walls, patrolled by musketeers and pikemen, were about as welcoming as the gates of hell. Thank heavens Lord Aiden had escorted her through the maze of buildings, though it wouldn't have been hard to guess the dank and archaic structure on the river, covered with pigeon droppings, was the prison. Nonetheless, she wanted to visit her father alone on this first meeting. Fortunately, His Lordship agreed to wait for her without a hint of annoyance.

"You have five minutes," said the guard after insisting she must see her father alone.

The heavy oaken door screeched on its iron hinges. Maddie peered inside and Da looked up from his cot. His face sunken with worry, he looked as if he'd aged a decade. Rushing forward, she opened her arms. "What have they done to you?"

"Maddie?" He blinked and held his hand to his brow, shading his eyes against the guard's torchlight.

With a boom the door slammed behind her. "Aye, 'tis me." She dropped to her knees and wrapped her arms around his leg. "I've been so worried."

"But why are you here, lass?"

"A hundred pikemen couldn't keep me away." She wiped away her tears. "Lady Mary wished to come, but she could not risk traveling in her condition."

Da smoothed his hand over Maddie's hair. "Thank God she is not here. The stress would have killed her and our unborn."

Honestly, it was for the best Lady Mary hadn't made the voyage to London. For the first time in Magdalen's life, she could help her father—prove her worth to the family. She rocked back on her knees. "Tell me what happened."

"I suspect you ken most of it. As Earl Marischal it was

my duty to ride to Edinburgh with my army. I have sworn my life to protect Scotland and will do so just as my forefathers did."

"So you rode to meet with Prince James Francis Edward Stuart?"

Da cringed at her use of the title *prince*, but he nodded.

"The walls have ears, do they not?" she asked in a whisper.

"Aye."

"And then the navy prevented the prince's armada from landing?"

"King Louis sent warships across the Channel. Indeed, the queen's navy did everything in its power to prevent a rising."

"How did they capture you?"

"They laid siege to my town house in Edinburgh. As simple as that." Da shook his head. "With the rising subverted, I assumed no foul." He slammed his fist into his palm. "I should have headed directly for Dunnottar. We could have withstood any backlash behind her fortress walls. 'Twas naïve of me to think the queen would understand my motives in meeting her brother."

"Albeit with the Keith Highland Regiment in tow." Maddie didn't need to ask if he would have marched on London had James been prepared for a revolution. She stood, clasping her hands together. "I want to help you."

"'Tis rare for a man accused of treason to be acquitted."

"But you did not take up arms. Not one drop of blood spilled."

Da nodded.

"Please, tell me what I should do. I know nothing of court. Lord Aiden tells me there are backstabbers lurking around every corner."

"Lord Aiden?"

"Son of the Duke of Atholl, a naval officer. He was on the wharf when my coach lost a wheel." Maddie bit her lip. "He's stationed aboard the *Royal Mary*—one of the officers who was at your Hogmanay masquerade."

Da arched his eyebrows. "I remember."

"You do?"

"Never mind that." With a wave of his hand, his expression grew dark. "His father is a backstabbing Whig for certain—but what about the son? Is he sympathetic to *the cause*?"

"I believe so."

"Believe?"

"He's a bit difficult to read—but he's said things—subtle things that make me want to trust him." She pressed the heels of her hands against her temples. "One must be ever so careful about what one says."

"True. But Atholl's son could be useful." Da eyed her. "Does he fancy you?"

"No—ah—I have no idea." Afraid Da might see her blush, Maddie turned and paced.

"A woman always kens."

"Possibly," she said over her shoulder. "He seems willing to help me, though a bit reluctant. His ship is only in port for a fortnight."

"Then use him—just ensure you keep him at arm's length."

Maddie stopped midstride. "I'm not certain I understand."

"You, my dear, are a bastard. Once the courtiers discover this, they will be disinclined to trust you—but Murray ought to be able to use his rank to introduce you to people who can help. If you can gain an audience with the queen, you could plead my innocence directly to Her Majesty."

Maddie nodded. "I've asked him to help. In fact, Lord Aiden suggested you but led a welcoming party to Edinburgh, not an army."

Da laughed, which brought on a fit of coughing. "Exactly the defense I have put forth. Let us never stray from it."

Chapter Seven

Magdalen's hands trembled while she stood outside the door of the Banqueting House at Whitehall. Everyone seemed to fit in except her. Worse, they were all dressed in finery the likes of which she'd never before seen. She wore a woolen gown of light green-and-black plaid; it was a gown she considered well tailored and fashionable, but it was nothing like the rustling silks and taffetas she'd glimpsed thus far. It was as if the gentry dressed to attend a royal ball, not a meal. Though all her life she'd been an outcast, she'd never felt so awkward before.

The doorman had insisted they be introduced separately, and he'd already taken Lord Aiden inside. Not without a rebuff from His Lordship, however. The gallant commander had grown red in the face, demanding that Lady Magdalen should have a proper escort. He'd capitulated only when the doorman explained that the queen preferred to greet newcomers individually even if they were husband and wife.

Maddie peeked inside the busy hall. Even the young officer looked bonnier than she. He wore a blond periwig and a navy blue doublet with long coattails, brass buttons, and gold trim atop. Lord Aiden looked ever so grand, with his dark blue-and-green kilt swishing across the backs of his knees. In the Scottish regiment fashion, the length of tartan belted around his waist was looped through the opening of his doublet, pulled around his back, and pinned at his left shoulder with an enormous brooch just like the one her father wore.

Goodness, he looked every bit the decorated officer. He even was more dashing than he'd been at Dunnottar Castle wearing a bandit's mask.

"The Lord Aiden Murray, commander aboard the *Royal Mary*," the doorman announced, his voice booming over the crowd.

Few looked up from their conversations, though Prince George of Denmark, lord high admiral and the queen's husband, stood and bowed. The prince was far stouter than in the paintings she'd seen of him.

Maddie couldn't make out the words, but by his gesture it was clear Prince George invited Lord Aiden to sit beside him.

Clapping a hand to her chest, she straightened and caught her breath. Where on earth would she sit now that Lord Aiden had been bidden to the royal table? He'd convinced her to attend the meal and said it was her opportunity to meet the queen because newcomers were always introduced.

Hot prickles sprang out across her skin.

I cannot possibly go in there now, even if I have to starve.

As she turned to flee, a guardsman blocked her path.

"You shall be introduced now, Lady Magdalen," said the doorman, coming up behind.

She gulped. "I do believe I am about to swoon."

The man offered his elbow. "You'll not be the first. I reckon half the ladies experience a bout of light-headedness the first time they are introduced to Her Majesty. Mark me, it shall pass."

Before Maddie could object further, the man marched into the hall. As they proceeded down the center aisle toward the dais, a few people glanced their way—but most ignored her.

Thank heavens.

The doorman will announce my name, I'll curtsy, and then I'll find a place to hide.

Now inside the enormous Banqueting House, Maddie couldn't help but look up. She'd heard about the ceiling, three stories high and painted in three scenes to depict the union of the crowns of Scotland and England and the peaceful reign of James I. On a gallery surrounding the entire hall, an ensemble of musicians played an assortment of dynamic modern music, barely audible above the hum of the crowd, though Maddie's sharp ears enjoyed the quick notes and harmonies, which would be a challenge on the harp.

While she was preoccupied with the sights above, her toe caught on her hem, sending her stumbling forward. The doorman tightened his grip on her elbow. "The ceiling is quite a sight, is it not?"

Maddie patted her curls, praying the queen hadn't seen her trip. "I've never set eyes on such a magnificent work of art."

They stopped in front of the dais and waited for the queen to glance their way. She was a large woman, which wasn't surprising given the double chin of the profile on her coins. Queen Anne wore her black hair parted in the middle, with curls trailing down the back of her neck. When she finally looked up, dark-blue eyes assessed Maddie from head to toe. Saying nothing, she gave a nod.

"May I introduce Lady Magdalen Keith," boomed the doorman, far louder than necessary.

Maddie dipped into a deep curtsy, bowing her head. "Your Majesty."

"I see by your gown you are Scottish?" the queen asked, her voice rich and full.

"Aye, Your Majesty."

The queen leaned forward and consulted with a tall man wearing a blond periwig. "Mar, you're a Scot. Tell me about Lady Magdalen."

"Illegitimate daughter of the Earl Marischal of Scotland, Majesty."

Maddie could have died.

The murmur in the hall instantly transformed into a series of hissing whispers. The crowd had been boisterous and inattentive until the Earl of Mar blurted the word *illegitimate*, and suddenly everyone stopped to listen and gossip?

Even Aiden gaped at her with a shocked, drop-mouthed stare.

Her cheeks burned. How on earth had she thought she might avoid the humiliation of her station in life? She should have fled when she had the chance. The embarrassment from her stepmother's disdain at the hospital paled compared to the mortification now making every inch of her skin perspire.

She glanced back over her shoulder.

I could run. But that would do nothing to help Da.

"The Earl Marischal?" said the queen, her voice condescending. "I take it you're here to plead for your father's innocence."

"Yes, Your Majesty. I believe him to be innocent."

Aiden shook his head in warning.

But Maddie stood her ground. When else would she have such an opportunity to voice her supplication to the queen?

Her Majesty took on an expression that made the word

haughty seem insignificant. "Why do you say that? Were you present when he marched his army to Edinburgh?"

"I beg your pardon, Your Majesty, but I believe you may have been misinformed. My father marched a welcoming party to Edinburgh." Maddie took in a deep breath, already feeling a noose tightening around her throat. "Would you not want your brother to be met with a welcome?"

The queen narrowed her eyes with a piercing stare. "You are outspoken for a bastard."

Aiden drew a hand to his forehead and cringed.

"Forgive me." Maddie again curtsied, bowing her head. "I wanted you to ken the truth afore my father's trial."

The prince nudged the queen with his elbow. "She is rather endearing."

"Hm." A slight smile turned up the corners of Her Majesty's mouth. "Have you any talents, Lady Magdalen?"

"I play the Celtic harp."

"Celtic?" The queen looked to her husband. "How quaint and provincial."

"I rather enjoy the Celtic harp," said Prince George. "'Tis soothing."

The queen arched her eyebrows and dismissed Maddie with a flick of her fingers.

"This way, my lady." The doorman grasped her elbow and led her to the back of the Banqueting House—all the way to the lowest tables—which was no surprise given the announcement of her bastard status. He held out a chair across from a couple who nodded, then swiftly glanced away.

As she pondered whether or not she should spirit out the door, a man slid into the chair beside her. "Lady Magdalen, might I introduce myself?" He offered his hand. "I am Reid MacKenzie." He cleared his throat. "Um, the Earl of

Seaforth. I dabble in legal matters and I'm a staunch ally of your father."

A flicker of hope made her sit a little taller. "Is that so, m'lord?" she asked in a whisper, not wanting to sound too interested, though practically jumping out of her skin to find a true ally. She assessed the man. Youngish, perhaps twenty, wearing his dark-blond locks trimmed to his shoulders rather than a periwig, he was dressed in silk breeches and waistcoat with a nicely tailored damask doublet atop.

"Have you found someone to represent your father?"

"Not as of yet."

The earl stroked his fingers down his chin as if thinking. "Have you been to London before?"

Maddie shook her head. "Never."

"It must be disconcerting to be in a hall with the most powerful nobles in the land."

"A bit, though I do not care much for titles and rank." She tried not to look bothered, though the past several days had to have been the most distressing of her life, starting with the visit from Lady Mary.

"Understandable." Seaforth reached for the ewer and poured himself a goblet of wine. "Though you do care what happens to your father."

She gave him a pointed nod. "That is why I am here, m'lord."

"Were you aware several other nobles were arrested and held in Edinburgh?"

"No, I was not."

His eyes shifted from side to side. "Yet your father was the only one sent to the Tower."

"Do you ken why?" Maddie whispered. This was shocking news indeed.

"Not exactly. My guess is it's because the Earl Marischal,

your father, has a duty to protect Britain's northern shores
from invasion. And everyone in London is well aware Prince
James's visit was a direct threat to the throne—and well
aware of your father's politics."

Since the earl hadn't offered to pour for her, Maddie
helped herself to the wine. "Perhaps, but I stand by my conviction that the prince should have been met with a welcoming party. And as a matter of fact, my father is ever cognizant
of his duty to queen and country."

"Is he?"

"Without question." She then reached for a slice of bread.

He passed her the butter. "Then you truly believe in his
innocence?"

"With my whole heart." Maddie leaned closer to the earl
and lowered her voice. "You say many nobles are being
detained at Edinburgh Castle?"

"Yes, including the Duke of Gordon."

"The duke?" Her stomach churned and she set the
uneaten slice on her plate. "My oh my, what does the queen
intend to do, execute half of Scotland's gentry?"

"All of London is awash with the same question, m'lady."

Maddie pushed away her plate. "What do you think it will
take to free my father?"

"Not certain. A public pledge of service to the queen. It
is common knowledge that Scotland is unhappy with being
forced into the Act of Union. I myself have been slighted,
along with my entire clan. Her Majesty needs a bevy of
northern nobles on her side...and with the Earl Marischal's
allegiances decidedly Catholic, no one doubts his loyalty
to *her brother*." Lord Seaforth glanced over each shoulder
as if he'd just uttered blasphemy. "But if your father can
prove himself a staunch supporter of Anne's rule...he just
might..."

"Might?" she asked.

"Keep his head attached to his neck."

Maddie gulped. The mere thought of her father meeting the headsman's ax made a clammy chill spread across her skin. "Can you help him?"

"I think I can."

"And what is in it for you, sir?" She stared pointedly. "Will your reputation not be sullied if you fail?"

He shrugged. "As I said, I'm a good friend of the Earl Marischal. Our clans are allies—always have been."

"And you believe my father to be innocent?"

He scowled and glanced away. "I believe your father will always act in the best interests of Scotland. The Tory Party needs him in London afore Parliament resumes. It is in Scotland's interest to see him proved innocent."

"I see." She glanced away. Everyone had their motives. She didn't want to trust Seaforth just yet...but her father could tell her whom she could trust. "Would you be willing to meet with Da on the morrow?"

"I could make time before the noon hour."

"Very well." She gave him a sharp nod. "Tomorrow morning at the Tower at, say, ten?"

"Agreed." Seaforth held up his goblet.

Maddie did the same, tapping her glass to his, but she nearly spewed the wine from her mouth when she saw Lord Aiden dancing with a woman. And not just any woman. This raven-haired temptress wore the latest French gown with her bodice cut so low, she might expose herself if the stays cinching her inordinately small waist gave her the slightest chance to breathe.

The music from the gallery above had grown louder.

"Are you all right, my lady?" asked the earl. "You look a bit pale."

Wiping her eyes, Maddie glanced away. "I'm well, thank you." Why should it matter if Aiden performed a court dance with a pretty courtier?

She bit her fingernail. "Do ye ken the lass dancing with Lord Aiden?"

Seaforth chuckled. "Why, that is the Countess of Saxonhurst. Unfortunately, she was widowed but one year past."

"She looks awfully young to be a widow." *Awfully happy as well.*

"Aye, though believe me, the woman is making the best of her circumstances."

Heat continued to spread across Maddie's skin while she watched the widow dance, laughing and throwing her head of black curls back as if she were a maid. How on earth could Maddie compete with a countess? Not that competing with anyone should be on her mind at the moment.

She was in London for one thing, and that was to see to her father's release. Now she'd met the Earl of Seaforth, perhaps it was best for Lord Aiden to kick up his heels and enjoy his holiday. Gracious, the man had done enough to help her already.

* * *

Dancing an Allemande, Aiden chuckled when the countess caught his eye and touched her lips with her fan. Never before had he received such an open invitation for a kiss, and to think Prince George had introduced them. Raven haired, her ample bosom swelling over the top of her bodice, the widow was exactly the woman Aiden had hoped to find by coming to court.

It should have made him happy to see a well-dressed lord sit beside Lady Magdalen. In fact, Aiden was thrilled—elated.

Perhaps she had found someone who could champion her in her quest to see her father cleared of the charge of treason and released from the Tower.

Aiden certainly couldn't prove the man's innocence in a fortnight.

He had no choice but to join the *Royal Mary* and sail two weeks hence, and if Lady Magdalen didn't find a champion by then, her father would in all likelihood lose his head. Aiden's leave had already been cut short by a day, a day spent ferrying Lady Magdalen through London to see her father with Miss Agnes in tow, no less. Even if he wanted to steal a kiss from the flaxen-haired lovely, the lady's maid would be certain to enter at the most inopportune time and clear her throat, just as she'd done last eve when Aiden had finally felt confident enough to slip his hand to the back of Magdalen's slender neck and lower his lips to hers.

He still could feel Maddie's silk-smooth skin against his fingers, roughened by hours passed on the ship tying knots. Their lips had nearly touched when Miss Agnes returned from the Banqueting House with a tray of food and a servant in tow.

Good God, the woman's timing couldn't have been worse.

Remembering the dance, Aiden stutter-stepped when the widow placed her small palm against his and promenaded in a circle. He took the opportunity to study the countess's face. Her eyes were wide set, her nose aristocratically long, and her lips plump—not as bonny as Maddie, but one quick glance down to the woman's cleavage and her face suddenly seemed lovelier.

When Aiden turned back to the men's line, the countess scandalously gripped his fingers and slid his arm across those oh-so-voluptuous breasts.

He practically moaned aloud.

Once he returned to the line, a single face stood out at the back of the room.

Lady Magdalen's.

Her eyes bored through him as if he'd committed a sin by enjoying a wee dance. She drew her hand to her chest, and her lips parted. He could even hear her gasp, though that could not be possible given the music and the hum of the crowd.

Ballocks.

He absolutely must find more suitable accommodations for the lass and her serving maid—especially if the countess proved to be the woman for whom he'd been searching.

I should not feel guilty about sending her elsewhere. Maddie didn't even tell me she was illegitimate. No wonder the earl didn't mention their relationship at the Hogmanay masque. He had a vested interest in his offspring for certain.

Again Aiden and the countess moved together to promenade in a circle.

"Are you not enjoying the dance?" Lady Saxonhurst asked.

"Very much. It is ever so invigorating."

"And the company?" She batted her long black eyelashes, her cheeks sporting quite a bit of rouge.

He grinned. The countess knew exactly what she was doing and the effect her advances had on him. "I must thank the lord high admiral for introducing us."

She let out a wee snort. "'Tis ever so kind of you to say."

At the end of the dance, the countess curtsied, keeping her head up and practically spilling out of her bodice. Aiden couldn't help but stare. He licked his lips—oh, to sink his head between those hills of pillowy softness and implore her to take him to heaven.

The queen clapped loudly, making the banter in the hall

ebb. "Lady Magdalen, would you do me the honor of playing the harp?"

All eyes shifted to Maddie, who suddenly looked like a doe in the sights of a musket. The man beside her stood and offered his hand.

Aiden clenched his fists. If that bull-witted boar made one errant move, it would be his last—and he'd best keep his eyes on her face. It hadn't slipped Aiden's notice earlier that Maddie's bodice scooped daringly low—not as low as Lady Saxonhurst's, but too low for the presence of strangers.

The countess started back to the dais, grabbing Aiden's hand with a huff. "It looks as if we've no choice but to listen to a bastard Jacobite play a woeful tune."

Aiden's hackles bristled as he followed.

Lady Saxonhurst sniffed. "Honestly, the urchin should be embarrassed to show her face in Whitehall, what with her father accused of treason, and her *questionable* birth."

"I beg to differ. In fact, I admire Lady Magdalen's fortitude." Aiden wasn't about to crumble and listen to the woman cut down the poor lass in front of everyone in the hall. "Her stepmother is with child and unable to travel. It takes a firm backbone to come to London alone and plea for leniency and justice."

"Dear Lord Aiden, you speak as if you have a soft spot for underlings such as she."

He gave her a pointed stare. "I believe Lady Magdalen has only the best intentions."

"You know the girl?" The countess looked as though she could spit out her teeth.

"Indeed I do." Aiden bit his cheek. He'd almost blurted out the fact that Lady Maddie was staying in his father's apartments. That wouldn't have turned out well for him or for the lass. "Her father was kind enough to invite the officers of the *Royal Mary* to a Hogmanay celebration, and we were introduced there."

The corner of Lady Saxonhurst's mouth turned up, somewhere between a sneer and a grin. "Truly? Do not tell me the woman dressed in the frumpy plaid managed to be charming and graceful, else I'll think you an utter fool."

Arriving at the table, Aiden held the chair for the opinionated woman. "Perhaps things in the north of Scotland are so far removed from London that all Scots appear a tad foolish when they first come to court." He helped her scoot in, then bent down so his lips were near her ear. "But I assure you, you're quite mistaken about the Earl Marischal's daughter. She has the grace of a swan."

"Please. She is but his illegitimate daughter—graceful or nay." Lady Saxonhurst shook her fan beneath his nose.

He straightened, lips pursed. "I'll grant you that."

With a sniff she reached for her wine. "Many a fallen woman has been gifted with grace, my lord."

Aiden clenched his teeth. Perhaps Lady Saxonhurst's bosoms were not as alluring as he'd first thought. After affecting a pleasant smile and bowing to the queen and her husband, he took his seat. Though hot under the collar, he didn't want to marry the widow, he just wanted to...ah... *learn* from her. As long as she kept her mouth shut they ought to be agreeable. And he'd never heard of anyone's talking while kissing—though if anyone could manage it, he surmised it would be the countess.

Light music hung above the crowd, and within two ticks of his pocket watch, the hall fell silent.

The strings of the Celtic harp took on a life of their own as blossoms of harmonies swelled throughout the hall. It was as if Lady Magdalen interpreted the lavish paintings on the ceiling and brought them to life. Aiden closed his eyes, and his toes kept time while his heart soared. How could one person make a single instrument so full of vigor? And the lass had been tucked away in the sleepy burgh of Stonehaven. Who besides her father had heard such utter brilliance? 'Twas like the music of a lark singing above the waterfall at the Glen of the Fairies. Magical and ever so enchanting.

"At least the little recital will be over soon," mumbled Lady Saxonhurst, swilling her wine.

He ignored the woman, though he opened his eyes. Fortunately, everyone else within sight remained riveted by Magdalen's performance. Goodness, her fingers worked so quickly, they moved in a blur.

When the tune ended, Aiden sat very still, his tongue dry. The only thing Lady Saxonhurst had been right about was that it had been over soon—too soon.

To his right the queen led the applause, a favorable smile playing on her lips. Prince George joined in, and soon everyone in the Banqueting House was on their feet applauding, though very politely like true Englishmen and -women. Aiden wanted to shout for more as sailors would do aboard ship, but such an outward display of bravado would be completely unacceptable at Whitehall, especially since he'd been invited to sit at the royal table.

Then his gut squeezed when the well-dressed man from the back of the Banqueting House greeted Magdalen on the gallery and kissed her hand.

Clenching his fists, Aiden sat forward. The bloody varlet took his time hovering over the lassie's hand—no doubt breathing in the same intoxicating fragrance Aiden had enjoyed only moments before entering the hall.

Pasty, fat codfish.

The worst thing?

The bastard didn't look portly in the slightest. He looked more muscle bound than a bloody ox.

Prince George nudged Aiden with his elbow. "It appears Lady Magdalen has found an ally in the Earl of Seaforth."

He ground his back molars.

Earl? That amorous bastard had best keep his distance.

Chapter Eight

*A*iden stared up at the gallery while Seaforth and Lady Magdalen started down the stairs. After excusing himself, he strode straight through the Banqueting House to the foot of the gallery stairwell. He'd be damned if he'd sit idle while the Earl of Seaforth took the liberty of kissing the innocent lassie's hand. For the love of God, she was Aiden's house-guest. He had a duty to protect her from licentious courtiers who saw young maids as their playthings.

"There you are, m'lady." As she descended the final step, Aiden took her hand and pulled her behind him, giving a cold stare to Seaforth. "Why did you not tell me you were such a practiced harpist?"

"You are acquainted with the lady?" asked Seaforth.

Aiden's arm muscles flexed beneath his doublet. "Best of friends."

Lady Magdalen wrenched her hand free. "Lord Aiden, please allow me to introduce the Earl of Seaforth, Reid MacKenzie."

Squaring his shoulders, the wet-eared earl gave Aiden a

deprecating once-over. Bloody hell, his face looked younger than a bairn's bum. "Ah, the sailor."

"Naval *officer*," Aiden corrected. "Commander aboard the *Royal Mary*."

"A Scottish frigate?" asked Seaforth.

Aiden folded his arms and tipped up his chin. "Aye."

Seaforth glanced to the lass. "And how have the pair of you become acquainted?"

"Lord Aiden and the *Royal Mary* officers attended a Hogmanay masque at Dunnottar."

Stepping in, Aiden blocked Maddie from Seaforth's view. "And the lady is in my care."

"Your care?" Seaforth scoffed, closing the distance so they were nose to nose, though Seaforth was forced to crane his neck. At six foot two, Aiden was a good inch taller.

Aiden didn't blink. The earl had no idea he could meet his end if he did not proceed wisely. "Someone must be responsible for her welfare whilst her father is incarcerated."

"But why you?"

Shoving between the two men, the lady cleared her throat. "Lord Aiden was kind enough to come to my rescue when my coach threw a wheel at Blackwall Port."

Aiden bowed. "Lady Magdalen, the hour is growing late, and I'm sure Miss Agnes will be anxious as to your whereabouts."

Maddie gave a defiant blink, then let out a long breath. "I suppose it is late." She looked to Seaforth. "Do not forget you agreed to accompany me at the Tower on the morrow, m'lord."

"How could I forget such a delight, m'lady?" He collected her hand and again hovered over it for far too long, planting a sloppy kiss. Then he tipped his head to Aiden. "It has been a pleasure, Lord Aiden."

Aiden moved in front of the lady. "The pleasure is mine, m'lord."

Stepping beside him, Lady Magdalen rested her hand on Aiden's elbow. "You were a bit short with the earl."

"Was I?" Aiden led her away at a quick pace, heading through a long passageway. "Do you allow every man you meet to ply your hand with adoring kisses?"

"I beg your pardon?" Maddie's voice shot up as she shuffled her feet alongside him. "It would have been rude of me to pull away."

This woman had him tied in knots. Aye, he'd aimed to find an education in the boudoir, but that didn't mean Lady Magdalen was fair game for any passerby. Damnation, his cravat was too bloody tight. "The earl was clearly smitten—who wouldn't be when faced with a woman as bonny as you?"

"So what do you recommend I do when a gentleman kisses my hand?"

"Don't look so bloody bonny, for starters." He couldn't help his scowl.

She yanked her hand away from his elbow. "You are making absolutely no sense at all. Would you prefer me to draw bags under my eyes with charcoal and drool whilst I'm at court?"

"Oh please, you ken what I mean."

She stopped directly in front of a window embrasure. "No, I do not. You are speaking as if it is a crime for a lady to try to look her best. Furthermore, you sound more controlling than a father."

"I—"

"You told me yourself you haven't much time to help me. What do you expect me to do? Grovel on my knees in front of the queen and beg for clemency? Ask her to release my father on the grounds that he's a good man?" She crossed her arms over her chest. "If you didn't hear Her Majesty, I am a *bastard*. Not only that, I have no choice but to make as many alliances as I can to help my father. Lord Seaforth said he is Da's ally."

"But—"

"And you are the son of the Duke of Atholl. I have no doubt your father was *not* among the welcoming parties in Edinburgh." She shoved his shoulder. "Was he?"

Aiden's cravat was definitely far too tight. "No. With the news of James's arrival, my father would have barred the gates of Blair Castle." He looked both ways down the empty passageway, then encouraged her deeper into the embrasure, lowering his voice to a whisper. "But that doesn't mean *I* would have. Had I not been aboard the *Royal Mary*, I would have taken the Atholl army and stood beside your da."

She blinked, coughing out a guffaw. "Why did you not tell me that before?"

"Because certain things are best left unspoken," he whispered loudly, backing her against the wall. For the love of God, she had to be the bonniest creature he'd ever seen. Aye, he'd dreamed of kissing her while enduring endless nights at sea. And now, as she stamped her foot and grew more indignant, the smoldering fire in his loins burst into a raging flame.

How could a man resist such temptation? His hands slipped to her waist, so small he could nearly touch his fingertips together.

Magdalen inhaled sharply. "M'lord?"

"Aye?" he growled, his tongue slipping across his lips as he enjoyed watching the rise and fall of her breasts with her quick breaths—breasts creamier and more enticing by far than the countess's.

"Y-y-you think me bonny?"

Had she only just realized what he'd said when they'd started down the passageway? "Any man who isn't blinded by your radiance the moment he walks into a room is utterly blind."

When she parted her lips to speak, he silenced her. With a slight dip of his chin, he captured her mouth and plundered it with reckless abandon. He slid his hands up her spine and drew her body into his. Oh yes, this was exactly what he'd been craving since he watched her from across the avenue in Blackwall.

With a wee moan, the lady turned to butter in his arms, matching his kiss with slow and rhythmic caresses of her tongue as if the harp music still swirled around them. Out of his mind with desire, he thrust his hips forward. Oh yes, yes, yes. Even though through layers of wool, he met soft woman. *Oh aye.*

His cock was stiffer than the hilt of his sword. Back and forth he ground the ridge of his erection against her skirts as his breathing sped. Each languid swirl of his tongue filled his chest with unquenchable desire and shot directly through his aching loins.

Heaven help him, if he wasn't in a public passageway, he'd tug up her skirts and slip between her legs. Yes, yes, yes, this was what he'd been waiting for. Forget the widow, he wanted to be inside Magdalen Keith. He wanted her to be the one to take him to the pinnacle of ecstasy.

She arched against him. His cock throbbed, leaking seed as he ground himself into her.

"Lord Aiden?" a woman's voice said from behind.

Aiden jerked away, running a hand over his mouth and turning. "Lady Saxonhurst." Devil have it, he sounded like an adolescent lad.

The countess smirked. "That rather looks like fun, though I suggest you find a bedchamber to finish swiving the tart."

Damn, he knew he should have kept his mouth shut until behind the doors of his apartments. "Forgive—"

Covering her mouth, Lady Magdalen rushed past them and dashed down the passageway.

With a guttural chuckle, the widow sauntered forward and cupped his ballocks. Aiden gasped. His cock was about ready to explode—and this woman knew it. His knees buckled and he braced himself against the wall in the nick of time.

The woman smirked with a teasing chuckle. "If you tire of the wench, my apartments are on the riverside, third floor." Then she pressed her breasts against him and smashed a kiss to his lips.

Aiden stood dumbstruck, every muscle in his body tense. On one hand, he ought to shove the arrogant countess up against the wall and give her exactly what she wanted— experienced or nay; the position of her hand told him all he had to do was tug up her skirts and slip inside. That's what MacPherson would do without a second thought. On the other hand, the woman Aiden wanted to kiss, the woman he wanted in his arms and every inch of whose succulent flesh he wanted to explore, had fled down the passageway.

The countess laughed. "You should see your face, Murray. 'Tis priceless."

Breaking from the widow's grasp, he bowed, collecting a modicum of composure. "Before I was interrupted, I intended to apologize for my brazen behavior."

"Hmm. It must have been that dreary Celtic harp. I noticed several gentlemen appeared smitten."

How on earth could this woman be so utterly wrong about everything? Pursuing the conversation further would only serve to incite Aiden's ire. Doubtless the countess didn't care for bastards, especially bonny bastard females. What she didn't seem to understand was that her cutting remarks only made her appear malicious and very unattractive.

"If you'll pardon me, I'd best head for my chamber, m'lady."

Lady Saxonhurst made an exaggerated roll of her hand. "Carry on then."

* * *

"Is everything well, m'lady?" asked Agnes as soon as Maddie entered her chamber.

Maddie sucked in a deep breath and hid her face in her hands. Agnes might be a servant, but the woman was the closest thing to a mother she had ever known. She couldn't admit that she'd thoroughly enjoyed kissing Lord Aiden in the window embrasure—that the two occasions she'd kissed him made up the highlight of her miserable life. She couldn't admit how impassioned she'd grown, how she'd swooned when he wrapped her in his arms and pressed his very hard, masculine body against her.

Oh, what a mind-bogglingly, wonderfully, delightfully solid male.

Nor could she admit how much her body craved more, but when they'd been discovered by the countess, she'd felt dirty and ashamed, as if the raw passion she'd shared with Aiden had been lewd.

How could such powerful and heavenly sensations be wrong?

Maddie hissed and shook her head. For pity's sake, the entire evening had been a disaster.

"Come, child." Agnes led her to the settee. "Tell me what's worrying you."

She pushed the heels of her hands into her temples and shook her head. "My entire life is a calamity."

"Oh dear." Agnes sank down beside her. "That doesn't sound good at all."

Maddie dropped her hands and looked to the ceiling. "As soon as I was introduced, the Earl of Mar announced to everyone that I am Da's illegitimate daughter." She again buried her face in her palms. "I could have died right then and there."

Agnes smoothed a consoling hand up and down Maddie's back. "Where was Lord Aiden when this was going on?"

"The doorman suggested we should be announced separately. Lord Aiden went in first, and then Prince George invited him to the high table. When the doorman escorted me to the dais, it was a complete and utter disaaaaaaster!" Maddie hated crying, but the humiliation that had persisted throughout the evening had her insides wound so tight, she could hold in her sobs no longer. With her next breath, tears poured down her face. "I hate London. I hate court and all the pompous, snooty people who think they're superior to everyone else."

Agnes produced a linen handkerchief. "There, there. I kent it was a bad idea to come here. Blast Lady Mary for forcing you into this situation."

If only Maddie were able to talk about Lady Saxonhurst and how the woman had shamelessly flirted with Aiden during the entire meal...and worse, how the countess had seemed sadistically amused when she'd caught Maddie in Aiden's arms.

Oh God, I'll never be able to show my face in the Banqueting House again.

A knock came at the door. "Lady Magdalen, is all well?" Of all the untimeliness—Lord Aiden's deep bass resounded from the passageway.

If only Maddie could melt into the settee and hide for the rest of her days.

What must Lord Aiden think of her? She'd completely forgotten herself in his arms—behaved like an utter tart pressing against him and allowing him to trap her against the wall.

"I'm well," she said, her voice far too high-pitched as she tried to mask the trembling.

"May I come in?"

Maddie shot a panicked look to Agnes and shook her head, mouthing, "*No*."

The lady's maid sprang to her feet and opened the door a crack. "I'm ever so sorry, Lord Aiden, my lady is not feeling up to having callers at the moment."

Aiden peered at her through the wee opening. "I understand. Please tell Her Ladyship how much I regret taking liberties. It shan't happen again."

"Liberties, Your Lordship?" Agnes threw an alarmed glare over her shoulder.

He cleared his throat. "I'll not embarrass her further by trying to explain. I only wish to add that her performance this evening moved me. I cannot recall ever hearing music played with such heart and reverence, and I do hope Lady Magdalen will see fit to play again very soon."

"Thank you, m'lord." After closing the door, Agnes turned and crossed her arms. "Liberties, m'lady?"

Maddie had known that was coming. She wiped her eyes with the kerchief. "He kissed me."

"And you allowed it?" Agnes strode back to the settee and plopped down beside her.

Holy crosses, why on earth had Lord Aiden mentioned liberties? And in front of Agnes. "It all happened so fast, I-I was swept away."

"Is that why you were so flummoxed when you dashed in here, or was it truly because of being named the illegitimate daughter of the Earl Marischal?"

Maddie heaved a sigh. "I suppose it was a bit of both."

"And you played the harp?"

"Aye, the queen requested it."

"The queen?" Agnes beamed as if Maddie's catastrophe had somehow become something to gloat about. "I imagine you captured the heart of every person in the Banqueting House."

She shrugged. "Some, perhaps."

"And how do you feel about Lord Aiden?"

"He's very nice. He has been most accommodating."

"And he's handsome. You cannot deny."

"Aye, then there's that." Maddie tried her best not to show any emotion whatsoever.

"But he kissed you?"

"Aye." *Will she please find something else to fixate upon?*

"Hmm. You mustn't forget yourself again, else your father will take the switch to my hide." Agnes patted Maddie's hand. "Well, my dear, after the excitement of this evening, I reckon you'll sleep well."

I reckon I'll not sleep at all.

Too many thoughts swirled through Maddie's head. Lord Aiden had clearly enjoyed the attentions of the countess throughout the meal. And the woman flirted shamelessly. Had she followed them? Did she delight in Maddie's humiliation?

If only I could sail back to Stonehaven at dawn on the morrow.

Chapter Nine

*A*iden awoke with a throbbing headache. As a matter of fact, he wasn't quite sure he'd slept. After begging for Lady Magdalen's forgiveness, he'd drowned his woes with a few good tots of whisky. The spirit had only served to make things worse. And this morning he was more confounded than he'd been when his head hit the pillow.

Yes, he liked the lass, but why couldn't she have arrived in London a fortnight hence? Even if she'd shown up a sennight later, it would have been better. He definitely would have achieved his goal by then. Now it looked as if he was down by the head and sinking fast.

So many times while sleep had eluded him he'd closed his eyes and tried to think about Lady Saxonhurst's bosom. With his every effort he managed only to see a pair of azure eyes gazing at him with complete trust, and Lady Saxonhurst seemed more like a dragon disguised in courtier's clothing.

Damn, he felt like a heel.

But weren't all naval officers supposed to be heels and

philanderers? Crass, coarse rakes, debauchers, and down-right expert lovers? "A woman in every port" was MacPherson's motto. Hell, MacPherson swived with such abandon, the lieutenant couldn't tell one wench from the next.

After slipping out of bed, Aiden poured water into the bowl and splashed his face. Dripping wet, he regarded himself in the looking glass.

A goddamned sailor with a conscience you are, you bastard.

His gaze slipped down to his cock, stiff as a board—too stiff to piss. Damnation, he'd thought abstinence was difficult aboard ship? Try staying at Whitehall with a bonny lass sleeping across the passageway. Every time he inhaled, he smelled lilacs and pure ambrosia of woman. Such temptation could drive a young man to madness.

A door opened and closed.

Aiden hastened to tuck his kilt around his hips while footsteps started. He threw open his chamber door. "Lady Magdalen."

She stopped and turned, her gaze sliding from his face down to his abdomen. With a wee gasp, her lips parted.

Glancing down, he reconsidered his hastiness. Perhaps he should have pulled a shirt over his head? Well, at least the years aboard ship had toned his form. He had nothing to be embarrassed about.

He leaned his hip against the doorjamb. "Where are you off to, m'lady?"

"Lord Seaforth agreed to meet me at the Tower by ten o'clock."

Aiden glanced inside his chamber to the mantel clock. "'Tis only half past eight."

"Aye, but I want to ensure I arrive in plenty of time. I wouldn't want to miss him."

He didn't like the sound of that one bit. "Are you planning to walk there?"

"I was."

"Alone?"

"No, silly, Miss Agnes just went to fetch her cloak."

"Miss Agnes needn't stress herself. I shall escort you."

The young lady blushed a shade of scarlet. "You mustn't put yourself out on my account. You are on holiday, after all."

"Which means I have nothing else I must do." *And there's no way I'll sit idle whilst Lady Magdalen meets with the Earl of Seaforth under my nose.* "Please, I'll be but a moment."

Her gaze again raked down his torso as her tongue slipped to the corner of her mouth. "Very well. I'll tell Miss Agnes she has earned a reprieve."

With a fluttering in his belly, Aiden bowed and ducked back into his chamber, wishing he'd employed a valet for the fortnight. He'd thought the maid would be enough. But damn it all, he'd planned on doing more undressing than dressing. Nonetheless, he'd had plenty of practice attending himself aboard ship.

The apartment bell sounded. "I've a missive," called a voice from the outer passageway.

Aiden pulled his shirt over his head.

What the devil? It had best not be a summons to the Royal Mary.

"I'll fetch it," Miss Agnes said as she approached, with footsteps clattering. "You shouldn't be answering doors to gentlemen's apartments, my dear," she added with a rather sharp tone for a servant, though she was right. Lady Magdalen could ill afford for her reputation to be sullied by her opening the door to the Duke of Atholl's apartments, especially when the duke's son was in residence... alone.

Aiden's gut clenched for the millionth time.

If only there were truly a scandal for the gossips to prattle about, I mightn't wake with an erection the size of Mount Olympus.

He made quick work of donning his hose, shoes, waistcoat, doublet, dirk, and sword, and a *sgian-dubh* in each of his flashes. He then found Lady Magdalen with Miss Agnes in the drawing room.

"Are you expecting to be attacked by highwaymen along the Thames, m'lord?" asked Miss Agnes.

Aiden draped his cloak over one shoulder. "Not at all, 'tis simply attire expected of a naval officer."

"Well, I think you look dashing," said Magdalen, blessing him with a radiant smile.

Aiden's heart skipped a beat. "My thanks." He bowed. "And where is the missive that just arrived?"

Lady Magdalen patted the pocket attached to her belt. "'Twas from the queen. She invited me to play the harp whilst she attends the card tables this afternoon."

He arched his eyebrows. "You must have made quite an impression on her."

"I trust that is a good thing." Maddie stood. "Unless she wants to flaunt a bastard's talents and make a spectacle... 'Ooo, look at the wee ill-born Scottish lassie. At least she has a talent to fall back upon. She'll be able to join a band of tinkers when she returns to Scotland.'"

"Magdalen!" Miss Agnes chided.

Aiden gave the woman a sharp glare, but held his tongue. Goodness, the serving maid must have been a beauty in her day, but the coif she continually wore atop her head made her appear frumpy.

"I see the queen's attention as a good sign. It will give her time to come to know you," Aiden said, offering his arm. "Shall we?"

Once they were outside, the wind off the Thames blew a chilly gale. "Would you prefer to take a coach?"

Magdalen clutched her cloak taut at the neck. "I like to walk."

"'Tis nice to find a lass who isn't afraid of the weather."

She chuckled. "I imagine you've met many a squall at sea."

"Aye, if there's one thing you can expect aboard ship, 'tis a strong wind. Besides, on the off day when the wind isn't blowing, the frigate drifts to nowhere."

"Do you like being in the navy?"

"I suppose."

"Why did you join?"

"I could have stayed home and supported my father, but a second son must blaze his own path. My brother John, the Marquis of Tullibardine, lurks in Da's shadow. He's a good man and will make a far better duke than I."

"I think you'd be a dashing duke—or marquis for that matter."

Aiden shrugged. "Well, at least we do not have to worry about that."

They walked for a time while he pondered his reasons for joining the navy. True, he had left home to elude the label of lesser son. It had been difficult growing up in a stately palace like Blair Castle ever aware that such a life was not for him. And honestly, he wanted to make his way—seek his fortune, be a man of substance, self-made, answering to no one.

"Have you given much thought to what you'll do once you retire from the navy?" Maddie asked.

"I've thought of making a life at sea. Before the Act of Union, I'd set my sights on becoming a navy captain."

"The merger with the English navy changed your mind?"

"Aye, the English senior officers look down on Scottish-bred officers. Do everything in their power to ensure only English-men are promoted as captains."

"Even if you've proven yourself?"

"Even then."

The lass gave an empathic nod. "That's kind of like being a bastard. Everyone thinks you're inferior because of your birth, and no matter how hard you work, you can't hide from your heritage."

He chuckled. "I'd never thought of it like that, but you're right. I suppose bastards have to make their way in this world just like second sons."

She glanced at him while her teeth grazed her lip. "Do you remember when we strolled atop the wall-walk at Dunnottar?"

"How could I forget?"

"Did you ever think fondly upon our...our...wee tryst?"

"Indeed, I lay awake in my bunk many a night remembering..." *Your scent, the softness of your lips...all the things I wanted to do...had there been more time.*

"Me as well," she whispered.

Aiden walked a little taller. In fact, he wasn't certain his feet were touching the footpath. The tingling of his skin, the lightness of his heart made him feel as if he were soaring. Until Lord Seaforth met them outside the Tower of London's gates.

The young man had an intensity about him—able-bodied, with a narrow-eyed stare that warned against crossing him. Oddly, he opted not to wear a periwig. Rather his wavy blond hair hung well past his shoulders—he descended from Viking stock for certain.

But Aiden was taller, older, probably smarter, and fur-thermore, Lady Magdalen was staying in *his* apartments.

Seaforth held out his hand. "Murray, I'm surprised to see you this morn."

Aiden gripped the earl's hand and bowed his head respectfully. "I couldn't allow Lady Magdalen to walk all the way from Whitehall without an escort."

"Do you trust him?" asked Seaforth, splaying his fingers.

"Absolutely." Maddie nodded with a smile. "Lord Aiden has been of great assistance to me."

Seaforth arched a brow. "Truly?"

"Why are you involving yourself, m'lord?" asked Aiden. "Do you have a plan?"

"I wish it were that easy," said Seaforth, motioning to the guard to lead on. "I want to meet with the Earl Marischal first."

Aiden followed, his jaw sore from his clenching his teeth. True, Seaforth wasn't as tall—mightn't be as fit, either— but he had the look of a rogue and shoulders as broad as the hindquarters of a stallion. Worse, he was an earl, a bloody firstborn son.

When Lady Maddie placed her palm in Seaforth's proffered elbow, Aiden hastened to her other side, his finger lightly brushing the back of her hand.

"It must be ever so disconcerting to see your father treated with such disdain," said the earl.

She drew her hand away from Seaforth's elbow, thank God. "It is."

Once they'd surrendered their weapons and had been admitted and taken through the labyrinth of cells, the Earl Marischal rose from his seat and shook hands with Seaforth. "Reid MacKenzie, what on earth has brought you to London? Has a session of Parliament been called?"

"Not as yet. As a ward of the crown until I attain the age of one and twenty, the queen thinks she's seeing to my education."

Aiden looked the earl from head to toe. "How old are you now?"

"Nineteen." Seaforth winked. "But not to worry, I ken who my da was, and Anne will not be changing political leanings ingrained in me since birth."

The Marischal scrutinized Aiden as pointedly. "And you, Murray? Do your political leanings align with your father's?"

Aiden held up his palms. It was common knowledge his father was no Jacobite. "I am my own man. Please do not allow my father's politics to sway your opinion of me."

"Ayyyyye?" asked Seaforth, his voice filled with uncertainty.

"If you haven't heard, the *Royal Mary* prevented the English warships from opening fire on Prince James's ships. That wasn't an accident." Aiden touched his finger to the tiny rose pin on his lapel—a secret Jacobite sign worn by the sailors aboard the Scottish naval ships. When anyone asked, the sailors would say 'twas in honor of Queen Mary. Little did the others know it was Mary, Queen of Scots, to whom they referred.

His eyes widening with recognition, Seaforth let out a long breath and clapped Aiden's shoulder. "'Tis good to hear," he whispered. "Perhaps we'll see Atholl's men at the next rising?"

"Many of my father's men side with..." He looked to the door and cupped a hand over his mouth and whispered, "Scotland."

Lady Maddie smiled. "I kent it all along."

Seaforth relaxed his stance. "'Tis a relief to ken *the cause* has allies in the Royal Navy."

"I assure you, Captain Polwarth is of like mind." Aiden looked to the lady and winked.

"That is all very well and good, but it isn't helping me gain a pardon," said Marischal.

Magdalen bobbed her head in agreement. "Aye, we haven't much time."

Lord Seaforth stroked his chin. "I've discussed it with the northern lairds. We are all in agreement that it is best if we can prevent your case from going before a jury."

"Aye?" asked Marischal with a smirk. "How do you expect to achieve that?"

"We need someone to bend the queen's ear."

Lady Maddie pulled the missive from her pocket. "It seems something good may have come from my harp playing last eve. I've been invited to play for Her Majesty this very afternoon."

"Excellent. You must make every effort to endear yourself to the queen's good graces," said Marischal.

She cringed and looked to Aiden. "I already have a black mark against me due to my illegitimate birth."

Her father flicked one of her curls with his pointer finger. "If anyone can overcome adversity, it is you, my dear."

"Indeed," agreed Seaforth. "This could be the opportunity we've been waiting for."

The older man looked to his comrade. "Imagine what intelligence Maddie could garner as the queen's harpist."

The lady drew a hand to her chest, looking rather dubious.

Sensing her reluctance, Aiden thrust his palms forward, bidding the men to slow down. "Perhaps Lady Magdalen should set her sights on this afternoon's performance before we turn her into a *spy* for *the cause*."

The two men peered at him as if he'd just drilled a hole through his own head.

"I agree with Lord Aiden," the lady said. At least someone remained in control of her sanity. "I'll play for the queen and first see if I can find favor for my performance. Once accepted, I'll request to be permitted a moment to speak, and only then will I make another attempt to explain about Da's welcoming party."

"If you have her ear, why not add how it would invite anarchy in Scotland if she decided to execute all the Scottish nobles held in Edinburgh?" said Seaforth.

Aiden shook his head. "I'm certain the queen is well aware that her popularity in Scotland is fragile."

"Aye," agreed Marischal. "Otherwise she would have introduced every last one of us to the headsman's ax by now. Keep in mind, if Magdalen pushes too far, it will be the last time she will be granted an opportunity to speak."

Seaforth let out a lengthy sigh. "And I suppose being overly zealous would hinder your plea for clemency."

Rubbing his hands together, Aiden looked between the accomplices. It appeared as though they had the makings of a plan. "Then 'tis settled. Lady Magdalen will not put herself in harm's way by spying, but she will work to encourage the queen to release her father and the nobles in Edinburgh."

"Agreed," said Marischal. "For now."

"What say you, m'lady?" Aiden asked.

Maddie pressed praying hands to her lips. "I'll do anything to see to Da's release."

"You are a brave woman," said Seaforth, taking her hand and squeezing it—a bit too bold a move in Aiden's estimation.

Grasping her elbow, Aiden tugged her away from the earl. "We must make haste. I'll hire a coach to take us back to Whitehall. That shall afford you ample time to prepare."

Chapter Ten

A Celtic harp stood in the drawing room awaiting Maddie when she and Aiden returned from the Tower. With the morning's missive, and now the delivery of the harp, it appeared a scandal had been avoided. Thanks to Agnes's shouting upon their arrival, everyone in London must know Maddie's bedchamber door was being guarded by the stalwart lady's maid.

Maddie followed Lord Aiden to the gaming hall as he carried the instrument as if it weighed nothing. Maddie had moved her own harp in Stonehaven enough times to know it weighed nearly three stone—not an inordinate amount, but lugging it through the long passageway and across the courtyard must be difficult without a wagon.

Now she knew why he hadn't bothered to send for a valet to help. The commander had to be hewn from marble.

Walking behind him, she enjoyed the view—perhaps more than she ought. She liked that he didn't bow to London fashion. His kilt accented his powerful calves and made him stand out as a proud Highlander. Though the Earl of

Seaforth had broad shoulders, she liked Lord Aiden's better. Solid but narrow hips supported his powerful shoulders, his waist fanning up into a V, sculpted perfectly by his well-tailored doublet. Maddie's knees had turned boneless when, earlier that morning, he'd opened the door wearing nothing but a plaid clutched around his waist.

Merciful heavens, did all men have abdomens with such defined musculature? It had been all she could do not to stare. And now watching him from the rear was every bit as amusing. He stood well over six feet, and wore his dark hair neatly pulled back and tied with a bow. It accentuated his long neck—indeed everything about him was long and lean. Not to mention sturdy. She much preferred his leanness to the Earl of Seaforth's burly form. Seaforth's build reminded her of a blacksmith's. Aiden? Well, the best way to describe him was as a stallion bred for the races. Especially when one was walking behind him and watching his kilt slap the backs of his legs with every step.

As they approached the hall, Lady Saxonhurst rushed toward them. "There you are."

"Am I late?" asked Maddie. "The missive said one o'clock."

"Regardless of what a missive says, you always arrive an hour early to any event requested by Her Majesty." The lady sniffed. "Though I daresay I have no idea why the queen is wasting her time with the likes of you."

"Perhaps she appreciates Lady Magdalen's talent," said Lord Aiden.

"Ha." The countess flicked her fan through the air. "You are so quaintly chivalrous, Commander. Why on earth did you not call a valet to carry that mammoth thing?"

"'Tisn't heavy." Lord Aiden winked at Maddie over his shoulder. "Besides, who wouldn't want to offer assistance to such a bonny lass as Lady Magdalen?"

Maddie had never seen anyone turn green, but Lady Saxonhurst appeared to grow chartreuse while she pursed her lips, apparently at a loss for words. And Aiden—er—Lord Aiden had again referred to her as bonny? Perhaps she just might float into the Great Hall on the coattails of such a charming compliment.

The countess cleared her throat and looked at Maddie with dagger eyes. "You shall proceed directly to the gallery. Speak to no one unless spoken to, especially Her Majesty. Keep in mind everyone at court is a person of *great* importance—there are very few *bastards* among us."

Maddie looked to Lord Aiden. "How could I ever forget?"

"Shall I go in with you?" he asked.

"Absolutely not," snapped Lady Saxonhurst. "You have not been invited."

Hesitating, the young commander pointedly shot his own set of daggers at the countess. "At least allow me to carry the harp to the gallery."

"Absolutely not, I say again." With a clap of the countess's hands, a servant came from the hall and took the harp. "Now up to the gallery with you, *Lady* Magdalen." The woman said *lady* as if it caused her a great deal of pain to utter.

Maddie tried to brush away Saxonhurst's impoliteness. It wasn't the first time in her life she'd met with snobbery, and she doubted it would be the last. Goodness, when one's own stepmother spurned one, what could one expect from the rest of society? Thank heavens she'd found allies in Lords Seaforth and Aiden.

After taking her seat in the gallery, she drew in a deep breath. Worrying about pompous and judgmental people would do nothing to help her free her father.

I must focus on that one thing only. Seeking Da's release is the only reason for my presence in London.

Tension eased from her shoulders as she began to play. As the music resonated around her, everything faded into oblivion. Aside from Agnes's care, playing the harp had been her only escape from her problems as a child. Music had kept her sane during her adolescent years, when she'd doubted her self-worth more than ever. In fact, the harp had probably kept her alive through those dark years when she'd believed herself an outcast from all of society. Then founding the Seaside Hospital for the Welfare of Women had given her purpose. Maddie's work helping others gave her dignity, and no one could take that away.

Her fingers plucking while her mind called upon the musical notes, she lost track of the time. But it didn't escape Maddie's notice when a woman ventured up to the gallery. Dressed in exquisite finery, the lass smiled. "I simply could listen to you play all afternoon."

"Thank you...Lady...?"

"The Duchess of Marlborough."

Maddie's head swooned a bit. "Oh my, Your Grace. You're the wife of the duke—the man who has been so instrumental in the war."

She chuckled. "Yes, I am very proud of my husband. And while he's away, the queen has employed me as lady of the robes—'tis the highest station a woman can hold."

"Please forgive my impertinence." Maddie straightened her harp, stood, and dipped into a curtsy. "It is ever so humbling to make your acquaintance, Your Grace."

"And I wish I could play as well as you." The duchess beckoned. "Come along. Queen Anne would like to have a word."

Maddie gulped against the sudden thickening of her throat. "With me?"

"Yes. And when you address the queen, you must let her

do the talking. You must not ask her questions unless she engages you in conversation. Do you understand?"

Maddie's stomach squeezed. There was a topic she was ever so anxious to broach with Her Majesty. Life and death depended on it. "I believe so."

With that, Maddie was whisked down to the queen's card table, though the cards had now been put away.

"Ah, Lady Magdalen." The queen smiled. "Tell me, where did you learn to play so beautifully? Did your father send you to the French court?"

"Why no, Your Majesty." Maddie's skin grew hot. With England at war with France, even she knew that admitting to having studied in King Louis's court would be akin to summoning the headsman for her father. Thank goodness she hadn't studied abroad. "My da gave me the harp when I was a wee lassie. Paid for lessons from an elderly gentleman in Stonehaven until I reached my majority."

Her Majesty appeared pleased with Magdalen's response. "Well then, you shall play for me in my antechamber every afternoon during your stay at Whitehall. Will that make you happy?"

"Yes, Your Majesty . . ." The queen had just asked a question. If what the Duchess of Marlborough had said was right, then the door was open for Maddie to ask one of her own. "But I would be a lot happier if my father were not incarcerated in the Tower."

Whispers hissed from the ladies-in-waiting, but Queen Anne chuckled. "You are persistent, though I am not convinced of your father's motives. What was it you said? He rode to Edinburgh with his army to welcome my half brother?"

"Indeed," Maddie said with such conviction even she believed it. "I understand many other Scottish lords did as well."

"Hmm." The queen pursed her lips with a leery gaze.

"I think—"

Her Majesty sliced her hand through the air. "I do believe I've heard quite enough of what you think, Lady Magdalen."

"Forgive me, Your Majesty." Maddie curtsied, wishing she could run and hide under the nearest rock. "I shall return and play for you on the morrow."

No matter how much she wanted to run away, she had a duty to help her father. She would return and play for the haughty queen as often as she could. In time Maddie would seize another chance to be heard, pray it wouldn't be too late.

* * *

After leaving Lady Magdalen at the Great Hall, Aiden went for a long walk. Bloody hell, he'd been at Whitehall for all of three days and had already had a gutful of politics. His plans for his leave had been thwarted, albeit due to his own flapping mouth.

An hour or so after leaving the palace, he arrived at Blackwall Port. As scheduled, the *Royal Mary* was moored alongside the pier for needed repairs. Carpenters' hammers echoed as he climbed up the gangway.

Captain Polwarth met him on deck with his fists on his hips. "Five and twenty years serving in the navy, and I've never seen an unwed officer return from a fortnight's leave after only three days."

Aiden feigned nonchalance. "Just thought I'd check on the repairs whilst I had a moment."

"Cannot stay away, can you, Commander?"

"I reckon not." Aiden shrugged with a smirk. "How is the hull looking?"

"Better than expected." Polwarth clapped him on the

shoulder. "Come, share a cup of whisky and tell me what's ailing you, lad."

Aiden followed the old man into his cabin at the rear of the frigate. He didn't have a mind to talk about Lady Magdalen and his mule-brained goal for his leave, but a tot of smooth Scottish whisky would go down well.

After pouring two cups, the captain gestured to a chair. "Pull up a stump and stay awhile."

"Don't mind if I do."

Polwarth took a seat behind his writing desk. "Now, tell me what a strapping young lord is doing mulling around a grungy pier when he has an entire fortnight's leave for the first time in two years."

Aiden groaned and turned the cup between his fingers. "This damned war with France is tearing all of Britain apart, for starters. Did you ken they have the Earl Marischal of Scotland locked away in the Tower of London?"

"I'd heard—read it in the gazette after we moored."

"'Tis a travesty if you ask me."

"Agreed, but you cannot do much about the state of affairs in a fortnight. Parliament isn't even in session." The captain sipped his whisky thoughtfully. "Devil's fire, you've been working yourself to the bone ever since you came aboard the *Mary*. You should be languishing in some woman's arms about now—I doubt a man with a face as bonny as yours would have difficulty finding a willing partner, if you ken my meaning."

"Bloody hell, not you as well." Aiden rolled his eyes. Damnation, the captain always had a way of driving straight to the point. "MacPherson has probably shagged every tart in London by now."

"Och, that lieutenant is all talk and swagger." Polwarth chuckled. "But if Fraser MacPherson thinks he has you fooled, a prankster such as he will squeeze every last drop of blood from you."

Aiden snorted with his next sip. Had his cabinmate been telling tall tales all this time? Just for a laugh? *Most likely.* "I've bloody well been trying to drum up a bit of female—ah—companionship. 'Tis just things haven't worked out the way I'd…imagined."

He then went on to tell the captain about Lady Magdalen and the visits to the Tower of London, the harp playing, meeting Lady Saxonhurst, who had completely ruined his plans and made being a bastard seem like the basest curse known to man, er, woman…and the fact that he felt a ridiculous and overwhelming need to protect the Earl Marischal's daughter.

When Aiden finished the confession, he didn't sip, he swilled the damned spirit.

Dear God, why couldn't he keep his mouth shut and bear his misery alone? He'd never spilled his guts like this to anyone—not even his brother, John. "Apologies, the whisky must have set my tongue to wagging."

"Sometimes a man needs to yammer on a bit." Polwarth took a thoughtful sip. "It seems it wasn't the countess who ruined your plans, lad."

"I suppose not. At first I was over the moon to see Maddie—I mean Lady Magdalen—again. It was as if fate had brought us together."

"Perhaps it did." The captain poured himself another tot, then pushed the flagon toward Aiden. "Does she have eyes for you?"

"I think perhaps she does." *But then she appears to look fondly upon Reid MacKenzie as well.*

"Hmm." Polwarth eyed him coolly, as he would an errant midshipman. "Mayhap I need to call the kettle black—did she kiss you back, laddie?"

A buzz twinged low in his gut. "Aye."

"Then what's your damned problem? Any lassie needs a man's attentions just as he needs hers."

Aiden choked down a hearty gulp. His damned problem? He was a miserable virgin, and before he tried to court Lady Magdalen, he needed *experience*. How in God's name could he say that to the captain without being laughed off the ship, demoted, and assigned to pumping the bilges for the rest of his naval career?

Polwarth held up his cup and smiled—not a friendly grin, but a knowing smile Aiden oft saw from a teacher who was just about to tell him the error of his ways. "Ye ken you've turned the color of my missus's scarlet petticoats."

Aiden closed his eyes and shook his head. "Och, it must be the spirit for certain. 'Tis potent."

The captain simply shook his head and sipped again. "Tell me, have you ever slept in a woman's arms?"

Aiden dropped his shoulders and stared at his palms. *May as well have out with it.* "No, sir."

"That explains everything. I think I ken the cure for your misery." The captain pulled open a drawer, a wry grin playing on his lips. "I picked this up in France back in '97. I reckon it just might put that mind of yours to rest."

"What is it?" Aiden opened the pamphlet. Christ, if he wasn't red before, he certainly must be now. His entire body went hot. "Hell's fire." He stared, turning his head sideways, unable to look away from a drawing of a nude couple with their limbs crisscrossing in every imaginable direction.

"That's about what I said when I first saw those sketches."

"Is this how...do people...I mean...so many different positions?"

Polwarth waggled his brows. "Aye, there's even a few maneuvers I haven't tried."

Aiden quickly folded the parchment and stuffed it inside his doublet. "Do you mind if I borrow this for—ah—a while?"

"Keep it as long as you need." The captain leaned forward and looked him in the eye. "Now go. I granted you leave because our next tour will be a long one. Could encounter a battle or two. I need you fresh and ready to weigh anchor, ye ken? I do not want to see you aboard the *Royal Mary* until we set sail."

* * *

Aiden took his time meandering back to Whitehall and stopped at Boodle's, a well-known gentleman's club on St James's Street. He'd been there once before with his brother, John, not long after he'd joined the navy. Tobacco smoke hung thick in the air while he found a green armchair in a dimly lit corner. He wanted to study the pamphlet in more detail, but he pulled it out only after the porter had brought his tot of whisky. After ensuring there was no one else nearby, Aiden drew the parchment from his doublet and unfolded it.

The only words were the title, scrawled across the top:

Situations de la Chambre à Coucher

He'd never imagined lovemaking could be accomplished in so many positions. Thirty-five in all. For the love of God, the woman could even be on top—or the man behind.

Oh, sweet Mary, that picture stirred his blood.

His skin grew hot as he studied each angle, the placement of the woman's shapely thighs, and how the man managed to insert...ah...himself.

Aiden threw back his spirit to calm the fire raging beneath his kilt. The problem? The whisky only made him burn hotter. He scanned down the page and his heart nearly stopped when he examined a sketch of a woman kneeling over her partner and taking him into her mouth, her fingers wrapped around the base of the man's shaft.

Mouths? MacPherson never alluded to that.

In the next drawing the couple had changed positions. Aiden nearly fell off his chair. The man actually had his face in the woman's... and her face expressed nothing but pure ecstasy.

He slammed the parchment shut and gulped, staring straight ahead.

"Are you unwell, my lord?" asked a passing porter.

"Another whisky, please," he croaked.

"Straightaway, my lord."

Aiden stole another peek inside. He rather liked the idea of lovemaking with the mouth. Oh yes, and, in addition to that, hands as well. Those were, well, surefire methods of preventing the birth of bastards.

Why hadn't MacPherson told him about such alternatives? Mayhap the captain was right, Fraser was more of a talker. Mayhap Fraser knew of only the one position, which now seemed rather dreary in comparison to so many others.

Chapter Eleven

Maddie lay awake listening to Agnes's light snores sail down from above stairs. She'd returned from the gallery anxious to tell Aiden about her conversation with the queen and had been disappointed to discover him away. And she grew further disappointed when he didn't return in time to take the evening meal.

He hadn't mentioned that he'd be away. Not that he needed to inform her of his plans.

But his sudden disappearance was odd all the same.

When the outer door opened and closed, Maddie slid from her bed and hastily donned her dressing gown. When she peered into the passageway, she found His Lordship opening the door to his chamber. "I'm so glad I caught you," she blurted, lest she miss him altogether.

He spun around, inhaling sharply. "M'lady. You're still awake?"

"Aye, did I startle you?"

"No." He stepped nearer, the scent of whisky and tobacco swirling around him. She couldn't put her finger on it, but there was something different about his eyes, something almost predatory. "Is Miss Agnes with you?"

"She's in her quarters—has been asleep for an hour or more." Maddie leaned closer and inhaled more deeply. Lord Aiden's scent was on the verge of being intoxicating. "I've never seen you smoke a pipe, m'lord."

"I don't." He drew a hand down his waistcoat, his eyes growing darker. "I stopped at Boodle's gentlemen's club to do a bit of reading."

"I see." She glanced away. "Was it invigorating?"

His breath caught—a very subtle sound, but he'd gasped all the same. Reaching out, he brushed his fingers along her cheek, staring at her more intently than ever before. "Very invigorating, lass." His voice sounded deeper as well.

Initially she'd wanted to tell Aiden about her conversation with the queen, but her tongue was tied. The thrill of his touch rendered her speechless. Though he had the most enchanting moss-green eyes, Lord Aiden had never gazed upon her with such fervor before.

Placing his hand at the back of her neck, he urged her nearer. Though the passageway was dark, the flickering lamplight from her chamber made his lips shine. Good heavens, she shouldn't have dashed into the corridor in her dressing gown. But now her breasts swelled with the thrill of his mouth growing nearer, his long lashes shuttering his eyes, the hint of whisky on his breath as it skimmed her forehead.

Aye, Maddie had enjoyed every kiss she'd received from Lord Aiden Murray. Enjoyed the light touch of his fingers on her cheek. Last eve she shouldn't have allowed him to kiss her in the window embrasure. She still shuddered at the humiliation of having been caught.

But now a shiver jumped up the back of her neck. Indeed, there was nothing to stop her tonight. With Miss Agnes fast asleep, not a soul would interrupt them. Heaven forgive her, she enjoyed kissing this man. His hands upon her were like a drug that once taken created an addiction.

She didn't know what came over her whenever he touched her, just as he was doing at this very moment. The hunger in his eyes made her blood thrum. And with a low growl, his lips clamped over hers. His tongue drove into her mouth as if he were starving—not for food, but for her.

Merciful heavens.

Maddie closed her eyes. Her emotions took over while her hands wound their way around his waist. On fire, she shuddered and arched toward him, craving more—more kissing—more closeness—*more*.

Aiden backed her against the wall, his big hands everywhere, rubbing up and down her body. Every place he touched begged for his fingers to sweep over and caress it again.

Her eyes flew open when his fingers swirled around her unbound breast. He met her gaze with a fiery, green-eyed stare. "Och, I've wanted you since the first time I saw you dancing in Dunnottar's gallery."

Maddie's eyes rolled back as his hand slipped inside her dressing gown and cupped her, skin to skin. With his touch her breast swelled and ached with a heavy longing that made her hips rock forward. Met with the same hard maleness she'd felt intimately touch her in the embrasure last eve, her hips rubbed while pressure built, like screaming inside, begging for more.

Kissing him, moving with him, her back against the wall, it wasn't enough.

With a deep guttural moan, he lifted her in his arms, carried her along the passageway, and kicked open his chamber door. Big, strong arms cradled her as if she weighed nothing.

Her mind cleared enough to realize he was headed straight for the enormous four-poster bed. "Lord Aiden, we mustn't!"

He chuckled into her hair. "Do you remember on Hogmanay, I asked you to call me Aiden?"

"Aye."

"I want you to call me Aiden now, Magdalen—Maddie—dear God, I'm mad for you." He rested her on the bed and knelt over her, untying his cravat. She'd seen him without his shirt that very morn. The image of a complete and utter Adonis would be burned upon her mind for the rest of her days. Grinning, eyes filled with passion, he slowly drew the lace away and cast it to the floor.

Her breathing sped up when he removed his doublet and tossed it aside as well.

With her last shred of lucidness, Maddie pressed her hand against his chest. Met with heat, the hammering of his heart thumped a steady rhythm against her trembling fingers. "We mustn't."

"I want you, lass, and I ken by your kisses you want me."

She chewed her lip, wanting him more than life, but forcing herself to be sensible. "Aye, but I cannot bring another bastard into this world."

"I've considered that."

Her heart nearly stopped beating. "You have?"

His deft fingers continued to unbutton his waistcoat while he arched a single eyebrow. "There are other ways to bring you pleasure aside from—ah—the direct route."

"Pardon?" she asked, her breasts swelling at the thought of seeing the rippled muscles in his abdomen.

But I am lying on his bed in his chamber. Sacrilege.

He pulled loose the bow at his nape and let his tresses fall forward. Dusky hair with highlights flickering amber by the coals in the hearth. Handsome as the devil. A more delicious man could not possibly exist. "Stay with me." His gaze trailed from her face to her breasts. "I promise I will not take your innocence."

"Kissing only?" she asked, heat pooling between her loins.

He tugged his shirt over his head and cast it aside. "And touching, Maddie." Rocking back on his haunches, he raked his gaze down her body—almost as if allowing her a chance to flee. "If you'll trust me."

Touching? He made it sound so risqué, so dangerous, so impossible to refuse.

Powerless to speak, she nodded as her hand grew a mind of its own and brushed across Aiden's hard, rippled stomach.

He closed his eyes and moaned. "That feels so good."

It felt good to Maddie, too, and before she had a chance to think, his lips touched hers as his hands untied her sash and spread open her dressing gown. Without her petticoats and stays, only a chemise of holland cloth separated her breasts from his bare chest. Desperate to feel his hardness, she slipped her hands to his back and pulled him closer.

When he moved over her, she whimpered. Too many erotic sensations coursed through her. Caught in a web of passion, Maddie kissed and rocked and swirled her hips. He slid between her legs, long and hard. A wanton streak she never knew existed demanded she rub in tandem with the motion of his hips.

* * *

As Aiden's cock nestled between Maddie's legs, he could have come right there...but he craved more. He wanted to be completely naked like the people in the drawings. And he was so close, he had to ease away a bit just to maintain control. Dear God, this woman's body was made for sin. And her scent? Och, Maddie's fragrance drove him to the brink of insanity. His every nerve ending trembled as he tried to remain lucid enough not to lose control.

Pulling back to his knees, he inched up the hem of her chemise.

When the linen reached her knees, she snapped her hands to her thighs. "But—"

"Trust me." With a cockeyed grin, he released his belt and let his kilt drop.

Her eyes fell to his cock—pointing straight at her. God save him, he liked having her eyes on him, the pink of her tongue slipping across her lip made him crave her lips on him, sucking him, her hand gripping his root.

But not yet.

"Now you," he said. It wasn't a request, but a command.

Trust filled her eyes as she moved her hands and allowed him to pull the chemise over her head.

Holy Christ, she was more beautiful than the woman in the drawings. More beautiful than anything he could have ever imagined. Long, sleek limbs, voluptuous hips, a slender waist and round breasts large enough to fill his hands with pure heaven.

Reverently he bowed his head and suckled the pert rosebuds tipping her breasts. He would savor Maddie this night.

His tongue moved from one breast to the next, teasing them to erect tips, and then he trailed kisses down her flat midriff. When finally he lay with his shoulders between her spread thighs, Maddie gasped and writhed with each new sensation as he relentlessly kissed her. The lassie's every mewl took him a little closer to the edge. He inhaled the full power of the fragrance that had driven him mad since the first time he'd met the woman—danced with her—touched his palm to her palm.

"I-I-I." She peered down at him. "What?"

"I want to watch your face while I kiss you here."

She tried to sit up, but he stopped her by splaying his hand on her abdomen. "Remember my promise, lass." Hell's fire, he'd never been so aroused in his life. God bless the captain and his wee pamphlet—it was exactly what he'd needed.

Maddie eased back against the pillows, her face pensive. But Aiden watched her as his tongue lapped. With a wee gasp her thighs shuddered around him. He slid his finger over her nub of flesh.

"Mercy," she cried out, arching her back.

Until he'd seen the sketches, he'd had no idea a woman could gain as much pleasure as a man.

He swirled his finger around the nub and then lower, finding her entrance slick, hot, and oh, so very, very wet.

His cock throbbed. *Aye, the big fella kens what he wants.*

Maddie's eyes rolled back when he slid his finger in and out, her hips moving in seductive swirls. Holding his finger inside her core, he licked the wee nub. Gasping, she bucked against him. Dear God, nothing stroked his cock, yet he could come just by licking her. Aiden flicked out his tongue and lapped again. The lass tasted of sweet butter mixed with nectar. He swirled his tongue faster with the rhythm of his relentless finger. Moaning like a woman possessed, Maddie tossed her head from side to side.

Gasping, she clutched the bedclothes in her fists. "I'm about to burst."

With a few more laps of his tongue, a high-pitched cry caught in Maddie's throat. When her body stiffened with a frantic gasp, he flicked his tongue faster, while watching the pleasure on her angelic face. Her thighs shuddered. Her core shattered around his finger, gripped it tight, then pulsed around it.

Sucking in deep breaths, she opened her eyes, her face radiant as a sunset. Her breasts heaved with every breath. "How can you make me feel like this?"

He grinned and trailed kisses from her hips to her slender neck. "A wee trick sailors learn," he hedged. Rising to his knees, he glanced to his waistcoat on the floor, the parchment still tucked away.

"I had no idea a man could make a woman shatter. From the way the women talk at the hospital, 'tis the men who gain all the pleasure." Her gaze slid down to his erect manhood. "But you, ah, can you gain pleasure without making a bairn?"

Dear Lord, he'd been praying she'd ask. His gaze again shifted to his waistcoat. No, she'd probably think him a lecherous beast if he showed her the sketches.

"Would it be all right if I touched, ah, your...?" Her shoulder rose to her ear while a lock of long hair covered one eye. Sexy as a wildcat.

"Aye, lass, you can touch me with your hands, and mayhap even your lips...ah...if it pleases you."

She gasped. "Just like you did to me?"

He held her heavy-lidded stare, and the corner of his mouth turned up as he nodded.

She grinned wantonly. "Well then, I think you should lie on your back."

Oh yes, Aiden was only too eager to comply.

Maddie slid an arm into her dressing gown.

"Wait." Aiden stopped her. "Would you leave it off?"

Blushing, she regarded the sleeve and pushed it away. Then she turned her attention to him. She rubbed her palm atop his abdomen. "It stirred my blood when I saw you without your shirt this morn."

"Mm."

"And now I want to ravish you." She traced her finger from the center of his chest to his belly button. "Just like you ravished me."

A low chuckle rumbled in his chest. "I am at your mercy, m'lady." A bit more seed dripped from the tip of his cock. God's bones, he prayed he could hold on a wee bit longer.

She began by suckling his nipples as he'd done to her. Every flick of her tongue, every caress of her fingers served to make him harder. When she actually placed her fingers around his cock, he sucked in a gasp. "Christ."

Maddie released him as if she'd wrapped her fingers around a hot brand. "Are you all right?"

"Better than all right," he croaked, guiding her fingers back.

"Can I hurt you?"

"Not sure."

"Have you ever done this before?"

"Nay."

"Then perhaps I should start slow?"

Slow wasn't in his vocabulary. Not now, when his cock was harder than an oaken bedpost. When she wrapped her lithe fingers around his shaft, a gasp caught in his throat. His blood coursed hot. Her lips bent toward him and opened wide—the most erotic picture he'd ever seen in his life.

Warm mouth surrounded him.

Aiden squeezed his eyes shut to stave off his need to thrust like a madman.

But when her hand squeezed, sliding up and down, he lurched into a frenzy. Losing his mind, he thrust with the rhythm of her hand. Maddie's naked body consumed his mind. Her intoxicating scent led him into a fervor of unbridled hunger. Euphoric tension on the verge of pain consumed him. Higher and higher he soared until a bellowing moan grated in his throat while the world shattered into a million pulsing stars of euphoria.

As the tension eased and the world became harmonious again, Maddie rocked back and slowly drew a hand across her mouth. "Fascinating."

Chapter Twelve

Maddie's feet barely hit the steps when she left the queen's antechamber and headed across the courtyard. Aiden had invited her to an organ recital by an emerging composer, George Frideric Handel, who was visiting from the Holy Roman Empire. Thank heavens His Lordship had given her enough notice for her to arrange for a new gown, and with the coin she had received from playing her harp, she could actually afford something stylish, fit for London society.

Agnes had gone to fetch the gown from the dressmaker, and Maddie couldn't wait to try it on. Her mind raced with thoughts of the accessories she'd need—a fan for certain, shoes, a velvet cloak. Mayhap Agnes could come up with a fashionable new hairstyle as well.

"There you are, m'lady." Lord Seaforth approached, taking long strides across the courtyard. "Where are you off to in such a hurry? I've been looking for you for two days."

She stopped short and drew a hand over her mouth. In the past few days she'd been so blinded by ardor, she hadn't been able to do as much as she'd wanted to further her father's cause—aside from trying to win the queen's good graces, or at least build enough favor with her to attempt another plea for Da's release.

But Maddie hadn't been sick with worry as a good daughter ought to have been. And now Lord Seaforth had been looking for her...for two days? She glanced to the folded parchment in Seaforth's hand and bit her lip. "I've been asked to play the harp for the queen."

"I ken, but you haven't been at the Banqueting House for a meal in three nights."

"No..." She pulled him aside. "I've been trying to avoid drawing attention to myself."

"You and Lord Aiden."

"I beg your pardon?"

"His Lordship hasn't been at the Banqueting House, either, m'lady." He looked both ways. "People are starting to talk."

She'd been in London for nearly a week, and she'd heard more gossip than she had in all of her days. "Sadly, that does not surprise me." She gave the earl a once-over. "Why have you been so anxious to find me? Have there been developments regarding my father?"

He handed her the parchment with a prideful grin. "Indeed. I have taken it upon myself to personally visit every member of the House of Lords who supports the Tory Party."

"Are they Jacobites?"

He quickly glanced over his shoulder and pulled her aside. "Wheesht—you must never use that word here. Those who lean that way refer to *the cause*, and I must advise you to do so as well."

"Very well. Are the Tories sympathetic to *the cause*?"

"Some are—but not all, though you'll never find anyone sympathetic to *the cause* in the Whig Party."

"Whigs and Tories? 'Tis as if you're speaking French. Why does this matter to my father's plea for clemency?"

"Because the queen has been subject to Whig plots to oust her."

"Oust?"

"Assassinate her and put her Hanover cousin, George, on the throne."

"Heavens! It seems everyone has an agenda."

"They do indeed." Seaforth pointed to the missive. "Support from the Tories is exactly what we need. With the Whigs out of favor, Anne leans toward the Tory Party even though there are more Roman Catholics in the membership."

"She fears Roman Catholics?"

"Popery," he whispered.

"I shall keep that in mind on the morrow when I am playing my harp." Maddie gave him a quizzical look. "This makes no sense to me. Why would the queen of England, Scotland, and Ireland fear the pope?"

"Because for Catholics God's law takes precedence over the law of the ruling class. You ken, King Henry VIII and his wives and all that."

"Aye, but that was an awfully long time ago." She shook the parchment. "So, Tory-siding lords have signed this document, and you reckon it will persuade the queen to give my da a pardon?"

"Aye."

She unfolded it and started reading.

"To paraphrase, 'tis a roundabout way of saying that as the Earl Marischal of Scotland, your da would have been remiss in his responsibilities if he hadn't taken his army to Edinburgh to meet Prince James. And that if said prince were to set foot ashore with intent to do harm to the inhabitants of Scotland or to his sovereign, then the Earl Marischal would have been in a position to act swiftly—as would the other lords now incarcerated in Edinburgh Castle."

"That is brilliant." She lowered her gaze. "And look at all those signatures."

"Twenty-three in total. I believe this document gives the queen the fodder she needs to pardon all those arrested." Lord Seaforth cringed. "Besides, where would she be if she executed half the gentry in Scotland?"

"She'd have a civil war on her hands for certain." Maddie folded the missive and handed it back to him. "Do you honestly think it will work?"

"If it doesn't, then I fear for the queen. This war with France and the one in the Americas is bleeding Britain dry. She can ill afford a war on her own soil."

She clapped her hands over her soaring heart. "Och, Lord Aiden will be thrilled to hear the news."

Seaforth's face fell. "Murray? You rather like him, do you not?"

Maddie averted her face as her cheeks sizzled. If she wasn't careful, she'd give herself away. "He has been very kind to me."

"'Tis a shame."

"Why?"

"He'll be off to sea soon."

"Do not remind me."

"And I..." He glanced away.

"What is it?"

"I'd hoped now that I've found a way to free your father you might look favorably on me."

She knitted her brows. "But you're an earl."

He grinned, making his hard features appear particularly boyish. "You've noticed."

"Are you not supposed to find a legitimately bred daughter of a peer to court?"

He shrugged. "I decided a long time ago I wouldn't court or marry for titles."

"A long time ago? You speak as if you're a man of thirty."

After inhaling deeply, he groaned. "Truth be told, I'd much rather be at Brahan Castle with my clan. The queen is bloody *grooming* me to be one of her staunch supporters in the Highlands."

"You do not sound overly enthused to be receiving the queen's royal treatment."

"Let us just say she has done nothing to change my loyalty to *the cause*. I'll be happy after the next session of Parliament. I've been granted leave to head for home."

"When do you plan to give her the missive?"

"The Earl of Mar and I are scheduled to meet with Her Majesty on the morrow."

"Oh, I do hope this works." Maddie grasped his hand between her palms and squeezed. "Thank you. From the bottom of my heart I thank you. For the first time since I arrived in London, I actually feel like something is being accomplished. I owe you a debt of gratitude."

Seaforth gave a sober nod. "The Tories will need your father when Parliament resumes next month. Let us pray it works."

When Aiden appeared at the far end of the courtyard, she waved, scarcely able to wait to tell him the news. But she slowed her pace when Lady Saxonhurst strode straight up to His Lordship, took his hands, and drew them straight to the tops of her bosoms. No more immodest a greeting had ever been given between mere acquaintances. Good heavens, Maddie hadn't paid much attention to the countess while she was playing her harp earlier, but the woman's bodice plunged scandalously low. Who could help but stare? If the woman took in a deep breath, she'd pop out for certain. Worse, she shamelessly rubbed the quite ample exposed flesh against the backs of Aiden's hands while she threw her head back and laughed.

The cackle resounded through the courtyard as the two couples moved closer to each other, Aiden's gaze unmistakably focused on the countess's cleavage.

"Are you all right?" asked Lord Seaforth, inclining his lips to Maddie's ear.

"Perfectly well," she said as she pulled him ahead. "Why are you asking now?"

"Because you're gripping my arm like you're strangling a chicken."

She quickly drew her hand away. "Apologies."

He chuckled. "Not that I didn't enjoy it, m'lady."

Now closer, Aiden looked from Maddie to Seaforth and scowled.

"Isn't it precious?" said Lady Saxonhurst. "Lady Magdalen and Lord Seaforth look so well suited, wouldn't you say, Lord Aiden?" The woman had the gall to push herself against Aiden's arm so that her bosoms smooshed together. Holy hexes, even Lord Seaforth gaped.

Maddie reached for Aiden's hand. "I have wonderful news."

Seaforth tugged on her elbow. "Mayhap this isn't the best time to share it."

"Why?" the countess asked. "Have you secrets? I dearly love secrets."

"Then they'd no longer be surreptitious." Shrugging from Lady Saxonhurst's grasp, Aiden pushed between Maddie and the earl, folding his arms. "Have you had a good spar as of late, Seaforth? I fear I'm growing a wee bit soft during my leave."

"Oh yes, I love to watch a good sparring session." The countess clapped her hands, fortunately forgetting about the news.

Though Maddie knew Aiden to be hewn of pure muscle, Reid MacKenzie was stocky and solid, and by no means looked like one with whom to trifle. She caught Aiden's eye and shook her head.

"Looking for a hiding, are you?" Lord Seaforth snorted, then wrapped his thick fingers around Aiden's upper arm. "Och, so you're concealing a set of cannons under all that velvet and lace."

Aiden drew his arm away, looking down at his opponent, who stood shorter, but only by an inch or two. "You have no idea what it's like to be the second son of a duke."

"Aye? But I ken what it's like to lose my da and become earl and laird afore my eighteenth birthday." Seaforth smoothed his palm over the hilt of the sword at his hip. "A wee sparring session would be welcomed. But let us keep it away from prying eyes. The Privy Garden in a half hour?"

"Agreed." Aiden bowed. "I am looking forward to it."

Maddie hastened after Aiden as he left to fetch his weapons. "Surely you do not mean to harm poor Lord Seaforth."

"Harm? Have you looked at the lad? He's the size of a behemoth."

"Have you looked at yourself of late? You're enormous, taller, and three years his senior."

Aiden gave her a sideways glance before he stepped into the stairwell. "'Tis just a sparring session, Maddie."

"What does that mean?"

"It means I aim to teach him a lesson about what happens when anyone touches you."

"Me? Am I the cause of this? What on earth did I do to spur you to such jealousy?"

"I saw you with Seaforth as soon as I entered the courtyard. He had his hands all over you."

"What?" Her mind flashed back. "No, he did not. He grasped my arm. He was simply excited about his plan to convince the queen to release my father."

"That's what you think."

"Pardon me? Your jealousy is completely misplaced." Well, not entirely, but Maddie wasn't about to say the earl had hinted toward his affection—and besides, Maddie had discouraged him. "He told me about gaining the support of the Tory Party and the fact that Queen Anne would risk civil war if she convicts my father and the other nobles of treason."

"It matters not what he said." After pushing through the door he stopped outside the drawing room with his fists on his hips. "It was the way he was looking at you that set my blood to boiling."

She hastened to follow him into the passageway. "Oh please. He kens I'm enamored with you."

"Aye? Well, I reckon he needs to know I'm no milksop. I might not be an earl, but I'm still a man. A commander in the Royal Navy, and I've a fine future ahead of me. Just because my brother stands to inherit doesn't mean I will not make something of my life."

She threw her hands out. "Was that ever in question?"

After pushing through the door to the Atholl apartments and striding into the drawing room, he whipped around and faced her, his green eyes practically boring through her skull. "It is *always* in question."

Maddie jammed her fists into her hips. "Och aye, just like owning up to being a bastard, I'd reckon."

With a grunt he dropped his chin to his chest. "I'm sorry." Sauntering forward, he reached out and twisted one of her curls around his finger—as if making a peace offering. "It seems we both are children born of nobles. Children who must find their own paths."

"At least you're legitimate. Though Da has always seen to my maintenance, I haven't been allowed to partake in family gatherings since the age of seven. Imagine how that injures a lassie's pride."

His hand slipped to her waist. "Then we both work hard because we've something to prove to all of Christendom."

"I beg your pardon, Lord Aiden, but I must ask you to remove your hand from Lady Magdalen this instant." Miss Agnes marched into the drawing room with fists clenched as if she were about to give Aiden a hiding.

Maddie leaped backward, her stomach squeezing. She'd rather be caught by just about anyone other than Agnes.

"Forgive me." Aiden's face turned red as an apple. "I must have lost my head. So sorry."

The lass could have burst out laughing. Thank heavens Agnes was unaware of how much touching they'd been doing behind closed doors.

"Do not apologize to me." Agnes grasped Maddie's hands. "Are you all right, dear?"

"Aye. You caught us at an awkward moment. We were discussing the problems with being noninheriting children of noblemen and found that our lots in life are really quite similar."

Agnes narrowed her eyes and looked between them. "Well, I do not want such a flagrant misstep to happen again." She shook her finger at Aiden. "I may be a lowborn servant, but I have been tasked with the duty to protect this lassie, and my authority has been *expressly* granted by His Lordship the Earl Marischal."

"Yes, m'lady. It shan't happen again." Aiden bowed, looking directly at Maddie. "Now, if you'll excuse me, I cannot be late to my sparring session with the Earl of Seaforth. After all, I am the challenger."

Maddie watched him stride out the door with prickles firing across her skin. What on earth did he mean, "It shan't happen again"? It had better happen again. She'd die if he spent the rest of his leave ignoring her.

She hastened after him.

Agnes caught her arm. "Where are you off to now?"

"To watch them spar, of course. I was there when they agreed to the challenge."

The woman gaped like a worried hen. "But you could be hurt."

"I promise to keep my distance. I assure you Lady Saxonhurst will be in attendance."

"The countess?" Agnes strengthened her grasp and tugged Maddie to the door. "Then you must go. We do not want that *courtier* gaining favor with our Lord Aiden, now do we?"

Maddie coughed out a snort. "But you just chided him for impropriety."

"Aye, but that doesn't mean I do not like the lad. A strapping young man like Lord Aiden just needs to be reminded of his manners from time to time."

"I'm glad you like him." Maddie stopped. "Afore I go, I need to tell you that Lord Seaforth has had a petition signed by the Tory Party for Da's release. He thinks the queen will honor it."

A flicker sparkled in Agnes's eyes. "Och, 'tis music to my ears."

"I thought the news would make you happy. I must pay another visit to the Tower on the morrow to tell Da."

Agnes drew her hands over her heart. "I do hope we'll be heading home soon."

A lead ball dropped in Maddie's stomach. She hadn't thought much past the next sennight. What if Aiden sailed away and she headed back to Stonehaven, never to see him again?

Chapter Thirteen

*W*hen Maddie arrived at the Privy Garden, Lady Saxonhurst was already there with a dozen or so other ladies who had come to watch the spectacle. Fortunately, they were sitting on benches at the far side of the garden. Maddie saw no reason to join them.

Stripped down to their linen shirts, the opponents circled, both wielding basket-hilted swords.

"Come," Aiden growled, his gaze honed like a hawk's. "Show us what you're made of, Your Lordship."

With a resounding bellow, Lord Seaforth barreled in, swinging his weapon over his head, baring his teeth, and by no means looking as if he was participating in a friendly contest. Aiden moved like a cat as he backed up, defending against the onslaught of hacking strikes.

When she blinked, somehow the tide had changed. Aiden grasped Seaforth's arm, spun him around, and angled the point of his sword at the young man's neck. "You're better than I expected."

"You haven't seen anything yet," boasted the earl. How

could he be so self-assured, given the blade held to his throat?

But when Aiden released him, they crouched and again circled. Seaforth lunged for the second time, and their swords clashed with earsplitting clangs. Just when Maddie was sure Seaforth would gain the upper hand, Aiden stopped him short.

On and on it went, with plenty of grunting and sweating.

When they stopped to remove their shirts, the ladies-in-waiting applauded and gasped, whispering behind their fans and making googly eyes. Indeed, both men were astonishing specimens of masculinity, enough to make any maiden swoon.

Maddie pursed her lips, not at all pleased with the ladies' flagrant adoration. Aiden's physique was for her eyes alone.

Lady Saxonhurst strolled over to Maddie. "Why is it every time I see Lord Aiden, you are nearby?"

They'd asked the master of the guard to keep mum about her staying in Atholl's apartments, though the longer Maddie continued to accept the House of Atholl's generosity, the more likely word was to leak out—especially as missives and harps arrived in the drawing room. "He and Lord Seaforth have been invaluable in helping me prove my father's innocence."

The countess harrumphed. "Well, you'd best not set your sights on Murray. He's a sailor, after all, and what with the war, his ship is likely to be sunk by one of those evil French galleons."

There it came again. A conjuring of the future that made Maddie's bones shudder. "How can you speak so nonchalantly about the fate of Commander Murray's ship?"

Saxonhurst tipped a shoulder toward her ear. "We all die, my dear. 'Tis just a matter of when."

Maddie studied the woman. Mercy, the countess was unduly blasé. "How, pray tell, did you lose your husband?"

"Consumption."

"Oh my. I am sorry."

"He was twenty years my senior..." The lady's voice trailed off.

Maddie didn't want to pry, but she suspected becoming a widow hadn't been entirely disagreeable for the countess. She returned her attention to Aiden, who was now showing a great deal of finesse, spinning, lunging, and wielding his blade while Seaforth clearly tired. "Well." She sniffed, straightening her Scottish spine. "If Lord Aiden's ability in the sparring ring is any indication, I'd place a wager in favor of his surviving the war."

"Oh, you are quaint. Is that how they breed bastards up in the far north?"

Unable to help herself, Maddie tsked. "Bastard or nay, I'd say Highland lassies look to the future with a fair bit more faith."

Smiling, Lady Saxonhurst patted her black curls. "Lord Seaforth will be undeniably delicious in a year or two. I do hope he continues to stay in London. I understand the winters are abominable in Ross-shire."

"Most likely the same as Aberdeenshire—but we all manage, m'lady."

The countess shuddered. "I could do quite nicely without winters."

That must have been the first thing the woman had said that Maddie actually agreed with.

"Will you be heading back to the Highlands soon?" Saxonhurst asked with a subtle arch to her brow. "I can imagine you marrying one of those big, strapping clansmen I've heard so much about."

Maddie shook her head and returned her attention to the sparring match—two well-built men shining with perspiration were difficult to ignore. "I suppose I'll need to return home as soon as my father once again finds the queen's favor. I am the benefactor of a hospital for women in Stonehaven."

"You?" The countess cooled herself with quick flicks of her fan. "My, how philanthropic. I never would have thought."

Maddie guessed that thinking wasn't one of Lady Saxonhurst's stronger suits. "I find imparting kindness makes each day a little brighter."

"How droll."

Grunting, Aiden leaped aside.

"Nicked you, did I?" growled Seaforth as he lunged.

Good Lord, Aiden's arm streamed with blood.

Maddie stepped forward, clapping her hands over her mouth.

Lady Saxonhurst grabbed her wrist. "Stay away. You're likely to be hurt."

"But—"

With an upward swing and a bellow to wake the dead, Aiden clashed with Seaforth's sword so hard, the weapon flew from the earl's grasp. Casting his own sword aside, Aiden lunged, grasped the earl's wrist, and bent it so far down, it looked about to snap. The younger man's knees buckled with the downward twist of his wrist. As he wrestled Seaforth to his back, Aiden pinned the earl's shoulder with his knee while his hand grasped the lad's throat. "Quarter?"

Seaforth's heels dug into the ground. "Och, I call quarter, ye bleeding bastard."

Aiden stood and offered his hand. "You're a worthy opponent."

"And you're a dragon."

A devilish grin played upon Aiden's lips. "I'll take that as a compliment."

"When does a man reach his prime?" asked Lady Saxonhurst, her hips swaying while she strode forward.

The earl stooped to retrieve his shirt. "Some say five and twenty."

Giving the younger man an exaggerated once-over, the countess slipped her tongue to the corner of her mouth. "Then I daresay you'll be besting the commander in no time."

Seaforth smiled, standing a fair bit taller. "Och, but I do not intend to ever again allow Murray to gain the upper hand."

"Well put," said Lady Saxonhurst.

As the two strolled off, Maddie examined the open wound on Aiden's arm. "This should be tended."

"Nay, 'tis just a flesh wound—nothing a wee bit of salve will not fix."

* * *

After purchasing a new suit of clothes befitting a duke's son, Aiden hired a valet as he should have done in the first place. One of the prerequisites of being a courtier was dressing appropriately, especially when attending a formal event at which the queen was expected to be present. This eve he'd spared no expense, from ginger periwig to shirt of holland cloth topped with a lace cravat. He wore an ivory silk waistcoat and a navy doublet with gold trim that would also be useful for naval events, but he refused to don a pair of English breeches. Fortunately, there were a number of Scottish nobles of the same mind in London, and he'd ordered a new kilt of red, navy, and black. As was the Highland custom, Aiden wore it belted at his waist, the length pulled from the lower right opening of his doublet around his back and pinned at his left shoulder with a silver brooch bearing the

Atholl arms. The valet had put forth a good effort to ensure there were neither wrinkles nor a hair out of place.

He regarded himself in the looking glass above the mantel in the drawing room, sliding one foot forward as he would do for a portrait. Not liking the image, he puffed out his chest and moved a hand to his lapel.

God's bones, take me to sea where I can cast aside these frills.

He turned sideways.

I abhor this damned wig. A man could sweat to death swathed in so much horsehair.

But he was a victim of his times. At least he hadn't been born in an era when he would have been expected to wear a coat of mail or plate armor. Turning his back to the looking glass, Aiden resorted to pacing and pulling out his pocket watch. The coach would arrive in five minutes, and Maddie hadn't yet made an appearance.

At least a light glowed from beneath her door, indicating she was within. It cast a hazy glow in the otherwise dark passageway. After pacing around the chamber a half-dozen times, he again eyed his timepiece. Another minute had passed. Perhaps he should knock on the door—perhaps Maddie's mantel clock had stopped and she was unaware of the time. Just as he started toward it, her door opened. A burst of light flooded the passageway, and with the tap of dainty footsteps, an angel emerged.

Aiden had known she'd purchased a new gown, but he hadn't expected this. His mouth went dry and he suddenly needed to take in two stuttering breaths to steady the thumping of his heart.

Christ, men aren't supposed to experience such heart hammering. Especially men bred for the sea. Damnation.

She smiled, and his goddamned knees wobbled. He

should have taken a healthy tot while he was pacing in the drawing room.

Her golden gown rustled as she walked forward with a matching fan in her hand. She moved the fan to her waist... just below her breasts. Creamy skin Aiden knew to be softer than spun silk swelled above a dangerously plunging neckline. His mouth went completely dry. If Maddie's serving maid had been anywhere but behind her lady, Aiden would have taken the lassie into his arms, pushed through his bedchamber door, and damned the recital.

"I hope I haven't made us late." Maddie batted her eyelashes as if she had no idea of the effect she had on his aching cods. "Miss Agnes spent ever so long curling my hair."

Aiden's tongue slipped over his bottom lip. "Your curls are exquisite. You are exquisite, m'lady."

Agnes cleared her throat, coming up behind with a cloak over her arm. "You'd best say so, m'lord. It took the greater part of the afternoon to make those ringlets."

Nay, there'd be no slipping into the bedchamber for a hasty sampling of those pearl-tipped bosoms.

"And how is your arm, m'lord? Has my salve done its magic?" Agnes asked.

"Can't feel a thing, thank you." Indeed, he felt nothing but his drumming heart.

Aiden glanced to his pocket watch—they still had a few minutes—and now that he knew Maddie was ready, there'd be no harm in making the coach wait for a minute or two. "Fine job, Miss Agnes," he said with more sobriety than he felt. "I think you deserve a healthy tot of fine spirit for taking such sterling care of Her Ladyship."

"Have we time?" asked Maddie.

Aiden led them into the drawing room and gestured to the settee. "A stolen moment will not set us behind overmuch."

Agnes gave a firm shake of her head. "You needn't make a fuss for the likes of me."

"It is no fuss. You take good care of your lady, and for that I want to thank you." Aiden poured three tots of sherry and offered each of the ladies a glass. "Shall we drink to Miss Agnes?"

Blinking, the woman drew a hand over her mouth, dipping her head and smiling broadly. "Heavens."

"Aye, we should." Maddie patted her lady's maid's knee and raised her glass. "To the woman who has seen me through one and twenty years of happiness. I have no idea what would have become of me if you hadn't been by my side. Sometimes I've felt as if you're the only person in all of Christendom who cares."

Aiden's gut twisted. He cared a great deal, but it was inconceivable that Maddie had been made to feel like an outcast from such a young age. He drank thoughtfully, watching the two women as they sipped. Even their mannerisms had become similar. "Miss Agnes, how long have you been serving Lady Magdalen?"

The woman's eyes glistened with pride. "Since the day she was born. The moment I held her in my arms I knew my purpose."

Aiden glanced to Maddie and knitted his brows. "Did your mother pass in childbirth?"

Shaking her head, the lass bit her bottom lip. "Nay. My mother knew I would have a better life if she gave me to my father. Only ..." Maddie looked away and took another sip.

"What?"

"The one caveat was that she could never set eyes on me again."

Agnes took a deep breath, frowning. "It was a good situation for Her Ladyship until the earl decided to marry."

"And that's when you were forced out on your own?" Aiden asked.

Maddie smiled—a smile with eyes growing dark with deep-seated pain. "Alas, the countess didn't want a bastard to remind her of my father's unchaste bachelorhood."

Grumbling under her breath, Agnes guzzled the remainder of her sherry. "We shan't discuss the Countess Marischal any longer. It sets both of our hackles to standing on end."

"Agreed." Aiden set his glass on the mantel and offered Maddie his hand. "Shall we be off, m'lady? We do not want to miss the opening. I hear it will be most spectacular."

Agnes stood and clasped her hands together. "I shall wait up. You are coming straight back, are you not?"

Maddie tapped the lady's maid's shoulder before they strolled toward the door. "I want you to take some time for yourself this night. Do something that will make you happy. You have nothing to worry about, my pet. I'll be in Lord Aiden's capable hands."

* * *

When they arrived at Westminster, it suited Maddie just fine to be seated straightaway. "We couldn't have timed it better."

"Indeed, and all eyes are watching you," Aiden whispered into her hair, making gooseflesh rise across her skin. "You are stunning, absolutely stunning this eve." Aiden followed the usher down the aisle until he stopped and gestured to their seats.

Maddie's eyes flashed wide. "In front?"

"I kent you'd enjoy it. You have more musical talent in one strand of hair than most of the people in attendance as a whole."

She squeezed her fingers around his elbow and inclined her lips to his ear. "Thank you."

"It gives me pleasure just to see you smile."

Once they took their seats, Aiden opened their program. "It says here that after his debut at Westminster, Handel is leaving to be the Kapellmeister to Prince George of Hanover."

She leaned in and read. "Oh my. Now I am even more excited to hear him. He must be very good."

They didn't have long to wait.

The nave of the abbey had been cordoned off and the guests sat in rows behind the enormous organ with pipes of all sizes extending upward to Westminster's vaulted ceiling. Maddie had been to cathedrals before, but had never seen an organ with so many stops and keyboards, five rows of ivory in total. Truly only a magician could make such a complex instrument sing.

After the queen and Prince George were seated with the usual fanfare, George Frideric Handel was introduced as an emerging composer born in Halle in the Holy Roman Empire. The side door opened and in walked the young maestro, clad in black robes, gray periwig, and lace cravat. Of medium height, he was shockingly young for a man who had already composed two operas. He bowed to the polite applause of the audience and took his seat. Despite the five keyboards, man and his instrument were diminished by the size of the enormous pipes above them.

As soon as his fingers struck the keys, Maddie was rapt, taken on a tour of heaven as if floating. Handel played pieces from his operas, *Almira* and *Nero*, and *Dixit Dominus*. That a man could be so young and have composed so much music amazed her.

Aiden threaded his fingers through hers. "You're playing along with him."

She gave him a quizzical expression.

"Your fingers were plucking your harp."

She chuckled to herself. But now that His Lordship had her attention, she realized she had been picturing the music in her mind's eye. And Aiden had been watching her the entire time. Maddie liked his attention, liked how his lips had parted and his eyes had grown stunned when she'd stepped into the passageway earlier that night.

Aiden had an untethered sensuousness about him—raw passion coursed through his blood. Maddie had never met a man who, with a blink of his eyes, could send her insides into a maelstrom of desire. He expressed more with a shift of the eye than most men did launching into a half-hour oration.

Her fingers trembled in his hand. She was so aware of his nearness, yet wanted to be closer. By the time the maestro concluded the first selection, Maddie had forgotten about her love of music. Aiden's touch, his glances, his warm breath on her neck when he'd lean to whisper a comment, combined to twist her insides into a sizzling vat of molten gold. She'd tasted pleasure and she wanted more—wanted him right then and there.

If only.

She snapped from her trance as the applause rose.

Aiden again leaned in, his lips but a hairbreadth from her ear—a mere fraction of an inch from kissing her there and making gooseflesh pebble down her neck. In fact, the gooseflesh had already risen. "I wish we were back at Whitehall."

She met his gaze—moss green, heavy lidded, and filled with the same sensuous desire whirring through her breasts, her heart, her most sacred places.

And in a church.

Maddie should be ashamed of her newfound passion,

unleashed and unbridled for only Aiden Murray to witness. But how could she focus on feelings of guilt? After years of hiding? After years of giving to others and denying herself? She wanted to be happy ... to experience life. This one time she would cast all caution aside and follow her heart—wherever it led.

Chapter Fourteen

*N*aked, Aiden slipped between the bed linens and rested against the headboard. He closed his eyes while a long sigh slipped through his lips. Every night since the first had been like this, waiting for Maddie to steal into his chamber, his heart hammering, his imagination taking over. He liked the growing anticipation, knowing that she'd come, but never certain when.

This night had been special. He'd already known that Maddie had uncanny musical ability, but her enjoyment of the organ recital had been palpable. She'd plucked an imaginary harp as if dreaming up harmonies in her head throughout the performance.

Of course Lady Saxonhurst had been there. This time she was on the arm of a man Aiden didn't know—someone of influence, no doubt. And at intermission he'd overheard the shameful gossip. It was almost as if the gentry wanted him to hear.

What is Lord Aiden doing entertaining a bastard?

'Tis an abomination. How dare that woman show her

face in public when her father is locked in the Tower and accused of treason?

Lord Aiden's reputation could be irrevocably tarnished. A commander can ill afford that. He'll never advance to captain.

And he's only a second son.

But mind you, he is next in line to inherit. The times are precarious and one must never tempt fate.

Aiden had thought about taking Maddie and leaving the recital, but that would have only served to make the snobbish nitwits think they were right. On top of all their foolishness, he had to admit that before he met Lady Magdalen Keith, he would have sided with the hypocrites. He'd been raised to a life of privilege, led to believe himself superior because of his birth and his family's wealth. The son of a powerful peer, Aiden spent his childhood living in an enormous castle filled with servants. His exalted position had instilled in him the erroneous belief that he was above any commoner and far better than any bastard.

How quickly the beauty had realigned his misplaced priorities. Or was it that now he'd set out on his own and become a man it was time for him to form his own opinions? Should a man not observe the world around him and come into his own? Was that not why men were born with the ability to reason?

Lady Magdalen Keith was the most alluring human being he'd ever met. Possessing a quick wit, Maddie was far more entertaining than any of his relatives. Aye, Aiden's brother, John, was a good man, but he didn't possess a certain human quality—one that endeared Maddie to his heart. Her unfettered concern for everyone around her spoke volumes about her character.

After his leave was up, he wondered if they'd ever meet again—possibly in Scotland next.

But such a notion is utterly unlikely.

He could only thank the stars Maddie was willing to give him his first taste of passion.

It is said a man never forgets his first love.

His gut twisted into a knot. Aiden didn't want to think about letting her go. How did other men do it? Fraser MacPherson found a woman at every port. He didn't rue saying good-bye, didn't pine—except possibly for a day or two; then he set his sights on the next adventure.

Dear Lord, why did Aiden's chest burn so? And he'd wanted to slam his fist into the Earl of Seaforth's jaw earlier that day when he'd seen the lout grasp Maddie's arm.

He chuckled.

At least I taught the whelp a lesson.

Then he looked down at the bandage covering the gash in his arm.

But the lad's only eighteen. Seaforth will be a force to reckon with; 'tis a good thing he's a Scot—and a good man

Such thoughts didn't ease the tightening in Aiden's chest. He never wanted to see any man touch Maddie again. The thought of their parting and going separate ways didn't sit well in the least. Who would court her next?

Damnation, our parting cannot be helped, and I will stop dwelling on it this instant.

With the latch's click, Aiden's heart thrummed.

The object of his desire slipped inside his bedchamber. Devil's bones, her smile could certainly melt away any wee pain in his chest.

"Agnes is finally asleep." The lady tiptoed to the bed. "I fear she's starting to suspect that we've grown a mutual fondness."

His cock lengthened as she slowly untied her sash and let the dressing gown fall from her shoulders. "Let us keep the good-hearted serving woman at bay for the next sennight, for I would go mad knowing you were alone in your bed only paces away."

"I'll do what I can—though she's wondering why I've taken to sleeping so late."

"It must be the London air."

"Oh, that *is* good. I'll use that on the morrow."

He slipped from the bedclothes, letting her see him naked.

She grinned, her gaze meandering downward and coming to rest on his manhood. "You are magnificent."

Stepping in, he fingered the satin ribbon on her chemise, then slowly tugged. "I'd go into battle to prove you are more so."

Maddie raised her arms while he drew the gown over her head and cast it aside. Her nipples constricted, making wee pebbles. "Is that what brought on the sparring session with Seaforth?"

He traced his finger around a supple breast, and his cock lengthened a bit more. "I suppose. Besides, it felt good to have a sword in my hand. Aboard ship the officers have an hour of swordplay every day."

"Ah, that explains why you're so practiced." Stepping closer, she tapped his bandage. "How is your arm?"

He drew her into his embrace, skin to skin. "Can hardly feel it." He bit his bottom lip. "As you are aware, a sailor is resourceful." He glanced to the pillow where he'd hidden his pamphlet. He'd decided to share it with her this night. "I have some drawings that I wanted to show you—but only if you wouldn't be offended."

"Offend the bastard?" She threw back her head with a chortle, grinding her mons against him. "I've been offended so much this eve, I doubt I could be injured further."

"Och, you heard the whispers, did you?"

"Only a deaf woman wouldn't have."

He cradled her chin in the crook of his finger. "I care not what any of them think."

She shrugged. "Nor do I."

After a kiss, he again looked to the pillow. "The pictures are . . . well, *erotic*."

A wee smile played on her lips while a naughty flicker sparkled in her eyes. "Similar to what we've been up to these past few nights?"

"Mm-hmm."

She circled her mons into his cock, deliberately this time. Dear God, no matter how much he wanted to maintain control, Maddie could turn up the heat of his passion like nothing he'd ever imagined. "Pictures? You mean to say someone actually was audacious enough to put pen to parchment?"

"Aye."

She snorted with laughter. "'Tis scandalous."

"*We* are scandalous." He gestured to the bed.

"Well then, show me these drawings, and I'll tell you if I cannot abide them."

They sat side by side as Aiden opened the pamphlet.

Maddie gasped and covered her mouth. "I'd never dreamed." She turned her head and looked at one picture in which the man and woman were each on one knee with their legs wrapped over each other's back. "That looks a wee bit uncomfortable."

"I daresay it does." Licking his bottom lip, Aiden pointed to the drawing with the woman seated on the bed and the man standing. "That one looks interesting."

"Aye, but we agreed not to . . ." She waggled her eyebrows at his member. "You ken."

"True, but a man can dream."

"Mm-hmm." She continued to study the drawings with great interest. She pointed to the picture at the bottom of the man licking the woman's quim. "We've done that."

He pointed to the reverse. "And that."

"And we've used our hands."

"I wish I could be inside you." He almost moaned.

She looked him in the eye, her teeth grazing her bottom lip. "What if I were to conceive?"

He glanced to the drawing showing a clear picture of the man buried inside the woman. God, he'd give an entire year's pay to feel her wet heat surround him.

"I've seen too many women succumb to the throes of passion, only to be left with a bastard," she said as if reading his mind.

He nodded. "Forgive me. 'Twas selfish of me to say."

"'Twas honest. I'd like nothing more myself." With a wicked waggle of her brows, she slid down and traced her tongue up his cock, sending his mind into a maelstrom of desire. "Let me bring you pleasure as I did last eve."

Lying back, Aiden gave in to the pleasure of Maddie's touch. Since they'd started this adventure, she'd grown defter and he'd grown a bit more endurance. Och aye, the longer he prolonged his peak, the greater the reward.

With her lips around him, he closed his eyes and imagined burying his cock inside her. His hips rocked back and forth, faster and faster, as she worked her magic, sucking, swirling her tongue, and milking him with her fingers. Though he tried to resist, passion hit him strong and hard, and he came with the force of a cannon blast.

Collapsing on top of him, Maddie chuckled. "I feel powerful when you bend to my will."

He ran his fingers through the wild honeyed tresses sprawling over his body. "Only you have that privilege."

Pulling her up, he claimed her mouth, a swirl of desire filling his chest, his cock growing hard again. But now he'd give Maddie pleasure. He coaxed her to her back and nuzzled kisses into her neck. "I cannot wait to eat you."

"Mm," she moaned. "You make it sound so sensuous."

He moved to her breasts, cupping them in his hands. He pressed them together and slipped his tongue through the crevice. "You are my goddess."

Down he went while his cock grew harder yet. She opened her legs and he moved between them, rose up on his knees, and stared into those fathomless blues. "Are you ready to reach for the stars, lass?"

Licking her ruby-red lips, she nodded.

With the first swipe of his tongue, Aiden, too, soared to the stars. *Heaven on earth.*

He could kiss Maddie until dawn and never tire. He loved how her pleasure made him feel like a man, like the king of the world. He was so rapt in his passion, Aiden barely registered the door slamming.

"Good God, what on earth is going on under my father's roof?"

Aiden's tongue stilled. Only one man on earth possessed a deep voice such as that.

In one move he leaped from the bed, grabbed his plaid, and covered his loins. "John? What the blazes are you doing here?"

His brother strained to glance around to Maddie. "The question is, what are *you* doing?"

Fortunately, she'd managed to pull the linens clear up to her neck—and now over her head.

Dear Lord, they'd been caught—and not by Agnes. Aiden wrapped the kilt around his waist. "Come. Let us allow Lady Magdalen a moment of privacy while she gathers her clothing."

"Lady Magdalen? Is she by chance related to Marischal?"

"Aye." Aiden pushed John out the door and to the drawing room. "I've allowed her to stay whilst she arranges for her father's release."

"Is that likely?" John, the Marquis of Tullibardine, plopped into a chair.

"It seems probable." Aiden scratched his head. "But what are you doing in London, and at this hour?"

"My regiment has been deployed. We sail for the Continent on the morrow. I came to Whitehall to sleep in a real bed for the last time in God kens how long. I'll be tenting it with the First Cavalry after we hit the Continent."

"Are things heating up on the front?"

"Haven't you heard? The French attacked the Allied forces in Bavaria. I'm surprised you're not in the thick of it."

"The *Royal Mary* is in port for repairs."

"You lucky devil." John glanced to the sound of a door clicking in the passageway. "In more ways than one."

"It's not what you think."

"No? What? Did my eyes deceive me?"

"She's not a harlot."

"You could have fooled me."

Aiden scowled. "Bugger off with the jesting."

John slapped a dismissive hand through the air. "I suppose it means nothing to me—after all, don't they say a sailor has a woman in every port?"

Chapter Fifteen

*E*arly the next morning, the porter brought in a tray of toast, jam, and herring. Aiden met his brother in the drawing room. Dressed in a red-coated cavalry uniform, John looked far too English for Aiden's taste.

"What regiment did you say you'll deploying with?" he asked.

"Marlborough himself. I'll be leading the First Cavalry."

"That's quite a responsibility."

"And an honor."

"Not to mention dangerous."

"No more so than traveling the byways around Blair Castle." Picking up a piece of toast, John used a round-tipped knife to carve off a slab of butter. "And you, you've never been one to shirk danger."

"Aye, but I'm not the heir. I'd expect you to be a bit more careful."

"Ever the practical one." John swathed his toast. "What news of the Colonies?"

"Not much. The French are carving out territory to the north—tempers are rising on that front as well."

"Next you'll be telling me the *Royal Mary* has been deployed to the Americas."

Aiden reached for the flagon of cider. "Holy hell, I hope not. We'd most likely succumb to the mercy of the sea. She's only a class-four frigate. The crossing is better suited to a galleon or the like."

"True, though you could request a transfer."

"Are you anxious to send me to the Americas, brother?"

"Not at all."

Aiden had thought about it at one time, though since the Act of Union, sailing off to the Colonies to represent Britain didn't sit well. John hadn't yet mentioned anything of home. "How is Mathilde?"

"Well." John chased down his bite with a swallow of cider. "Still not with child, but we'll resume our efforts upon my return."

Aiden gave his brother a wink. "Not an unpleasant thing for a soldier to dream about."

"Not at all."

When a floorboard creaked, Aiden turned his attention toward the sound. Wearing her cloak, Maddie tiptoed toward the door. He immediately stood, with John following suit. "Lady Magdalen, are you stepping out before you break your fast?"

She snapped around and gaped at him, her face blushing red as raspberries. "Lord Aiden, you are up early this morn."

John cleared his throat. "My brother always rises with the first crow from the roost."

Maddie shifted her gaze to her feet.

Aiden had no doubt she was embarrassed half to death. Dear Lord, if he'd known his brother was planning to pay a visit, he never would have risked… "Ah, I haven't properly introduced my brother, the Marquis of Tullibardine." He gestured from John to Maddie. "Lady Magdalen."

"I recall." John bowed deeply. "'Tis lovely making your acquaintance."

"What does he mean he recalls, m'lady?" asked Agnes, pattering through the hallway.

Maddie bit the corner of her mouth. "Ah, there was a wee commotion when the marquis arrived last eve."

Agnes frowned and looked between the two men, though her gaze didn't linger. "I do hope all is well?"

"Indeed," said Aiden. "His Lordship will be sailing for the Continent—at what time, John?"

"Orders are to be aboard ship at midday."

The bell sounded. "A missive for His Lordship."

"I'll fetch it," said John, walking to the door. "Though I've no idea why you haven't employed a valet for the duration of your leave."

Stepping nearer, Maddie mouthed, "I'm sorry."

Aiden spread his palms, affecting an aghast expression. She had absolutely nothing to apologize for. "What are your plans for this morrow, m'lady?"

"Agnes and I are off to the Tower to tell Da about Lord Seaforth's petition." Her smile brightened the entire chamber. Thank heavens she wasn't entirely flummoxed by last eve's debacle. "I am certain it shall do much to lift his spirits."

Aiden tugged on his lapels. "It would be an honor to accompany you."

"Oh, that is kind, is it not, m'lady?" said Agnes.

John stepped back inside holding up the opened missive. "I'm afraid this is for you, Aiden."

Knitting his brows, Aiden took the parchment and read.

Then a lead ball dropped to the pit of his stomach. His face grew hot.

God, not now.

Maddie craned her neck, her expression alarmed. "What is it?"

"I've been ordered back to the *Royal Mary.*"

"When?"

"I'm to report immediately."

"My word," Maddie whispered, drawing her fingers to her mouth.

"Didn't you say the ship is in port for repairs?" asked John.

"Aye, minor repairs, but she's still seaworthy." Aiden eyed his brother. "What does Marlborough have planned?"

John arched one eyebrow and studied the two women. "An all-out sweep of the Continent—by land and sea. He aims to put an end to this bloody war once and for all."

Having been in the navy for two years, Aiden had heard the same more than once. But perhaps the Duke of Marlborough was serious this time. Aiden reached his hands out to Maddie, but quickly snapped them to his sides. Touching her in the presence of his brother and her serving maid would be completely and utterly improper.

She remained surprisingly composed. The only thing giving away her disappointment was the stricken look in her eyes. "Do you have any idea when you'll return?"

"None." He raised his palms while a chasm spread in his chest. "We could be gone for months."

"We'll most likely be back in Stonehaven by that time," said Miss Agnes.

Maddie drew in a sharp breath. "Will the *Royal Mary* again visit Stonehaven?"

"I cannot be certain." Unable to stop himself, he stepped forward and grasped her hands tightly between his palms.

Damn propriety. "I thought we had several days. I wanted to join Lord Seaforth in working to see your father released, or at least stand beside you whilst you presented the petition to the queen."

She blinked, her eyes watery. "Not to worry."

The walls closed around him. "But more than anything, I wanted to spend the remainder of my leave—ah—with you."

John cleared his throat—the lout.

A tear slipped from Maddie's eye. "Me also."

Damnation, Aiden's tongue was tied. He wanted to pull her into his chamber and declare his undying love. Promise that he would return as soon as possible. Tell her he would meet her in Stonehaven for Hogmanay, or sooner. Mayhap make a promise of marriage, ask for her pledge to wait for him.

For how long?

Only God knew. And his fate rested in the Almighty's hands. If Britain truly intended to pull out all stops and end the war, then he could be away for a year or more, if the *Royal Mary* didn't end up at the bottom of the Channel.

Aiden shuddered. He'd never given much thought to a cannonball's sinking his ship—he'd always thought about the adventure—but looking at Magdalen's bonny but stricken countenance made ice pulse through his veins. He must come back for her.

He raised her hands to his lips. Closing his eyes, he kissed them—imparting all the affection swelling in his heart. "I will endeavor to see you again, God willing."

His pathetic words conveyed but a pittance of his true feelings.

Indeed, Maddie knew as well as he that they couldn't make commitments. Their liaison had been a tryst. An affair.

Right?

He gulped.

Why did his heart feel as if it had been ripped from his chest and crushed in a pair of scorching-hot tongs?

* * *

A lump the size of Maddie's fist remained fixed in her throat for days. She sat on the stool while Agnes combed her hair. At least while Aiden was in London, her plight hadn't seemed as dire. Perhaps she'd neglected her daughterly duties somewhat, but what else could she have done? Gaining a pardon was a dreary job of waiting for days, mayhap months. Having Aiden near had made the hours fly by, made the waiting tolerable.

A sennight ago Lord Seaforth had presented his petition to the queen. He hadn't allowed Maddie to attend Her Majesty alongside him. He'd thought her presence would be too distracting and draw attention away from the true purpose of the document, which served to express the political prowess of the Earl Marischal of Scotland and the other peers still incarcerated in Edinburgh Castle.

Maddie's shoulders drooped. *What a miserable state of affairs.*

"My heavens, m'lady," Agnes said, pulling her hair and pinning it too tightly. "Ever since Lord Aiden left, you've been as listless as a rag doll."

Heaving a sigh, Maddie rolled her eyes to the ornate ceiling frieze. At least they'd been granted leave to continue to stay in the Atholl apartments. "I'm so worried."

"About your da, or about Lord Aiden?"

"Both."

"What more can we do?"

"Lord Seaforth said to wait—and for me to continue to play my harp." She busied herself by studying her fingernails.

"I think music is the only thing that has kept me sane in the past few days."

Agnes primped fastidiously. She always did that when something weighed heavily on her mind. "I've prayed every moment that Lord Seaforth's petition will be successful."

"As have I."

"I miss Lord Aiden, too."

"You do?"

"Aye, he was ever so gentlemanly. He would be a good match for you, m'lady."

Maddie's heart fluttered—the blasted thing. "If only we weren't at war. Who kens when I'll ever see him again?"

When the bell sounded, Agnes went to answer the door, leaving Maddie sitting before the looking glass.

Many times her mind had conjured images of the fleeting moments she'd spent in Aiden's arms. Their liaison had been wrong in so many ways, yet Maddie refused to feel guilty about it—except the night when John had caught them. To his credit, the Marquis of Tullibardine had been courteous toward her—especially when he'd been within his rights to throw her out of the Atholl apartments for her scandalous behavior. If the marquis harbored any ill sentiments, he'd masked them well.

Unfortunately, Maddie had met many people who were kind to her face yet abhorrent behind her back. Though if the marquis was anything like his younger brother, he'd act honorably and with discretion.

She sighed. It was unlikely she would ever again have the opportunity to meet Aiden's brother.

"M'lady." Agnes hastened inside. "A guard is here. The queen has requested an audience."

The lump in Maddie's throat felt as if it grew two sizes larger. "The queen?"

Agnes clapped her hands together, looking like a wee lass at Yuletide. "I pray your father will be released and we can return to Stonehaven within the sennight."

Standing, Maddie reached for her lady's maid's hands. "Please let it be so."

"You mustn't tarry. Go and bring the good news swiftly."

As she followed the guard, Maddie's palms perspired and her stomach squeezed with her every nervous thought. Ushered into the queen's presence chamber, Magdalen dipped into a reverent curtsy.

"Come forward," commanded the queen in her imposing tone as she sat on her high-backed throne.

Maddie had never seen this chamber before and took in the grandeur as she moved deeper inside. Life-size portraits of past kings hung on the walls, and on the ceiling a renaissance mural of angels gazed down at her. The queen's throne sat atop a red carpet raised by a small dais. Behind the great woman was a velvet drape with the royal coat of arms embroidered in rich golds. The drape continued to the ceiling, making a canopy, as if the queen needed to be shaded indoors.

"Have you enjoyed your time in London?" the queen asked.

"Yes, Your Majesty." What else was Maddie to say? She hated London, and now that Lord Aiden had been called to sea, she desperately wanted to see her father freed from the Tower so that she could return to Scotland.

Her Majesty's smug smile looked very similar to a frown. "Such news makes me happy. I do quite admire your music."

"Thank you, Your Majesty."

The woman shifted in her seat. "I have considered the petition submitted by the Earl of Seaforth on your father's behalf."

Maddie drew in a deep breath and stood taller. "My father is a loyal servant to the crown. I ken in my heart he is innocent and—"

"Silence. I do not need to listen to the pleas of a bastard." How quickly the tides could turn with Her Majesty. Seconds ago she'd spouted praise, and now she barked with disdain.

Maddie pursed her lips. Holy crosses, how daft could she be, chattering like a hen?

Queen Anne sniffed with a flutter of her fan. "Now then, I have a proposition for you."

"Aye?" Maddie asked reticently, almost afraid to speak aloud lest she be reprimanded.

"If you agree to be my personal harpist, I will release your father to attend the next session of Parliament. And if he supports my defense against those nobles attempting to abolish the Act of Settlement, I shall consider absolving him entirely of any suspicion of treasonous acts."

The perspiration under Maddie's arms stung. She could barely take a breath. "You mean for me to remain in London, Your Majesty?"

"Well, you couldn't very well play your harp for me sitting in some drafty hovel in the north of Scotland."

"No...Apologies." Maddie dipped into another curtsy. "Forgive me." There was so much to consider while the queen impatiently drummed her fingers on the armrest. Everyone and their grandmother knew the Earl Marischal supported the movement to abolish the Act of Settlement. Discriminating and a political sham, the act had put an end to the true monarchy by stating that anyone who practiced the Catholic faith or married a member of the Catholic faith would lose his or her right to inherit the throne.

But couldn't Da side with the queen on this one thing? It would ensure his freedom.

On the other side, how long was Maddie expected to remain in London?

The queen snapped her fan closed and clapped it in her palm. "I sense you are hesitant about my offer."

Dear Lord, I could ruin our lives with my next utterance.

Maddie curtsied deeply. "Your offer is quite generous, Your Majesty. I consider such a proposal not only generous, but a greater honor than a lass of my station could hope for. And I am certain to the depths of my soul that my father will stand beside Your Majesty whilst you face your enemies in Parliament."

A faint smile played on the queen's lips—one that reflected a great deal of cunning. "I thought you'd be overjoyed; thus I've taken steps to reinstate your father's apartments. You must vacate the Duke of Atholl's residence at once. I should not have allowed you to remain there this long."

"No, Your Majesty?" Maddie's face burned as if held to hot coals.

"Oh please, I'll wager you are not impervious to the gossip. If it weren't for your lady's maid's being in attendance, I would have not been able to ignore the situation as long as I did."

Again she curtsied. "Thank you, Your Majesty. We were in dire need. I do not ken what I would have done if Lord Aiden hadn't come to my aid."

"Hmm." Her Majesty glanced away. "The realm could use more white knights such as he." Then she flicked her fingers at Maddie. "Move into your new quarters today. The Duchess of Marlborough will keep you apprised of your harpist appointments."

Maddie curtsied for what seemed like the hundredth time. "Thank you ever so much, Your Majesty."

As she made her way back to the Duke of Atholl's apartments, Maddie tried to focus on the positive. Her father would be freed. For the first time since she was seven years of age, she would spend time under the same roof with him—at least until this session of Parliament ended.

Regardless, her stomach twisted in knots and her shoulders drooped a bit more with her every step. How would she survive the gossip without Aiden to guide her through the mire? Merciful Father, she missed him something awful. Things were so dreary without him at Whitehall.

Agnes would be disappointed for certain. And what would happen to the hospital? She'd never intended to be gone for so long, and now who knew how long she'd have to bear the ladies-in-waiting's wicked stares and snooty jibes?

Blast it all, she should be overjoyed that Da would finally be freed, and if playing her fingers to the bone for the queen was the price she had to pay, then so be it.

Chapter Sixteen

London, 14 June 1708

*O*ver a month had passed since Da's release from the Tower. They'd received news of the birth of his daughter, whom the countess had named Anne after the queen in an attempt to gain favor. Fortunately, both mother and child had come through the ordeal well.

Maddie sat across the table from her father, porridge spoon in hand. "Every time I hear anything about the war, I nearly stop playing." Honestly, every time Prince George visited the queen, Maddie's ears homed in on the conversation, trying to garner any news about the *Royal Mary*. "Were you aware the Royal Navy engaged the French in cannon fire, in an effort to protect the Netherlands' trade routes?"

Da looked up from his gazette. "I beg your pardon?"

Maddie blinked. "Why are we protecting the Netherlands' trade routes?"

Flicking his hand as if he were swatting a fly, Da huffed. "The queen believes there's an imminent threat of French domination."

"I have no idea why we have to involve ourselves in the war on the Continent. Haven't we enough to worry about on our own soil?"

"My sentiments exactly. I swear that woman engages the French merely to thwart our efforts for *the cause.*"

Maddie shrugged. "She no longer thinks the prince poses any sort of threat."

Da set the gazette on the table. "What's that? Do you ken this to be true, lass?"

"Aye, I heard it from the queen's mouth but a sennight ago."

"Why did you not tell me sooner?"

Maddie scooped a spoonful of porridge. "I thought you were already aware."

Da leaned nearer, stroking his clean-shaven chin. "What else has Her Majesty said about her brother?"

"Not much." Swallowing, Maddie composed her thoughts. "She believes him to be a coward, of course. You ken they're calling him the *Pretender.*"

"Aye." Da narrowed his gaze. "What else?"

"Not certain. She receives reports on his whereabouts, but they're dull mostly. James attended a ball or the opera or he dined with the Duke of Berry." Maddie held up her finger. "Oh, there was a rumor of his betrothal, but that turned out to be false—after all, he's only twenty."

Da slapped his hand on the table. "I cannot believe you have been holding this information from me. Do you have any idea how important it is that you divulge everything you hear, especially when it pertains to *the cause*?"

Maddie rested her spoon beside her bowl, a prickly

sensation spreading across her arms. Then she leaned forward and lowered her voice. "Are you asking me to spy on the queen?"

"Och, dear gel, everyone at court spies. Surely you've been here long enough to realize that. How else are we to make informed decisions?" He slapped his folded gazette. "We surely cannot find it in this compilation of gibberish."

True, Maddie had been listening in, trying to learn anything about the fleet or the *Royal Mary*'s whereabouts. "You're saying you want me to relay reports about *the prince*?"

Da leaned forward and jammed his pointer finger into the table. "You cannot be so naïve to think we are not in a war—and mark me, I am not referring to the French. Aye, you did what you had to do to free me from the Tower, and for that I am grateful. But I do not intend to see that woman rule Scotland or Britain any longer than necessary. She is a poorly educated buffoon—as is her bumbling, rheumy-eyed, self-appointed-admiral husband. You may fancy yourself a musician, but you will always be my daughter and loyal to the Highland way of life. Never forget your duty."

"I haven't. *My duty* is the reason I came to London in the first place."

"'Tis good to hear you say it." He patted her shoulder. "Now, I want to be apprised of everything that is said about France, the war, and any wee word about repealing the Act of Settlement."

Maddie shook her head. "Ye ken the queen would rather die than allow the succession of a Catholic on the throne."

"That could be arranged."

"Da!" She clapped her hand to her chest. "What are you saying?"

He spread a bit of conserve on his toast. "'Twas but a jest, my dear."

Chewing her bottom lip, she shook her head. "Somehow spying seems wrong."

"Not at all. All I am asking is for you to relay to me things you have heard. For all that is holy, lass, you'll just be doing more of the same." He eyed her as he often had when she was a small child. "You've earned a position in the queen's court that few other women of your station could hope to attain. Now you must use it for the good of your clan and kin."

"Very well." Maddie let out a long sigh. "'Tis unlikely she'll say anything of import in my presence, but if I can be of assistance to *the cause*, then so be it."

* * *

Behind him the rising sun cast a pink glow across the shore. Scotland. Aiden hadn't stepped on home soil since the last time they moored off Stonehaven. Unfortunately, this mooring would be briefer than the last.

The *Royal Mary* had intercepted a French galleon lying in wait for a cargo ship headed for Britain. Though neither he nor Captain Polwarth condoned the war with the French, they still had a responsibility to protect home's merchant ships.

They'd followed the galleon all the way up to Norway until she opened her cannon doors and fired a warning shot across the *Royal Mary*'s bow.

"She has eighteen guns ready to fire, Captain," Aiden had said from his position at the helm.

"I reckon we've done our duty. The cargo ship is well under way. What say you, Commander? Shall we change course for Stonehaven and replenish our hold?"

"Och aye, sir." Aiden's heart soared until the captain announced only the purser would step ashore, and a host of sailors to transport supplies.

Now Aiden watched the small burgh of Stonehaven approach with a heavy heart.

MacPherson stepped beside him and leaned on the rail. "Why so glum?"

"There's someone I need to see, and the captain has said no leave."

"Have you asked him?"

"Nay."

MacPherson thumped Aiden on the shoulder. "Well, no one ever obtained a thing they wanted without asking."

"Right." He stepped back and looked astern. Bloody hell, this was his chance to see Maddie again. And he was so damned close. What good was the rank of commander if he couldn't bend a few rules now and again?

A half hour later Aiden stood at the stern of a skiff, rowing for shore. He had an hour. Plenty of time.

He hopped onto the pier before the skiff had been tied and hailed the first man he saw. "You there, can you tell me where I might find the Seaside Hospital for the Welfare of Women?"

The man gave him a leering once-over. "What business have you there?"

"Lady Magdalen is an acquaintance of mine. I have a message for her."

"Och, I was wondering. You didn't look like a wife beater to me." Pointing, he gave an overblown explanation of how to turn left at the first street, walk two blocks, and take another left. Fortunately for Aiden, he was a Scot and accustomed to being told to watch out for every storefront along the way.

The hospital was impossible to miss. Standing alone, the whitewashed building was small and quaint. He could picture Maddie there, running things in her own little world, protected from the malicious gossip of court, yet making a difference for those who needed her care.

A bell rang when he opened the door and stepped inside.

It was eerily quiet. He waited, taking in the small entrance hall, the sparse furnishings, the slight scent of vinegar—used for cleaning, no doubt. He examined a landscape portrait of Dunnottar Castle painted on canvas, with a storm brewing in the distance. No matter how one looked at the fortress, it always made for a grand sight, sitting atop its immense promontory, dominating the sea with its majestic presence.

"May I help you?" asked a woman from behind.

Though it didn't sound like Maddie, Aiden's stomach fluttered as he turned. "I'm looking for Lady Magdalen. Is she about?"

"No, I'm sorry, she's presently away." The woman eyed him from head to toe with a distrustful glint in her eye.

What was Aiden to expect? This was a hospital for battered women, and he hadn't even bothered to introduce himself. He swiftly bowed. "Forgive me. I am Commander Aiden Murray from the *Royal Mary.*"

The woman dipped her head politely. "Mrs. Boyd, at your service."

"I assisted Her Ladyship in London a few months past and stopped in to bid her good day."

"Oh dear, you haven't heard? The queen has asked my lady to be her personal harpist."

Aiden felt as though he'd received a blow to the gut. "She's still in London?" Oh no, Maddie wouldn't be happy at all.

"I'm afraid so, m'lord. Things just aren't the same without Her Ladyship here."

"I doubt they are." A sad smile played on his lips. "Has there been any word as to when she might return?"

Mrs. Boyd glanced aside while she shook her head. "No.

Her last letter said she was staying at Whitehall with her father. 'Tis quite an honor to be asked to play the harp for the queen."

"Indeed it is." Aiden bowed, deeper this time. "If you would kindly tell her I stopped by when she does return, I would be grateful."

"Of course." Mrs. Boyd gestured to a table displaying an open book. "I'm certain she would be tickled if you signed the guest log—no one ever does."

"My thanks." Aiden picked up the quill and dipped it in the ink pot, biting his bottom lip. He wanted to say something personal, but nothing that would be scandalous. In the end he decided to keep it short.

My Dearest Lady Magdalen,

A dark cloud has shadowed my day now that I have missed you. For your smile would have brought a month of sunshine into this sailor's heart. Adieu, m'lady. Until our paths shall once again cross.
Lord Aiden Murray, Commander, the Royal Mary

Chapter Seventeen

London, August 1709

Maddie couldn't believe it had already been a year and four months since she'd first stepped onto the pier at Blackwall Port. Aside from her brief interlude with Lord Aiden, her life had been dreary, with nothing to look forward to. And spying didn't sit well, either. The only positive thing that had come of it was she'd proved herself useful to her father for the first time in her life.

Having finished her afternoon set, she started collecting her things when Prince George entered the queen's antechamber. "I have news."

The queen flicked her wrist at Maddie and Lady Essex, who happened to be the only two in attendance. After a curtsy Maddie followed the countess out the door and pretended to proceed through the passage in the opposite direction. At the corner Maddie glanced over her shoulder.

Clearly suspecting nothing, Lady Essex had meandered

on her way, which was the normal state of affairs. Few if any of the queen's ladies-in-waiting paid Maddie much mind, unless they had something spiteful to say.

Steeling her nerves, she tiptoed back toward the door. Whenever Prince George came in with news, Maddie paid extra attention, intently listening for anything about the *Royal Mary*. Goodness, it had been a long time since she'd had word. A year ago Mrs. Boyd had written that a Lord Aiden Murray had asked for her and signed the hospital's guest book with a fervent hand.

But he hadn't sent a letter.

At least not one that had reached London.

And Britain was solidly embroiled in two wars—the War of the Spanish Succession on the Continent and Queen Anne's War in the Colonies. Hostility surrounded them, and the queen was forever meeting with her cabinet ministers, all the while growing paler and heavier. It was no wonder her temperament had suffered as well.

"The French are pushing in on our fishing rights in Newfoundland." The prince's voice resounded through the timbers.

"This is preposterous," the queen shouted. "First they attack our ships in the Channel and now they're after the Colonies? Have we engaged them? Do they have warships?"

"I dispatched the *Royal Shrewsbury* and the *Royal Newcastle* this very morning. But it will be two months before they're in a position to engage."

"I want it contained," said the queen. "Blast the French out of the sea. I will not tolerate another underhanded attack from them."

"Though fishing is not really an attack, my love."

"You say not?" the queen shrieked, sounding on the verge of hysterics. "They are invading our territory and taking the fish out of the hands and the mouths of our colonists.

Next our troops in the colonies will be starving because the French have pushed and pushed until there is nothing left."

"Yes, you are right as always."

"We must take every step to stop Louis." A loud bang resounded with the queen's mounting ire. "The king of France supports popery and will stop at nothing to sink his wiles into every corner of Christendom!"

When someone tapped Maddie on the shoulder, her heart nearly leaped out of her chest. She whipped around, excuses already filling her head.

Lady Saxonhurst shot her an accusing glare. "Exactly what are you doing listening at the queen's door?"

Usually Maddie tried to be a bit less obvious when actively spying rather than overhearing as she did when playing the harp. But she'd been so excited about the possibility of hearing something about Aiden, she'd done nothing to make herself look unobvious.

She blurted the excuse refusing to leave the tip of her tongue. "I hoped Prince George had news of the *Royal Mary*."

The countess blinked at first, then her eyes filled with haughty laughter. "You cannot be serious. How long has it been since the *Royal Mary* was in port?"

"Over a year." Maddie bit her lip. She'd wanted to say one year, three months and twenty-two days, but that would only invite more scorn.

"I thought Lord Aiden adored you in a puppy-dog sort of way, but my dear, he's a naval officer. Hasn't anyone told you never to fall in love with a naval officer?"

Maddie pursed her lips, refusing to play along with the woman's banter.

But Lady Saxonhurst jammed her fists into her hips. "Aside from enemy ships, there are pirates on the high seas.

All manner of woes can befall a ship. She can suffer a cannonball to her hull, an ill wind, sea creatures that rise from the deep and drag a ship and her crew to their watery graves."

"Please stop." Maddie held up her palm. "I do not need to worry any more than I already do."

The countess's jaw dropped. "My word. You *are* in love with him."

"I did not say that."

"Truly you are if you risk being caught outside the queen's antechamber like a *spy*."

Maddie's mind raced, searching for something to turn the conversation away from her. "And what brought you back this way? Is it not time to dress for the evening meal?"

"That is none of your concern." Lady Saxonhurst's eyes narrowed, giving that leering glare again. "I'm afraid I'll have to report you to the Duchess of Marlborough."

"I beg your pardon?" Maddie thrust her hands to her sides. "I just humiliated myself baring my soul to you, and you're planning to report me?"

"This might be the first time I've confronted you, but I've seen you listening in on the queen's private business before. Goodness, at times you even look like you're paying more attention to the queen than to your music when you're plucking that ridiculous harp."

"Please." Maddie resorted to pleading. "I merely wanted news of Lord Aiden's ship."

"Hmm, we'll have to let the Duchess of Marlborough decide what is to be done." The countess turned on her heel and paraded off, in the direction whence she came, no doubt.

Maddie crossed her arms as she watched the woman's retreating form. Aye, she'd noticed the countess watching her—the woman had been doing that since she arrived at Whitehall. She'd also noticed the countess keeping company with Lord Blackiron, a Whig and an earl Da detested with vehemence.

The pair of them deserve each other.

* * *

An hour later Maddie sat with her father in the drawing room of the Earl Marischal of Scotland's apartments.

"I want to go home." She jammed her needle into her embroidery. "Haven't I been here long enough?"

"No. Dammit, lass, for once in your life you are providing an invaluable service to me—to Scotland—and all you can think about is that little hospital in Stonehaven." He marched to the sideboard and poured himself a brandy, since good Scottish whisky was in short supply this year due to the queen's trade embargoes.

"But now that Lady Saxonhurst suspects me, she won't leave me alone. I feel it right down to the tips of my toes. It's as if she suspected I might be spying right then and ventured to the queen's antechamber just to catch me."

"What the devil are you saying?"

Maddie tossed her embroidery aside. "There was no reason for her to be in that part of the palace. She tapped me on the shoulder. Right before that I may have heard a very faint footstep—but she crept up on me. I am absolutely certain of it."

"Do you think Blackiron has put the countess up to her own bit of spying?"

"As you've said a hundred times, everyone at court spies. I just do not see why I'm to be reported to the Duchess of Marlborough for listening in to a harmless conversation."

As soon as the words slipped through Maddie's lips, the valet entered the drawing room. "Lady Magdalen, you've been summoned by the Duchess of Marlborough."

Maddie rolled her eyes to her father and mouthed, "See?"

Da pointed at her directly. "'Tis a slap on the wrist and that is all. You must be more careful, but as long as the queen requires your presence here, I require your ears. Do you understand?"

With a nod, Maddie curtsied. "Yes."

Of course Father was right. After the highest-ranking lady admonished Maddie's behavior and berated her for her admitted affection for Lord Aiden, she was dismissed with a "This behavior will cease immediately" and a "Your only duty is to play the harp for Her Majesty, and nothing else."

The warning bit, though. Never in her life had Maddie felt imprisoned. But now Lady Magdalen Keith was a prisoner of the queen, only allowed to play her harp and ordered not to have a whimsical thought outside of music. And on the other side, she must listen to everything that was said while she was in the queen's presence. Da grilled her every night. Anything Maddie didn't know, he probed into further, asking more questions that she usually couldn't answer.

He said she was providing a valuable service, but she didn't see it. She was just listening to a litany of posturing. The country was rife with war. It was a wonder that France hadn't invaded and put King Louis XIV on the throne because of all the backstabbing nobles. It was almost as if the entire aristocracy of Britain were vying over who could cast the greatest insults.

Well, Maddie wanted none of it.

At least the people in Stonehaven were the salt of the earth. They worked their fingers to the bone, going home to their families every night. They didn't have time to gossip or spy or plot about how they'd stab each other in the back—figuratively, of course.

Chapter Eighteen

*A*iden peered through his spyglass. "The sloop is flying a black flag, sir."

"How many cannons?" asked Captain Polwarth.

To be sure, Aiden counted again, though he'd already made an assessment

"Seven on her starboard side—fourteen most likely in total. There are two and fifty men on deck, but a sloop typically holds five and seventy."

"I am aware, Commander." The captain grinned. "But the odds are not bad."

Returning the spyglass to his eye, Aiden focused across the water to the pirate captain, who was dressed in black, including his feathered tricorn hat. His arms waved through the air—as he shouted a barrage of orders, no doubt. Men on the deck ran to and fro, some with bows and others with sabers in their hands. The ship slowed.

"They're heaving to," Aiden reported crisply.

"What's our dead reckoning?"

Having expected this question as soon as the sloop had

been spotted an hour ago, Aiden had calculated their position. "A hundred leagues from Lizard Point, sir." He used that reference because it was the southernmost point on the British mainland.

The captain stood ramrod straight. "And from Portsmouth?"

Indeed, Aiden had figured that distance as well. No ship navigated the English Channel without knowing how far it must sail to reach the largest shipbuilding port in the kingdom. "One hundred, five and seventy leagues northeast, sir."

"Cannon three at the ready. We'll fire a warning over her bow," Captain Polwarth ordered.

"Cannon three!" MacPherson's voice bellowed from the gun deck below.

"Tack to port."

"Tacking to port," echoed MacBride from the helm.

Aiden continued to watch through the spyglass. Pirate activity off Britain's coast had escalated in the past several months, and this wouldn't be the first Bermudian sloop the *Royal Mary* sent to a watery grave.

Men without scruples, pirates preyed on Britain's merchant ships, but the smaller-bodied sloops were ideal for a ship the size of the *Mary*. They were sleek and fast, with a narrower turning radius than the heavier frigate, but Aiden's crew outnumbered the pirates. Though they were matched for cannons, he would place any wager on the *Royal Mary*'s crew. His men were disciplined, lean, and trained to be deadly.

And this wasn't their first time facing the dragon-hearted varlets who lurked on the seas, waiting for their chance to plunder cargo sorely needed by Britain's own.

As the *Mary*'s boom swung, the sails collapsed before they once again filled with the breeze. The captain raised his spyglass and waited.

Tension rested on Aiden's shoulders like the points of sharp knives.

The only sounds on deck were those of the sails flapping and the waves breaking against the hull. His pulse pounded through his veins with the thrill of anticipation.

When the ship sailed broadside, not a hundred feet from the sloop, the captain gave a nod.

"Fire!" Aiden bellowed.

"Fire," repeated MacPherson from below.

Boom!

The deck shuddered with the force of the blast. Aiden's ears rang while the cannonball whistled through the air. With a dunking splash, water washed over the sloop's deck while the captain ordered the *Royal Mary* to heave to.

Aiden lowered his spyglass. "A bold move, sir." Giving the pirates a broad target, they were baiting the thieves to engage in an all-out sea battle.

Polwarth glanced his way with a reckless grin. "I aim to send the milk-livered swine to their graves."

A cannon barrel jutting through the sloop's gunport flashed, a boom and a hissing whistle followed. Aiden stood very still and held his breath.

"They've sealed their fates," growled the captain.

Splash!

The shot missed the hull by only a dozen yards. The ship bobbed and rocked with the waves caused by the shot, but with another shift of the sails, the *Royal Mary* continued to drift on a path to engage in battle. Receiving a nod from the captain, Aiden raced down the steps and across the main deck. "Archers, at the ready!"

Still standing at the helm, the captain continued to shout orders. "All cannons, set your sights."

"Setting sights, sir!" bellowed MacPherson from below.

Aiden drew his flintlock pistol and held it aloft. "Muske-teers, charge your weapons."

"'Tis a good day for a fight, sir," snarled a weatherworn seaman.

"Agreed." Aiden charged his weapon with his powder horn, then rammed a lead musket ball. "They will feel the iron might of Scotland in their very bellies."

A roar rose from the deck as the men shouted the battle cry, "For Scotland!"

The *Royal Mary* might have come under the flag of Brit-ain, but her crew would never forget their roots.

After hours of posturing, it took only minutes for the *Mary* to maneuver close enough for the captain to give the command for the cannons to fire all guns.

"Archers, take aim," Aiden bellowed. "Fire!"

As he watched the arrows soar, cannon blasts from the gun deck shook the ship. Aiden spread his feet to main-tain his footing. "Muskets, take aim," he shouted over the whistling and deafening cracks from cannonballs smashing timber.

Across the water, flashes from the sloop's gunports flared. Aiden leveled his pistol at an officer on the far deck. "All men, fire at will!" he ordered as his finger closed around the cold trigger. Adjusting for distance and the movement of his target, Aiden moved the pistol to the right. His finger closed. The flintlock snapped with a bang.

Flaming arrows soared from the enemy ship.

"Take cover, sir," shouted the sailor beside him. The whistle of approaching cannon fire registered in the back of his mind. Slowly he dipped down below the ship's rail as he watched his target fall to the enemy's deck.

With his next blink the *Mary*'s deck erupted in a barrage of showering splinters. Something stabbed his arm. Fires ignited.

"Douse the flames!" Aiden yelled.

"Cannons, reload!" MacPherson bellowed belowdecks.

Aiden glanced to his arm. A thick splinter of wood was lodged in the muscle. He clenched his fist against searing pain. At least the fragment hadn't pierced deeply enough to ruin the use of his hand. Gnashing his teeth, he yanked the splinter out and cast it aside.

Steeling his mind against the hot, shooting pain, he panned his gaze up to the poop deck. "Archers! Where are my archers?"

Beside him a musketeer clutched his chest and fell. A whoosh of air hissed through the man's lips, and then the sailor's eyes stared vacantly at the sky.

Damned ill-breeding pirates.

Aiden reached for his comrade's musket and powder horn. "I will avenge you."

"Fire!" an archer shouted from the poop deck.

"Charge your weapons!" Aiden countered. "Water barrels, stand at the ready to douse any fires. The only way to beat them is to match them trick for trick." He eyed their captain and pulled the trigger. The man stumbled backward, grasping his shoulder. Dammit, the ball should have pierced the man's heart.

Running forward, Aiden grabbed a barrel of tar and heaved it up to the deck with the archers. "Set it alight."

"But—?" Tommy MacGrath objected.

"Do it, I say, and pummel that boat with flaming arrows." He pointed. "And mark me, if the fire spreads I'll hold you personally responsible."

"Aye, sir." Crouching low, Tommy pulled a flint and knife from his pocket and set to making a spark.

Across the deck Polwarth waved his arms through the black smoke, but the deafening sounds of battle swallowed his orders. Behind the captain a cannonball crashed through the upper deck—too bloody close to the bow.

Shouting, the pirates levered planks across the span of water between the boats. One, two, three ramps clapped the *Royal Mary*'s rail.

"They aim to board us," hollered Tommy.

"Musketeers, affix bayonets." Aiden handed his musket to an archer, then drew his sword. "Prepare to fight for your lives, men!" But he wasn't about to wait for the bastards to cross the planks. Running to the first, he hacked at the hardwood. Over and over he swung his blade.

Down the deck MacBride followed suit, using a carpenter's ax.

As the timbers gave way, at least ten pirates fell screaming into the sea.

By the time Aiden hacked through the plank, two more boards had been leveled into place.

"I'll carve out your liver for that," growled a pirate, leaping onto the deck.

The hair on the back of Aiden's neck stood on end as he whipped around in time to block a deadly blade from lopping off his head.

Crouching, Aiden crossed one foot over the other, sizing up the man while the entire deck erupted in a maelstrom of combat. From the carelessness of the brute's first swing, Aiden doubted the man had much finesse, but that didn't matter when you were as big as a horse and wielded an enormous blade.

Aiden kept the rail to his back while he crouched and waited for the bastard to strike.

"Are you milk-livered?" the pirate growled.

The fine hairs on Aiden's arms stood on end.

The bastard's eyes shifted. Lunging in, the pirate jabbed his sword forward.

Faster, Aiden met the thrust with a clang that reverberated through his arm. Using his momentum, he spun. Eyeing the man's throat, he sliced his blade across neck sinews. The pirate's eyes bulged, then his knees buckled.

Rushing into the thick of the fight, Aiden didn't watch his opponent fall. The man would bleed out before his face hit the deck.

On and on he fought while the listing of the ship registered. Around him muskets cracked, the dying howled, and water splashed as bodies hit the surf.

Black smoke stung his eyes. His muscles burned. Every clash of steel reverberated through his bones. This is what Aiden had trained for all his life. And he'd be damned if he would meet his end this day. Rage pulsed through his blood.

"Bring that fire under control, sailors!" MacPherson yelled.

But Aiden couldn't stop. He surged ahead, swinging his sword like a madman, cutting down every ruthless, filthy pirate who had the misfortune of stepping in his path.

With his next swing, a bit of plaid caught his eye. His weapon stilled, ready to strike. "MacBride," he choked out while smoke seared his throat.

"Lower your sword, ye mad Scot."

Wiping his brow, he slowly turned in place. Good God, they'd fought them off. The sloop was down by the head and sinking fast. "Good work, men," Aiden hollered, sweeping his gaze to the source of the smoke.

Seaman Ellis cracked open a water barrel, and the flood across the deck doused what remained of the flames.

Aiden marched to the quarterdeck only to find two men

kneeling over the captain. He pushed beside them. The man was out cold. "Is he breathing?"

"Aye."

"Take him to his cabin straightaway and notify Dr. Laidlaw."

"Yes, sir."

Aiden straightened and regarded the dirty faces of his men. "How many dead?"

"Ten, sir."

"Prepare them for burial at sea." He crossed himself. "How many wounded?"

"Two dozen, sir."

"Take them belowdecks and see to their care straightaway." He looked to MacBride. "What are the damages?"

"She's taking water in the bow, sir."

"Is she breached?"

"'Tis in the forward cargo hull, but..."

"But what?"

"We must make haste."

"Unfurl the sails. Set a course north by northeast. Steady as she blows." Aiden looked to the helmsman. "Are you ready to take us to Portsmouth, Mr. Ferguson?"

"Aye, sir. More than ready."

"Mr. MacGrath, please report on the fire damage."

"Timbers on the main deck charred bad, sir—no one can cross them. The mainmast has been hit, too."

"The sails?"

"Untouched, sir."

"Will the mast hold?"

"As long as we aren't hit by a howling tempest, we should make it to Portsmouth, sir."

Aiden looked to the sky. Above sailed a covering of clouds. The wind was steady, but only God knew what lay ahead. With only five and seventy leagues to Portsmouth, they'd need a bit o' luck to make it before either the *Royal Mary* sank or the mast crashed to the deck.

"I'm stepping aft to check on the captain. If anything changes, I want a report of it immediately."

MacBride saluted. "Yes, sir."

Chapter Nineteen

*M*addie continued to play the harp while the cabinet ministers entered Queen Anne's antechamber. Straightaway her fingers began to perspire, making the strings slippery.

After plucking a sour note, she stopped and looked to the Duchess of Marlborough for direction. Her Grace rolled her hand through the air, indicating for her to continue.

"Things are heating up. The duke is marching for Malplaquet, straight down King Louis's throat," said the Earl of Nottingham.

"We'll send them to hell this time, Your Majesty," said the Earl of Rochester.

The queen frowned, making her double chin more pronounced. "I do believe that is exactly what you said right before the Duchess of Marlborough's husband led my troops into the disastrous Battle of Oudenarde."

The earl opened his snuffbox, seemingly unperturbed. "Ah, but this time we have the ground advantage, Your Majesty."

The queen shook out her skirts and adjusted her seat. Of

late Queen Anne hadn't looked well. She'd had trouble with swelling in her extremities and complained of gout.

To better hear, Maddie selected a quiet, simple tune that she could play in her sleep. Nonetheless, another sour note blared through the chamber when the lord high admiral, Prince George, marched into the antechamber, his face redder than Maddie had ever seen it.

He bowed to the queen. "I have grave news."

As prickles spread down Magdalen's arms, her fingers plucked the harp strings faster. Ignoring the frown from Lady Saxonhurst, Maddie inclined her ear as far as she could without tipping her instrument.

"Go on, my love," said the queen.

"The *Royal Mary* has incurred a damaged hull in a battle with a pirate ship...barely made it to Portsmouth."

Maddie's fingers ran down the strings in a cacophony of jumbled notes. A lump the size of her fist stuck in her throat. Shaking, she couldn't continue playing. She righted the harp and scooted forward in her chair.

"And the pirate ship?" asked the queen, while all eyes in the room focused on the admiral.

"It was a sloop—sunk, but not before cannonballs struck the *Mary* midship and near her bow. According to the report, the dastards boarded the ship and engaged in a bloody sword fight." The admiral shuddered. "Worse, she was only a hundred leagues from our very shore."

The queen drew her hand over her heart. "My God, attacked by the French, and now we have pirates sailing this close to home? What of the crew? You said our ship made it to Portsmouth."

Maddie stood, wringing her hands.

"Ten dead, dozens severely wounded. Captain Polwarth himself sustained injuries, and has been taken to hospital."

"Dear Lord," said the queen, turning white.

Maddie's mind raced. Ten killed? Oh no, Aiden had to have survived. And if he hadn't been injured, he would now be in charge on the ship. "Forgive me for interrupting, Your Majesty, but may I have leave to travel to Portsmouth forthwith?"

The Duchess of Marlborough snapped her fists to her hips. "Lady Magdalen, how dare you speak out of turn? Collect your harp forthwith and leave us at once."

The queen held up her hand. "What on earth would you hope to accomplish in Portsmouth, child?"

Maddie dipped into a hasty curtsy. "The crew is almost entirely Scottish, and I had the pleasure of meeting the ship's officers in Stonehaven. Not to mention, you may be aware that I oversee a hospital there, I...ah...I provide a great deal of healing to the community." Maddie wasn't about to admit the hospital was for women. "If nothing else, I should be able to bring comfort to the wounded."

Lady Saxonhurst snorted, but kept her lips pursed, perhaps for the first time in her life.

"Why did you not tell me this before?" asked the queen.

"Forgive my impertinence, but as Her Grace pointed out earlier, it is not proper for me to volunteer information."

The queen eyed her. "I do believe it would send a message of goodwill if we sent a party to care for the crew of the *Royal Mary.*"

"Indeed, dear," said the admiral.

The queen frowned at him and cleared her throat while the other cabinet ministers mumbled to themselves.

Prince George dipped his head politely. "Forgive me, Your Majesty. But I agree. Especially since their captain is recovering from his injuries. A royal party bringing words of encouragement, and perhaps Lady Magdalen's harp, would be most welcomed."

"But do we want to show favoritism to a Scottish ship?" asked the Earl of Nottingham.

"It would be seen as reaching out a hand of peace to our northern neighbors," said Lady Saxonhurst. Why the devil was she siding with Maddie—and saying something nice about Scottish subjects?

"Well said. I shall allow it." The queen flicked her fingers through the air. "Lord High Admiral, you shall lead the excursion to Portsmouth and take Lady Magdalen and her lady's maid with you. But I shall expect both of you back here in time for the Michaelmas feast. Am I understood?"

The prince bowed. "Yes, of course. I wouldn't miss Michaelmas feast with you for anything, my queen."

Maddie bowed her head and curtsied. "Thank you, Your Majesty." As she hastened out, Lady Saxonhurst fluttered her fingers with a coy wave. Odd. The countess had never been remotely friendly. But Maddie couldn't worry about the woman's devious smile, not when her heart was about to pound out of her chest. Besides, whatever the countess was thinking didn't matter.

The conniving lady-in-waiting could revel in that which her petty little mind was scheming. Maddie had far more to worry about. The good news? She was heading for Portsmouth, and prayed she'd find Lord Aiden Murray in good health.

* * *

Aiden faced the master carpenter and snarled, "Do you think I care about how many other ships are in sore need of refit? The *Royal Mary* and her crew just prevented pirates from sailing up the Thames and pillaging London, you lackwit. I want first-quality timber that will withstand years at sea. Do you understand me?"

The man scratched his head. "But the wood I brought aboard is of the best quality we are able to put our hands upon."

"Och, I reckon you're blowing pish up my arse." Aiden beckoned him to a plank one of his seamen had just shown him. "Look at this." He jutted his finger toward the worm-eaten timber. "Infested with termites. I should throw you and your poor-quality wood off this ship."

"I beg your pardon, sir, but the *Royal Buccaneer* received repairs with the very same wood."

"That's a pack of lies. The *Royal Buccaneer* did not sail with this poor quality." *Not an English ship, for certain.* "Mr. Guthrie!" Aiden hollered.

"Aye, sir?"

"I want you to personally inspect every piece of beech, birch, hickory, or ash wood brought aboard this ship. If any shows signs of rot, toss it over the side without recompense."

The shipbuilder spread his palms to his sides. "But sir, you cannot."

Aiden stamped his foot. "I can and I will."

A royal yeoman marched up the gangway. "All hail the arrival of His Royal Highness, Prince George, lord high admiral of the queen's Royal Navy."

Aiden averted his gaze to the overstuffed peacock. A visit? From the admiral? Now? Dear God, there was a hole in the deck the size of his bunk and a third of the crew was belowdecks wounded, or down with scurvy.

"Bloody hell," groaned MacPherson under his breath.

"'Tis the last thing we need." Aiden marched across the main deck. There was nothing to do but to meet the admiral with their best foot forward, albeit a weak one. "All hands, muster to the main deck for inspection!"

Prince George placed his foot on the ship just as Aiden

arrived at the gangway and bowed deeply. "Your Highness, it is indeed an honor for you to show your support for Her Majesty's seamen who fought valiantly for queen and country."

"Indeed, Lord Aiden. It is with great respect I visit this Scottish vessel of our navy, albeit a small frigate." The prince slapped Aiden on the back. "I hear you sank the pirate ship not a hundred leagues from our shore."

"That is true, Your Highness. Though we did incur damages and casualties." Aiden led the prince toward the hole in the deck, where stood the mule-brained master carpenter. "I was just rejecting worm-eaten timbers, though this gentleman tells me the higher-quality wood is reserved for English-built galleons."

Out of the corner of his eye, he caught flashes of red coats as the prince's men paraded onto the ship. Then swishes sounded, decidedly female. That was odd. Women didn't board warships—and the queen hadn't been announced, so it couldn't be Her Majesty.

Before Aiden had a chance to see if his ears had deceived him, the prince bent down and picked up an offending piece of wood. His face turned apple red. "This is unforgiveable, sir."

The carpenter bowed. "Forgive me, Your Highness. I was unaware of the importance of the *Royal Mary* to Her Majesty's fleet."

The prince looked sideways, drawing a deep breath through his nostrils. "All of the queen's ships are important."

Aiden grinned. Perhaps the royal visit this day wouldn't be a complete disaster.

The carpenter tapped his fingers together obsequiously. "But we do have the *Royal Essex* in for refit, Your Highness."

"The *Essex*?" asked the prince. "Why didn't you say so,

sir? Of course first pick must go to a racing galleon. She's one of the fastest in the fleet. Then do your best to see to it the *Royal Mary* receives the very finest quality available."

"Yes, Your Highness." The carpenter shot a smug look to Aiden before he bowed.

When the man dipped down, Aiden stared into the loveliest blue eyes he'd ever seen in his life. A pair of inordinately large azure eyes—eyes he'd thought about every hour of every day for the past year and a half. His heart leaped, his palms perspired, his fingers trembled. And then she smiled. Dear God, a winsome smile that could melt the most hardened of hearts.

Gulping, he stepped forward. When the master carpenter straightened, Aiden scooted aside and performed a bow of his own. "M'lady." He looked to the woman standing beside Maddie. "And Miss Agnes. Ladies, please forgive my impertinence. I was unaware you had come aboard."

Lady Magdalen Keith curtsied, shuttering her gaze with long eyelashes. "No apology needed, m'lord. Though it lightens my heart to see you are well."

Aiden's arm, wrapped in a bandage beneath his doublet, throbbed as if on cue, though he showed no outward sign of discomfort. "Indeed, m'lady. I was one of the lucky ones." He glanced to the prince. "Captain Polwarth has been released from hospital and is recovering in his cabin, Your Highness."

"Lady Magdalen and I have come to visit the infirm." The prince gestured to a porter carrying a Celtic harp. "And the lady will play for them."

"Ah yes, the wounded crewmen are belowdecks. I am certain your visit will warm their hearts."

Lieutenant MacPherson moved beside Maddie. "I would be happy to assist you to descend the steps, m'lady. They can be treacherous, especially with so many skirts."

Aiden clapped the swine on the shoulder and dug in his fingers. "*Third* Lieutenant MacPherson, please see to it the captain is informed that His Royal Highness Prince George is aboard the *Royal Mary* and will pay a visit to the captain's cabin directly after he has met with the injured." He offered his elbow to Maddie. "Shall we, m'lady?"

The mere touch of her lithe fingers on his arm sent goose-flesh pebbling across his entire body. He inclined his lips toward her ear. "I've missed you."

"And I you," she whispered every bit as quietly.

The admiral and his entourage descended the ladder first.

"I have so much I want to say." Aiden stepped on the first rung. "You'll need to bare your ankles, I am afraid. I'll block you from view whilst you descend."

"My thanks." Maddie nodded, her eyes filled with happiness. Aiden hoped his reflected the same. "And will you catch me should I slip?"

His heart hammered like a woodpecker's beak. "It would be an honor to do so, m'lady."

"And me as well?" asked Agnes as she followed.

"Of course, and it is ever so good to see you, Miss Agnes." Aiden offered his hand while Maddie hopped from the last rung. Unfortunate she didn't fall, for he would have enjoyed cradling her soft curves in his arms, if only for a moment. Still, he couldn't help staring into her lovely eyes, though the light was dim belowdecks. "I—"

"Lady Magdalen, come along," said the prince. "The wounded will be heartened by your lovely face, and then they will be enchanted by your music."

She cringed at Aiden apologetically. "Anon?" she asked in a hurried whisper.

"I wouldn't miss it for all the gold in Christendom."

Though his fingers drummed against his thighs, Aiden

stood by while the royal party paid their respects to the injured. Then Maddie played her harp. Dear Lord, he'd forgotten how she could make the music swirl in the air. Her soothing tune calmed even the most anxious of men—almost even stilled the drumming of Aiden's fingers, but not quite.

Fraser MacPherson moved alongside him. "Do you ken the lass?"

"Aye."

"Why have you never spoken of her to me?"

"Mayhap you do enough talking for the both of us." Aiden leaned in to his cabinmate and further lowered his voice. "Hands off."

Fraser held up his palms, a sly grin spreading across his lips. "You're the commander of this ship. But I'll be damned. You surely had the wool pulled over my eyes."

Aiden returned his attention to Maddie's performance. He'd never spoken to anyone about the fleeting sennight of passion he'd shared with her, and he never would. Such liaisons were secret, to be treasured and remembered by him—and hopefully by the lady.

After the performance ended, Aiden stepped forward and gestured toward the aft steps. "Lieutenant MacPherson, would you please lead the admiral and his party to the captain's chamber?"

"Aye, sir." Fraser smiled as if pleased to be asked to perform such a task. Aiden should have led the entourage himself, but he had a plan.

Grasping Maddie by the elbow, he held her back and allowed all others to pass, then led her to an empty alcove used for kitchen stores. He clasped her fingers between his much larger hands. "We haven't much time, but I must tell you how greatly it touches my heart that you are here."

Her breath caught with a wee gasp. "I prayed for your good health every night."

"I'm certain your blessings have kept me safe." If only he could dip his chin and kiss those lips, shiny and pink in the dim light. "Have you been in London all this time?"

"Yes. The queen asked me to be her harpist." Aiden ran his thumbs over the tips of her fingers, which were hard with calluses. She looked down as if embarrassed. "I received word that you visited the hospital in Stonehaven."

"I did." He grinned. "I signed the guest book."

"Mrs. Boyd sent me a letter telling me so."

"Did she tell you what I wrote?"

"Aye." Even in the darkness, Aiden could see her blush.

"I've written you so many letters." He squeezed her hands tighter and held them over his heart.

"You have? But I haven't received a one."

"That is because they're all still in my sea chest."

"Why?"

Aiden shook his head. Dear Lord, he was a damned fool. "After I found you hadn't returned to Stonehaven, I feared you may have found another."

"Oh no."

"And I feared your father might have other plans for you."

"Truly, Da has had plans for me, but marriage hasn't been in the offing."

"That is good news indeed, m'lady."

"Lord Aiden? Where have you absconded to with my lady?" Miss Agnes's voice rang through the dank passageway.

Aiden raised Maddie's fingers to his lips and kissed them. "I want to see you again."

"Then you shall. The prince is planning to invite you and the officers to the keep at Southsea Castle for the evening meal. I do hope you can come."

"I will—"

"There you are." Miss Agnes stepped beside him. "Whatever has made you tarry? And with Prince George waiting. Lord Aiden, you ought to be dazzling him with your brilliance."

Ushering the lady ahead, Aiden took the matron's arm. "Forgive me, Miss Agnes. Lady Magdalen and I have much catching up to do, and I'm afraid I led her astray."

Maddie glanced over her shoulder and winked. God bless her.

Chapter Twenty

Maddie's visit to the *Royal Mary* could have come straight from a fairy tale. The lady's heart had nearly leaped from her chest when Aiden pulled her into the alcove and clasped her hands between his. Oh, how she longed for him to kiss her in that moment. Though it would have been inordinately improper for him to do so, she'd licked her lips and inclined them to him, hoping he knew exactly what she wanted.

Well, at least he'd kissed her fingers.

And now she sat at the long dining table in Southsea Castle's great hall. Built atop a promontory at the mouth of Portsmouth Harbour, the castle was a drafty medieval relic, every bit as archaic as the old keep at Dunnottar Castle. The walls were of a dank gray stone, and there were no windows aside from the arrow and musket slits. Built to defend the harbor, the fortress presented a glum and uninviting picture. Even with a roaring fire in the immense hearth, the great hall was cold, and the table was rough-hewn, as if the attendees had been thrown back in time two hundred years.

Maddie didn't care in the slightest. Lord Aiden Murray was present. She would endure a feast in a pigsty just to be near him. He'd been seated practically across the hall, but that was the way of things. He occupied a seat near the admiral, and Captain Polwarth had risen from his sickbed to join them. Though pale, the captain assured everyone that he was on the mend and that by the grace of God he'd received only a glancing stab to the thigh. The captain sat at Prince George's left. The governor of Portsmouth sat to his right, and the governor's wife was the only other woman at the table.

Beside her was an annoying lieutenant everyone called MacPherson. He leaned too close when he spoke, and his breath smelled of rotten onions. However, something about him was familiar.

"Were you at the masque with Lord Aiden on Hogmanay in 1708?" Maddie asked.

The lieutenant smoothed his knuckles down his lapels. "Why yes, I was there." He sucked in a sharp breath and held up his finger. "Oh, my word. Were you the sprightly lass in the blue gown and matching mask?"

"Indeed, my gown was blue," she admitted. "Were you wearing a mask with a beak?"

He sat straighter as if proud. "Aye, m'lady. That was me."

She couldn't help but laugh from her belly. That certainly explained why she found him so annoying.

At the other end of the table, Aiden glowered. But his angry stare didn't focus on Maddie. He looked as if he could ask Mr. Beak-Nose out to the courtyard for a friendly—or not-so-friendly—sparring session.

"Whyever are you laughing?" Mr. MacPherson asked.

She tapped her fingers to her lips and quickly regained her composure. "As I recall, your mask was a bit silly looking, is all."

"Silly looking?" He sniffed and reached for his glass of wine. "I thought it was rather dashing."

She stifled her snort by moving her fingers to her nose. "Then you mustn't have been near a looking glass when you put it on."

The man looked absolutely aghast. "I indeed was not. It was the Earl Marischal who provided the masks. Perhaps he should have omitted that one from the selection."

"Not to worry." She glanced up as a servant placed a slice of roast beef on her plate. "I'm certain the mask suited you."

"Hmm. So you think me silly?"

Maddie fixated on her plate. "Not at all."

Mr. MacPherson turned his attention to the servant. "Two slices, please."

At least he said please.

"I understand the prisoners of war at Carisbrooke Castle are growing numerous," said a gentleman farther down the table. Thank goodness someone had changed the subject.

"I reckon we should ship them to the Colonies," said Captain Polwarth. "As prisoners of war, they aren't criminals. They might do well for building trade in the New World."

"You must be jesting." Prince George frowned and belched. "News of the war in the Colonies is worse than on the Continent."

"Wouldn't it be nice if everyone could stop fighting?" Magdalen said with conviction. It wasn't until she looked up and put the bite in her mouth that she realized everyone at the table was gaping at her. Well, at least Aiden smiled. Dimples, a sly grin, shiny green eyes. Nothing else mattered.

Mr. MacPherson nudged her with his elbow. "That is exactly why I enjoy having womenfolk at the evening meal. They do say the most diverting things."

Maddie shot the buffoon a look, then sliced off another piece of meat. Goodness, she must pay attention to what she let slip through her lips. A crowd of naval officers surely didn't need to be told it would be nice to have no wars, especially when their ship had nearly been sunk to the bottom of the sea by a band of vile pirates.

"How was the journey from London, Lady Magdalen?" asked Aiden, watching her from behind his wineglass.

She chewed delicately and swallowed before answering. "Not too dreary in the slightest. Only one squall, and it passed within an hour."

"'Tis good to hear." Aiden placed his glass in front of his plate. "I do believe it is a two-day journey. Is that right?"

"Two days if you ride hard," said Prince George. "But it took us three with a wagon and two coaches."

Aiden continued to watch her. "I find it difficult to believe that Lady Magdalen would need a wagon for her portmanteaus. Did they not fit atop her coach?"

"It wasn't the lady's luggage that required the wagon," said a red-coated officer named Walther—Maddie had been introduced to him when they'd assembled for the journey outside Whitehall's gates. "One needs pikes, bows, arrows, muskets, and powder when leading a royal entourage."

Aiden nodded. "Och aye, of course. Forgive me."

A sentry entered the hall, his footsteps slapping the flagstone loudly. "Pardon the interruption, Your Highness, but I have an urgent missive for Lord Aiden Murray."

He pushed his chair back and waved his hand. "Here, sir."

Maddie set her knife down and leaned forward.

Aiden broke the seal and his face blanched. The words "Dear God," slipped through his lips while his complexion grew even whiter.

"What news?" asked Prince George, growing redder in

the face as if he was upset the missive hadn't come to him first.

Captain Polwarth snatched the missive from Aiden's fingers and handed it to the admiral. After reading, the prince stood, his face now somber. "I believe all present should hear this."

My Dearest Son,

I am writing to inform you that I have received confirmation that John has succumbed to a musket ball wound to the chest in the Battle of Malplaquet. He fought bravely for Queen and Country, and is now with our Lord in Heaven.

It is with a heavy heart that I inform you of your inheritance. You are now the Marquis of Tullibardine and the heir to the Dukedom of Atholl.

As you may be aware, as I write this, I am in London for Parliament. I have sent for your mother. I require your presence at Whitehall forthwith.

Your father,
His Grace the Duke of Atholl.

Aiden wiped a hand across his brow, looking shocked and out of sorts. "If you will excuse me, Your Highness, I must prepare my kit."

"Yes, of course." The prince bowed in concert with Aiden. "This is grave news. I'm certain my lady the queen will wish us to return to London directly."

"And I am able to resume my post at the helm of the *Royal Mary*," said Captain Polwarth.

"Thank you, sir." Aiden's gaze shot to Maddie as he again

bowed. "Forgive me. I had hopes this evening would be merry for us all."

The prince resumed his seat. "I will have a retinue ready to ride at dawn."

Aiden gave a nod. "I will be honored to ride with you, Your Highness."

"Indeed, Lord Tullibardine."

Aiden took a step back, his expression shocked. After one more bow, he swiftly took his leave.

Prince George looked to Mr. Walther. "The carriages and wagon will only slow us down. I shall appoint a retinue to accompany Lady Magdalen to London."

Maddie gulped. Heaven's stars, Aiden had just learned of his brother's death and she was to follow, riding in a carriage for three dreary days? "But I am skilled with a mount. It would give our new marquis great solace to have me beside him. Our families are *very* close."

The prince's eyes grew wide. "Is Tullibardine's care the reason why you were so anxious to travel to Portsmouth, m'lady?"

Her cheeks burned as she nodded. Now was no time to grow bashful. She squared her shoulders and tipped up her chin. "Indeed, I was aware of Lord Aiden—I mean Lord Tullibardine's post on the *Royal Mary*. When there was no report, I needed to confirm for myself he survived the pirate attack."

"Och, Murray can fight with the might of five seamen, m'lady," said Captain Polwarth. "He's the last member of the crew you should be concerned about."

The prince stabbed a bit of roast beef with his fork. "It stands to reason that the Duke of Atholl and the Earl Marischal of Scotland would be allies—and I'll say the queen will be heartened to hear it. I shall allow you to ride with us, my lady."

* * *

As he stuffed a shirt into his satchel, Aiden's jaw clenched. His mind raced with all the memories of growing up in John's shadow. His brother had always been the serious one, had always questioned everything, had always been cautious and practical.

John's sense of loyalty had sent him to the army and to the Continent.

Taller and stronger, Aiden should have been the one marching in Marlborough's army.

Damn the bloody Act of Union. If England hadn't forced Scotland to merge, John would have stayed at Blair Castle. Bless it, Scotland and France had been allies for centuries, and now Queen Anne was using Scotland's sons to fight her wars—just as every English monarch had attempted to do since the beginning of time.

And now Prince George wanted to accompany him to London? In court the man had proved himself a dull-witted bore. And he'd proved so again by ordering first-quality timber for the *Royal Mary* in one breath, and in the next telling the master carpenter that the *Royal Essex* came first. No one needed to tell Aiden where Scotland ranked with the royal family. Highlanders were placed on the front line because they were deemed expendable. John had been placed in harm's way because the queen's emissary, the Duke of Marlborough, saw only a Scot. He didn't see an intelligent heir with a love of his clan and country. An honest man whose integrity would put to shame every noble in London—especially the backstabbing English.

And now he was dead.

And now Aiden, the adventurer in Clan Murray, the rebellious son, the opinionated, defensive, curious son, was left to take up the reins. Dear God, Aiden no more wanted to be a marquis than he wanted to pluck his nose hairs.

He threw the satchel on his cot while a silent bellow ripped through his throat.

Damn you, God. If you wanted to take a Murray, why did you not choose me?

Chapter Twenty-One

*I*t came as a surprise to see Lady Magdalen riding with the admiral's retinue. Aiden had naturally assumed she would return with the coaches. Even odder, the prince had insisted that she ride beside Aiden. He'd said clan and kin should stay together at a time like this. Though it was easy to assume why Maddie had asked to travel with the men, they were no kin. Lord knew the Keiths and the Murrays rarely saw eye to eye on anything.

Except that Magdalen Keith is the bonniest lass in all of Britain.

Still, Aiden would have preferred it if Maddie hadn't come. His entire world had just crashed down around his ears, and he was in no mood to talk to anyone—not even the woman he'd dreamed about every night for the past year and a half.

Aye. His life had completely plummeted into the depths of the icy sea with that missive.

If only he could grab Maddie's bridle and ride north. If only they could ride endlessly until they reached home. He'd take her to his hunting cottage in the Blair wood, fish in the River Tilt, live off the land with her for the rest of their lives.

If only.

He pursed his lips and tightened his grip on his reins.

Duty first.

Aiden was no more able to make an offer for Lady Magdalen's hand than he had been when he'd been a second son working for the damned queen aboard the *Royal Mary*. With war heating up in every corner of Christendom, he could be dead in sennights and meet his brother at the pearly gates. Now that he was a marquis, the queen would probably promote him, but such a promotion would only be a ploy to send him and his hapless crew into the thick of battle to be sunk by a French galleon with bigger cannons. Aye, the queen had proved quite intolerant of the Scotsmen who supported her to the north.

She'd proved herself parochial and terrified of Catholics out of fear of a coup by His Holiness, the pope.

That was exactly the reason more than half of Scotland looked to the exiled King James, recognized as Britain's only true sovereign by King Louis of France.

Indeed, Queen Anne would send the new Marquis of Tullibardine to a lowly sloop with a handful of guns and rotting timbers. What did she care if the timbers were rotting? Tullibardine and his crew would be served up as sacrificial lambs, just as the *Royal Mary* had been on dozens of occasions. It was only because of the superior skill of the crew that they'd come out alive. And now her repairs would be done with third-rate, worm-eaten timbers.

I would take a Scottish crew any day.

"You look deep in thought." Maddie's sultry voice snapped him from sinking deeper into his foul musings. Though Aiden was no fool. He and his crew had been treated as lesser men because he had been born in his beloved Scotland, and for that he'd harbor a chip on his shoulder the size of Blair Castle. "I have a great deal to think about."

He glanced her way. Why did she have to continually look at him with concern filling her eyes? And those goddamned eyes had to be so alluring. Did she not know he couldn't pick up where they'd left off? No matter how much he wanted to kiss her. No matter how much he wanted to lean over and yank her off her mount and into his lap. No matter how much his body craved the thrill of pressing against hers or his mouth yearned to cover her lips and taste her deliciousness. No matter what he felt in his heart. From now on it didn't make a difference what *he* wanted. His decisions must be for the good of the clan…and for the good of the goddamned alliance. His life was no longer his own.

I belong to Clan Murray.

And to Atholl.

And to the bloody queen.

"I'm ever so sorry for your loss," she said so softly, Aiden almost asked her to repeat herself. But he'd heard well enough.

Pain stabbed his heart. "John was a good man. Better than I."

"In the brief time I met with him, I could tell he was a man of integrity."

Aiden snorted and forced himself not to smile. Dammit. He couldn't smile. He didn't dare smile. True, John had caught them in a compromising situation, but Aiden never should have been so bloody daft. He'd been young and stupid and selfish. Worst of all, he never should have entertained a liaison with Lady Magdalen Keith. He didn't deserve her affections.

He cleared his throat and addressed her with his most sober expression. "And you? Have you settled into life at court?"

"Heavens no. If I were there for a hundred years I think I'd still abhor living at Whitehall." Frowning, she glanced down and rubbed her reins between her fingertips.

"You seem a wee bit distraught," he said. Christ, he'd been wallowing in his own misery and hadn't thought about hers.

"Mm." She sniffed. "I miss Stonehaven and the hospital." Then she looked over each shoulder before she leaned closer to Aiden. "And the queen's ladies seem to relish every opportunity to drive a knife into my back."

"Let me guess...Saxonhurst is at the center of it."

"Of course. And now she's developed a friendship with Lord Blackiron and she's even worse than before." Pursing her lips, Maddie shook her head as if stopping herself from complaining further.

"Where is the Earl Marischal?" he asked.

"He's still at Whitehall. Part of the agreement of his release from the Tower was that he remain and support the Treaty of Union."

Good God, the earl would sooner slit his wrists than support the union, and Aiden could wager the queen knew it, too. "I think it is good you have him."

"Agreed." She smiled. "Else I would have gone completely mad by now."

Aiden wanted to dig deeper, but this was no time to discuss court grievances. Even the mention of backstabbing ladies-in-waiting could make its way back to the queen.

* * *

After riding until dark, they stopped at Poyle Manor in Guildford, the stately home of the sheriff of Surrey and his family. Maddie had been assigned to a bedchamber she would share with the sheriff's daughter, who seemed nice enough though she was but a child.

After the evening meal, Maddie wanted to go anywhere but above stairs with the chatty lass. Her head throbbed, and worse, her heart felt as if it had been tied in a knot. She had no idea where to find Aiden. Not that it would have been proper for her to chase after him. Some of the gentlemen had retired to the drawing room with Prince George, though the marquis had declined the invitation and left the dining hall before anyone else. All Maddie could do was sit and watch.

Moments ago the sheriff's daughter had been called above stairs by her nursemaid to ready herself for bed. Maddie took advantage of the opportunity to collect her thoughts and ventured outside.

If only she could be alone with Aiden and truly have an opportunity to talk with him. He'd been so despondent during the day's ride. It was as if he didn't want her near.

Obviously he was grieving, and no one could fault him for that. Was he so filled with grief that he didn't want to see her? Or did his indifference go deeper? Though he'd tried to visit her in Stonehaven, aside from the fleeting moment of passion aboard the *Royal Mary*, Aiden had been rather tepid toward her.

Had that moment been stirring only for her? She couldn't be certain.

Maddie sighed. Now that Aiden had suddenly become a marquis, he would most likely shun her. The Marquis of Tullibardine surely would want to marry a highborn woman, not a woman like Maddie who'd been given a courtesy title. Heaven's stars, she'd been shunned enough in her lifetime. Her stepmother and the snobbish ladies at court had made clear to Maddie her place—and it wasn't at Whitehall. There she was but a tinker among the privileged.

Right. So why on earth would I think Lord Tullibardine would be any different? He's a Murray. Will he now side with the Whigs? Dear Lord, this is a disaster.

Stubbing her toe, she stumbled forward but caught herself before she completely fell on her face. Though the weather was balmy for late September, darkness cast a blanket over the manor's gardens, making it difficult to see. Ahead a light shone through the doorway of the stables. Maddie turned and looked at the house. A chat with a stable hand might be far more diverting than listening to Miss Woodroffe chatter. Perhaps Maddie could pay a visit to the gelding she'd ridden that day and offer him some oats.

After she stepped through the doorway, the soft neigh of a horse down the alleyway caught her attention. Moths' wings clicked against the glass of an overhead lantern, the only source of light.

"Hello?" Maddie said, stepping farther inside while straw and dirt crunched beneath her feet.

No one responded.

Spying a barrel, she pushed back the lid and found exactly what she'd been looking for. She took a scoop from the wall and filled it with oats, then proceeded through the stable, peeking into every stall along the way. In the second to the last, her sorrel gelding snorted when she stopped. He looked at her with big, soulful eyes.

"I'll wager you're weary after the day's journey." She carefully slid back the latch and slipped inside, then pulled the door closed behind. But she wasn't fast enough with the oats. The horse shoved his nose in the scoop and pinned her against the wall.

"Move off me, you beast." She pushed his nose, only to

be rewarded with a stamp of the hoof, mere inches away from her foot. "Goodness, and I thought you a gentlemanly horse."

When she tried to pull the scoop away, the gelding pinned his ears. Maddie's stomach squeezed. Ear pinning definitely wasn't a good sign when one was shut inside a stall with a horse. Worse, with one more slurp of his tongue, the oats disappeared.

He shoved his nose into the scoop, giving another stamp.

"Whoa, big fella," said a deep voice as the stall door creaked open.

"Aiden!"

"Slip out behind me." He slapped the gelding's hip with a coil of rope, giving her enough space to skitter sideways out the door.

After Aiden shoved the bolt back in place, he faced her. "By the way you rode, I would have thought you'd have more sense around horses."

"I am quite adept with them—at least I thought so. My garron pony in Stonehaven is a fair bit better trained in manners than this hackney."

"Well, 'tis a good thing I was here, else you could have been in dire straits."

"Thank you for coming to my aid." Knitting her brows, Maddie peered through the stable—she'd walked the length of it and hadn't seen a soul. "Where were you?"

One corner of his mouth turned up, making a dimple dip into his cheek. "In the loft. I needed some time alone to think."

Maddie cringed. "And I spoiled your solace. Forgive me."

"Not to worry. I'm accustomed to being surrounded by people at all hours."

"I would imagine you are." She bit her bottom lip. Why

must she feel awkward at this moment? She hadn't gone to the stable in search of Aiden—and he could have let the horse pin her against the wall. She would have found a way out of the incident. Somehow.

He kicked a bit of straw. "I suppose you'd best go back to the manor. We have another long day ahead of us on the morrow."

Her heart sank right down to her toes. "I'm waiting until Miss Woodroffe has a chance to fall asleep first. She's rather chatty."

Aiden almost chuckled. "If her conversation at the evening meal is any indication, I can understand why you're here."

"Ah well, she's only thirteen, and we're sharing for just one night." Maddie made a pretense of examining her clasped hands. "What do you think will happen now that you're a marquis?"

"I have to admit, the news came as a shock. I always believed my brother more suited for the role of heir." He let out a long sigh. "With war surrounding us, I assume not much will change. I imagine I'll be sent back to sea."

He'd been away so long already, and the only time she'd been happy at Whitehall had been the fleeting days when he was there. But never in a hundred years could she tell him how she really felt. "I wonder if our paths will ever cross again."

"I can hardly think about the morrow, let alone the distant future." He combed his fingers through his dark tresses. "Do you think you'll return to Stonehaven soon?"

"I hope so. If not, I fear one of Lady Saxonhurst's accusations about me will be taken seriously."

"I doubt anyone listens to the countess overmuch."

"Thank heavens."

"Have you seen much of the Earl of Seaforth?"

"Nay, he left for Ross-shire not long after you sailed from London."

"Good for him. I kent he missed his clan and kin."

"Do you miss yours?"

"Indeed, m'lady." He glanced away, and his Adam's apple bobbed as if he was thinking of something to say.

Maddie wrung her hands. It was difficult to imagine that at one time they'd talked into the night with seemingly endless things to discuss. Now she stood there awkwardly, wanting to look him in the eye and declare her love, but knowing she could not embarrass herself, nor could she put him in such a thorny situation.

He swiped a hand across his mouth with an emotionless stare in his eyes. "It has been a pleasure seeing you again, m'lady."

Ah yes, that was her cue. Regardless of Miss Woodroffe's mindless prattle about her gowns or her hair or the color of her new bedclothes, Maddie had no recourse but to leave the marquis in peace. Besides, he'd said he needed time alone to think. Her presence in the barn was unwelcomed.

She curtsied. "Good evening, m'lord. Thank you for coming to my rescue."

"It was my pleasure." He bowed. "Sleep well."

Turning, Maddie hung her head while fighting her body's urge to collapse in a heap. She'd gone to Portsmouth in hopes of finding Aiden well, and she'd found a man who had matured and moved on. Perhaps he'd never been in love with her. Perhaps he'd gone to Stonehaven simply to be friendly. After all, he was a young man, and through her work at the hospital for women, Maddie knew all too well that young men were lusty. By their very natures, as they matured, noblemen sought out marriageable women to bear their children.

She'd fallen for his charm. She'd fallen for his kisses and his passion and his good looks, and had mistaken it all for love. She'd fallen for his muscular body and the power exuding from his every move.

Aye, she'd done everything she'd promised herself she would never do. Well, almost everything. The sad part? She didn't regret one minute of their affair. Maddie would treasure those fleeting moments in her heart for the rest of her days.

Chapter Twenty-Two

*A*iden accompanied his parents back to Whitehall after the funeral at Westminster. Though they could easily walk the three blocks, Da had ordered a coach. The wheels screeched, adding a morose melody to the somber overtone of silence. The air surrounding them was as heavy as it was thick, and it weighed on Aiden's shoulders.

But it wasn't until they were behind closed doors in the Atholl apartments that Da pulled Aiden aside. "I thought you should be aware I appealed to the queen to end your tenure with the Royal Navy."

Though his mouth was dry, Aiden gulped. "Why? I have only a year remaining." If he chose not to sign another contract.

"Think, Son. It would kill your mother to lose another of her strapping lads. Did you not hear her wails of grief resounding through Westminster's halls?"

"I ken she's hurting, but I doubt that would sway Queen Anne. She has been with child what...nineteen times, and not a living heir to show for her efforts?"

"I have already received Anne's response, and she has granted my request, providing you sign an oath upholding the Act of Union and the Act of Settlement."

Stepping back, Aiden folded his arms across his chest. "What if I refuse?"

Da smirked, his periwig shifting, but his eyes bored into Aiden with the force of a driving nail. "Do you honestly want to send your mother to an early grave?"

He didn't want to have this conversation, and his father's using Ma to force Aiden to pledge allegiance to acts of Parliament he staunchly condemned was a bitter tonic. Throwing out his arms, he faced the hearth. "After three years in the navy, I firmly disagree with the Act of Union, and I'm none too happy with the Act of Settlement, either." Damnation, now was not the time to tell his father they stood on opposite sides of *the cause*, but Aiden couldn't be wrung like a rag. On the surface the queen seemed harmless enough, but her policies did nothing for the prosperity of Scotland.

Da moved in behind him. "Oh please. These are but trivial matters to us. The Murrays still rule Atholl lands—which, mind you, have grown exponentially since Her Majesty *The Queen* granted me the dukedom. We are one of the most powerful clans in Scotland, a force that is even felt here in London."

"Indeed." Over his shoulder Aiden regarded his father's gaunt face. "But what is the true cost? Our clansmen are divided for certain, and most of them side with me."

"You are wrong. I—"

Aiden thrust his finger under the duke's nose. "The queen supports sanctions against Scottish wares whilst her people grow poorer."

Da swatted Aiden's finger away. "Since when did you become the bleeding heart? Scotland's commoners have always struggled. We do what we can for our clansmen and -women, but honestly, they are vassals to do our bidding. You ken that as well as I."

"Do I, indeed? If you have paid no attention to your daily gazette, I am simply stating fact. Nothing I have said is remotely an exaggeration."

"Well, you'd best shove those facts into a strongbox and toss them into your beloved sea." Da sliced his hand through the air. "You are my son and as such you will do my bidding in this matter. Presently you must set your sights on finding a wife. Your brother marched off to war before impregnating his wife and, by God, that is not going to happen with you."

"I beg your pardon? We are but minutes from leaving John's funeral and you expect me to drop everything and find a wife?"

"Whilst you are at court, yes. There is no better place to make an alliance."

Aiden rolled his eyes to the ceiling. As long as he was disagreeing with his father on every imaginable subject, he might as well blow a musket hole through this topic as well. "Then I choose Lady Magdalen Keith."

"The harpist?" Turning scarlet, Da looked as if he could spit out his teeth. "Are you jesting?"

Aiden smiled for the first time in days. "She's enchanting and bonny. She has wit and intelligence."

"And she's a bastard."

All it took was those few words to wipe the grin off his face. Aiden's gut churned with bile. Och aye, the Duke of Atholl prejudged as much as every other noble in London. "If you must have an answer, I choose Lady Magdalen."

Throwing up his hands, His Grace sputtered. "No, no, no. I did not say I needed an answer today." He took a few paces, then turned, pointing his finger. "I *absolutely forbid* you to marry the Earl Marischal's bastard. I expect you to find a proper wife. For the love of God, Whitehall is swarming with eligible heiresses."

Aiden stood his ground, every muscle clamped and tense. "But I'm not interested in the others."

"Your mother will take to her sickbed if she should hear such irresponsibility uttered from your lips."

"I tend to call it truth."

"Well, that is why you are a young, inexperienced lad. All young men need to sow their wild oats. That is why I agreed to allow you to enter the navy."

"And John to join the army?"

"Exactly, and look where that led the family." Da stamped his foot. "Damn it all, do you truly want to destroy your mother's hopes, and at a time like this, when she has just lost her firstborn, when she is in a most vulnerable state?"

"Of course I don't want to hurt her. It's just—"

"Promise me this. Spend the next month or so casting your net. That is all I ask. Refrain from fraternizing with the Keith woman especially whilst your mother is in mourning. A scandal would destroy her." With a stern countenance, Da grasped Aiden's shoulder and squeezed. "Do not dishonor the family by denying my request."

Aiden nodded. What else could he do? He was a Murray, and the heir. Besides, marrying Maddie had never come into the equation. Honestly, marrying hadn't come into his equation at all.

"I'm sure someone will catch your eye." His Grace marched toward the passageway. "Good God. I doubt the Keith woman even has a dowry."

Aiden watched his father's retreating form. *Who bloody cares? I doubt any other woman at Whitehall can hold a candle to Lady Magdalen, dowry or nay.*

A hollow void spread through his chest. The next fortnight just might kill him.

* * *

After the return from Portsmouth, things grew even more unbearable for Maddie. Aside from the newly titled Marquis of Tullibardine's ignoring her and flirting with every unmarried lass at court, Lady Saxonhurst had grown increasingly adversarial. Da continued his nightly inquisitions, asking Maddie about everything she'd witnessed while playing for the queen—not that anything untoward ever happened when she was present. The attendants were always excused when someone came in with sensitive information. Nonetheless Da repeatedly told Maddie she was providing a valued service.

The queen didn't care for her afternoon tea. More pirates have been spotted off the coast of the Isle of Lewis. That didn't concern the queen overmuch, because Lewis is part of the Hebrides in the north of Scotland.

Maddie chewed her thumbnail as she headed out for her afternoon serenading session.

Honestly, that tidbit of information about the pirates must have provided some value. After all, Lewis is only a day's sailing from English waters.

"Why so glum?" Da asked from the drawing room.

Maddie stopped, finding Miss Agnes there as well. She forced a smile. "I suppose Miss Agnes is pulling your ear about returning to Stonehaven? I've been ready to return home for over a year."

"I ken, my dear. Goodness, my infant daughter has never even seen my face."

That made Maddie's throat thicken. She probably never

would see her new half sister. She looked to the floorboards and nodded.

"Unfortunately, as long as I'm forced to remain at Whitehall, it only makes sense for you to remain here as well. Besides, we haven't been able to spend this much time together in years."

Ever, if my memory serves me right.

"We have naught but to carry on and make the best of it," said Agnes.

Maddie gave her lady's maid a sharp look. The traitor. Agnes was supposed to be on her side. "I'll remember you said that in a year's time, when we are still here."

Agnes cringed and batted eyelashes at the earl, for heaven's sake. "Do you think it will be that long, Your Lordship?"

Da patted the servant's hand. "Dear Lord, I hope not."

Maddie had seen and heard enough. "I'd best be off before I end up late." She curtsied and hastened out the door.

It was only about a five-minute walk to the royal apartments, though she had to cross through the main courtyard. Stepping out into the blustery wind, Maddie stopped short and clutched her arms across her midriff. For all that was holy, Aiden was taking a stroll with Lady Annabel, daughter of the Earl of Sussex.

Maddie quickly ducked inside and hid behind the door until they passed. Why did her insides feel as if they had been ripped from her body every time she saw the marquis with yet another courtier? Worse, Maddie actually liked Lady Annabel. She was the only maid of honor who had actually treated her with a modicum of respect.

Two weeks had passed since the funeral, and the new Marquis of Tullibardine hadn't said a single word to her. Not that she'd been close enough to him for a conversation. On the few occasions when she'd seen him, he'd conveniently been across the room—or, as in this instance, Maddie had ducked out of sight because he was strolling past deep in conversation with a noblewoman, and always an unmarried one at that.

Once certain Aiden—er—Lord Tullibardine had had plenty of time to stroll past, Maddie hurried across the courtyard and dashed to the queen's apartments. As soon as she stepped inside, she was met with the haughty expression of Lady Saxonhurst. "You are late."

Maddie tried to catch her breath. "Hardly."

"I'll wager you were in a secret meeting with your father." The countess leaned in. "Talking about how you will do away with the queen so you can see her half brother on the throne."

Maddie's stomach was already twisted in knots, and now she had wicked Saxonhurst to fend off. "Absolutely not. Where do you come up with this hogwash?"

"I do not need to look far, my dear. You Scots are all backstabbers."

"Lady Magdalen?" the queen called in her wispy voice. "I do hope you are planning to cease chatting with Lady Saxonhurst and take up your harp sometime this day."

After shooting the countess a narrow-eyed glare, Maddie curtsied. "Straightaway, Your Majesty."

Chapter Twenty-Three

*A*iden didn't care to attend the Hallowmas eve ball, but a nobleman did not turn down an invitation from the queen, especially when staying at Whitehall. To appease his parents, he'd been making an attempt to meet the maiden ladies at court. Regrettably, with news of the ball, their numbers had grown considerably in the past sennight, which made Aiden's head hurt all the more. If his mother introduced him to one more giggling, daft-headed nymph, he might do something rash—like draw his dirk and run it across his own neck.

It would have been a hell of a lot easier to play the merry courtier if Lady Magdalen Keith were not present. But it seemed every time he looked up, she was staring at him as if she'd like to grab his dirk and help him run it across his neck. He couldn't blame her. If he'd been in her shoes, he probably would have made a scene by now.

But Maddie showed more couth, more style, and more maturity than all the other women swarming around him like diving magpies.

With resolute forbearance, he faced his dancing partner as the minstrels began an Allemande. Across the aisle Lady Annabel smiled. Aiden halfheartedly returned the expression. Of all the maids to whom his mother had introduced him, Lady Annabel was the most tolerable. In fact, she possessed a pleasant demeanor and had a reasonably pretty face. Her nose was a bit too long, but he liked her light-brown hair and her blue eyes—though they were not quite as blue as Maddie's. Lady Annabel was of average height, which suited Aiden well enough, and she hailed from a respected family, though her father sided with the Whig Party. She danced forward and locked arms with him, her gaze downward, where a demure lass's gaze ought to be. A few days ago when he'd strolled through the courtyard with her, she'd been quiet and reserved. Aiden definitely preferred a soft-spoken woman to some of the more brazen lassies he'd met of late. In truth, Lady Annabel embodied everything he'd thought he wanted in a woman.

But there was one thing lacking.

He felt no emotion for Lady Annabel whatsoever. Aye, he respected her just as he would any lass, but he wanted more. He'd once thought he had found more. The first time he'd seen Lady Magdalen, he'd been dumbstruck. The entire evening at that Hogmanay celebration nearly two years past, he'd not been able to draw his eyes from her.

Would he ever be rendered dumbstruck again?

As he promenaded with Lady Annabel's hand on his arm, he made the mistake of looking to the crowd. Standing beside her father, Lady Magdalen played the wallflower, staring at him as if frozen, her eyes wide with hurt, her bow-shaped lips parted.

Aiden's gut roiled. Self-loathing came to mind. He hadn't sought her out—hadn't even spoken to her since the night in the stables at Poyle Manor. There had been so much to do in assuming the role of marquis. Because of his duty, combined with his mother's doting and her taking over his social calendar, he'd had no time to himself.

No opportunity to think, to sort out his priorities.

But every time he saw Lady Magdalen watching him from across the Banqueting House, or across the courtyard, or, as now, across the ballroom, guilt crawled up the back of his neck like a slithering serpent. He owed her an explanation. He owed her an apology for taking advantage of her when she, in good faith, had accepted his hospitality and he in turn had seduced her. He'd behaved like a lecherous cur— a debaucher akin to Fraser MacPherson. He'd been a young and irresponsible sailor with one thing on his mind.

Lady Magdalen Keith deserved so much more. She needed a man who would protect her from lusty naval officers and hideous ladies-in-waiting who had nothing better to do than to strut like peacocks and issue insults at Maddie's expense.

He continued with the dance, skipping in line and holding Lady Annabel's hand. All the while his self-loathing grew deeper.

She leaned nearer him, her gaze shifting back toward Maddie. "Are the rumors true?"

"I beg your pardon?" He had an inkling of what she planned to ask, but he feigned ignorance, assuming nothing.

"Lady Saxonhurst told me that Lady Magdalen is…" She cupped her free hand over her mouth. "A spy working to oust the queen and place that vile James on the throne."

Aiden smirked. "You mean she's a *Jacobite*?" He whispered the offending word into her ear softly enough to ensure no one else overheard.

Lady Annabel gasped as if he'd cursed. "Never let anyone

hear you mumble such an utterance anywhere near White-hall or Kensington."

Aiden bowed his head at the lassie's featherbrained admonishment. If for one minute she thought him that daft, she should release his arm and remove herself from the Alle-mande. But as always, he ground his teeth and let it pass. After a turn with the neighboring woman, he again joined elbows with Lady Annabel. "As to your question, m'lady, I wouldn't believe a single word voiced by Lady Saxonhurst."

Annabel giggled. "I thought the same."

The next time Aiden glanced to Maddie, her father was nowhere in sight. To his dread, Lord Blackiron and Lady Saxonhurst bookended the lass. When Blackiron pointed his finger beneath Maddie's nose, her eyebrows drew together and she shook her head vehemently. High color flooded her cheeks. Whatever was being said, Aiden imagined it wasn't truthful, or nice. His every muscle tensed. Dear God, if they were not in the presence of the queen, Aiden would relish sparring with the pasty codfish without even inviting him outside. Fists would do. Simply keeping company with the countess made Blackiron guilty of *something*.

Luckily, the music ended. After leading Lady Annabel off the dance floor and politely excusing himself, Aiden strode directly toward the threesome, clenching his fists and imagining slamming them repeatedly into Blackiron's beastly visage.

"You look bonny this eve, Lady Magdalen," Aiden said, meaning every word. Maddie always looked beautiful, but tonight she lit up the room as if hundreds of candles sur-rounded her. She wore red. He'd never seen her in red before, and the color suited the lass, making her appear even more ravishing than the blue gown she'd worn at the Hogmanay masque or the gold she'd worn at the organ recital. A red feather crowning her honeyed tresses swept over the top of her head.

Dear God, *she* should be revered as a princess, with all the lords and ladies in the hall bowing to her.

Looking at him with wide eyes and nothing that could be mistaken for a smile, Maddie twirled her fan in her left hand, seemingly as an admonishment, to which she had every right. "Thank you for your kind words, m'lord," she clipped.

Lady Saxonhurst gave him a once-over. "Tullibardine, I've noticed that now you're a marquis, you've been keeping company with more respectable fare."

"Whatever do you mean, m'lady?" Aiden shot a glare to Blackiron, then offered his elbow to Maddie. "My mother has asked me to remember my manners and extend kindness to new faces whilst at court. A man at sea for months can oft forget proper etiquette." This he said directly to Maddie, who had yet to accept his proffered lifeline. "And I believe I have been unduly absorbed with meeting my mother's expectations whilst regrettably ignoring some of my dearest friends." Hopefully Maddie understood he referred to her.

"I would be very careful whom you claim as a friend, my lord." Blackiron sneered. "The void between the parties is growing, and you'd best find yourself on the right side."

Since Maddie still hadn't taken his cue, Aiden grasped her arm and pulled her behind him while he stepped in front of the earl. "Och, you sound certain of this impending doom. My advice is that you'd best watch your back. With such drivel spouting from your mouth *you* could end up with one of your English daggers in it."

The earl sputtered through his buckteeth. "Are you threatening me?"

Aiden leaned in, making Blackiron crane his neck. "Oh no. I've no need to make threats, m'lord." He turned to Maddie, again offering his elbow. "The minstrels look as if they're about to play another set. Would you dance with me?"

"I—" Maddie glanced from Saxonhurst to Blackiron. "I'd be delighted," she said, though her tone was none too certain.

Aiden swiftly led her away.

"Hmm, I do believe the Marquis of Tullibardine is out to ruin his reputation." Lady Saxonhurst's shrill voice cut through the hum of the crowd.

Stopping midway to the floor, Maddie drew her hand away. "Thank you for coming to my rescue, m'lord. I'm sure you would prefer to return to dancing with Lady Annabel now."

Aiden faced her. He reached out to grasp her shoulders, but before his fingers touched the red damask, he snapped his hands away. Such a display of affection at a royal ball would do nothing for the lassie's reputation. "Forgive me, m'lady. But it is you with whom I wish to dance."

She shook her blasted fan under his nose. "Did you not hear the countess? Simply speaking to me could tarnish your reputation."

"Do you think I care about what anyone in this hall thinks?"

"You do not? What about acting upon your mother's bidding?"

"My actions have been only to appease Her Grace during her time of mourning."

Anger flashed through the lady's eyes with the force of a slap. "So you mean to say you are not enjoying meeting with every court maiden who strikes your fancy?"

"I beg your pardon?"

Maddie stood a little straighter, her defiant lips disappearing into a straight line. "Tell me, have you shown the unsuspecting lassies your pamphlet of pictures? Have you preyed on their innocence as you did mine? Do you intend to cast them aside without a simple apology or farewell?" She spit the words from her mouth like the hissing of a cat.

With curious heads turning their way, Aiden stepped closer to speak more softly. "How dare you accuse me of—"

"Pardon me, m'lord, but I do not need your pity." She spun away with a whoosh of her skirts and marched for the door like Queen Zenobia leading the Palmyrenes.

The Earl Marischal moved in beside him, a glass of brandy in his hand. "What on earth did you say to my daughter?"

Dear God, the last thing Aiden needed was a tongue-lashing from Maddie's da. He threw out his hands. "I thought she needed rescuing from the vultures, so I asked her to dance."

"Figured you were being valiant, did you?"

"I did, though I reckon the lady has her reasons for shunning me."

The earl sipped from his glass. "Lady Magdalen is a complex woman. She's bright, for certain. But mind you, never take my daughter for granted."

Aiden nodded. "I understand she has had to face a number of rebuffs throughout her life."

"Aye, but each setback has made her stronger. Mark me, Lady Magdalen will never lie down and die. She's a fighter." The earl jabbed Aiden in the shoulder with his finger. "The reason I allowed you to take her up to the wall-walk at Dunnottar was because I thought you might be a good match for her—and an alliance between our clans wouldn't hurt, either. If you want the lass, you'd best not cross her... Ye ken?"

Aiden gulped. "Aye, m'lord."

Chapter Twenty-Four

*M*addie was sick and tired of living at Whitchall. Had she known being treated like a common tinker was to be her fate, she would have insisted her stepmother send someone else to see to her father's release.

Crossing the courtyard, she looked to the sky, fully aware she could never turn her back on her father. But now? Now he'd become insufferable. Just this morning she'd asked for leave to return to Stonehaven and received the same refusal as before. "I need you here, my dear."

And to the question, "When do you plan to return to your wife and bairns?" he'd replied, "Yule, God willing."

God willing?

Yule was two months away, which seemed like an eternity. And God must will it first? What if the queen demanded they stay in London for another year?

I will die.

Maddie missed her quiet, solitary life. It was easy to hide at the hospital. No one ever broke her heart there.

And how daft could she have been, thinking she was in

love with Lord Tullibardine? He could no sooner marry her than a guttersnipe. Aye, there might have been a remote possibility for them to wed if he'd remained a second son and not an heir. But alas, their tryst had been only a dream, a fleeting sennight of passion between two very young and idealistic people.

From the day Maddie was born, she'd been destined to become nothing—a spinster—a harpist to play soothing music for highly strung, spoiled aristocrats.

She took a few deep breaths before entering the queen's apartments. She'd learned ages ago not to allow emotion to show, and right now Maddie had enough ire pulsing through her blood to set all of Queen Anne's cabinet into an uproar.

Calm and serene.

She smiled and proceeded on her way, walking much slower than she had been.

When Maddie entered the queen's antechamber, the chandelier had been lowered for cleaning. The enormous fixture sat on the table atop a drop cloth. A servant hastened through the door, carrying a bowl filled with lumps of wax.

Lady Saxonhurst gestured to a crate of candles. "Lady Magdalen, would you be so kind as to replace the candles?"

"Certainly." Maddie offered a guarded smile. Perhaps being pleasant was the countess's way of apologizing for her abhorrent behavior last eve?

The servants had already pulled out the old candles and cleaned the chandelier of wax, but for some reason they'd all left without finishing the task. Carefully Maddie twisted in two dozen candles, ensuring each one rested tight in its holder so that none would fall.

"It looks like you've done this before," said the Duchess of Marlborough.

"Aye, at the hospital we replace the candles in the entry every fortnight."

"Wonderful." The Lady of the Robes rubbed her hands together, surveying the chamber. "We want everything to be perfect for this day's meeting with the cabinet."

"The chamber looks pristine, Your Grace." Maddie pushed in the last candle and stepped back.

A servant returned and lit all two dozen tapers before the chandelier was raised.

"That is why the queen asked for you to play your harp, but you mustn't bring any attention to yourself whatsoever. Do you understand?"

"I do." Maddie didn't recall bringing undue attention to herself before—unless there was a matter of life and death, as there had been with the announcement of the *Royal Mary*'s battle with the pirate ship.

"You will sit in the corner and pluck something soothing. The queen says her ministers are always much more amenable with soothing music in the background."

Maddie touched her fingers to her lips and bowed. "I am pleased that I can be of service in a small way."

"Everyone has a role to play," said Lady Saxonhurst as she adjusted a vase of roses sitting atop the sideboard.

Not much later the queen entered with her cabinet ministers and all the ladies left the chamber except Maddie. As instructed, she moved to her Celtic harp set up in a corner and began to play.

Prince George appeared rather bothered, and paced behind the queen in her enormous chair at the head of the grand walnut table with lion's feet. "I understand unrest in the Colonies is escalating, and we must do something to quash it forthwith."

The Earl of Mar shook his head. He'd proved grounded in

his opinions. Maddie liked him, and he was the only Scot in Queen Anne's cabinet. "The only way to maintain order is to enlist more men."

The admiral stopped pacing and planted his palms on the table beside his wife. "How do you intend to pay these additional conscripts?"

Clearing his throat, the Earl of Surrey sat back. "We must raise taxes in the Colonies. I've heard word commoners are growing wealthy off their crops."

The queen harrumphed. "I do not think—"

A screeching groan came from overhead.

The chandelier jolted.

Hot wax rained down on the table.

Maddie's fingers grated over the strings as she gasped.

Another deafening screech.

Shoving the harp to the floor, she sprang to her feet, racing for Her Majesty with her arms outstretched.

Beside the queen, Prince George shoved Her Majesty aside, pushing the woman off her throne just as the chandelier came crashing down, splintering the table and smashing into the queen's seat.

The chamber erupted in a cacophony of disorder while the queen recoiled on the silk carpet, her gown hitched up to expose a pair of stocking-clad calves.

Maddie dashed forward and pulled down the queen's skirts while the ministers used their cloaks to snuff the flames spreading on the shattered wood. "Are you all right, Your Majesty?" she asked, wringing her hands.

Prince George lumbered to his feet. He offered his hand to the queen. "My dearest, you must be beside yourself. Did I hurt you, my love?"

The Earl of Mar hastened to grasp the queen's other elbow. "Please, allow me to help."

Nodding, Queen Anne allowed the men to help her lumber to her feet. "I am unscathed...I do believe. Perhaps a bit riled."

"That certainly is understandable, Your Majesty," said the Earl of Sussex as he righted the throne.

The door opened and in rushed the Duchess of Marlborough, leading the queen's ladies-in-waiting.

"What on earth happened?" asked the duchess.

Lady Saxonhurst stopped midstride, sucking in a high-pitched gasp. Then she shook her finger at Maddie. "This is her fault. I asked Magdalen to replace the candles, and while she did it, she loosened the chandelier from its support. I am sure of it."

Clasping her hands to her chest, Maddie shrank backward. "I did no such thing."

"Call the guard!" Prince George glared at Maddie as if she'd just attempted murder. "Someone restrain this woman before the entire ceiling comes crashing down upon us."

Every person cringed and looked to the ornate relief above.

In seconds six guards armed with pikes barreled into the chamber. "We heard the commotion from the courtyard."

"It was Lady Magdalen," Saxonhurst shrieked, again pointing to Maddie. "She's the Earl Marischal's daughter—a man formerly imprisoned for being a traitor."

"I-I merely replaced the candles." Maddie instinctively backed away from the guards, but still they seized her wrists. Jolting at the affront, she twisted against their grasps with little effect. "Everyone kens as well as I that my father is innocent."

The countess snorted. "Oh please. We all know he intended to march straight to London with the *Pretender*."

"I cannot abide treacherous urchins in my court," fumed

the queen. "I should have known not to open my arms and allow an ungrateful Highland woman into my inner circle. Trusting Scots is akin to trusting the serpent in the Garden of Eden. Take her to the Tower. I never want to set eyes on her again."

Maddie's gaze snapped to the Earl of Mar, who merely shook his head.

Would no one rise to her defense? "This is absurd." Maddie again struggled against the guards' iron grips while they strained to tug her toward the door. "I did nothing but replace the candles as Lady Saxonhurst directed. How on earth could I be held responsible for this? How many other people touched the chandelier this day?"

The queen turned her face away. Lady Saxonhurst stepped into Maddie's view, a smirk playing on her lips. "You have said quite enough."

Digging in her heels, Maddie narrowed her eyes at the evil countess. "'Tis you, is it not? At every turn you've tried to falsely implicate me."

"Oh?" The countess spun and faced the cabinet ministers. "You heard her. Now the earl's bastard daughter is attempting to cast the blame to me...and when that *spy* has been caught in the act."

"Take her away," commanded Prince George. "She will hang from the Tower's gallows!"

Maddie's throat closed as the guards muscled her into the passageway. Her mind raced. She'd done nothing but give up the things she held dear to remain at court and play the blasted harp for the ungrateful queen, and this was how she was repaid? A clammy chill coursed over her skin as her breathing grew shallow and stuttered.

Hang? Oh God. This cannot be happening.

"Please! Someone fetch my father!"

* * *

As Aiden made his way to the sparring court, a booming crash came from the queen's apartments. In the blink of an eye, a mob swarmed toward the source of the sound.

"'Tis the harpist. She rigged the chandelier!" someone shouted.

The crowd erupted into a rumbling mass of dissention.

Aiden's gut gripped as he pushed ahead, straining to see over the tops of heads. But he didn't need to push inside the passageway to know Maddie had been framed.

The harpist rigged the chandelier? Preposterous.

When Prince George's voice carried outside the halls with a deep bellow, declaring she would be hanged from the Tower's gallows, Aiden darted away from the crowd and ran for the stables. The mob would soon be shouting for a swift trial and execution, and the Earl Marischal would be powerless to stop them.

By the time they figured out that Maddie was innocent, it would be too late.

The more Aiden considered the direness of her plight, the faster he ran. Ahead a groom led a saddled hackney toward the barn. Dashing straight for him, Aiden reached for the reins. "I need this mount."

"But 'tis Lord Blackiron's horse."

Aiden shoved his foot into the stirrup, chuckling at the irony. "It is he who is behind my urgency to make haste."

Before the groom could utter another word, Aiden mounted and dug in his heels, spurring the horse to a gallop. Shod hooves smacked the cobblestones.

Aiden prayed that for once time would be in his favor.

Chapter Twenty-Five

*A*fter slapping manacles on her wrists, two guards shoved Maddie into a coach with iron bars on the windows and bolted the door shut. Trapped within, she pounded on the side. "I am innocent!"

"Lies," shouted a woman's voice, followed by taunts and jeers from the crowd.

"Never trust a bastard," a man bellowed.

As the coach pulled away from Whitehall, it seemed every person in London had come to shout taunts at Maddie. Something hit the bars and oozed down the inside of the door—it stank like horse dung. Maddie pushed herself into the far corner, praying the nightmare would end.

Tears filled her eyes as she frantically twisted her wrists against her shackles. Shoving the right bracelet downward, she squeezed her fingers together and tugged with all her might. As she twisted, a bit of skin scraped off. Blast it. The manacles had been locked so tightly around her wrists, there wasn't the least bit of give.

The coach swayed and bumped over the cobblestones,

but mercifully, the farther they traveled from Whitehall the more the shouts ebbed. Thank heavens the vile courtiers weren't running alongside the coach with their taunts.

Maddie pressed her face into her palms. Her mind raced. How in heaven's name would she free herself from this mess?

Please, Da. Make haste.

Though her father was her only hope, she feared there would be nothing he could do. He was still under scrutiny for marching his army to Edinburgh to meet King James.

Aye, she'd replaced the candles in the chandelier. She had been all but ordered to do so by the countess. Everyone had seen her.

Who else touched it?

Innumerous servants for certain.

She closed her eyes and recalled that the Duchess of Marlborough had been the one to wind it back into place—but the duchess had used a crank on the wall, and of all the ladies-in-waiting, the duchess was the closest with the queen and the least likely to do anything to harm Her Majesty. In fact, the Duchess of Marlborough's husband was Britain's champion general leading the troops on the Continent.

Perhaps her father could find a solicitor to help prove her innocence? Would there be time, or would her hanging be ordered for the morrow?

Her entire body shuddered.

This cannot be happening.

Who would be so evil as to do such a thing? Maddie's mind went straight to Lady Saxonhurst. *That woman somehow staged the whole affair to make me look the guilty party.*

But that made no sense. The countess was but a distant

cousin to the queen. She had no right to the succession, though she abhorred Jacobites. If she was responsible, what was her motive? Blackiron?

The pair of them had accused her father of being a Jacobite at the Hallowmas eve ball. And everyone knew Blackiron to be a staunch Whig.

Maddie whimpered in the darkness of the coach.

If the countess wasn't involved, if she truly suspected Maddie of treason, then who had rigged the chandelier? Had it been an accident?

What if Queen Anne had been killed? Had someone truly tried to assassinate her?

Maddie groaned. The reason for the accident didn't matter. She was on a course to her execution, and she doubted there was a soul in all of London rational enough to discover the true cause of the incident.

Ice pulsed through her veins.

She clutched her fingers around her throat.

I am going to be hanged by the neck until I expire.

She sat frozen in the corner of the coach, too frightened to blink. Too frightened to swallow. What would it feel like to die? To have a rope slid over her head and tightened around her neck, and then, with a fatal push, to have the life choked out of her?

She could feel it now. The coarse hemp rope cutting into her flesh and constricting.

Oh God, help.

Three miles took an eternity to traverse, but when the coach came to a halt, Maddie wished it had kept going, had left the city and headed north, had taken her far from this nightmare and the queen and court and all the horrible courtiers. She held her breath and listened for taunts, but the only noise was of the guards hopping from the driver's seat, followed by the soles of their shoes slapping cobblestones.

The door opened and the light from the setting sun blinded her. "I-I was merely playing my harp," she tried to explain.

A thud and a grunt sounded.

Maddie clutched her fists beneath her chin. "It was Lady Saxonhurst who asked me to replace the candles."

Two more grunts followed. Something smashed into the side of the coach, then sounded as if it dropped to the ground.

Maddie's fists refused to stop shaking, no matter how tightly she squeezed her fingers. "The c-c-c-countess has behaved *horribly* toward me the entire time I've been at Whitehall."

"Maddie, come!" Through the glare Aiden's face appeared, surrounded by white light as if he were an angel sent from heaven.

Had fear killed her?

She sucked in a sharp breath. "Have I already died?"

"Nay, you are as alive as I." He thrust out his hand. "We must hurry."

Shaking like a leaf in the wind, Maddie reached out with her manacled wrists. Aiden grasped her hand and pulled. Before her feet hit the ground, he had cradled her in his arms. Big, strong arms surrounded her and renewed her strength. Lord Almighty, the power that surged from him was palpable...

But why was he there?

Where had he come from?

"I, ah..." Blinking, she glanced down. One guard lay flat on his face, and the other rested askew against the coach wheel.

"What happened?"

Aiden hastened toward a hackney stallion. "I readjusted their priorities."

"You wha—?" Her body sailed through the air. Maddie had known Aiden was strong, but she'd never thought him powerful enough to toss her onto a horse as if she weighed no more than a bag of oats. She'd barely had time to find her seat when, with one leap, he launched himself behind her and dug in his heels. After two trotting steps, the horse picked up speed into a canter.

"We must haste," Aiden growled in her ear.

Clutching the stallion's mane, she glanced back at the guards now starting to rouse. "To where?"

"Blackwall Port." Aiden's voice rolled with the cadence of the horse.

"Is the *Royal Mary* there?"

"Highly unlikely. She'll be in Portsmouth for another month."

"But—?"

"Wheesht." The reins cracked on the horse's shoulders. "Lean forward. We must ride like hellfire."

"The prisoner's escaping!" yelled a deep voice, made softer by the growing distance.

Picking up speed, they nearly plowed into an old man with a barrow. Aiden steered the hackney around coaches and street vendors like Satan was on their heels.

After pulling to a stop at the wharf, Aiden hopped down, then reached up to Maddie. "I'll find us a boat."

"Why are you helping me?" she asked, placing her hands on his shoulders as his big hands closed around her waist.

He grinned as he lowered her feet to the ground. Aye, in the face of certain death, the Marquis of Tullibardine smiled with those boyish dimples as if he hadn't a care. Then he looked at her wrists and cursed. "*Damnation.*" Reaching into his sporran, he glanced over his shoulder. "Hold still."

She nodded and watched while he twisted a metal pick into one of the padlocks. With a flick of his wrist, it sprang open. He did the same thing to the next, then scooted sideways and dropped them into an empty barrel.

"How did you do that?"

"An old navy trick." He grabbed her hand and pulled her toward a two-masted brig, her sails unfurled and picking up wind.

"Where are you sending me?"

"Home." He tugged her arm.

The skin had been rubbed raw, but at the moment Maddie would follow this man anywhere, even if he didn't love her. Even if he had made her feel like a used carpet for anyone to wipe their feet upon. The Marquis of Tullibardine had come a long way toward exonerating himself.

With purpose he strode up the gangway, "Where are you headed?" he asked of a seaman.

"Alnwick."

"Indeed, luck is with us. Can you take on a pair of passengers?"

A man dressed in a doublet with gold trim and looking like a captain with periwig and tricorn hat pattered down from the helm. "We've no cabins to spare. You'll have to bed down belowdecks."

Aiden dug in his sporran. "That shouldn't bother us overmuch, given it is a short jaunt to Alnwick."

"The fare is four crowns."

"Four?" Aiden looked as if he was about to pull Maddie off the boat.

"The extra weight will slow us down."

"Hardly," Aiden grumbled under his breath, but he placed

the required fare in the man's outstretched palm. "When do we sail?"

"As soon as you step off my gangway so the men can draw it in."

"Very well." Tugging Maddie's raw wrist, Aiden pulled her onto the deck. "I am Mr. Blair and this is my lady wife."

"Captain Child." His gaze sliding to her breasts, the captain shoved the coins in his purse, then held out his hand to Aiden. "What is your business in Alnwick?"

The gangway scraped the deck as two sailors pulled it aboard.

"Edinburgh, actually." Frowning, Aiden brushed his fingers over the ship's rail and then rubbed them as if he'd met with unseemly dirt. "I am an officer aboard a Firth ferry and must make haste to rejoin my crew."

Maddie gave him a sideways glance. His lies sounded like the honest truth.

Captain Child squinted, looking beyond them. "You're not in any kind of trouble, are you?"

Aiden glanced over his shoulder. Maddie did, too. A retinue hastened toward the wharf. "No trouble at all." He pulled her to his far side, blocking her from view from the shore.

"How long will it take to sail to Alnwick?" she asked.

"Weigh anchor," hollered the captain before he answered, "We'll sail through the night, madam. I suggest you and your husband head aft and make yourselves comfortable."

As they moved toward the rear of the brig, Maddie kept her head down, letting her shoulders fall forward as she leaned into Aiden as if she were elderly. "Do you think they've seen us?"

"Not yet," he whispered, and he pulled his tricorn hat lower on his brow. "But once they identify Blackiron's horse, it won't take long for them to fit the pieces together…and the harbormaster will ken where this ship is sailing."

"Do you think they'll follow us to Alnwick?"

"Aye, but I do not plan on staying there long."

"Why are you helping me?"

He spread his palms with a shrug. "I heard the crash and someone shouted that the harpist had rigged the chandelier. I reckon that's all it took. I kent if I didn't take action straightaway, you'd be locked in the Tower, and once you were inside, there'd be no chance for rescue."

"But you'll be implicated in this horrible sham."

"I reckon so, m'lady."

The ship rocked and groaned as she began to sail into the Thames, headed for the open sea. "So you're my knight in shining armor?" she whispered.

"Nay. I do not even own a coat of armor—at least I don't think I do. I haven't seen a report of my assets as of yet."

"I'm sorry to be such an unmitigated bother. Why didn't you leave me aboard the ship and return to Whitehall?"

"Are you jesting? Do you not remember the guards I knocked unconscious? Both of them will be pointing their fingers my way when they come to."

"Oh, my word. I've placed you in an untenable situation."

Aiden grasped her hand and held it to his heart. "Not at all, m'lady. In fact, a great weight has been lifted from my shoulders."

Maddie knitted her brows. "Pardon?"

"At this very moment, I feel like a bird released from its cage."

"Stop that brig!" a dragoon shouted from the shore, still only fifty yards away.

Both Maddie and Aiden peered over the ship's rail and watched the redcoats stand helpless as the brig picked up speed. The problem? Several members of the crew watched the dragoons as well.

Aiden pulled her down a set of steps. "We'd best stay out of sight in case they decide to start shooting off their muskets."

Maddie squeezed his hand tightly. "I've ruined you."

"Nay, m'lady. It is I who have ruined myself."

Chapter Twenty-Six

*A*fter their near brush with the soldiers on the wharf, Aiden had found a pallet of straw belowdecks near the bow, and as far as they could be from the crew's hammocks. Once they were settled, he'd gone to the galley to ask for a bit of bread and bully beef. Other than that, they'd stayed out of sight. Aye, the crew had seen the soldiers, but thus far no one had sought them out to ask why they had been so anxious to board the merchant brig. With luck the crew would continue to mind their own affairs.

However, there was nothing like being surrounded by potential enemies to keep a man on edge. Once they'd eaten their meager meal, darkness came on fast—not that there had been much light belowdecks, but at least there had been shadows. Now Aiden could barely see his palm in front of his face.

Maddie remained quiet. He tried to put his arm around her shoulders to provide comfort, but she scooted farther away. How could he blame her? Should he expect her to turn around and pretend he hadn't carried on like a lout for the past few sennights?

He patted the hay. "You'd best try to sleep."

She chuckled, her sultry voice stirring. Aiden had forgotten how much her voice could move him. "I do not think I can."

"Aye, but there's naught to do but wait. It will be morning before we moor off the coast of the River Aln."

"Have you been there before?"

"Aye, off the coast. Alnwick is inland about five miles. The ships moor in Alnmouth Bay and riverboats ferry the wares to the village."

"Oh." She sat in silence for a time, sighing now and again. "Aiden?"

"Mm."

"What will happen to us?"

He'd been thinking about that, too. "As soon as we reach Alnwick, I aim to send a missive to your father. He is our best chance to help us prove your innocence."

"And *your* father?" she asked. "Do you think he will help?"

"Knowing my da, he'd be much more inclined to help if first presented with proof of your innocence." Aiden clamped his lips together. He couldn't tell Maddie that his father had all but forbidden him from seeing her. Not that the Duke of Atholl had any say in the matter now. Besides, telling her the truth would only serve to hurt her feelings all the more.

The night wore on, and finally the lass gave in and fell asleep, curled into a ball, her back against Aiden's thigh. Her every breath made his heart swell—as if he'd found a new connection to her. If only they could stay connected forever, he'd pledge an oath never to move his leg. Even her warmth soothed him. Raising his hand to caress her, he hesitated. She mightn't want him to touch her, though his fingers itched to do so. Letting out a long breath, he placed his hand on her shoulder. When she didn't rouse, he rubbed, ever so gently. If he could turn back time, he'd go back to the day she came aboard the *Royal Mary*. Though that was the same day he'd received word of John's death, he would still act differently if given the chance.

He should have sought Magdalen's succor rather than push it away. If only he'd allowed himself to fall into her embrace. But no. He was a Murray, and Murrays always bottled up their emotions and pushed away succor.

Over and over he replayed the twist of events that had led a marquis and an earl's daughter to the darkness of the bow of a rickety merchant brig. But idle time aboard a swaying ship always lulled him to sleep. Leaning his head back against the timbers, he closed his eyes. He carried a sword and a dirk, plus a dagger tucked into each of his hose, and he prayed to God that would be enough weaponry to see them safely to Edinburgh.

If all goes well.

Fortunately, they had a head start on the English, even if the queen's navy did pursue the brig up the coast. With luck he'd spirit Maddie into the Highlands, where they could wait until the whole misunderstanding was resolved.

His eyelids grew too heavy to stay open. It wasn't until a beam of light shone down from the hatch that Aiden again opened his eyes. The rolling of the sea had ebbed to a smooth sway, a clear indication that they were again sailing through shallow waters close to shore.

"Drop anchor," a man hollered above.

Aiden wriggled his toes and tightened his buttocks. His blasted arse had gone numb during the night, and he flexed his knees to ease the pins and needles. He didn't want to do it, but he had no choice but to shake Maddie's shoulder. "We've arrived."

"Hmm?" Stretching, she sat up and scooted away. Aiden's thigh chilled.

"Did you sleep well?" he asked.

"I think so." She rubbed her eyes. "Better than I thought I would. And you?"

He grinned. "Put me on a rocking ship, and I can sleep standing upright." Though he would have liked to stay there a bit longer, he needed to go up top and have a look at their mooring. With luck the captain would let them sail ashore with the first skiff of supplies.

Aiden stood and offered his hand. "We'd best go have a chat with Captain Child."

"And something to eat. I'm starved."

He was hungry, too. "Very well. A chat with the captain and then we'll see if we can't find an oatcake."

Stepping onto the deck, Aiden shaded his eyes. Though there was cloud cover, the light of day still hurt. But his senses had told him right. They were moored but a half a league from the sandy shore.

"Move the empty barrels portside," said the captain from his place near the helm.

"Aye, Captain." A pair of sailors rolled and stacked quarter casks against the rail. Each was fitted with a metal loop attached to its iron belly band, used for tying the barrels down to prevent them from rolling out of control in rough seas.

"Are you picking up cargo?" Aiden asked. He'd assumed they were taking wares to Alnwick.

The captain strode toward them, his eyes narrow and his chin tipped up. "These are for brandy. It seems they don't distill enough in London," he said with a sure hint of irritation in his voice. Aiden didn't think much of it until the man's eyes shifted and his hand slipped around the handle of his cutlass. Footsteps sounded on the deck behind.

Instinctively Aiden pushed Maddie against the rail, then trapped her with his back, guarding the lass against attack. His fingers slipped into his basket hilt.

"I wouldn't draw my weapon if I were you," said the captain.

Aiden glanced right. Two sailors closed in. "What is the meaning of this? Are you in the habit of threatening paying passengers?"

"We all saw the dragoons on the wharf." Captain Child slid his thumb over the dagger in his belt. "You're in some kind of trouble, and I'd reckon someone's willing to pay a bounty for your capture."

Dipping into a crouch, Aiden drew his sword with his right hand and his dirk with his left. "Jump!" he shouted over his shoulder.

A sailor lunged. Aiden deflected the blade downward.

"What?" Maddie screeched.

"Jump!" With a backhand he sliced his dirk across the attacker's throat. Eyes bulging, the man clutched his neck while blood streamed through his fingers.

"I can't," Maddie said, her voice filled with terror.

Christ, Aiden couldn't look back. Fighting forward, he cut down the man on his right while kicking the captain to the deck.

Seconds were all he had before he'd have to fend off another onslaught of charging attackers.

In a heartbeat he spun, dropped his sword, and hurled Maddie over the rail. Her scream rang in his ears, but he'd end up with a blade in his back if he dived in after her now.

In one fluid motion, he swooped down for his sword and fought off another two seamen while he tossed a quarter cask over the side. Shouting, more crew members rushed him. Aiden glanced back, praying Maddie had swum for the barrel.

His sword clanged, knocked from his hand. Blindly he leaped over the rail, plunging downward with the speed of a cannonball.

Sorry I cannot linger, you bleeding bastards.

Before he hit he searched for Maddie. Damn it all, she was nowhere to be seen. Only the quarter cask bobbed in the water.

With a slap his body slammed into the surf as if he were falling onto a slab of rock. Icy water stabbed him while the air whooshed from his lungs. But this was no time to go soft. Shoving his dirk in his belt, he opened his eyes and used his legs to spin. A flash of white flickered.

A hand!

Though his lungs burned with the need for air, he dived straight for Maddie. After three powerful strokes, he clamped on to her hand. She thrashed, her eyes wide with terror. Yanking her up, Aiden kicked with all his might, but her skirts were too damned heavy.

"Kick," he yelled while salty water filled his mouth and throat.

She must have heard him, because in the next moment she grew lighter and the life-giving surface grew near. He sucked in a huge gulp of air as his head broke through, and then with all his might he pulled Maddie up.

Gasping, she sputtered and coughed while her head kept dipping below the waves. "I—" She sank under. Aiden gnashed his teeth and drew her up.

"—can't swim." She went under again.

A musket cracked. A ball smacked the water a foot short of their heads.

Spying the cask, Aiden wrapped his arm across her chest and swam to it.

"Fire!" roared the captain from the deck.

"They're s-shooting at us," Maddie shrieked.

Aiden grabbed the metal loop on the cask. "Hold on to this, use it to protect your head so you don't end up with a musket ball in your skull."

All around them shots hissed through the air and pierced the sea. Swimming for his life, Aiden refused to look back. His muscles burned, drained by the cold and his efforts to pull Maddie up from the depths, but he focused on the shore and swam with all his might.

"Keep kicking," he growled through clenched teeth, tugging her with his left hand.

"I...am."

"Harder. Faster." Soon the captain would be lowering the skiff and the crew would be after them. It didn't matter how much their muscles burned, they must swim for their very lives.

"What...next?" she asked, still breathless.

"Hit the shore and run like hell." Water splashed in Aiden's mouth with his every word.

"I don't like our odds." Maddie's head dipped under again. Clearly she was tiring.

"Och. We'll be all right." He used a wave to help project them toward the shore. "Keep kicking no matter how much your limbs burn and beg you to stop."

The lass did, too, and in no time their feet hit the sandy bottom. Panting, Aiden continued to pull Maddie in his wake as he ran, but her wet skirts were even more difficult now that they were on sand. Stopping, Aiden bent down to tear them.

She batted his hands away. "No."

"You can hardly move."

"We're in the middle of nowhere and you want to rip my gown?"

"Can you hold up your skirts?"

"But—"

"Do it or I tear off your overskirt right now."

Aiden took her hand and ran straight for a copse of trees just beyond the beach. He needed a mount. Fast. In the trees they had cover, but it wouldn't protect them for long. And Maddie was slower than treacle. He stopped at a clump of broom. "Climb under and hide."

Sucking in gasps of air, she looked at him as if he were daft.

"Hide, I said. I'm off to find a horse. Hurry."

She did as he asked, then he took a switch and covered their tracks. After turning full circle, Aiden sprinted north.

* * *

Holy crosses, Maddie had thought she'd been petrified with fear when they shackled her wrists and locked her in a coach with iron bars, but that was nothing compared to being tossed over the side of a ship and nearly drowning. And then the blackguards had fired musket balls at them.

Her teeth chattered as she crouched under the thick brush. Aiden had picked her up and thrown her overboard like a sack of grain.

She could hardly think for the cold.

But when she blinked, she saw a picture of Aiden fighting in front of her. He'd guarded and protected her from attack. If they'd stayed aboard the ship, he wouldn't have been able to fight them all. Still, he'd just tossed her into the sea. How many lassies did she know who could swim—and with layers of skirts and petticoats?

A twig snapped in the distance.

Holding her breath, Maddie listened, her eyes shifting back and forth.

"This way," a man's voice said.

Footsteps grew nearer.

Taking shallow breaths, Maddie shifted backward until something sharp prodded her shoulder. She didn't dare cry out. She squeezed her fists against her mouth while her heartbeat thundered in her ears.

A pair of worn boots stopped directly in front of her hiding place. "They came past here for certain."

The boots turned and faced the brush.

Gracious Father, they're so close, they can hear the hammering of my heart.

"Do you know who they are?" asked another.

"Nay, but the queen's men were after them."

"Outlaws, yes? Do you think the captain will share the reward?"

"If he doesn't, he'll have a mutiny on his hands."

A sickly chuckle rolled from one of the sailors. "Did you see that blighter fight? He's been trained well—better than me for certain."

"Perhaps so," said the man with the worn boots. "But he's not likely to take on all three of us and live."

Three? Oh God, what if they set an ambush?

More footsteps crunched the ground, moving away from Maddie's hiding place. "Come. It looks like they went this way."

After the footsteps faded, Maddie pushed up to her hands and knees, crying out with a muffled grunt when the thorn in her shoulder dug in and scraped down her back with the sound of tearing fabric. She bit her knuckle until the pain subsided to a dull ache. If the men were good trackers, they'd soon realize only one set of tracks led north, and she didn't want to be there when they returned.

On her belly she slithered through the brush until she

came to a large oak. Reaching for a branch, she tugged up her filthy, wet skirts and threw a leg over. Once she found her balance, her strength returned and she climbed high enough not to be easily spotted from the ground.

Hugging the tree tightly, she panned her gaze across the scene, peering through the golden autumn leaves. To the east the beach was only about a quarter mile away, and the brig sat at anchor while two skiffs rowed toward her and one away.

The foliage was too thick for her to see anything inland. Taking tiny steps on the branch, Maddie swiveled around. To the north a horse and rider cantered over the crest of a hill, straight toward her.

Aiden!

Out from the foliage below, the three sailors rushed toward him, swords drawn. Maddie's heart lurched. One wielded a musket. He knelt and leveled the weapon at his shoulder.

No! Maddie's throat constricted as she tried not to scream out loud.

Aiden leaned forward on the mount, spurring his horse straight for the musketeer. With a puff of smoke, the blast from the gun cracked like a bullwhip.

At the same time, Aiden leaped his mount as if there'd been a fence in their path. Gaining speed, he was nearly upon them.

Did he leap over the shot?

The shooter sprang to his feet and skittered backward, tugging the bayonet from the musket.

Not fast enough.

Aiden cut the musketeer down with a swing of his dirk.

Bellowing, the other two charged.

Aiden spun the horse in place, his dirk clashing with a

sword. He pulled a dagger from his sleeve and threw it into the heart of the other man. The second man clutched at the knife in his chest and dropped to the grass.

The blackguard with the sword attacked the horse's flank.

Aiden spun in time. Targeting the sailor's unprotected temple, he slammed the pommel of his dirk in a deadly strike. The man dropped on his face.

Leaping from his horse, Aiden grabbed a sword and then remounted as if the movement had been choreographed. Slapping his reins, he galloped toward Maddie's hiding place.

Scurrying down the tree, Maddie called out, "I'm here!"

As his mount leaped over the brush, he reached down and grabbed her hand. "Jump."

Wet skirts and all, Aiden pulled her onto his lap, both of her legs draped over the horse's shoulder.

She slung an arm around his waist and latched on while the horse took up a canter. "I cannot believe you dispatched all three of them."

He glanced down to his leg. Blood streamed from his calf onto the sorrel horse's barrel. "Not without a graze from the damned musket ball. The arse must have been a sharpshooter."

"My word," she gasped. "We need to find a healer straightaway."

"Nay, 'tis only a flesh wound. We must spirit north as fast as this old nag will carry us."

Maddie turned her attention to the horse's mane and drew her fingers through his coarse hair. "He's fearless."

Aiden grunted. "He'll do for now."

"Where did you find him?"

"The farmer over the hill—charged me double the going price for an old gelding."

"He didn't happen to sell you food?"

"There wasn't time, lass." His arms tightened around her. "Can you hold on until I spirit us away from here?"

"Aye." After nearly drowning and then being terrified she'd be caught by their pursuers, she didn't have much of an appetite—but it wouldn't be long before she started shaking with hunger.

For now all she wanted to do was flee England nestled between Aiden's powerful arms.

"Sit back," he said as if he could read her thoughts. "It will be a long ride."

The icy breeze cut through her wet garments and she curled into Aiden's warmth. "Do you think Captain Child will send someone after us?"

"You can count on it, lass."

Chapter Twenty-Seven

*M*idafternoon they stopped in an English village. The signpost indicated they'd arrived in a wee burgh called Wooler. The horse needed to be rested, and Maddie was so dizzy from hunger she couldn't see straight. Aiden ushered her into an alehouse. Dark inside with mahogany-paneled walls, it held a bar, stools, and a few tables. Aside from the barman, the place was empty.

Ever the gentleman, after holding her chair, Aiden sauntered up to the bar. "Two pints of ale and two bowls of pottage, please."

The barman poured the ale and Maddie's mouth watered when Aiden returned with frothy tankards. "This will set you to rights until the food comes."

"Thank you." She took the handle and drank greedily, then wiped her mouth with the back of her hand. "Feels better already."

"Good." Aiden guzzled the entire contents of his tankard and motioned for the barman to bring another. "Do you think someone truly tampered with the chandelier?"

She shook her head, watching the bubbles foam across the top of her ale. "I have no idea. It could have been wear. As I recall, that wing of Whitehall was built by King Henry VIII. The chain could have been two hundred years old."

"Interesting point. But what about Lady Saxonhurst? What were she and Blackiron saying to you at the ball?"

Maddie groaned. "I swear that woman was a thorn in my side throughout the duration of my time at Whitehall. She and Lord Blackiron continually try to force me to admit that my father is a Jacobite. Do you think they had something to do with it?"

"Mayhap, though the old chain seems more likely. Rigging a chandelier? It seems unlikely. The thing could have fallen in the middle of the night when no one was about."

"True."

The barman approached with two bowls. "Lamb pottage, sir."

"I'm starved." Maddie nodded at the man, showing her gratitude.

"My thanks," Aiden said, taking up his spoon. "Ye ken what I reckon?"

Maddie took a heavenly bite, the stew warming her insides. "What?"

"I'd wager Saxonhurst is an ornery witch who cannot leave you be because you're bonnier than any of the other ladies at court, and on top of that you do not have a perfect pedigree. She thinks her birth status gives her the right to bully you."

"I cannot believe the Duchess of Marlborough tolerates her. She never chides the countess for anything." Maddie took another enormous bite.

"Mayhap they are cousins."

She hadn't thought about that possibility. All the gentry seemed to be related in one way or another. "But why is Blackiron playing into her hands?"

"He's a buffoon if you ask me. He's a Whig as well, and the Whigs have fallen out of favor with the queen. If they can reveal the Jacobites in the Tory Party, the Whigs think it will strengthen their position in Parliament."

"But what does that have to do with me?"

After taking a bite, he pointed his spoon her way. "Och, I think you're being used as a pawn to get to your father."

"And now I'm not even there for them to tread upon." Maddie ran her spoon around the bowl, scooping up the last dregs. "Woefully, with Lady Saxonhurst's allegations, the Whigs have lost their conduit to my father."

Aiden looked to his empty bowl and smacked his lips. "Well, we can only hope the truth will prevail. Until then, we must ride."

She eyed him as Agnes often did her. "You'd best allow me to have a look at your leg first."

"Nay." He batted his hand through the air. "Not here."

Feeling almost alive after a bowl of meaty pottage and ale, they were once again on their way, looking over their shoulders to ensure they still weren't being followed. With food in her belly, Maddie's fear of being chased ebbed into exhaustion. Everything hurt, from her grazed shoulder to her bum from spending hours seated across Aiden's lap. Though she couldn't deny that having his arms wrapped around her as he maneuvered the reins made her melt a little on the inside. And why shouldn't she allow herself to relax into him? There was naught else to do, and he hadn't complained—in fact, he'd even encouraged her to lean back.

She closed her eyes, surrounded by brawny male. Swirls

of yearning weighed her breasts. Would the entire journey to Stonehaven be fraught with unfulfilled longing? It seemed the more she resisted her yearnings, the fiercer they grew. Helpless to stop her silent desire from flooding to her nether parts, she rested her head against his chest and sighed.

"Mm." His deep voice rumbled against her back. He didn't need to utter another sound for Maddie to know desire coursed through him as well. Though only desire of a carnal nature.

Lust, not love.

Maddie crossed her arms and hugged her shoulders to will away the intensity of her feelings. Must she continue to remind herself that what they'd once shared had been merely pleasure of the flesh—the profession of fallen women? Never again would she succumb to hot passion without love, without marriage.

"How is your leg feeling?" she asked, trying to sound indifferent.

He shifted against her back. "It bloody hurts."

"You should have allowed me to look at it when we stopped in Wooler."

His shoulder nudged hers almost playfully. "And you should have allowed me to look at your scratch."

"It doesn't hurt overmuch."

But there hadn't been time.

And she was still in trouble—and might be in hot water for the rest of her days.

At dusk about four hours later, they crossed the River Tweed into the burgh of Coldstream.

Aiden inclined his lips to Maddie's ear. "We're in Scotland, lass." The words made gooseflesh pebble across her skin.

She looked up into his green eyes and her stomach flipped. Why couldn't the man have eyes of steel-cold gray like his heart? Moreover, the stubble that had grown in since they'd left London made him look incredibly dangerous—and, to Maddie's chagrin, all the more desirable.

Forcing herself to glance away, she swept her gaze across the wee burgh. "I do not ever again want to leave Scotland's soil."

"Agreed, though we still must prove your innocence."

Such words made the chill in the air even frostier. Maddie rubbed her arms. "'Tis growing cold."

"Aye, and neither of us has a cloak."

"Even a woolen blanket would do." She chanced looking at him again. Merciful fairies, how her lips pursed with want to kiss him—even if only once. "Have you given any thought as to where we'll stop for the night?"

He pointed up the road. "I'm hoping the alehouse up yonder has rooms to let."

"An inn?"

"Mm-hmm. I still need to send a missive to your da, and as you said, we're not equipped to ride through the night."

"Do you think 'tis safe to stop so close to the border?"

"I reckon we'll find out. Besides, even if Captain Child reported us to the Alnwick sheriff, he'd have no jurisdiction in Scotland."

"What about the army?"

"Och, that's a different story."

"So they're probably coming after us?"

He gave her a sober arch of a single eyebrow. "Most likely, though I'd wager they're at least a half day's ride behind."

"And they'll have to stop to rest their horses as well?"

He winked. "I'm banking on it, lass."

After they left the horse at the stable yard with orders for the stable boy to give him an extra ration of oats, Maddie followed Aiden across the street. A shingle outside the alehouse read "Castle Inn."

"I'll do the talking," Aiden said over his shoulder, then held the door for Maddie.

Inside the patronage was small—a few scraggly-looking men seated at the bar and a pair seated at a table.

A stout woman came from around the bar—as solid as a mighty oak, with a square jaw. She would fit right in at Stonehaven. "Have a wee peek at what the wind brought in. You pair look as if you've been through the wars."

"Nay." Aiden stood a little straighter and hooked his thumbs in his doublet lapels, while his gaze swept across the hall. "My wife and I have been traveling for days. You wouldn't happen to have a room and a warm meal?"

The barmaid eyed him from head to toe. "A guinea for the room, sixpence and a quarter for two meals. But you'll have to sign the guest log."

He gave a nod. "Thank you, Mrs. . . . ?"

"Swinton. And you are?"

"Mr. and Mrs. Grant from Inverness." The lie rolled off his tongue as if he'd repeated it a hundred times. He dug in his sporran and handed the woman the coins.

"Inverness? My, you are a long way from home." Mrs. Swinton carefully counted the change in her palm. "I could send up a warm bath for another two pennies."

Maddie shook her head. "That will not—"

Aiden squeezed her shoulder. "A bath would be lovely, thank you."

Maddie shot him a narrow-eyed glare. "Well then, if you could please send up a salve as well, matron."

Aiden gaped at her as if she'd uttered a curse, holding up a finger to indicate silence.

Shaking her head, Maddie ignored his admonishment. She had a tongue to speak for herself. "Mr. Grant caught his leg on some yellow gorse, and I'm afraid he received a nasty scrape to his calf."

Mrs. Swinton glanced down to his blood-soaked hose. "Goodness, that does look nasty."

Aiden pressed his palm in Maddie's back. "Och, it just needs a bit of cleaning up and 'twill be good as new."

"I reckon you should listen to your wife." The innkeeper bustled toward the stairway. "Follow me, and we'll set you to rights."

At the top of the stairs, she led them down a passageway while old, dry floorboards creaked beneath their feet.

The woman pulled a ring of keys from her belt. "The bed has fresh linens, and there's a stack of firewood beside the hearth." She opened the door. "I'll have the lad bring up your meal before your bath, shall I?"

"Aye, thank you, matron." Aiden bowed as Maddie walked inside.

Maddie stood in the center of the chamber and stared. The room was nothing if not stark. One narrow bed sat shoved against the wall. The hearth was small, with an iron screen. In one corner was a wee table with two rickety wooden chairs, and under the window was an even smaller table with a bowl and ewer atop.

"I could take your overskirt and mend it," said Mrs. Swinton. "Have it returned to you by the morning."

Maddie glanced to her shoulder. "I wouldn't want to be a bother."

"Thank you," said Aiden. "Would you please send up a needle and a spool of thread?"

The woman shrugged. "Very well, if that's what you would prefer."

After Mrs. Swinton closed the door, Maddie moved her fists to her hips. "There's only one bed," she whispered.

Aiden unbuckled his sword belt. "I'll sleep on the floor."

She nodded. "But what about the bath? Surely you're not planning to bathe?"

"As you noticed, I need to clean my wound. If it would cause Your Ladyship too much consternation, then I suggest you keep your back turned. Though..."

"What?"

"After your dip in the sea and crawling under brush and then riding all day, you might feel better if you cleaned up a bit as well."

Her gaze drifted downward to his abdomen, then lower. A curl of desire coiled deep inside her—that place where only Aiden could satisfy her longing. 'Twas a potent fire stirring, reminding her of the scorching-hot passion they'd once shared, and it made her gaze linger. But no, she couldn't allow him to take advantage of her yet again, no matter how heroic he'd been. Snapping herself from her moment of insanity, she looked him in the eye. "So now you believe you have the right to lord it over me? Do you think because of your undeniably handsome face that I will bend to your sexual whims this time?"

Drawing his eyebrows together, he took a step back.

Throwing up her hands, she in turn stepped nearer. "You rescued me from certain death, and for that I reckon I owe you my life, but parading around the countryside like we are married?" She harrumphed. "'Tis ghastly."

His jaw dropped, those green eyes flashing with ire. "What would you have me do? Firstly, 'tis a good cover for us. Secondly, if I paid for two chambers, there would be no way for me to protect you—not to mention, the coin in my sporran isn't going to last forever. And lastly, if anyone caught wind of an unwed maid traveling with a roguish marquis, it wouldn't be my reputation ruined forever."

"Ugh. I ken all that, but are you not taking things a bit far?" She stamped her foot, throwing out her hands. "You ordered a bath and suggested I have one, too. Do you plan on bathing fully clothed?"

"I—"

"I believe you *have* overstepped the bounds of propriety."

"But—"

She shook her finger under his chin. "Let me make it perfectly clear, Your *Lordship*. I am no man's whore." She sneezed.

"Bless you." He pulled a kerchief from his sleeve and handed it to her. "I also want to make it clear that I have never thought ill of you."

She swiped the cloth across her nose. "Well then you are one of the few at Whitehall."

"All anyone needs to do is take a wee bit of time to come to know you." Cocking his head, he stepped even closer. "In fact, I think very highly of you."

She blinked. His face looked stone-cold sober. But how could he think her anything but a tart after what they'd done? She'd gone to his chamber at night and had taken part in unspeakable things with him. How could he look at her and not think of their impropriety? Truly, at one time she'd thought he harbored the same emotion for her that she did for him, but his recent behavior at Whitehall had proved her hopes to be those of a fool. She stamped her foot. "And I'll not have you play me for a simpleton."

"I would never even consider doing such a thing."

She sneezed again.

"See," he said. "Another reason I ordered the bath was

because you were chilled to the bone earlier this day. My mother always said a bath keeps the sniffles at bay."

Maddie wiped her nose one more time, folded the damp bits inside the kerchief, and handed it back to him. "I will not strip bare in front of you."

He stuffed the cloth back into his sleeve and studied her.

Goodness gracious, why did he have to look at her like that? She knew he didn't love her, and she'd told him she wouldn't be played for a fool. But he still had the most confounded effect on her insides.

"I..." Reaching out, he grasped her hand. The look in his eyes was unreadable. A storm brewed beneath his heavy lids as if he were angry or warring with conflicting emotions. "God bless it, Maddie, I owe you an apology."

"For wha—" Before she could finish, he pulled her into his powerful arms and covered her mouth with his lips. His tongue slipped inside, tasting like the wildness of the sea, fevered with hot passion. He devoured her as she stood helpless against her own need for him.

Overwhelmed by the shock of his advances, Maddie's knees turned to wobbly mush. When she next inhaled, Aiden's scent filled her nostrils like a drug. Spicy, masculine musk made her swoon. The strength of his embrace was the only thing supporting her as her thighs trembled.

Clinging to him and rising on her toes, she pushed into his hard maleness, her breasts flush against his chest, aching for his hands to caress them. As he trailed his lips down her neck, Maddie sucked in a deep breath to try to clear her swooning head. It felt so good, but she had to make him stop. In a blink she gained a modicum of sanity. "I-I cannot allow you to seduce me."

* * *

Aiden stilled his lips and inhaled.

Seduce? Why the bloody hell did she accuse me of seducing her? I do not want a one-sided affair.

Hell's fire, if his cock grew any harder, he'd come right there, pushing himself into her hip. And she'd melted like butter in his arms. She'd kissed him back with every bit of pent-up passion he'd been restraining for sennights. And she felt so damned good with her body pressed against his. Soft, pliable breasts were still molded into his chest, the ridge of her mons brushing his cock right where he wanted to be stroked.

His gaze slid to the bed. All she had to do was say yes and he'd carry her there. In seconds he could raise her skirts and slide inside her wet core. Bury himself deep inside. Make love to her as he'd dreamed of doing every goddamned night since he'd sailed from Whitehall for the war.

But she must want me as much as I want her.

A knock came at the door.

"Your supper, sir."

"Come." Aiden dropped his hands and stared into Maddie's eyes.

Filled with the same pained expression he'd seen many times, she slowly drew her fingers over her lips—lips swollen from the force of his kiss.

Had he been too aggressive, too brutally impassioned with her?

The lad placed a tray on the table. "Shall I start the fire, sir?"

Aiden didn't even look his way. "Thank you."

Maddie broke the intensity of their connection by shifting her gaze to the table. "We should eat."

"Aye." He held the chair for her and gestured with his palm. "M'lady."

"Thank you."

After Aiden took his seat, the lad stacked a piece of wood on the crackling fire, then faced them. "The kettles are on the boil for your bath, sir."

Aiden glanced to Maddie and considered canceling the bath. But truth be told, his leg ached as if he'd been sliced open with a rasp. "My thanks."

"Do not forget the salve as well," Maddie said.

"Straightaway, madam," said the lad before he slipped out the door.

Lady Magdalen broke off a bit of bread and popped it in her mouth. "I could grow accustomed to meals delivered to my bedchamber."

Aiden couldn't help but snort.

Chapter Twenty-Eight

A big wooden tub sat in the middle of the chamber, wafting steam. Removing his doublet, Aiden looked to Maddie. "I do not want to make you feel uncomfortable."

She turned her back. "Go ahead then. Don't mind me."

He removed his shoes and untied his flashes, then gingerly pulled his hose away from the wound. Bloody hell, a half-inch deep gash three inches long looked like mincemeat. Worse, it was encrusted with grime from the trail. Wincing, he straightened and unfastened his belt, sending his kilt to the floorboards. After whipping off his shirt, he stood totally naked, his back warmed by the fire while he gazed at Maddie, willing her to turn around and rush into his arms.

When she didn't, he stepped into the water. The sting made him hiss like a kettle blowing steam.

"Are you—?" Maddie spun around, then clapped a hand over her mouth, her eyes horror-struck. "Sorry."

The corner of Aiden's mouth turned up, and he glanced downward. *Now she bloody turns around.* And rather than running to his arms, she looked at him as if he were a sea monster.

"No." He held up his palm and lowered himself into the tub. "The water stings, is all." The only problem with a tub this size? His damned knees were up around his chin. He swirled some water against his cut, clenching his teeth so he wouldn't hiss again.

"Can I examine your wound?"

As it was below the surface, he couldn't see it himself. Grunting, he raised his leg out of the water and rested his foot on the edge of the tub. "It'll be set to rights in a day or two."

Now Maddie gasped. "Gracious, it looks sore."

"I'd be lying if I told you it wasn't."

"Does it hurt to walk?"

"A bit, but we're not doing much walking."

"No." She looked at his eyes again. This time her gaze didn't harbor as much hurt. In fact, she met him with the gaze he remembered from long ago, though a tad older and wiser. "Are you planning to use that soap?" she asked.

He reached for the cake he'd placed atop the drying cloth on the floor beside the bath and held it up to her. His gut tightened when she frowned. Then she took it with a pursing of her lips—almost as if she were trying not to smile.

"Shall I wash your hair?" she asked in a sultry tone that made his heart melt.

"Thank you." He leaned forward and let her massage in the suds. Aiden loved the clean fragrance of soap, especially this bar, scented with wildflowers. Closing his eyes, he succumbed to Magdalen's magical touch as her fingers eased away his burden. Moving behind him, she ran the soap down his back in a swirling pattern while her fingers plied muscles he hadn't even realized ached. When she hit a knot, he leaned into her touch and moaned. "I am in heaven, m'lady."

She leaned so near, he could feel her warm breath upon

his neck. "'Tis the least I can do for my knight in shining armor." Och, there was the sultry voice he adored.

He chuckled. "Is that all it takes to get you to take note of me—pull you from the prison coach, fight off a crew of hostile sailors, take a musket shot to the leg?"

Her hands stilled. "My word, when you put it like that, I realize how incredibly insensitive I've been."

"Nay, m'lady. It is I who have been insensitive." He glanced over his shoulder. Her ruby lips parted with her blue-eyed stare. God's bones, if he weren't wedged into the tub with one leg hanging over the side, he'd kiss her.

She rubbed the soap down his arm, his skin tingling all the way to the tips of his fingers. "What was your childhood like?" she asked, as if needing to change the subject from one that might hurt a bit too much.

"Being the son of a noble, I never wanted for anything. My da was a marquis when I was born. He received a dukedom when I was eighteen." Aiden grinned, thinking back, "I was given ample education—so much so, I tested out of most courses at university."

"Impressive."

He sighed. "It wasn't all work. John and I did everything in our power to ensure we had the governess flummoxed most days."

Maddie laughed, her voice smooth as silk, rolling with the feminine chuckle Aiden loved. He cupped her face with his palm. "In all my childhood, I do not remember ever seeing a face as bonny as yours, Lady Magdalen Keith."

Blushing, she handed him the soap. "And I cannot recall ever being flirted with so unabashedly."

He swirled the cake over his belly. "You think I'm flirting?"

"Perhaps you're so adept at it, you do not even recognize when you are."

"Nay." He scrubbed the soap around his loins, wishing it were she who was doing so. His voice grew deeper. "I was but merely telling the truth."

Maddie inhaled sharply, her tongue slipping to the corner of her mouth while she watched his eyes.

Would she kiss him again? God, he hoped she would. Hoped she'd forget what a daft blighter he'd been at Whitehall. Hoped she wanted him in the way he wanted her. Devil be damned, if they weren't in this predicament, he'd propose right here and now.

But that would be too irresponsible—even for him.

"Are you sure you do not want to climb in?" he asked, making a splash above his lap. "The water's still warm."

She shook her head. "I couldn't. Besides, there isn't room."

Pursing his lips, he nodded. Mayhap a proposal was what she needed to overcome her reluctance. He could be such an arse. She'd asked him about his childhood, and he'd droned on about how normal it had been. Maddie had told him her childhood had been spent in isolation. She'd told him she didn't want to end up like the women in her hospital, or to bear a bastard.

Aye, he knew all these things about the lass, and they made him want her all the more.

A long pause passed between them while they stared at each other. She bit her bottom lip. White teeth slowly scraped over rosy-pink flesh.

Did she have the slightest inkling how seductive she looked?

She stood and wrung her hands. "Shall I turn my back whilst you dry off?"

"Uh…aye."

Aiden wasn't at all convinced he wanted to move, but she was right, he couldn't stay in the cramped tub much longer.

Once she turned, he stepped out and dried himself. The only problem was that his clothes were draped over the chair in front of Maddie.

He attempted to tie the cloth around his hips, but the damned thing fell short by a good ten inches. "Would you mind handing me my shirt?"

"Oh...certainly." As she reached out, she swept his entire stack of clothes to the floor. "Goodness, I am so clumsy."

Aiden lunged forward to snatch his shirt in tandem with Maddie. "I've—"

"—got it," they said together.

She faced him, grasping one side of the linen while he had ahold of the other. "Sorry." Heaven help him, the firelight flickered in her eyes.

"I want ye, lass," he whispered hoarsely.

She licked her lips, her gaze dropping down to where he clutched the cloth in front of his loins.

"I want you, too," she whispered almost inaudibly.

But that was the only thing Aiden needed to hear. Dropping the cloth and the shirt, he swept her in his arms and smothered those delectable pink lips with one claiming kiss. She met him swirl for swirl as he ground himself against her. His need gripped him like a steel vise. "I've wanted you since the first time I laid eyes on you," he growled into her hair.

She kneaded magical fingers up and down his back. "I shouldn't be doing this."

"Aye, you should, and when we escape this mess, I will make you my wife, so help me God."

"Yes," she gasped.

In the blink of an eye, he had her gown unlaced and shoved it from her shoulders.

Deftly he hiked up her chemise and petticoats, moved

his hands to her waist, and lifted her up. "Wrap your legs around me."

Maddie did as he asked.

His knees nearly gave out when her slick core rubbed up and down his cock.

"Do not get me with child," she said in his ear.

"If such a miracle should occur, we shall have to visit a priest with haste, my love." He clenched his teeth against his urge to shove her against the wall and take her right there. For Christ's sake, the bed was but three paces away.

Those had to be the three longest paces of his life. Her breathy sounds of desire roared in his ear. With every step, he could feel her skin growing hotter, her urges growing hotter just like his.

He set her on the bed as gently as he could, then he climbed on top of her. "I cannot wait."

"Nor can I."

Kneeling between her legs, he coaxed her hand lower. "Guide me inside so that I'll not hurt you."

His eyes rolled back when Maddie encircled him and squeezed with just the right amount of pressure. Then she chuckled and their gazes met, heated and on the verge of madness.

Moist heat encircled the tip of his cock, slick, wet, and hot as fire.

No words were necessary after her nod, and he slipped inside—but just a fraction.

Her breath caught.

Aiden squeezed his bum cheeks taut. He stared into her eyes and panted, waiting for her to give him a sign.

With a sigh she gave another nod.

Ever so slowly he slid through the length of her until he met a pillow-soft wall. With a sultry moan, Maddie rocked her hips. Hot woman milked him, surrounded him like a glove. Moving her grip to his buttocks, she showed him what she wanted. Rocking, swirling. In and out.

Merciful heavens, all the dreams he'd had of making love to her paled in comparison to this moment. This one joining of souls took his heart and made it soar. This single moment made all the nights apart and the endless yearning worthwhile. Finally he'd claimed her for his own, and by God, he would make it forever.

She arched her back, and her moans came swiftly. Aiden matched her frenzy with a deep guttural moan as he drove his cock into her again and again, the tight rippling of her inner walls taking him beyond the point of ecstasy. Maddie's fingers sank deeper as her gasps came in short bursts. While she focused on his eyes, a gasp caught in the back of her throat.

Her fervor, her unbridled passion sent him over the edge of pure madness. Throwing back his head, Aiden roared with his release.

As he kissed her, he swore he would never again hurt this woman. He wanted to hold her in his embrace and protect Lady Magdalen Keith forever.

Chapter Twenty-Nine

*I*f someone had told Maddie she was floating on air, she would have believed it. She sighed, as the remnants of sleep still made her dazed and she was a wee bit drunk on love. Not ready to open her eyes, she curled into the soft feather mattress. Last night had been an eve to write stories about, to sing odes about, and to compose passionate harp music for. She'd resisted Aiden with every fiber of her being, but when he uttered the words *I will make you my wife*, her entire outlook changed.

How could she have been so daft? The man—the marquis— had risked his reputation, his life to come to her aid when no one else saw fit to raise a finger to help her. For pity's sake, no one in the queen's antechamber had said a word about how absurd it would be to even think of accusing her of sabotaging the chandelier. Where had it broken and how had it fallen? Surely these questions could be answered with an examination. Who had lowered the chandelier in the first place? How long had it been down before Maddie arrived?

But all these questions faded into oblivion when compared

to the past day and a half of being on the run. She and Aiden had been thrust together in a race for their lives. The oddest part? For some insane reason, the terror of having been arrested and the fear of being pursued now felt worth enduring. She would run to the ends of the earth with Aiden. As long as he was by her side, she could do anything. By the grace of God, she would remain faithful to him for the rest of her days.

Had she finally found her place? Had she finally found love in a man with whom she could raise her own family? A family she'd been deprived of as a child?

Oh Lord in heaven, how much she did love Aiden Murray. It mattered not that he was a marquis who would one day become a duke. She almost wished he were still Aiden Murray, commander and second son. Life would be simpler if she were married to a sailor. But then, sailors were never home, and Maddie couldn't imagine spending months on end without the big Highlander in her bed.

For the love of humanity, when they'd shared passion in the Atholl apartments a year and a half ago, she'd thought him the bravest man she'd ever laid eyes upon. Little did she know that Aiden had some growing yet to do. Perhaps not in height, but in the time he'd spent away at sea, he'd become a full-fledged man. His chest had grown larger and even more muscled. His arms were thicker, too. Everything about him was powerful and every bit Highland male.

Mm, mm, what a man.

If all men were thusly appointed with banded muscle and rippling flesh, not a woman would ever entertain the notion of leaving her bedchamber. Though she was not a small wisp of a lass, he could lift her with one arm. He could fight off three attackers at once—even with a nasty gash in his leg.

And he said he would make her his wife.

Happiness swelled in her breast.

Maddie slid her palm over the bed linens and opened her eyes. The man of her dreams no longer slept beside her. She rose up on her elbow. "Aiden, my love?"

When he didn't answer, she sat up straight, clutching the bedclothes under her chin.

Across the chamber a plate of cheese and bread sat beside a wooden cup. She slid into her chemise, tied her petticoats around her waist, then tied her stays loosely in front. If they would be riding all day, she didn't need a cinched waist making her woozy. After securing her hair in a plait, she pattered to the table. Maddie hoped Aiden wouldn't be away for long.

After she ate, she used the needle and thread to mend the tear in the shoulder of her gown. When that was done, she paced in front of the hearth for a time before taking a seat and pouring a second cup of cider.

Maddie nearly spilled the drink down the front of her chemise when the door opened. Aiden grinned as he stepped inside. "You found the food."

"Thank you." She glanced at the parcels in his hands. "You've been gone for a time."

"Aye. I dispatched the missive to your father."

"Do you think it is safe?"

"I took precautions. Signed it 'Commander Murray of the *Royal Mary*.' I'm guessing the redcoats in these parts will be looking for a marquis."

Maddie took a careful sip. "Good thinking."

"I purchased another horse—one a bit more robust than the gelding." He set the parcels on the table.

"Oh?" She pretended to frown. "I rather liked riding double with you."

"Me as well, but the old fella will last a lot longer with one rider, and the lighter of the pair of us at that. We can ride faster if we run into trouble."

"Do you think we will?"

"One never kens. I'd reckon news has reached Edinburgh by now. If I were Captain Child, I would have dispatched missives from Alnwick with every vessel sailing north."

"Blast."

He untied a parcel and held up a large woolen plaid. "I reckoned we would look a wee bit suspicious wearing cloaks, so I opted for your blanket idea—an arisaid for you, and I'll tie an additional plaid to my saddle." He nodded to her gown. "You'd best dress."

She stood. "What's in the other parcel?"

"Oatcakes, bully beef, and a water skin."

She grinned, stepping into the heavy damask and sliding her arms into the sleeves. "You thought of everything."

He moved behind her and took up the laces. "If we stick to the byways we can skirt around Edinburgh. Once we slip past Stirling, we'll be out of danger."

"How far is it from Stirling to your lands?"

"Sixty miles or so."

"Sixty? Why, that's a two days' ride, is it not?"

"Aye, but Stirling is the gateway to the Highlands. Once we're past her walls, it will be easier to stay hidden."

* * *

Riding over unfamiliar roads, Aiden would have felt a fair bit more comfortable traveling by sea. He didn't know the Lowlands well. Even his father preferred to take a transport from the port in Leith before riding horses to London to attend court. Aiden's heart lightened a bit when they passed a signpost reading "Edinburgh Castle 48 Miles." If all went well, they might be able to traverse the distance in a day.

Maddie slowed her mount. "I thought you said we're not riding through Edinburgh."

"We're not. When Craigmillar Castle comes into view we'll turn west—give the burgh a wide berth, then skirt around the Firth of Forth. We can cross just north of Stirling."

"I'm glad you have it all planned, because I hardly ken north from south." She tapped her heels and trotted alongside him. "Aside from my stay in London, I've never been more than fifty miles from Stonehaven."

"Mayhap I should take you across the Channel to the Continent after this is over. There is ever so much to see beyond our island."

She patted her gelding's neck. "Take me into the midst of a war?"

"I doubt we will be at war forever."

"Well, no, thank you. I want to go home and stay put."

Honestly, building a life in the Highlands had its appeal. They'd live in Blair Castle, and have the protection of the Atholl men. As long as the crown didn't meddle in his affairs, all would be splendid.

Five or so miles northwest of Coldstream, Aiden stopped looking over his shoulder. No one had followed. He'd even looked back when they crested a hill. Aside from a farmer with a wagonload of hay, there was no one on the road this morning. And the road was adequate—two wheel tracks all the way, as if it was used frequently, and the milepost was a testament to that as well.

As long as they didn't encounter a battalion of dragoons, they should be fine. Even if they did, Aiden doubted there'd be trouble. News of Maddie's escape and his involvement might have reached Edinburgh. He thought it unlikely that soldiers scouting this far south would have yet received word—though not impossible.

When they crested the next hill, a gust of wind hit them hard, making Maddie's arisaid billow. She pulled it closed and peered up at the sky. "It looks like rain."

The first setback.

Indeed, low-hanging gray clouds sailed on a path straight for them. "Aye, this time of year we can expect rain near every day."

Maddie shook with chattering teeth. "Should we look for shelter?"

"Och, you're not afraid of a wee bit o' rain, are you, lass?"

"Just tired of being wet."

"Mayhap if we pass a barn we can wait out the squall." The path led into a copse of trees. The wind blew their golden leaves in spirals as they showered to the ground. The gale howled and the trees groaned. With the racket, a sense of dread snaked around Aiden's neck. He spurred his horse to a canter. "Let us haste out of the wood."

When he turned back to ensure Maddie followed, the dread hit him in the gut like a block of ice.

Four riders wearing flour sacks over their heads were closing in on Maddie's gelding.

He'd heard many a tale about lawlessness on the borders, and the sight of the outlaws made his blood run cold. "Faster!" Aiden hollered, holding back long enough for her to catch up. "Reivers."

She glanced back. "Oh God."

"Dig in your heels." Damnation, neither of them was wearing spurs, and he bet everyone in the mob behind them wore a set.

Driving rain stung his face as they galloped through the wood. His heart thundered while Aiden desperately searched for a farmhouse—or any sign of humanity they could run to.

These were outlaws for certain—fabled border reivers

who preyed on their English neighbors and anyone else who happened to pass through their lands. The horses snorted as their hooves pummeled the earth.

Aiden pulled up when, around the bend, they were met with a white-masked varlet aiming a pistol their way.

Good God, they set a trap.

Charging down a path to the right, he grabbed one of Maddie's reins and led her in the only direction not blocked by outlaws. Harder and harder he kicked his heels while the skies above flashed with lightning, followed by a thunderous boom.

Blinded by spitting rain, he pushed the horses forward, demanding more speed.

The trees opened to an enormous outcropping, forcing Aiden to pull to a stop. Fanning their horses into an arc, the outlaws surrounded them. Aiden had led them straight into their snare.

Aiden pulled Maddie's horse behind him, then drew his sword, his hand slipping on the wet hilt.

"You're outnumbered, mate," said the tallest through his makeshift mask.

Aiden sliced his sword through the air in an X. "I can take the lot of you, ye milk-livered backstabbers."

The men encroached, walking their horses closer.

"I mean it." Aiden slashed his sword again while rainwater streamed into this eyes. "Stay back."

"Give us your purse," said one.

Aiden shifted his gaze across the bedraggled lot of bandits, buying time. "Is that all you want? A wee bit of coin?"

"And the lass," said a shorter one. He didn't have a firm grip on his sword, and was clearly the weakest of the lot.

"Not on your life." Baring his teeth, Aiden spurred his mount toward the weakest and with an upward blow knocked the sword from the blighter's hand, sending him toppling backward.

In a blur the outlaws attacked from all sides. Aiden spun his mount, praying Maddie was all right. As the blades hacked and jabbed, he couldn't spare a blink to glance her way.

Hit from behind, he crashed over his horse's withers only to meet a blade swinging toward his face. As he countered to the right, his horse bucked and reared. Unable to keep his seat, Aiden crashed to the mud. His backside hit hard, but the pain didn't register. Springing to his feet, he charged the nearest assailant, cutting the cur across the flank.

Bellowing, the outlaw countered with a pommel strike to the top of Aiden's head. His eyes rolled back and his gut churned as he tightened his fist around his sword.

His stomach heaved.

His knees buckled and the world went black.

* * *

Shivering with cold and lying in the mud, Aiden forced himself to open his eyes. Through the misty rain he made out two corpses but five paces away—the two he'd struck down before being bludgeoned. His skull pounded as if it had been cracked in half. He slid his hand over his hair, then regarded the sticky blood covering his fingers. Moving to his knees, he vomited over and over again, until he brought up yellow bile that burned his throat raw.

His gaze swept the surroundings for Magdalen. His shoulders dropped like an anvil the size of the Bass Rock had been chained around his neck.

Christ, he felt like shite—worse, the rain had soaked him clean through. He pressed the heels of his hands to his temples, willing the world to stop spinning.

Throwing back his head, he bellowed, "Maaaaaaddieeeee!"

Hunched over in a crouch, he waited for her to respond. A chill iced through his blood, though it did not surprise him when he heard nothing but the call of the birds in response. Grunting like an ox, he lumbered to his feet and swiped his hand over his eyes to clear his vision.

The bastards had taken everything—his sword, dirk, and sporran, his horse, and, worst of all, Maddie. He couldn't even begin to think about what they would do to her.

Rubbing his arms, he snorted. At least the miserable curs hadn't found his daggers. They must have thought him dead like their comrades, else someone would have run him through. He stumbled over to one of the corpses. "Where the bloody hell are you from?" he asked, nudging him with his toe.

The man's lifeless body flopped. Well, Aiden would find out soon enough. Damn it all, he'd flashed a bit of coin in Coldstream. Someone must have tipped the bastards off, though they could have been highwaymen lying in ambush, waiting to plunder the first passerby.

Aiden searched the dead men for weapons and came up empty.

Bloody marvelous. Stranded in the Lowlands with nothing but two daggers and the sopping-wet clothes on my back. No greater marquis vagabond hath there ever been.

Carefully he stepped around the clearing and examined the tracks. One of the horses had thrown a shoe, making it easier to track.

Aiden coughed back his next heave and wiped his mouth on his arm. He'd follow Maddie to the ends of the earth if needed. No, he'd not behave like a wilting flower and succumb to a knock on the head. He was a Murray, goddammit. He'd fought in countless sea battles and had survived. No illbreeding band of outlaws would get the better of him.

And if they lay one finger on my woman, I'll sever their ballocks and stuff them down their throats.

Stumbling ahead, Aiden focused on the print with the missing horseshoe. A mile later his head didn't hurt quite so much. Aye, he felt like shite, but he pushed his pain to the back of his mind and focused on one thing.

Magdalen Keith.

Another mile and he hastened his pace to an easy trot, all the while imagining the many ways in which he would kill the miserable outlaws—men who were too cowardly to show their faces. Men who had no right to traverse the soil of his beloved Scotland.

Chapter Thirty

*T*he hairy brute who appeared to be the band's leader pulled Maddie from her mount and shoved her into a horse stall. "Two of my kin died because of you and that backstabbing bastard who tried to butcher us."

Butcher? Aiden was defending us.

She scooted out of reach of his boot. She wouldn't put it past this monster to try to give her a kick. Her throat was sore from tensing, and from suppressing anguished wails while they forced her farther away from Aiden's body.

"Och, 'tis a good thing I struck him on top of his skull," said a second man, holding up Aiden's sporran. Then he glared at Maddie. "We should have killed the wench with the Highlander."

Her entire body tensed. Her breathing came in short gasps. She'd watched it all. After the blow to the head, Aiden had dropped like a sack of grain to his face.

Dead.

God, no. I still cannot believe it.

She couldn't think straight. Her wrists bound, she clenched her fists against her body while she shook.

The brute eyed her while he grumbled, "Kill a wench as bonny as this one? Nay, nay, I aim to claim my reward from her afore we do her in."

Sweat stung under her arms. Pulling down the corners of her mouth, she glared at the murderer standing before her. A lowlife of the worst sort. "You. Will. Not. Touch me."

"Ye think not?" He laughed like an evil banshee. "Och, MacFee, the wee lassie is spewing threats."

Maddie kept her eyes on the brute while she slid to the far corner. Why couldn't he leave her alone? She swept her gaze across the stall, looking for a way out. She had no weapon—not even an eating knife.

The beast sauntered toward her. Ugly, with bushy eyebrows and a black beard that took up most of his face, he should have kept the flour sack over his head. "I aim to have a wee bit o' fun with you." He reached for his belt and tugged.

Maddie shook her head. "You'd best stay back."

With a yellow-toothed sneer, he cast the belt to the ground. "Or what? Ye think you can come after a burly man the likes of me?"

"If you lay a finger on me, you'll live to regret it." She prayed. Surely her father would rain vengeance—if anyone ever found her body.

Dropping to his knees, he reached back and grabbed her plait, pulling hard. "Now I suggest you scoot down flat on your back and spread your legs. Make it easy on yourself."

A mixture of terror and revulsion made the air whoosh from her lungs. She couldn't breathe. "No," she shrieked, and spit in his face.

"Bitch," he snapped, wiping away the spittle with his

shoulder, and pulling her plait so hard her neck was about to snap. "You prefer it rough, do you?"

Thrashing her head from side to side, she pounded her bound fists against his chest. "Leave me be!"

He grabbed her chin in a dirty palm and licked her across the lips. "Ha ha." He pressed his body against hers. "Struggle all you want, lass. I like it when my wench has a bit of kick."

"Bhreac," called MacFee from outside the stall. "Come have a look at this."

"I'm busy," growled the black-bearded swine.

"You want your bare arse shot whilst you swive the wench?"

The brute pushed Maddie against the wall. Her head hit hard. Then he turned his face away. "What are you on about, MacFee?"

"Come."

Bhreac pointed to Maddie and scowled. "I'll be back." Then he picked up his belt.

Maddie gulped, watching his retreating form. She couldn't allow him near her again. He closed the stall door, the iron bolt scraping into place. Locked inside with no escape, she hid her face in her palms and silently screamed. Oh God, how had she ended up in this mess? Accused of trying to assassinate the queen, and now captured by a band of lawless tinkers? And with Aiden's lifeless body lying in the mud back at the outcropping?

How could she escape these murderers?

Aiden needed a proper burial. Though she'd seen the blow to his head with her own eyes, she still couldn't believe he was gone.

God, no. It cannot be.

"You called me away for this?" Bhreac's deep voice seeped through the wall.

" 'Tis a document seal."

"I bloody well ken what it is."

"But 'tis fancy—with a stag's head, like it belongs to someone important."

"Och, that pair were tinkers for certain. What I want to ken is how much coin did you find?"

"A few guineas mainly...uh...but the booty isn't why I called you out here."

"Fuck," Bhreac growled. "What are a mob of dragoons doing riding on our lands?"

Maddie's heart hammered. What was worse, facing the noose or being raped and having her throat cut? Her entire body froze. She could scarcely breathe.

"Dunno, but I wouldn't be surprised if it has something to do with this seal."

"Well, whatever you do, don't show it to the bastards. Hide the booty. What little there is. I'll go silence our wee plaything." With another scrape of the bolt, Bhreac stepped into the stall holding a rag in his hand. "Tell me true. Why would we have dragoons breathing down our necks?"

Maddie cringed. "Because they're hunting highwaymen and shipping them to the Colonies, I'd reckon."

"Bitch." The lout lunged forward and gagged her with a filthy rag, tying it behind her head. "I'm warning you, not a peep, or you'll be the first to die."

When the sound of horses approached, he moved to the door.

"Jesus," cursed MacFee. "I kent we should have brought the bodies back here for burial."

The hoofbeats grew nearer, then stopped. "Hello the barn," said a man with an English accent.

"Hiya."

"We found these corpses a few miles north of here.

You wouldn't happen to know who they are?" asked the Englishman.

"Good God." Bhreac sounded almost believably bereft. "They were kin."

"You have any idea what happened?"

"Nay." Footsteps crunched the ground. "Wonder what they were doing up there?"

"We thought the same. We're following a man and a woman, but their trail went cold after we found this pair run through."

Pair? Maddie's heart skipped a beat. *Run through? Where is Aiden?*

"They murdered my cousins?" Bhreac bellowed as if he'd been shot with an arrow to the heart. "Who are these outlaws?"

Maddie choked back a gasp through her gag.

"Gave a name of Mr. and Mrs. Blair to Captain Child. He said the couple stowed away on his ship—looked like they were running from Her Majesty's soldiers when they sailed from London."

Pardon? Maddie sat forward. *We were paying passengers, for pity's sake.*

"Do you reckon there's a reward for these murdering varlets?" asked the black-bearded cur.

And now the pillaging thief is looking for more booty.

"Might be. Haven't heard of one as of yet, but if they plundered your kin, they'll hang for certain," the soldier said with conviction. "I've sent a missive to London, telling them we're on their trail. Odd, though…."

"What's that?"

"The tracks led us straight here."

"Er…well, ah, thanks for bringing our kin," Bhreac mumbled. "After we've given them a right Christian burial, we'll be seeking our vengeance."

"You'd best let the government troops take care of justice—but if you come across any more information as to the whereabouts of that pair, I'd be obliged if you reported it to the garrison in Kelso."

"Will do. Thank you, Captain."

"Richardson."

Maddie sat very still and listened to the horses ride away. If she had tried to cry out through the gag, she would have been arrested and taken back to London. And where was Aiden? The dragoons had found only two bodies. Was there hope?

She sank her fingers into the hay and touched something smooth.

"Give me that seal," growled Bhreac from beyond the wall before the latch to the stall scraped and the door opened.

Gradually Maddie moved her hands and folded them in her lap.

"Mrs. Blair, is it?"

She gave a single nod.

"Well then." He moved forward and held out Aiden's seal. "Tell me why your husband was carrying this."

"A-oi-a-oi-a," she garbled through the gag.

"Bloody hell." He slipped back and untied the rag. "Speak fast, for I am not a patient man."

Maddie spat out gritty dirt. "'Tis a document seal, you buffoon."

"Of someone important, for certain." He twisted the rag between his fists. "You ken what I reckon?"

Not giving him the satisfaction of a reply, she looked away.

"I reckon you're in trouble with the government, and moreover, once Captain Richardson receives a reply from London, my guess is there will be a reward for your head, and I aim to claim it—and the same for the ornery varlet you were traveling with."

Her chin tilted upward. "I thought you said you killed him."

"I did. But dead men don't disappear."

* * *

Aiden hid behind an old ruin of crumbling stone and watched the soldiers ride away from the decrepit barn. Beside it stood a sod shieling with grass sprouting from its thatched roof. With the absence of a chimney, smoke seeped out one end.

So it appeared Captain Child had sent the dragoons after them from Alnwick.

The entire borderlands would be crawling with redcoats itching to make a name for themselves.

At present, however, Aiden harbored more worry about the outlaws who'd kidnapped Maddie. During the entire interchange between the brigands and the troops, he'd feared the bastards would hand her over to the authorities. Stealing her back from a few scraggly outlaws would be a hell of a lot easier than breaking her out of some prison guarded by innumerous dragoons.

He'd run from the clearing and dodged the soldiers as they rode up and back along the path he was following, and now his legs were spent along with his throbbing head.

Chasing after a mob of dragoons on horseback could have set him back days, but if Maddie was still with the outlaws, his chances were better.

Once the redcoats were gone, Aiden crouched low and scurried to the back of the barn, where he'd be out of sight. Pulling an ax from a chopping block, he almost grinned. For once fortune might be with him.

Now I have a weapon, you bastards.

"I thought you said you killed him." Maddie's muffled voice came through the wall, thank the Lord.

"I did. But dead men don't disappear," came the gruff voice of one of the lowlife maggots who'd attacked them.

Aiden's blood boiled.

At least she's still alive.

"I'll ask you once…why are the dragoons looking for you?"

"You're mistaken."

Something banged loudly. "You rutting bitch, you'll give me answers."

Maddie shrieked with pain.

Tightening his grip on the ax handle, Aiden sprinted for the entry.

More shouts came.

Against his gut instincts, he forced himself to stop at the open door. He pressed his back against the wall and peered around the doorjamb.

One of the attackers stood at the entry to a horse stall, chuckling.

Another is in there with Maddie.

Aiden checked both ways.

Where's the third blighter?

Then he looked to the smoke seeping through the shieling roof.

In the cottage?

He'd find out soon enough.

Taking in a deep breath, Aiden wielded the ax over his head and rushed inside. Silently, he cleaved the first murderous varlet in two and crouched, ready for attack, as he shifted his gaze into the stall.

The man standing over Maddie whipped around, brandishing a dirk. "What is—?" With a snort he scooted forward. "I should have plunged my blade through your heart when you were lying there like a dead man."

Stepping through the doorway, Aiden readied the ax and

eyed his quarry. He crossed his feet in a grapevine, circling to the side. "Are you all right, Maddie?" he asked while staring at the beefy swine.

"Aye," she said.

"But *you* won't be." The brute lunged forward with two hissing slashes of his knife.

Sucking in his gut to avoid being cut open, Aiden hopped back. He hefted the ax over his head, then down in an arc. With a half-turn, he used the momentum to continue the circle, heaving an upward chop.

The bastard hopped aside, spinning and aiming his blade at Aiden's flank. He missed his target by a hairbreadth and stumbled toward the wall.

Aiden saw his chance. He swung the ax and hit the blackguard square in the back.

The man roared as he crashed face-first to the ground.

"Arrggh!" Aiden used all the strength in his arms to dislodge the ax, then tottered back, quickly regaining his feet and raising the weapon over his head. Bellowing and baring his teeth, he lunged for the kill.

The dirk's blade flashed in the corner of his eye as the man rolled. Blood poured out of his mouth while he pushed himself up and slashed the knife at Aiden's throat.

Aiden twisted to elude the strike and stumbled off balance. Gripping the ax, he stutter-stepped into the wall.

"No!" screamed Maddie behind him.

Aiden used the wall to push off for another attack.

The man staggered back.

Both hands over her head, Maddie sprang between them.

Aiden jerked sideways, missing her by an inch.

The man's dirk angled upward.

"No!" she shrieked again, slicing a blade across the murderer's neck. Gasping, she skittered out of the way. The black-bearded face elongated in a stunned gape. And then the man dropped to his face.

Casting the ax aside, Aiden rushed to Maddie and wrapped her in his arms. "Thank God you're alive."

"I-I-I . . . a-a-a-and you as well!" She leaned into him as he pressed his lips to her hair.

"Och, I cannot believe your bravery."

"I-I, he-he was about to kill you."

"Nay, 'twas the other way around, lass. But thank the stars you saved me a wee bit o' time." He closed his eyes and squeezed her tighter. Dear God, he'd almost lost her. He buried his nose in her hair, breathing in her scent, the sweetness calming the savage beast within. "Come, let us away from all this death."

She held up her bound hands. "This rope has burned my skin raw."

"Christ, how many times must you end up in bondage?" He made quick work of untying her wrists. "We must make haste."

She rubbed her skin and hissed. "The redcoats are after us."

"I saw them—they're on our trail, aye?"

She nodded. "Captain Child alerted them."

"The milk-livered fiend." Aiden looked to the stall doorway. "Where is the third man?"

"Not certain. Bhreac said something about food when we first arrived."

"Then I reckon he's in the shieling."

Maddie looked to the dead man. "So much blood." She held up her stained fingers, then wiped them on the dirty straw.

"Come." Standing, Aiden helped the lass to her feet. "I hate to make you rush, but there will be time to clean up once we're away from here."

"You're not going anywhere," said a menacing voice from the door.

Aiden whipped around and dived for the ax, his fingers missing it by an inch.

The third outlaw brandished a musket, holding it to his shoulder with a finger twitching on the trigger. He didn't look a day over sixteen. "Halt, else you'll be the first with a ball of lead in your belly."

Holding up his hands, Aiden moved in front of Maddie to protect her from a shot. "I can make you a wealthy man if you give me your weapon." He inched forward and stretched out his palm, keeping it steady.

The cur scooted back a step and coughed out a nervous laugh. "Right, you're a pair of murdering tinkers, you are."

"You're wrong," Maddie said from behind. "He's a marquis. Bhreac has his seal in his pocket."

When the outlaw shifted his gaze, Aiden leaped forward and grabbed the musket barrel, twisting it upward. The man's finger closed on the trigger. An earsplitting boom blasted through the stall, followed by a shower of debris falling from the wall.

Gnashing his teeth, Aiden continued to twist the musket until it broke from the man's grip. Using the upward force, he smashed the butt into the outlaw's face.

The varlet's head snapped back with a roll of his eyes and he toppled backward. Aiden stretched for Bhreac's dirk and crouched over the man.

"No." Maddie grasped his shoulder. "He's only a lad."

"Aye, and he just tried to kill us." Aiden tapped the wastrel with the toe of his shoe. He was out cold. Satisfied, Aiden pulled Maddie out of the stall and bolted it shut. The lad could use the ax to free himself when and if he awoke. "It'll be dark soon and safer to travel with those dragoons about.

Go to the cottage and pack up whatever food you can find. I'll collect weapons and saddle a pair of horses."

"Straightaway."

He caught her arm before she left and pulled her in for a kiss. Chuckling, he pushed the hair away from her face. "Where did you find that rusty knife?"

"Under the straw."

"'Tis a miracle the thing was sharp enough to cut through flesh."

"Thank heavens it did."

He brushed his finger over her silken cheek. "Thank heavens for you, lass."

Chapter Thirty-One

The wind blew so hard, Maddie clutched her arisaid around her shoulders and hunched behind the horse's withers. Little good that did. Her teeth chattered and her ears hurt from the cold. She'd have given a year's allotment just to sit before a hearth in an overstuffed chair with her feet up on a stool.

"How are you holding up?" Aiden asked.

She stilled her shivers long enough to answer. "I'm c-cold."

He looked to the east—looming and dark as the rest of the sky. "I reckon it will be dawn in a few hours."

"Then will we stop to rest?"

"Aye." When they hit a burn Aiden pulled up. He pointed. "What's that yonder?"

It looked like a lean-to. "An animal shelter?"

"That'll do. Though I wish we'd come upon a forest."

"I don't think that's likely on the borders—at least that's what I've heard."

The sky did lighten a tad once they dismounted. Taking a few steps proved torturous. After countless hours in the saddle, everything hurt. Her movements grew sluggish. Sighing, she untied the food parcel and bedroll from the back of her horse. At least they'd found enough supplies at the shieling to manage for a time.

Indeed, the structure they entered looked like a dilapidated animal shelter of some sort. There were holes in the roof and the ground was damp.

Aiden tossed his bedroll against a wall. "If you can pull out some cheese and oatcakes, I'll set to cutting rushes to make up a pallet."

"Very well." Maddie couldn't decide what she needed more—sleep or food. Fortunately, Aiden had made the decision for her.

She set out the food on a linen cloth, then gathered some kindling for a fire. When she pulled out the flint, Aiden stilled her hand. "No fire."

"Honestly?" Her heart sank. "But it's freezing—not just a wee bit cold. I wouldn't be surprised if it started snowing."

"We'll huddle together in the back. It'll keep us out of the wind."

"No fire?" she tried again.

"Nay, but not to worry, I'm as warm as a brazier."

"You're not cold?"

He grinned. How could his dimples look so bonny at a time like this? "I didn't say that."

After their meager meal, they bedded down atop the rushes. Aiden had Maddie face the wall on her side and spooned his body behind hers. With a woolen blanket beneath and two on top, it was a great deal more comfortable than being on the horse in the wind, but nothing like the narrow feather mattress they'd shared in Coldstream.

It didn't matter. Maddie pushed comfort from her mind and focused on the warmth of Aiden's body pressed against her back, the strength of his arm draped over her waist and holding her tight. Weariness made her limbs heavy, and she closed her eyes for what didn't seem like anywhere near long enough.

* * *

When Aiden opened his eyes, daylight shone through every crevice in the shack. He didn't want to be awake. Aye, it was worth enduring the rock pushing into his hip to have Maddie's soft curves spooned against his body. Her enticing bottom nestled against his loins. He closed his eyes and savored her. Even though she'd ridden through hell and had been locked in a horse stall, she still managed to smell like a vat of simmering lilacs. The only problem—if he didn't rise and relieve himself in the next minute, Maddie wouldn't be so happy sleeping anywhere near him ever again.

Once he stepped outside, he moved around the corner and assumed the position. A heavenly smile turned up the corners of his lips with the release of pressure while his bladder emptied. Last night he'd hobbled the horses, and now they grazed nearby with their saddles on—an inch of snow atop them. He couldn't be too careful with dragoons patrolling the border like red ants.

Then his tongue went completely dry. Smoke rose in the distance. He looked closer and saw white tents dotting the hilltop. Good God, an encampment of government troops loomed not even a mile away.

Aiden quickly adjusted himself while gaining his bearings. To the northeast the beginnings of society lined the horizon, with small farmhouses peppering the green hills. Last night they'd ridden all the way to the outskirts of Edinburgh for certain—right where Aiden wanted to be, except for the troops practically breathing on top of them.

Slipping back into the shelter, he hated to rouse Maddie,

but they needed to sneak away north as quickly as possible. He shook her shoulder. "Come, lass, we must make haste."

She batted his hand away. "No."

"Maddie, the redcoats can see us."

Sucking in a gasp, the lass sat bolt upright. "What did you say?"

"Quickly. Take care of your needs whilst I roll up our things. We ride as soon as you're ready."

Aiden worked fast, then used the lean-to for cover while he tied the bedrolls and food parcels behind the horses' saddles. When Maddie reappeared, he was tightening her gelding's girth strap. "Mount up," he whispered. "We'll start out nice and slow as if we were out for a Sunday ride."

She nodded, her eyes filled with trust.

"Let me give you a leg up." He cupped his hands and she stepped into them as she'd done several times now. "Remember, we are Mr. and Mrs. Grant."

"But do you not think the dragoons will know that from Coldstream? I'll wager they spoke to Mrs. Swinton at the inn."

"Bloody hell," Aiden cursed. But Maddie was right. "Let's use Armstrong. That's a good Lowland name. Mr. and Mrs. Armstrong from Ayrshire." He mounted and took up his reins. "You ready, lass?"

"I am, and once the redcoats are well behind us I'll pay you a guinea to sleep on a real bed this night."

"Do you have one?"

"Not here, but I have several in my hiding place at home."

"Aye, so you're a hoarder, are you?" He chuckled, trying to look normal while glancing back at the dragoons' camp.

"I'm practical. I'd call it saving for an emergency."

Aiden cringed as red-coated riders crested the hill. "Well, lass, you'd best gird your loins, 'cause we're having an emergency of our own just about now."

When Maddie turned her head, she gasped. "Do you think we should make a run for it?"

"Nay. Let us go with the plan. If we run they'll suspect us for certain." Aiden steered his mount around a stone so he wouldn't appear obvious when he again looked back. There were a bloody dozen of them. "Pray they make a turn and leave us be."

Unfortunately, their praying had little effect. Within a mile the redcoats stopped them.

Aiden pulled on his reins while Maddie did the same beside him. "Good morrow, soldiers. May I help you with something?" he asked, rolling his *r*'s with a Highland brogue thick enough to be mistaken for a Shetlander's.

"We're looking for a pair of riders—a man and a woman much like yourselves," said a dragoon dressed in a sergeant's uniform.

Aiden frowned and scratched the stubble on his chin. "I'd reckon you see a number of couples traveling on any given day."

"What is your name?" asked the sergeant.

Aiden looked the man in the eye, affecting his most sober expression. "Mr. and Mrs. Armstrong from Ayrshire."

"What brings you all the way to the Lothians?"

"Vising my wife's kin in Dunbar—a-a wedding."

Maddie smiled and nodded as a good wife ought.

"Hmm." The sergeant looked warily at the lass. "And from where in Ayrshire do you hail?"

Aiden's mind raced. He'd sailed past Ayr a few times— that would have to do. "Ayr, of course."

"Then you must know the governor. He's a good friend of mine."

Damnation, the dragoon was persistent. "Nay, I cannot say I've had the pleasure of meeting him face-to-face."

The sergeant squinted. "Tell me, what's the governor's name?"

Good God, mayhap Aiden should have omitted the face-to-face part. He made eye contact with Maddie and gave her a sharp nod, praying she'd know what he meant. "Forgive me, but I cannot remember, sir."

The man pointed to a pair of sentinels. "I'm afraid we'll need to take you to Edinburgh Castle for further questioning and proper identification."

"Not this day." Aiden kicked his heels while he slapped Maddie's steed's backside. Breaking through the circle of soldiers, they took up a gallop. Once free, Aiden chanced a backward glance. Good lass, Maddie stayed right on his heels. But the dragoons were not far behind.

With no time to talk, Aiden slapped his reins and kicked his heels, praying for a miracle.

Chapter Thirty-Two

*F*roth coated the horse's neck while he snorted loudly with exertion. No matter how hard Maddie kicked her heels, with every step her mount lost ground to Aiden's larger, faster horse.

Her heart thundered as the redcoats drew nearer.

Ahead Aiden's hackney splashed through a burn.

Gripping her gelding's mane, Maddie leaned farther forward and requested a jump. The horse's rear dipped as the beast skidded to a stop. Holding on for dear life, she dug in her heels. "Go, go, go!"

"Not this time." Thundering up from behind, a soldier reached for her bridle.

At the top of the hill, Aiden turned.

"Don't bother with him." The sergeant waved a dismissive hand. "The missive we received from London this morn said they want the girl."

As a dragoon locked her wrists in manacles, her heart sank. No matter what they did, it was her destiny to be marched up to the gallows and hanged with her hands bound. "I am innocent," she said.

"Aye?" The man clicked a padlock in place. "That's what they all say."

Perhaps they are all innocent. I would believe that, given the sham by which I have been accused.

* * *

When Aiden realized Maddie had been caught, it was too late. Riding to her rescue and fighting a dozen dragoons would be suicide, and then she'd have no one to fight for her. He followed at a distance, but when the troops turned east on Glasgow Road, it was clear they were taking her to Edinburgh Castle, and he opted for a more circuitous route to the city—one where he'd be less conspicuous.

Now he sat at the back of an alehouse on Grassmarket Street, staring into a tankard of ale and weighing his options.

The sound of heavy boots clomped toward his table, and a big Highlander stopped beside him, wearing a bold kilt and a sword sheathed at his waist.

Aiden slipped his hand to his dirk while his gaze moved from the man's belt up to his broad torso. "You're blocking my view."

"Och, Murray. The last time I saw you, you were kicking my arse at Whitehall."

Good Lord, Reid MacKenzie, the Earl of Seaforth, had put on about two stone of muscle. Springing to his feet, Aiden shook his friend's hand. "Bloody oath, 'tis good to see you."

"Is your ship moored in the Forth?"

Aiden gestured to the seat opposite. "Nay. I've been beached. Regrettably, my brother was killed on the Continent, making me the Marquis of Tullibardine."

"Marquis?" Seaforth gestured for the barmaid to bring two ales. "You outrank me."

"Mayhap, but I could use your help."

The earl's mouth twisted with curiosity. "Aye?"

Leaning forward, Aiden lowered his voice and relayed everything, including Maddie's run-in with Blackiron and Saxonhurst at the ball.

When Aiden finished, Seaforth sat back. "Blackiron and Saxonhurst are snakes for certain. They deserve each other if you ask me. And you say a chandelier fell after it had been lowered for cleaning?"

Aiden took a swig of ale. "Aye, it could have fallen for any number of reasons, with sabotage being the least likely."

"Too right. Do you ken if they're conducting an investigation?"

"They damn well had better be, unless the judicial system has completely collapsed under our incompetent aristocracy. Regardless, I dispatched a missive to the Earl Marischal from Coldstream two days ago."

"And what do they plan to do with Lady Magdalen now they have her locked in Edinburgh jail?"

Aiden thumped his fist on the table. "That, my friend, we need to find out."

"True, but you're not the one to do it."

The hairs on Aiden's nape stood on end. He needed to do *something* before he jumped out of his bloody skin. "I'll not sit idle while Her Ladyship suffers in the bowels of the castle's dungeon."

"Agreed, but first I'll have my man-at-arms make some inquiries." Seaforth downed his ale and stood. "Come. My town house is only a block away. No one will be looking for you there."

Chapter Thirty-Three

Alone and cold, Maddie crouched in a corner of the tiny cell and stared at nothing. A dim glow came from the passageway, but it was not enough for her to see much of anything, which was probably for the best. Judging by the stench, she didn't want to see overmuch. She hadn't eaten a morsel of food since they threw her into Edinburgh Castle's jail. Her fingers shook uncontrollably—worse than they usually did when she was hungry.

Surely they didn't starve people to death in this hellhole. *Do they?*

She'd slept some, but couldn't be certain if it was day or night. The eerie glow from the passageway hadn't changed much. It had flickered a time or two, but that was all.

Her hearing had grown more acute in the darkness. Sounds of moaning and misery resounded from somewhere below. She guessed she was imprisoned in a cell halfway between purgatory and hell—hell being from whence the eerie voices arose.

Something metallic scraped above, like a key in the lock

of the gate of Dunnottar Castle. Sitting erect, Maddie looked toward the sound. Footsteps neared, as if they were descending stairs, coming closer with each step. More than one set of shoes clapped the stone in a stoic cadence. At least the visitors appeared to be in no hurry.

The light grew brighter and the footsteps more even.

Two dragoons stopped outside her cell, their leathery faces appearing like skulls in the torchlight.

Maddie held up her hand to block the blinding glare. It hurt her eyes like the sun. "Who are you?"

"Our names are not important." The man used no courtesy.

She clenched her teeth. "I beg to differ. I want to know who my jailors are."

One shoved a key into her cell's lock. "I'm Corporal Payson, dragoon in charge of recording your confession."

Maddie stood, keeping her back to the wall. "Confession? But I am innocent—how can I confess to a crime I did not commit?"

"You'll confess. They all do." The door screeched on its iron hinges.

Dear Lord, they couldn't do something rash. Could they? She licked her lips, looking beyond Payson to the other blank-faced sentry. "Is it morning? I haven't been given anything to eat or drink since I was tossed into this *vile* cell."

The corporal sauntered toward her, his face blank, unfeeling, and unreadable. "Eating will only make you puke."

She clutched her fists beneath her chin, her nerves fluttering like moth wings. But this was no time to cower. "How dare you use such vulgar language with me? I am the daughter of an earl, not a tinker."

The man grasped the chain between her manacles and yanked. "I don't give a rat's arse who you are. Word is you plotted to assassinate the queen."

"No. How many times do I have to repeat that I did nothing but change the candles on the queen's chandelier? I swear it. I will pledge an oath before the magistrate, before His Holiness the pope, if necessary."

With a shove in her back, the corporal marched her out of the cell. "You're a Catholic, are you?"

A clammy sweat sprang across her skin. Dear Lord, she knew better than to mention His Holiness. "I am but an honest Highland-born woman."

The guard holding the torch inclined his head toward the bowels of the prison. "This way."

With no choice but to trudge onward, Maddie tried to avert her eyes from the horrors. Half-starved men dressed in rags, their eyes sunken and ghostly, stared at her through iron bars. Coughing at the stench, she moved her hands to cover her nose and mouth. "These conditions are deplorable."

"It is a jail, miss."

" 'My lady,' " she corrected him.

Marching onward, the dragoons ignored her until they entered a chamber with a chair, a bucket, and a table pushed against the far wall.

"Sit," ordered the corporal.

Maddie did as commanded while the other dragoon removed one manacle and forced her arms behind her, then locked them to the back of the chair. "You think I am so dangerous that I must be chained?"

No one uttered a sound.

"Have you received word of the investigation into what truly caused the chandelier to fall?" she asked, trying to sound as haughty and in command as Queen Anne herself.

"No."

The other dragoon moved behind her and placed his heavy palms on her shoulders.

Maddie swallowed and looked up at him, but he didn't meet her gaze.

Corporal Payson took a cloth from the table and dunked it into the bucket. "I'll ask you one more time. Were you involved in the plot to assassinate the queen?"

Maddie watched the water drip from the cloth. "Of course not. How many times do I need to say it?"

The corporal's jaw twitched when he nodded to the man behind her. After sliding one arm across her shoulders, the brute grasped her forehead, yanking it back.

Maddie gasped. Her mouth opened wide as her neck kinked with the force.

A snarl stretched across his lips as the sadistic swine wadded the cloth and jammed it into her mouth. "You are guilty as accused." He smashed his hand over the rag.

Maddie's eyes bulged as she convulsed, trying to shake her head from side to side. The rag wasn't drenched in water. Vinegar filled her throat, threatening to drown her. She couldn't breathe. She kicked her legs, her lungs craving air.

Yanking the cloth from her mouth, the corporal glared. "Confess."

Tears stung her eyes. "I cannot."

He slapped her across the face. "You pox-ridden whore, how dare you thwart the truth?"

Her cheek stung as if a hundred angry bees had unleashed their ire. "I am telling the truth!" she shouted, her voice hysterical. Trapped with these vile beasts, she had no place to hide—every horrid thing she'd ever heard about government troops had proved to be true.

By God's grace, she would not bend to their will.

Every muscle in her body tensed as she helplessly watched the dragoon dunk the cloth again. Barely wringing it out, he stood over her. "Admit to being in collusion with the Earl Marischal of Scotland, you filthy Highland bitch."

"Never! My father would nay stoop—"

The soured cloth again filled her mouth.

Gagged her.

The bitter liquid gurgled in her throat, threatening to take her to the drowning depths of hell.

Eyes rolling back, Maddie fought to keep her wits. The memory of craving air while sinking deeper into the sea filled her mind with fear. Her fingers splayed as she stretched her wrists against her manacles. The corporal pushed the cloth harder and deeper this time. "I will not abide liars and murderers!"

Praying for death to take her from this nightmare, Maddie lost control of her limbs as they shook. With her hands chained behind her back, her fingernails clawed at nothing. Her toes curled. Her lungs burned, her eyes rolled back.

Again the corporal pulled the cloth from her mouth. "Admit your deviousness."

"I will never," she snarled back, the conviction infusing her with strength. She knew enough about the law to know confessing would send her to the gallows. Regardless, she was doomed. The only thing she had left was the truth. She refused to give up her honor by lying.

She endured the cloth twice more, gagging and gulping, but forcing her mind to a place of strength. She learned to control her urge to kick and scratch. She overcame the violent tremors and retches. The last time Corporal Payson shoved the vinegar-drenched cloth in her mouth, he levered the heel of his hand up—trying to make her swallow it.

But she clenched her teeth and stared him in the eye.

I vow I will never yield to tyrants.

He took his time drawing the rag from her mouth.

Maddie gave him a steely-eyed glare, swallowing and clearing her throat so that she would be heard without question. "I am the daughter of the Earl Marischal of Scotland, and I do not lie, nor do I engage in plotting against Her Majesty. I will die before I confess to a crime I did not commit."

* * *

A fortnight had passed, and Aiden was ready to wring Seaforth's neck. The earl continually yammered about gaining an audience with the Duke of Argyll. The only problem was that the goddamned duke kept eluding Reid's requests. Argyll was the greatest known backstabber in all the gentry. He'd even had a hand in the Glencoe Massacre, the bastard.

Aiden had the patience of a stallion sniffing a filly in heat, and sitting idle while they built their case and waited for some sort of word from London drove him to the ragged edge. Every waking hour his mind devised ways to launch a rescue. But the goddamned fortress was impenetrable. They locked the prisoners in a dungeon below ground with no windows and no way out.

Aiden knew well enough. He'd dubbed the passageways *the catacombs of hell* long ago when he'd walked through the prison with his da. Aye, he knew the abominable conditions in which Maddie suffered. And every time he closed his eyes, an image of the torture chamber came to mind—archaic and medieval. Some of the most heinous devices ever made resided in that dank hellhole.

Well, he'd had enough. No longer would he tolerate hiding in Seaforth's town house. After securing his weapons, he found the earl in his drawing room.

Seaforth leaned back in his chair. "You look like you're off to fight a battle."

"I'm achieving nothing here. I've decided to ride to Blair Atholl and ready my army."

"To do what, exactly? It would take ten thousand men to seize Edinburgh Castle. That is a fact that has been proven many times over."

Aiden gripped the hilt of his sword. "I'll find a way."

"You'll get your throat cut."

Christ, he'd had a gutful. "You think me a bumbling fop, do you?"

"Of course not. No man who can take me on in the sparring ring is any sort of fop. I've received word from Argyll. Says he's making room in his calendar for a meeting."

"Aye? Mayhap he'll find the time come Yule—"

"M'lord." Seaforth's man MacRae marched into the drawing room. "They have Lady Magdalen locked in the pillory in Grassmarket Square."

"The pillory? They're treating her like a bloody commoner." A fire roiled in Aiden's gut. "This is the last straw." Grumbling under his breath, in two strides he reached the door.

But Seaforth was just as fast, his big hand clamping around Aiden's elbow. "Think before you charge out there like a mad bull."

"You're telling me to think?" He narrowed his eyes. "You'd best release me before you force me to do something rash. I am not only your senior peer, I have two years in the navy under my belt. I'll not cower in these rooms while Her Ladyship suffers the wrath of the mob with her head and wrists trapped between two locked planks of wood."

"By going out there you will risk all we have put in place to see to her release. Not to mention, if anyone discovers you're staying under my roof, we'll never gain an audience with Argyll."

Aiden yanked his arm away from Reid's fingers. "Dammit, can you not see I have no choice? What kind of man would I be sitting but a block away from where the only woman I've ever loved is suffering public humiliation?" He glared into his friend's eyes, ready to fight his way out the door if need be.

Reid's expression softened, though he narrowed his eyes. "Go, but if you're followed do not come back here until well past the witching hour—and use the servants' entry behind the close."

Aiden grasped forearms with his friend, giving a Highland handshake. "Ye ken I would never put your house in jeopardy. And I truly am grateful for your unfettered hospitality. I'll stay clear. Mark me."

With that he slipped out through the servants' quarters and made his way to the Grassmarket. He stopped dead in his tracks when the pillory platform came into view. The wind rushed from his lungs as if someone had thrown a fist to his gut.

A crowd of hecklers surrounded Maddie, shouting jeers and taunts. Her head and hands hung limp as if she'd given up the fight. Her dress was torn and filthy, her lovely blonde tresses in a matted mess.

Clenching his fists, Aiden ran. Two dragoons guarded the rear of the platform, while another pair stood across the square, looking on with their arms folded. The two across the way had muskets slung across their backs.

Take one thing at a time.

As he barreled past the first dragoon, Aiden laid the unsuspecting varlet flat with an elbow to the jaw. The second saw him coming and drew his sword while the crowd grew louder. Aiden snatched his dirk and stopped in a crouch. Circling, he took in deep breaths, resisting his fierce desire to bury his blade in the varlet's gut. "Give me the keys and I might let you live," he growled.

"Not on your life."

"'Tis Tullibardine," someone yelled from the crowd.

"Aiden!" Maddie shouted.

His attention drawn away for a split second, Aiden sensed the dragoon lunge. He hopped aside in the nick of time as the man stumbled forward. Quickly gaining his footing, the dragoon slashed his sword through the air. "So the rumors are true. A marquis helped the vixen escape." He chuckled like a rogue. "Perhaps if I feed the bitch your cods, she'll confess to being a traitor just like her father."

The crowd grew more frenzied, the shouts louder.

A bellow ripped from the depths of his bowels as Aiden charged in. Sword and dirk clashed with a deafening clang of iron. The men were locked in a battle of wills and strength, their faces contorted with determination. Their weapons shook. Steel scraped until their cross guards met. Stronger than an ox, his opponent bared his teeth. "I like a challenge, but you have no place to run."

"And you are torturing an innocent maid," Aiden hissed with a snarl.

"And you're next. I can see my cat-o'-nine-tails streaking your back with its iron teeth."

Strength surged through every fiber of his being as Aiden gnashed his teeth and shoved the brute to the cobbles. Ready to run the man through, he froze when a shot rang out.

Maddie screamed.

The crowd went wild.

Aiden followed through with his strike, but the dragoon rolled.

Another musket fired.

"Aiden, run!" Maddie shouted.

He glanced toward the two musketeers across the way. Barreling toward him with bayonets affixed, they'd multiplied by ten.

"Are you shot?" he yelled.

"No. Run!" she shrieked.

Aiden peered out from under the platform. Musketeers lined the rooftops across the way. Dear God, if he tried to climb the gallows steps, they'd both be shot before he reached the top.

"Know I will free you. Know I will not stop until I can hold you in my arms!" As he shouted the words, he slunk into the crowd, keeping his head down, running away with the mob while the dragoons advanced.

Aiden pushed into the center of a group heading down a close. Glancing over his shoulder repeatedly, he wended his way through the closes and markets that lurked on the city's fringe. He discarded his doublet, plucked a hat from a vendor's table, and stole deeper and deeper into the dark alleyways walked only by the impoverished and destitute.

Chapter Thirty-Four

After the rioting throughout the streets of Edinburgh, Corporal Payson didn't force Maddie to suffer public humiliation by locking her in the Grassmarket pillory again. In fact, she didn't see the black-hearted monster after that. Instead Queen Anne's dragoons left her alone for nearly a month, locked in her dank cell no larger than a broom closet. The bucket at the back hadn't been emptied, and the stench made her eyes water.

With not even a handful of straw to lie upon, Maddie's body ached. The last day she'd been free, she had teased Aiden about sleeping on a feather mattress. Mercy, she'd give her entire dowry for a bit of straw and a meal. Three times a day a sentry stopped by with a bucket of water and a crust of bread—scarcely enough to keep her alive.

She combed her dirty fingers through her matted hair, the chain between her manacles hitting her nose. Would they leave her there to rot until she died? What had happened to Aiden? With no news, she had no way of knowing whether he had been shot or had fled.

But he'd told her he would free her—those fleeting words he'd shouted as he ran from the Grassmarket had buoyed her heart enough to keep her from sinking into a morass of misery.

No one had spoken to her for a month. At least she thought it had been a month. She used a link in her manacles to scratch a notch in the iron bars the third time the sentry came past each day. The emotionless old man just scooped water from the bucket and handed her the ladle without a word. He wouldn't answer a single question.

Not only must she endure being locked in a tiny cell in solitude, the screams and shrieks from those incarcerated deeper in the bowels of the dungeon made her skin crawl. All day and all night someone howled, "Set me free" over and over. Though the pitch was high, the eeriness of it made Maddie wonder if the prisoner was woman or man. Mercy, if she could set her hands on the keys, she'd release the poor tormented soul.

Keys scraped an iron lock in the distance, making her stomach jump. Though it was now a familiar sound, she didn't think it was time for a meal. But perhaps the monotonous hours had melded together since the sentry had awakened her with his last pass. With nothing to indicate whether it was morning or night, she'd become totally disoriented.

Multiple footsteps slapped the stone stairs. Craning her neck to see who might be coming, Maddie used the iron bars to pull herself to her feet. Her legs had grown weak.

Three men carried a torch, and she shaded her eyes against the sudden brightness when they stopped outside her cell.

"Have you received word of my innocence?" she asked, as she had countless times.

"Still harping on about being innocent, are you?" One of the guards unlocked the door. "We've received word you're to be shipped back to London to swing from the Tower's gallows."

Maddie's fingers started trembling again. "Why not hang me from the gallows here and be done with it?"

Where is Aiden?

"Orders are for you to pose as an example to the people of London—show them what happens when someone tries to *murder* the queen."

"I did no such thing."

"Tell that to the magistrate in London." The guard grabbed her arm and yanked her into the corridor. "Now keep your mouth shut, else I'll be forced to gag you."

The mere thought of a gag made perspiration spring across her skin. Maddie could only imagine the sort of filthy rag these monsters would shove in her mouth. It was useless trying to talk to them anyway. They never listened—just mindlessly carried out their orders no matter what.

After marching her outside, the guards made her stand in the back of a wagon and tied her wrists to a post behind the driver's bench. No cowering inside a coach this time. Surrounded by a retinue of dragoons, she was paraded through the streets of Edinburgh as if she were a heinous criminal.

People stopped and heckled. More came out of their shops, throwing rotten food and wadded parchment. The taunts burned her ears:

"The pox to you!"

"Illegitimate swine!"

"Tie her to a stake in the Forth and let us watch the tide rise over her head!"

Maddie shuddered. That had to be the most hateful taunt she had ever heard in her life. How could these people judge her so harshly when she'd done nothing wrong?

The wagon rolled to a stop beside the Leith wharf where

a large eighteen-oar sea galley waited, bobbing in the water. The ship's mast rocked to and fro while the crew labored busily. Men unfurled sails, and one coiled rope while others loaded barrels of stores. They worked efficiently, not a one looking in her direction.

Maddie gasped when the Earl of Seaforth hopped onto the wharf. He gave her a pointed look and held his finger to his lips, then swiped it sideways as if wiping his cheek.

Had Seaforth turned backstabber? He was a queen's man, after all.

"I'll sign for the prisoner," said the earl. "And you'd best give me the key to her manacles. She'll need to relieve herself at some point."

"I'm sending Sentinel Roberts with you to guard the prisoner," said the dragoon.

"Och, I'm certain my brawny Highland men can handle a wee lassie." The earl took a quill from the sentinel and dipped it in the dragoon's pot of ink, then scrawled on the parchment. "Besides, with a full crew I have no room to spare on my ship."

After unchaining her manacles from the pole, another sentinel all but pushed her down the two rungs at the back of the wagon. Stumbling forward, Maddie nearly fell into Seaforth.

He looked down his nose at her and sneered. "MacRae, take charge of the prisoner."

As a Highlander stepped ashore and grasped Maddie's elbow, the dragoon in charge spread his palms to his sides. "I really think we should send our man—"

With a slice of his hand, Seaforth cut him off. "You dare question an earl? I said there was no need for your sentinel to sail with us. Bloody oath, if it will ease your conscience, I shall deliver Lady Magdalen to the Tower myself."

With a loud sigh, the man bowed. "Very well, m'lord."

MacRae led Maddie to the sea galley. "This way, m'lady. Mind the first step. 'Tis rather steep."

"Thank you." This was the first time since her capture that anyone had been courteous. Taking her skirts in bound hands, she raised them only as high as was necessary to take the step without falling.

MacRae followed. "We made a place for you near the stern, where you won't be bothered by the oarsmen."

"That is very kind," she said, though with a tad of sarcasm in her voice. After all, the earl was being paid to ferry her to her death.

Unfortunate a soul cannot die from being mortifyingly, disgracefully, and hideously humiliated.

Seaforth hopped down onto a rowing bench without using the steps. "Weigh anchor," he bellowed, heading for the rudder. "Man the oars and prepare to set a course for the open sea."

Maddie was none too happy to discover she'd be sitting beside the backstabbing earl while he navigated the galley. However, with the heavily armed dragoons staring at her from the wharf, she decided to sit where MacRae instructed. And once they sailed out of earshot, she'd be giving Reid MacKenzie a piece of her mind even if he was an earl.

The backstabber is doing the work of Satan.

"The anchor is stowed, m'lord," shouted a man from the bow.

"Shove off, oarsmen. Head with the wind and make the MacKenzie sail billow..." The orders spewing from Seaforth's mouth seemed as if they would never end.

But the sail flapped, and the mast groaned with the creaking of the boom until suddenly the wind filled the canvas, while the crew of eighteen manned the oars and rowed them to open water. It took only minutes for the galley to pick up speed, and she was on her way on the long voyage back to London.

Maddie wished a sea monster would rise from the depths and devour her in one gulp. If only this nightmare would end. She was tired, her body weak. And now she had to suffer the same punishment in London?

Because she'd changed a few miserable candles?

"M'lady," Seaforth said, leaning toward her and placing a blanket about her shoulders. "I feel it is my duty to inform you that we are not heading to London." He looked back toward the shore. "But I'll not point the galley northward until we've passed Tantallon Castle in North Berwick. By then we should be well away from prying eyes."

Maddie's heart fluttered. "You—we—where?"

"I need you to act like a prisoner going to her doom. Now be a good lass and hang your head like you were doing. We'll take the manacles off after we've turned north, m'lady."

Sitting back, Maddie looked at her hands, then buried her face in them, for she couldn't have wiped the smile from her mouth if she'd been hit between the eyes with one of the oars rowing her to freedom. "I have but one question."

"Aye?" rumbled Seaforth.

"Where is Lord Tullibardine?"

"All will be revealed. Now speak no more."

* * *

As he pulled on the oar with all his might, it was everything Aiden could do not to remove the bonnet from his head and rush back to Maddie. In the few glimpses he'd chanced, the poor lass looked as if she'd been through the bowels of hell.

In the past few days he hadn't shaved, and he'd combed his

hair forward to cover most of his face—even wet it with sea-water for added effect. He looked like a heathen swine, but no one on the wharf had been any the wiser to his presence.

It took a bloody eternity for the galley to pass Tantallon Castle near the Bass Rock, protruding from the white-capped waves with its squawking gannets. The seabirds made the big rock appear white.

When a gannet screeched overhead, Aiden finally allowed himself to turn around. Staring at her folded hands, Maddie hadn't noticed him, but Seaforth grinned and tapped her shoulder. Then he pointed. "Lady Magdalen, I believe there is someone quite anxious to see you."

When she looked up it was as if a ray of sunshine burst through the clouds and lit up her filthy face. She sprang to her feet. "Aiden—ah—I mean, Lord Tullibardine!"

Reid produced a skeleton key. "Allow me to unshackle your wrists, so you can give His Lordship a proper welcome."

After securing his oar, Aiden leaped from one rowing bench to the next until he reached her.

Tears glistened in Maddie's lovely eyes as she drew a hand over her mouth. "I'm afraid I am not fit to be seen, m'lord."

"Och, no." He stepped up to her and pulled the lass into his arms. "I care not if your hair is combed and curled and your face is scrubbed clean. I want to hold you in my arms and never let go."

Her body trembled and shook as she buried her face in his shoulder. Aiden himself teared up. Dear God, the past month had been murder, but they'd done it. Seaforth had insisted on patience, and when the order came to ship Maddie back to London, they were ready. Closing his eyes, he pressed his lips to her forehead. "I never want to allow you out of my sight again, my love."

"But—but—" She couldn't still her breathing enough to finish.

Aiden smoothed his hand over her matted hair, hair that should always be brushed silken smooth and flowing in the wind. But that could be remedied easily enough. "Shhh," he cooed. "Let us sit, and when you are ready, you can ask whatever comes to mind."

Chapter Thirty-Five

Maddie sat on the bench and listened, her hands trembling while Aiden explained how Seaforth had invited the Duke of Argyll, acting governor of Edinburgh Castle, for an evening meal while Aiden sat behind the servants' door and listened in. Seaforth eventually got around to asking about news of Lady Magdalen and what was to be done with her.

Just that day the duke had received word that she was to be shipped back to London for a trial and public hanging. Seaforth said he had business in London and could take her. No sense diverting a navy ship for a prisoner, he'd added.

Seaforth pulled on the rudder handle and laughed. "It was difficult to keep a straight face when Argyll asked me if I'd seen Tullibardine."

"What did you say?" asked Maddie.

"Told him I'd only met the marquis once and he struck me as someone smart enough to know when to stay out of sight."

Aiden slid his hand over Maddie's shoulder and pulled

her close. Closing her eyes, she leaned into him. She loved everything about the man Aiden Murray had become—his musky scent, his strength, his perseverance.

"We're turning west into the Firth of Tay," said Seaforth.

Maddie sat straight and drew a hand to her chest. "How are you going to explain my disappearance?"

"Got that all planned." Reid grinned like a lad. "When we arrive in London I'll file a report saying we hit a squall late at night and the prisoner threw herself overboard. I'll say we searched for an entire day, and then I declared you dead."

"Dead?"

Aiden gave her a squeeze. "You can reappear once we prove your innocence."

"And in the interim?" She should be happy, euphoric, but she couldn't shake the dread or the fear lurking at the back of her mind.

"We'll have to keep you out of sight." Aiden looked between Maddie and Seaforth. "I've sent word for my men to meet me at the Inner Tay Estuary. From there we'll ride north to Blair Castle."

"Is it safe to stay there?"

"Aye, we'll have the protection of the Atholl men."

Maddie's shoulders sagged. "It will be a miracle if I can ever return to Stonehaven again."

"Do you want to resume your duties at the hospital?"

"I've done nothing but pine for home and the hospital ever since I arrived in London."

Aiden's mouth formed a thin line and he looked away.

She blew a long sigh through pursed lips. "I just want to go home."

"Och." He patted her hand. "Things will work out. But you must trust me."

"I do."

He pulled her to her feet. "Have you sailed the Firth of Tay before?"

"Nay." Goodness, the chilly breeze off the water was ice cold.

It was beautiful.

Aiden pointed. "To the south is Ferry-Port on Craig—gateway to the waterway. And see there to the north?"

A city sprawled along the far shore, with grand town houses billowing smoke from their chimneys that an icy wind carried out to sea.

"Aye." Maddie decidedly loved bitter-cold gales. Any weather was preferable to the misery in Edinburgh's jail. She shuddered as the memory of that place lurked in her mind like a black-robed villain.

"That's the burgh of Dundee," Aiden said. "Many a battle was fought there during the time of William Wallace and Robert the Bruce."

Maddie looked from shore to shore. "'Tis nowhere near as wide as the Firth of Forth."

"Nor as long," said Seaforth.

Aiden took Maddie's hand in his warm palm and kissed her fingers. "Do you remember what I said when we were in Coldstream—words I've never uttered to any other woman?"

Butterflies swarmed in her stomach. Oh, heaven of heavens, she wanted to marry Aiden more than anything, but not when she was to be proclaimed dead—not until her name was clear. "I can never forget." This was not a conversation to have in front of the Earl of Seaforth and his men.

Aiden grinned. "Good."

* * *

At the Tay Estuary, Aiden breathed a sigh of relief when the Atholl men stepped from the forest and helped pull the galley onto the sandy bank. Though it had been years, Aiden recognized them all, with Thomas, the captain of the Atholl Regiment, in the lead. A big Highlander at six foot five inches in height, Thom had proved his value to the clan a hundred times over. Any man with Thom's sword guarding his back would be emboldened to ride into hell if necessary.

After Aiden helped Maddie to disembark, they bid good day to Seaforth. Aiden then shook hands with each and every Highlander in the regiment, calling them by name and thanking them for their loyalty and introducing Lady Magdalen Keith.

Thomas bowed, giving her hand a light peck. "The women at Blair Castle are expecting you, m'lady."

She looked to Aiden with a startled expression. "They ken I'm coming?"

"My missive only said there would be a guest in my company." He patted her shoulder. "Not to worry, lass. It was carried by Seaforth's runner."

She drew her fists under her chin, her shoulders hunched as if she feared retribution.

"The horses are waiting just beyond the wood, m'lord," said Thomas.

After smoothing a hand down her back for reassurance, Aiden grasped Maddie's elbow and led her forward. "Excellent. And has there been any word from the duke? Anything about my disappearance?"

"Afraid not, m'lord."

Blast. Aiden would have liked some news from London. Perhaps something to suggest he'd been pardoned—or that he was being pursued. His not knowing anything didn't help circumstances in the least. "I want Atholl spies posted at

Edinburgh Castle. If so much as a word about me or Lady Magdalen is mentioned, they must send word immediately."

"I already have men dispatched, m'lord."

"You're a good soldier, Thom." Aiden didn't want to make Maddie any more uneasy than she already was. He grinned and waggled his eyebrows in an attempt to lighten her burden. "We'll be at Blair Castle by nightfall, and I'll have the chambermaids draw you a soothing bath."

* * *

During the ride north, Maddie continually looked over her shoulder. Though the dragoons thought she was on the Earl of Seaforth's sea galley heading for London, she couldn't shake the feeling that a regiment of government troops would charge out of the woods and attack—or be lying in wait over the crest of the next hill. With trembling fingers she clutched the arisaid tightly beneath her chin to appear as inconspicuous as possible.

"Blair Castle ahead," Thomas shouted.

Tears welled behind her eyelids. As she peered through the trees, her arms went limp. Whitewashed and majestic, Blair had to be one of the stateliest castles in all of Scotland. It wasn't an archaic castle surrounded by a motte and bailey with cannons atop, but the magnificent and sprawling home of a powerful family.

Once they'd dismounted, Aiden led her up the steps and through a relatively modest doorway, given the grandeur of the castle. However, on the inside her impression of stateliness was not dashed in the slightest. Spacious and two stories high, the richly paneled walls in the hall displayed row upon row of antlers.

A matron quietly stepped into the hall.

"Ah, Mrs. Abernathy." Aiden dipped into a brief bow.

The woman clasped her hands and peered at Maddie as if she'd been dragged in by the dogs. "Lord Tullibardine, I cannot tell you enough how delighted I was to receive word you would soon be arriving at Blair." Her voice, however, sounded anything but delighted.

Maddie pressed her hand to her forehead and shifted her gaze to the floorboards. She hadn't seen a looking glass since leaving Coldstream over a month ago—or a comb, or a facecloth, or a decent meal, for that matter.

Aiden grasped Maddie's hand and gave it a gentle kiss. "Allow me to introduce Lady Magdalen. She has suffered unjustly at the hands of certain Atholl enemies. Please see to it you draw her a bath. She needs new clothing, her hair combed and curled. Anything Her Ladyship requests is to be granted. I want you to treat her like a queen. Am I understood?"

The woman curtsied, though she didn't smile. "Very well, m'lord. I've already set the water to warming, knowing how much you like your baths."

"You are a good woman, Mrs. Abernathy."

There came a wee smile. The head housemaid beckoned Maddie with a wave of her hand. "This way. I think you'll be happy with the chamber we've prepared for you, m'lady."

Maddie followed, uncertain if she'd ever again feel safe enough to be happy.

Once inside the chamber, she stood clutching her arms tightly across her midriff while Mrs. Abernathy stoked the fire, drew the drapes, and pointed to the bowl and ewer with soap and drying cloths, and then to the privy closet. Now that Aiden was no longer by her side, Maddie backed against the wall and watched while the servants brought in a tub and filled it with buckets of water. One brought in a dressing gown, new stays, new shift, and a new kirtle and arisaid.

"How did you ken I'd need these things?"

The woman watched the servants officiously. "Lord Tullibardine ordered them in his missive."

Nodding, Maddie tried to smile in gratitude.

Each one regarded her as they walked past. She read pity and disdain in their expressions.

After the last servant left, Mrs. Abernathy faced Maddie, wringing her hands. "You have been through quite an ordeal, have you not?"

A tear rolled down Maddie's cheek as she nodded. Mercy, she felt numb.

"Can I help you into the bath?"

"I'll do it." She wiped her eyes. "Is there a comb?"

"There's one on the table beside the ewer, and a dressing gown over the chair when you're ready."

"Thank you."

Maddie waited until the woman left before she began the process of peeling off the layers of fetid clothing—garments she'd been wearing for ages—garments soaked in blood, sweat, grime, and the putrid things the citizens of Edinburgh had thrown at her.

With each layer stripped came a flood of tears. All her life she'd been an outcast, a pustule on the face of society. She'd tried to be strong. Every single day of her life, she'd tried to be a good person, tried to help others, tried to bear her burden by holding her chin high. But she couldn't do it anymore.

As she sank into the warm water, her stomach convulsed. It felt as if someone had reached down her throat and pulled out her insides. She clutched her fists to her mouth. Her throat burned with her silent wail. Curled into a ball, she huddled in the tub with her mouth barely above the water. She wanted to drown, but the raw memory of being choked with the vinegar-drenched rag prevented her from sinking any farther.

Rocking, wallowing in her wretched misery, Maddie cried and cried and cried, until there was nothing left. Wrung out to the edge of her wits, she sat in the now-cold water and stared at nothing, unable to move.

"Maddie?" Aiden's voice came through the door timbers.

"Go away," she croaked, her voice hoarse and raw.

"You've been in there for hours. Do you not want to eat?"

She shook her head once, too tired to speak again.

When Aiden entered, she closed her eyes and sank deeper into the water, her teeth beginning to chatter.

After staring for a moment, he turned and bolted the door. "I shall wash your hair as you did for me."

She cast her gaze to the water. The mop was so matted, she'd be better off shorn. When she didn't move, he placed his hand on her shoulder and coaxed her forward. Maddie closed her eyes while his fingers massaged up a lather. He seemed to know not to speak. His hands worked quickly yet gently. He washed everything from her head to her toes, and Maddie let him, sitting there like a lump. Once she was clean and rinsed, he dried his hands on a cloth and sat back.

"Are you ready to step out of the tub?"

Though shivering, she couldn't make her body move, still couldn't raise her head or look at his face. "I am unworthy of your care, m'lord," she whispered, blinking back tears.

He took up a cloth and stood. "I beg to differ. Come. I'll dry you and then we shall wrap you in a warm dressing gown and I'll have some broth brought up."

She straightened her spine, but that was all the movement Maddie could muster.

"Och, what did they do to you in there?"

She didn't want to talk about it. "'Tis over."

"You'll catch your death if you remain in that cold water." As the words left his lips, Aiden sank his arms into the bath and hauled her out dripping wet. Ashamed, she crossed her arms over her breasts and leaned into him.

He set her on a chair near the fire and rubbed her dry. "I've seen this with soldiers. They fight like the devil, but once they're back in the mainstream of life, they feel lost."

Maddie nodded, her teeth still chattering. That was how she felt, completely lost. "I'm a misfit."

He shook out the dressing gown and wrapped it around her shoulders. "You are an angel."

"They all stared at me like I was a leper."

"Who?" He pulled her to stand and coaxed her arms through the sleeves, then tied the sash.

"The servants." Her teeth stopped chattering.

Wrapping his arms around her body, he ran his palms up and down her back. "Nay, they just need time to come to know you is all. Not a one kens what you've been through."

She shook her head. "Nay. I'm a freak." Her tongue was tied, jumbled by all the things she wanted to scream out loud. She clutched the robe closed, listening for odd noises as she'd done in prison. What if they came after her? She'd die if they locked her up again. "I'm so afraid."

Aiden led her to a stool and urged her to sit. "I will not *ever* let you out of my grasp again." He picked up the comb and started working the knots out of the ends of her tresses, being meticulous yet gentle. "A piece of me died when the dragoons took you away."

A lot more than a piece of me died after a month in the bowels of hell. She closed her eyes against the fear. "I do not ken if I'll ever be the same again."

"It will take time, my love."

Keeping her eyes closed, she shook her head. "You

cannot hide me here forever. Eventually the queen's men will discover I'm alive."

He smoothed gentle fingers over her hair. "I pray in time you will run through the fields of Blair Atholl with your golden tresses sailing in the wind."

Maddie couldn't imagine ever again running free without a care. She glanced at Aiden in the looking glass. He was a marquis, an important peer of the realm. And what was she? A wretched bastard.

Chapter Thirty-Six

As usual, Aiden found Maddie in the library, sitting with her ankles crossed on the bench built under the recessed window. Over the past sennight it had become the only room she visited aside from her bedchamber. She'd even taken all her meals in her chamber. Though he knew it would take time for her to recover from her ordeal, he worried. She'd become so withdrawn. Her unabashed smile, her quick wit, and her relish for life had faded like an old watercolor.

On the outside she appeared much the same as the Maddie he knew, though thinner. And now when he looked into her eyes, he saw terror lurking there, and he was powerless to replace the darkness with joy.

The few times he'd tried to touch her, she'd been guarded—a pat on the shoulder, a squeeze, gentle lips pressed to her forehead Magdalen permitted. But she shrank away from anything more intimate.

She didn't look up from her book as he approached. Very unlike her as well.

"What are you reading today?" he asked.

She turned the cover so he could see. "*Hamlet*."

"Do you like Shakespeare?"

She shrugged. "I suppose."

There was just enough room at the end of the bench for him to sit. "I used to read here when I was a lad. 'Tis quiet."

"Aye."

Tapping his fingers on his knee, he peered out the window. "It looks as if we might see some snow."

"Oh?" she gave another monosyllabic response while turning a page.

Aiden sighed. "I'd like it if you joined me in the dining hall for your nooning."

She glanced over the top of her book with panic written across her features. Her eyes grew wide like a doe's.

"Please. It is only one floor below. I shall escort you there myself."

Her lashes fluttered. "Would it make you happy?"

"Very."

She closed the book—a good sign. "And you'll accompany me?"

"Indeed I will."

"M'lord." Thomas strode into the library with a missive in his hand. He held it out. "It bears the seal of the Earl of Seaforth."

Maddie looked on while Aiden ran his finger under the red wax. He inclined the parchment toward the sunlight to keep her from seeing its contents, but she leaned closer.

There wasn't much said—he'd met with the Earl Marischal to tell him the bird had flown to Blair—secret code for "Maddie is safe." Her father had started an investigation into the cause of the accident, and the admiral had ordered all troops on land and sea to detain the Marquis of Tullibardine upon first sight and ferry him to London with haste.

Gasping, she covered her mouth.

Aiden took note of the date—the news was only a sennight old. Seaforth had sent it with great haste. He looked to Thomas. "Has there been increased redcoat activity in the nearby townships?"

"Benjamin's retinue rode in but an hour ago. Campbell's dragoons are in Dunkeld asking questions."

"What kind of questions?"

"About your whereabouts." Thom's gaze shifted to Maddie. "And if they've heard anything about Her Ladyship."

She clenched her fists at her temples and cringed. "'Tis my fault. I should have asked Reid to push me over the side of his galley and do away with the pretense of my death."

Aiden tossed the missive on the table and hastened to her. "No, no, no."

"But I have ruined you for certain."

He grasped her hand and squeezed. Hard. "Dammit, woman, I told you before that everything I have done, my every action, has been of my own volition." Standing, he pulled her to her feet and looked to Thom. "Saddle two horses and outfit a pack mule with as much food as it will carry. Send Mrs. Abernathy to Lady Magdalen's chamber to help Her Ladyship pack a traveling bag."

"Straightaway, m'lord." With a bow Thom marched out the door.

Aiden turned to Maddie. "Go to your chamber and collect your things. Can you do this for me? I have one thing I must do before we ride."

"But where are we going? Will they not find us?"

He eyed her intently. "No. They will not."

"I thought we were safe here."

"Aye, the Atholl guard will keep us safe. I just fear for the other souls in my care. I cannot risk retaliation against my clan. In the mountains my men will make use of God's fortress. Now haste ye."

* * *

Maddie set her book aside and watched Aiden march out of the library. How much longer could she expect him to risk his life for her? By all that was holy, the man had already earned a sainthood on her behalf. Standing, she turned until she was peering out the library window. In the distance a mighty river coursed through Atholl lands. The wind blew hard this day, and leaves scattered. But the trees were bare, all except the pines.

No longer could she hide. No longer could she allow Aiden to risk his reputation or his life for her. He was a marquis and heir to one of the greatest dukedoms in all of Britain. He could not throw away his future because he'd fallen in love with a societal misfit.

She lived with the yoke of fear drowning her. She couldn't sleep. Every creak of the old castle made her cower.

She made a snap decision. Then she raced through the passageway, down the stairs, and out the nearest door. A cold wind picked up her skirts and chilled her to the bone. Gaining her bearings, she ran for the river. She sprinted as fast as her legs would move, the icy air burning her lungs.

Maddie would never return to London, and vowed she would never again suffer in Edinburgh's jail. Moreover, she would never ruin Aiden Murray, Marquis of Tullibardine.

Her actions were taken out of love for him. A woman of her rank would only be an anchor around his neck. On and on she ran. Catching her toe on a rock, she stumbled and hit her knee.

Wincing, she looked at the damage. Blast, blood streamed down her shin.

I cannot stop.

With a hiss she swiped the blood away and forced herself to stand. When she took a step, her knee buckled. Clenching her fists, she urged herself to move forward and nearly went cross-eyed from the pain.

I'll allow only a wee moment.

She leaned forward and braced her hands on her thighs, breathing deeply while the pain subsided. At least she'd made it halfway. When she started again, she limped but nonetheless was able to carry on.

It served her right to be injured. Who was she to hide in the great Blair Castle? Tears stung, but she wiped them away and ground her teeth. She'd done enough crying, wallowed in enough of her own misery.

Reaching the bank, she stood and watched the river swirl. Water rushed loud and fast, the force of the wind making white-capped waves.

A hollow void as black as the midnight sky spread through her chest. She buried her face in her hands and asked the Lord for forgiveness. Begged for understanding.

She slipped her foot forward. A splash of freezing water leaped up and soaked her shoe.

Taking one last breath, she stepped into the torrent and dived for the deep rushing water.

Chapter Thirty-Seven

*D*amnation, woman, you will be the death of me!" Aiden shouted above the rush as he hauled Maddie from the river and threw her across his horse's withers. Thank God he'd caught her before she'd sunk past her knees. The water was so cold ice wouldn't melt.

"No!" she screamed. "I can no longer burden you."

The buttocks prone to him were too goddamned tempting. He spanked her with a hard slap. "I will decide when and if you ever become a burden."

She cried out and gave his thigh an ineffectual smack. "But I am ruining your life. I am putting you in danger."

"Damnation," he growled. "How many times do I need to say I am already in deep? We are in this together, whether you like it or not."

"You are being foolish."

"And you're not? Jesus Christ, you want to drown? You want to end your life? Do you have any idea how much that would have cut me to the quick?"

"I—"

"Don't you ever do anything so foolish again." He resisted the urge to spank her once more before he pulled the horse to a stop at the stables. "Promise me!" he shouted so loudly the sound even made him jolt.

"Forgive me," she said softly, but not like a simpering fool. Aye, some of the old Magdalen still lurked somewhere in her heart, and he vowed to find it again.

After helping her slide to her feet, he hopped down and pulled her into his embrace.

"No." She shook her head and pushed his chest, but Aiden was far stronger than this wisp of a lass.

"Can you not see how much I love you?" Grabbing her chin, he glared into her eyes, but when he saw so much fear in them, he hesitated, licking his lips. "I love you. Did you hear me?"

"Aye," she whispered. "I love you more than life."

About to burst, Aiden lowered his lips to hers and kissed. He plied her mouth with everything he was worth, showing her how he could be gentle, how much he adored her, and how reverently he worshiped her.

For the first time since he'd brought her to Blair Castle, Maddie softened like clay in his arms, responding to his kisses. Dear Lord, the lass had been to hell and back. Aiden only prayed this mess would soon be set to rights. With Reid Seaforth and the Earl Marischal working to clear her name, his hopes stretched higher than ever before.

Taking a deep breath, he leaned his forehead against hers. "We must go."

"I'll follow you anywhere...until..."

"Until?"

"You no longer want me."

"Such a day will never come. I swear it."

* * *

When Aiden kissed her, it was as if a spark restarted her heart, as if life began anew, and Maddie's heart swelled while she rode behind him through the thick woods, climbing into the mountains. The air grew cold and she could see her breath, but with the gloves and sealskin cloak Aiden had given her, she was comfortably warm. By dusk they had arrived at a wee cottage nestled alongside a loch. Surrounded by enormous trees, the cottage made a picture bonny enough for a portrait.

After entering the clearing, Maddie pulled her horse to a stop. "There's smoke coming from the chimney."

Aiden gave her a semblance of a smile—rugged, yet still angry. "My men had a half-hour head start."

"Who kens we're here?"

"Thom and Benjamin. I trust both of them with my life." He dismounted, then held his hands up and slowly guided her to her feet. "We'd best go inside."

Trusting him, she nodded and let him take her hand.

"I hope you like it. John and I spent many a summer's day here as lads."

"And no one kens this place is here?"

"Few. Da uses it for hunting. The inner circle of Atholl men have been here, otherwise no. My father is a private man, believes it is important to keep some things hidden from the rest of the world." Aiden opened the door and ushered her inside.

Maddie moved to the center of the cottage and rubbed her hands. Above, an oil lantern cast a golden glow. At one end was a stone hearth with a blackened iron cooking grill and utensils. Before it stood an oblong table with a bench on either side. On one side of the hearth was an old rocking chair, and across from that a stool.

At the far end of the cottage was a box bed, wide enough for two. Her heart fluttered as she moved toward it, her feet skimming a dirt floor. Feeling warm for the first time in months, she unfastened her cloak and let it slip across one arm. "'Tis homey."

"I ken it is rustic as the Highlands. Nothing like the castle, but—"

"I like it better than the castle. I have no idea why, but I feel safer here."

He took her cloak and tossed it atop the box bed along with his. Then he pulled her into his arms. "There's one more thing we must do before I can let the men return to Blair Atholl."

Her heart fluttered like butterfly wings. "Oh? And what is that?"

"I aim to marry you."

"Here?"

Grinning from ear to ear, he couldn't have looked more like an angel if he'd tried. "If you'll have me."

She peered around him and saw no one. "Do you mean to say Thomas is a priest?"

"Nay. I want to marry you in the Highland way. The way of our ancestors."

Gooseflesh pebbled across her skin—everything felt surreal. "Now?"

"Aye." His eyes twinkled as, taking her hand, he knelt. "Lady Magdalen Keith, you would make me the happiest man in all of Christendom if you would do me the honor of being my wife."

A wee tear dribbled down her cheek. True, she didn't want to cry anymore, but she'd make an exception this once.

"What say you, my love?"

"I say yes." She strengthened her grip on his hands. "You are finer to me than anything on this earth, and if it will make you happy to have my hand, then I willingly give it."

It didn't take long for Aiden to fetch the two Atholl men who had made the cottage ever so cozy for their arrival. Maddie greeted them both with a warm smile, the empty chasm in her chest all but gone. "Thank you for taking care of us. It meant ever so much to arrive at this delightful cottage and have it warmed by the fire."

"Much obliged, m'lady," said Thom, holding up a leather thong.

"A strip of leather?" asked Aiden.

The old guard shrugged. "Couldn't find a bit of ribbon anywhere. Sorry."

"Very well then. Carry on."

Benjamin raised a knife. "Give us your hands." First he made a wee incision in Aiden's palm, then he took Maddie's and did the same. It bit, but she didn't make a sound. Benjamin pressed their palms together, then Thom stepped forward and wound the thong around their hands. "By binding your hands, the blood coursing through Lord Tullibardine combines with that of Lady Magdalen. Once your blood is merged, you will no longer be one man and one woman, but a couple. Once your blood commingles, you, Lord Tullibardine, will be a part of Lady Magdalen, and Her Ladyship a part of His Lordship. You will be bound in the eyes of the Highlands, in the eyes of your ancestors, and in the eyes of God Almighty."

"Let it be done," Aiden said, gazing into her eyes—those boyish dimples making her stomach leap. "I will love you until I take my last breath on this earth."

Maddie smiled, her heart full and heavy with love, shoving aside the chasm that had tormented her. "And I shall love you with every fiber of my being throughout eternity."

The wound on her palm pulsed with life, Aiden's strong blood mixing with hers. Though earlier that day she had been filled with despair, this was the happiest moment in her life. At last the man she'd loved for years had pledged his adoration in such a way that no one could repeal it.

As Thom removed the leather binding, Aiden joined his lips with Maddie's. She barely heard the door shut as the two loyal guards took their leave. Melting into the warmth and tenderness of his kiss, Maddie could have been floating on air.

"Are you hungry?"

"Oddly, no."

He grinned—dimples—handsome as a devil. "Then let me take you to heaven."

Aiden slowly removed every last stitch of her clothing. Then, standing very still, he held his arms out while Maddie unpinned his plaid, loosened his belt, and let his kilt fall to the ground. She bent to remove his hose and his shoes, but before she straightened he'd already whipped his shirt over his head.

Together they climbed into the box bed and sealed their love with a night of endless passion, of worship, taking pleasure in the beauty of their bodies and reveling in the strength of their bond.

While she made love to Aiden, Maddie didn't think about the future or the past. All that existed was Aiden, a man with whom she'd fallen in love and a man with whom she would live out the rest of her days.

Chapter Thirty-Eight

*I*t didn't take much for Aiden and Maddie to settle into a routine. He should have brought her to the shieling in the first place. Had he known the depth of her despair, he wouldn't have hesitated. Fortunately, the isolated cottage was exactly what she needed to heal. The entire world was shut out. He hunted, fished, and set traps, and together they prepared their own meals, which wasn't difficult—not even for a man who had grown up surrounded by servants.

He often thought about staying there forever.

Perhaps they could, especially if Thom brought oats, leavening, and flour now and again.

He saw no reason to leave anytime soon, and hadn't even broached the subject with Maddie.

A fortnight had passed when they sat at the table about to dig into a meal of lake trout and oatcakes. Beyond the cottage the sound of horses neared.

Maddie glanced up, a horrible look of terror filling her eyes for the first time since they'd arrived.

Aiden headed for the musket he kept loaded by the door.

"Hide in the bed." Moving to the window, he lifted the curtain and peeked out. Sure enough, horses moved through the foliage. Opening the window ever so slightly, he cocked his weapon and slid it through the gap.

"Hello the cottage," hollered a voice Aiden could never mistake.

Quickly he removed the musket. "'Tis my da."

"His Grace?" Maddie asked, as if she couldn't believe the Duke of Atholl would ever come calling at such a rustic outpost.

She moved beside him as Aiden threw open the door. Not only had Da brought a dozen men with him, the Earl Marischal rode in as well.

And they weren't smiling.

Aiden braced himself for a battle of words. "Welcome, m'lords."

"My God, Son, do you have any idea what this looks like, hiding out in the Highlands with a fugitive?"

"Former fugitive," said the earl. His face cracked a wee smile, though he gave his daughter a pointed look. "Maddie, are you well?"

She curtsied. "I'm quite well, thank you."

The duke dismounted. "I think we need to have a word in private, Son."

Aiden didn't budge. "Anything you have to say to me can be uttered in front of my wife."

The Earl Marischal beamed. "Good on you, lad."

But Da's eyes bugged as he gripped his fist over his heart. "I beg your pardon? Do not tell me you've gone off and married a bastard?"

Sliding his arm over Maddie's shoulders, Aiden pulled her tight to his body. "I have, and I'll thank you for never referring to Her Ladyship thusly again."

The earl slapped His Grace on the back. "That means our families are allies, John. That should make the queen happy."

The duke mumbled a string of curses under his breath.

"We were about to have our nooning. Will you join us?" Maddie asked.

"Have you any whisky?" His Grace gave her a bull-headed look as he marched through the door.

"What news of court?" Aiden asked.

"With Lord Seaforth's help, we proved that the chandelier fell of its own volition. The chain links were worn right through," said the earl.

"Aye, but it practically took an act of Parliament to convince the queen to drop the charges and reinstate your title." The duke climbed onto the bench. "Bloody ungrateful lad loses his title days after earning it, then runs off and elopes with a ba—"

Aiden sank his fingers into his father's shoulder. "Pardon me?"

"Runs off with a lady born out of—"

Aiden pounded his knuckles on the table. "*Lady* will do."

The duke cleared his throat and swiped an oatcake from the plate. "Ye ken Mother will have one of her spells."

Aiden waited until Maddie and her father sat, then took the seat beside Da. "Ma will be fine—and happier than a lark when bairns come."

The two men looked to Maddie. "Are you...?"

"Not that I know of." She turned redder than an apple. "So what of Lady Saxonhurst? Was she implicated in the investigation at all?"

The earl shook his head. "That woman feels it is her duty to cause a stir at her every opportunity."

"Unbelievable," said Aiden. "I would have thought she had some hand in it."

"Well, the whole debacle was an accident, plain and simple." The duke bit into his oatcake. "I wanted you to ken the news and to take you back to Blair Atholl before the snow sets in for winter."

"I think we might spend the winter here." Maddie's blues flashed with mischief. "What say you, Aiden?"

He mulled it over. "It was the only option a few moments ago, but in a month's time, the snow will be up to the rafters."

The Earl Marischal wrapped his arm around Maddie's shoulders. "Besides, your mother is awaiting you at the castle."

Maddie's eyes grew round as silver coins. "I beg your pardon?"

He gave her shoulder a pat. "I figured it was about time I told you. Miss Agnes is your mother. She was my first love—my only love, really. But unlike you, I couldn't marry her because she is a commoner."

A chuckle pealed through Aiden's lips. "I always thought you pair looked like kin."

"They do." The earl poured himself a cup of water. "I do not think I will ever tire of looking at mother and daughter when they stand together."

Aiden raised his cup. "I ken I'll never tire of gazing upon my Maddie. She has won my heart forever."

the standard of Mar and the Che

uprising. He was also one o

Prince Charlie, op

at Saint-Nazaire

ognized by the

continued

until h

Thank you for joining me for *The Highland Commander*. This was a deliciously fun story to write, and I enjoyed taking my Scottish characters to eighteenth-century London. One of the interesting facts in the book was the incorporation of the "Screw Plot": In 1708, a chandelier fell and was assumed to be a Whig assassination attempt on the life of Queen Anne. Because the time period was close and the scandal too tempting to expand on, I felt it added a bit of spice to the story when the heroine, Maddie, was blamed for a similar incident and ended up running for her life.

Aiden's character was loosely based on William Murray, Marquis of Tullibardine (1689–1746). Murray matriculated at St Andrews University in 1706. In 1707 he entered the service of the Royal Navy as an officer and in 1709 became the Marquis of Tullibardine after the death of his brother, John, who was killed in action in the battle of Malplaquet.

The House of Atholl was divided over the rebellion and William opposed his father, the Duke of Atholl, who sided with the government. Tullibardine was one of the first to join

valier in the 1715 Jacobite
the seven followers of Bonny
June 22, 1745, embarked with him
the Loire. Lord Tullibardine was rec-
acobites as the rightful Duke of Atholl and
o be a prominent figure for the Jacobite cause
s death in 1746.

The marquis did not marry, making it convenient for me to introduce the fictitious and illegitimate daughter of the Earl Marischal of Scotland, Magdalen Keith. Although William Murray, Marquis of Tullibardine, never married, such a state of affairs wasn't the happy ending Aiden deserved.

Also of note, because I adore the grandeur of the Banqueting House at Whitehall and wanted to use the Whitehall location in the London scenes, I stretched the timeline a bit. In 1698, a fire destroyed much of the Palace of Whitehall, though the Banqueting House still survives to this day.

The Earl of Seaforth promised a dying
friend to look after his daughter.
But when his new ward turns out to
be a beautiful young woman, the earl
finds the only thing that needs
guarding is his heart...

Keep reading for a preview of

THE HIGHLAND
GUARDIAN

Chapter One

The North Sea, off the coast of England, 14 May 1711

*T*he gale blew through the English Channel like a savage rogue, making foam gush and spray from the sea's white-capped swells. When, finally, the Earl of Seaforth's sea galley sailed past the Thames estuary, Reid MacKenzie blew out a long breath, having navigated the treacherous crossing without incident. But relief was short-lived. In his wake the Royal Navy's racing galleon gained speed, creeping closer with every league.

Nicholas Kennet lowered his spyglass. "They're following us, I've no doubt now."

"Stay the course," bellowed Reid. He wasn't only an earl, he was captain of his eighteen-oar, single-masted galley, and he'd dive to Davy Jones's locker before he allowed one of the queen's vessels to bully him into dropping anchor and submitting to an inspection. These were precarious times, and a man had to keep his opinions secret lest he be misunderstood.

"Someone must have tipped them off in Calais," said Kennet. The Englishman had proved loyal to the Jacobite cause, and he'd become a friend and confidant over the past several months.

"Even if they did, they have nothing on us."

"Except we paid a visit to King James."

"What of it?" Reaching inside his cloak, Reid smoothed his fingers atop the leather-wrapped missive he carried in his doublet. A missive for those loyal to *the cause*. "Many a nobleman has traveled to France to meet with His Highness."

Not a seafaring man, Mr. Kennet turned a ripe shade of green. He was a wealthy coal miner from Coxhoe in the northeast of England and had proved his loyalty with bequests of coin. "But none were carrying a message as incriminating as ours."

The man hadn't lied. After enduring nine years of Anne's rule, the Jacobites had made an ironclad plea to James Francis Edward Stuart, the rightful heir to the crown. An appeal Reid had been certain the prince wouldn't refuse. With her failing health, Anne's days were numbered, and it was imperative to gain her half brother's agreement to take the necessary measures to ensure his succession to the throne. Reid had been confident James would accept a temporary shift to the Protestant faith.

But he'd been wrong.

"The *Royal Buckingham* approaching portside, m'lord," said Dunn MacRae, chieftain of his clan and Reid's most trusted ally.

"Damnation." Reid pulled out his spyglass and trained it on the upper deck of the navy ship. A red-coated buffoon wearing a feathered tricorn hat dashed aft, flailing his arms.

"Shall we heave to?" asked Dunn.

"God, no. That would only make us appear guilty." He

snapped his glass closed and addressed his crew. "Stay the course. Maintain present speed. Let the bastards sail past and find someone else to chase. We're nae pirates, and we've done nothing wrong." *Aside from carry a missive calling the Jacobite clans to prepare for the succession.*

"Is that why you're not flying your pennant, m'lord?" asked Kennet.

Reid leered out of the corner of his eye while his mouth twitched. "No use broadcasting I've paid a visit to France." He pointed to the navy ship. "Given a good wind, that galleon will beat us every time, but she cannot sail up rivers. If we can keep her guessing until we reach the estuary of the River Tees, I'll have you sitting by home's hearth before the witching hour."

"Seaforth," said Dunn MacRae, his voice steady—too steady. "She's opened gunport one."

Reid didn't need his spyglass to make out the black cannon pushing through the open port like a deadly dragon. He swiped a hand across his mouth. "How near are we to the Tees?"

"Two leagues. I can see Tees Bay from here, m'lord."

"Tack west. Aim the bow for the shallows."

"Aye, Captain!" bellowed every man aboard the galley as the oarsmen increased their pace. Reid might be an earl when his feet were on land, but at sea his clansmen called him Captain.

"Surely they will not fire." A gust of wind blew Nicholas's hat and periwig to the timbers, and he scrambled over a bench to retrieve them.

Dunn pulled on the rudder while the boom swung across the hull, shifting the single sail. Ignoring the Englishman's question, Reid watched the galleon as it sailed alongside them. "They'll most likely launch a warning shot across our bow."

"Dear God. This is preposterous," said Nicholas, shoving his wig and hat low on his brow. "If I hadn't witnessed it myself, I never would have believed Her Majesty capable of such piracy."

The flicker of a torch flashed through the gunport. "You'd best believe it, my friend." Reid turned with a scowl. "Bear down on your oars, lads!"

The flash burst from the gunport and flared bright before the sound of the cannon blast boomed through the air. Reid's skin crawled at the high-pitched whistle from the approaching cannonball. He ducked below the hull, praying the British ship had set her sights correctly for a warning shot. But as the whistling missile neared, hope became but a wayward prayer hurtling through the wind.

With his next breath, the bow of his ship splintered into a thousand shards. The blast boomed with a thunderous roar of water that gushed into the hull, instantly soaking the men and pulling them into the frigid whitecaps.

"Swim for your lives!" Reid yelled as he climbed atop the rowing bench. Casting his cloak aside, he prepared to plunge into the icy swells of the North Sea.

"Help!" Nicholas shouted, his voice strained.

As he took a quick glance over his shoulder, Reid's blood turned cold. Dear God, a spike of wood at least a foot long protruded from Nicholas Kennet's chest.

"Jesu." Reid waded through the rushing water of his sinking ship and hefted his friend into his arms. "Hang on. Shore's in sight. I'll have you to safety in no time."

Strengthening his grip, the Earl of Seaforth clenched his teeth and leaped into the sea. He was engulfed by biting salt water attacking him like a thousand knives, and air whooshed from his lungs. The current dragged him downward, threatening to tug Nicholas from his grasp. Bearing down with a surge of power, Reid kicked fiercely, battling the undertow, his lungs screaming for blessed air.

If the sea claimed him this day, it would not be without a fight. Ever since he'd faced off against the Marquis of Tullibardine and lost, Reid MacKenzie had not allowed a day to pass without pushing himself to gain more strength. To better himself.

His head broke through, a desperate breath filling his lungs. Arching his back, he shifted his grip under Nicholas's arms to ensure the man could breathe as well.

The shore appeared to be miles away as a wave lapped over Reid's head and drew him under. But he kicked his legs and clutched tight his comrade's chest, his arm holding fast just above the spike. The freezing water sapped his strength, but he clenched his teeth and refused to stop. Swimming on his back with Nicholas secured against his chest, Reid pumped his legs, propelling them toward the shore.

Behind, his ship was gone, sunk into the North Sea's merciless depths without a trace. The galleon had heaved to as if the men on deck laughed at the poor Highland sops who fought to reach the shore before the sea swallowed them as well.

With his next breath Reid looked to the coast as his teeth chattered uncontrollably. It was nearer now, and hope infused his muscles with renewed power. But when the next thundering wave broke over their heads, the taunting sea gave Reid no choice but to clutch his arms tightly around Nicholas and pray to God they'd bob to the surface before the air in his lungs expired.

The next thunderous wave swept them up and spit them out onto the sandy beach like a pair of dead mackerel. Salt water blew through Reid's nose while he staggered onto the shore. Coughing and sputtering, he dragged Nicholas in his wake.

"Good God," Dunn hollered, running up beside him to lend a hand. Once clear of the surf, they rested Nicholas on the sand.

Sucking in gasps of air, Reid dropped to his knees and placed his hand on his comrade's forehead. "We'll have ye set to rights in no time, mate."

Dunn caught his eye, thinned his lips, and gave a shake of his head.

The stake protruding from the man's chest was akin to a bayonet.

"Please," muttered Nicholas, his voice weak. "Swear you will care for my daughter."

Reid's gut clenched. "Daughter?" *Shite.*

"She's alone—her mother gone."

"Are there any other heirs?"

"None."

"Christ." The last thing Reid needed was a ward.

Nicholas gasped and clutched Reid's cravat. "Swear it."

He had no choice. "I give you my word. The lass will be cared for."

As if a great weight had been lifted from his chest, Nicholas Kennet released his last breath with an eerie sigh that faded into the rush of the surf.

"He's dead," said Dunn, now surrounded by men drenched and shivering.

Reid moved his hand to the man's nose and felt not a thing. Suppressing his ire, he closed Nicholas's eyelids. Such a pity. And for naught. He glanced to the galleon, looming in the deep water. Through the shroud of early dusk, the wind again filled the sail as the naval ship resumed its course and got under way. "Is the crew accounted for?"

"Aye," said Graham MacKenzie, lieutenant and navigator. "Davy has a gash on his arm, but no other casualties."

"Thank God for that." Reid stood and looked to the town of Hartlepool. "Quickly. The tower of a church stands yonder. We'll take the body there for a proper burial."

The MacRae chieftain gave a somber nod. "Then you'd best find something to occupy his daughter. You're far too important to *the cause* to waste your time playacting at guardian."

Reid ground his back molars. Dunn was right. He needed to think of some way to see to the heiress's maintenance without becoming involved. And fast.

* * *

The brass knocker on the Coxhoe House door hung from a lion's mouth. Reid had used it once before, but during that visit he hadn't been introduced to Kennet's daughter. They'd been in too much of a hurry to sail across the Channel for their meeting with the exiled king.

Exhausted and sore from sleeping in a copse of trees to elude capture, he clenched his fist before knocking. With the missive from King James still secured in his doublet, the last thing he needed at the moment was to take on the role of guardian of a spoiled heiress. But it couldn't be helped.

"Go on. Have it over with," said Dunn from behind, as if speaking Reid's conscience.

Fixing a somber frown in place, he gave the knocker three good raps. "Do you recall the butler's name?" Reid whispered.

"Gerald."

The door slowly opened with an interminable screech. The gaunt butler regarded them, eyes peering over a pair of round spectacles. "M'lord?" He drew his graying eyebrows together as he craned his neck and looked beyond the men. "This is a surprise."

"Good morrow, sir." Reid took in a deep breath. "I bring grave news."

The butler drew a hand over his heart as his face blanched. "Do not tell me Mr. Kennet..."

"He perished off the coast of Hartlepool. One of Her Majesty's galleons attempted to fire a cannonball over our bow."

"But the bastards sank His Lordship's sea galley," finished Dunn.

"Dear God." Gerald stumbled backward and ushered them into the entry. "Forgive me. I need a moment to compose my person."

"Of course." Reid and Dunn stood aside while the old man closed the door and hung his head, clearly distraught.

Gerald slowly drew a hand down his face, and after a few deep breaths and gasps, he addressed them. "The pair of you look like you've been through the wars."

Reid glanced to his doublet, shirt, and kilt; matted by salt water, peppered with sand and dirt, he looked a fright. But nothing could be done about that now. "We were forced to swim for our lives. After reaching the shore, we took Mr. Kennet's body to Saint Hildas for burial, then slept in a copse of trees."

Gerald glanced eastward. "Do you think they're after you?"

Reid shrugged. "They've nothing on us. The galleon even continued on her voyage. They may have been trying to implicate me for some misdeed, though I have far more grounds upon which to seek damages than they have to accuse me of a traitorous plot." He didn't utter the word *Jacobite*—strange walls had a way of hearing things they shouldn't, especially in England.

"I reckon they kent it as well," said Dunn.

The butler nodded, his face drawn.

MacRae gave Reid a nudge.

Dash it, Reid knew his task was not yet finished, not by half. "Forgive me, I ken you must be sorely smote by this news, however 'tis my duty to inform you that Nicholas Kennet's dying wish was for me to see to his daughter's maintenance."

"Aye," agreed Dunn. "The earl vowed a sacred oath."

"You, my lord?" Gerald scratched his chin, the furrow between his brows growing deeper. "I might have thought Mr. Kennet would have appointed someone a bit older."

Swiping a bit of sand off his sleeve, Reid gave the man a scowl. Regardless of his age, the oath he'd sworn was an inconvenience, but duty was duty. "Och, if only the Earl Marischal of Scotland had been there, rather than me."

The butler cringed. "Are you not up to the task, my lord?"

Reid guffawed and grasped his salt-encrusted lapels. Hell, he was one of the wealthiest, hardiest men in Scotland, and an elderly butler was questioning him? "Of course I'm up to the task. I'm the Earl of Seaforth, for God's sake. I gave my word, and once given, I am honor bound. Now bring the wee lassie to me. I must notify her of this unfortunate turn of events forthwith."

"Straightaway, my lord." Gerald started off, but stopped before he reached the stairs. "Perhaps it would be best if she heard the news from me first. After all, I have known Miss Audrey since the day she came into the world."

Reid arched his eyebrows at Dunn. It certainly would make his lot easier if he didn't have to tell a child she was now an orphan. "If you think that's best, then I shall allow it."

Bowing, the butler gestured to a pair of double doors.

"Thank you, my lord. If you gentlemen would kindly make yourselves comfortable in the parlor, I shall have refreshment brought to you straightaway."

"Very well, but I should like to speak to Miss Audrey as soon as she is able to receive me." Since the butler had referred to the lass in the familiar, Reid figured it was best if he started doing so at once. After all, a guardian should be on a first-name basis with his ward.

Dismissing Gerald with a bow of his head, he led Dunn into the parlor. Decorated with Parisian plasterwork, the hearth was the centerpiece, surrounded by an ornate relief depicting vines and leaves, and intermixed were rose-painted porcelain plates. The gilded chairs' seats, arms, and backs were embroidered with countryside scenes. Reid chose the largest, with a high back, near the fire. Dunn took a seat on the other side, crossing his feet at the ankles.

Weariness caught up with Reid as he brushed the sand off his doublet. He needed a meal, a bath, and a bed, in that order.

"Have you given any thought as to what you'll do with the lass?"

Reid's gut twisted into a knot. He didn't have many options, and he most certainly didn't need a child disrupting order at Brahan Castle—especially when he was away more often than not. "Boarding school, of course."

"Brilliant. I should have thought of that."

It wasn't brilliant, though that was where most heiresses went for finishing in this day and age.

The tension clamping Reid's shoulders had almost eased when a high-pitched scream resounded above stairs. The sound wasn't that of a young child, but that of a feral animal in deathly agony. Not only did the knots in his shoulders stab him with relentless fury, a lump of lead sank to his toes. If only he were on the trail back to Brahan Castle. If only he were anywhere but in the Kennet parlor. Upset females were in no way his forte. As a matter of fact, he'd made a practice of heading the other way when a female grew distraught.

Dear God, what have I got myself into?

About the Author

Amy Jarecki is a descendant of an ancient Lowland clan and she adores Scotland. Though she now resides in southwest Utah, she received her MBA from Heriot-Watt University in Edinburgh. Winning multiple writing awards, she found her niche in the genre of Scottish historical romance. Amy writes steamy edge-of-your-seat action adventures with rugged men and fascinating women who weave their paths through the brutal eras of centuries past. She loves hearing from her readers and can be contacted through her website at AmyJarecki.com.

Fall in Love with Forever Romance

PRIMROSE LANE
By Debbie Mason

"[The Harmony Harbor series is] heartfelt and delightful!"
—RaeAnne Thayne, *New York Times* bestselling author

Finn Gallagher returns for a visit to Harmony Harbor only to find that the town's matchmakers have other plans. Because it's high time that wedding planner Olivia Davenport gets to plan her own nuptials. And finding true love is the best reason of all for Finn to move home for good.

Fall in Love with Forever Romance

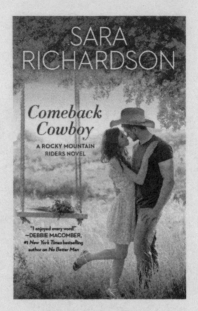

COMEBACK COWBOY
By Sara Richardson

In the *New York Times* bestselling tradition of Jennifer Ryan and
Maisey Yates comes the second book in Sara Richardson's Rocky
Mountain Riders series. When Naomi's high school sweetheart comes
riding back to town, this self-sufficient single mom feels something she
hasn't felt in years: a red-hot unbridled need for the handsome cowboy
who left her behind. As much as Naomi's tried, a woman never forgets
her first cowboy...

Fall in Love with Forever Romance

ON THE PLUS SIDE
By Alison Bliss

Thanks to her bangin' curves, Valerie Carmichael has always turned heads—with the exception of seriously sexy Logan Mathis. But Valerie is determined to get Logan's attention, even if it means telling a teeny little lie to get a job at his bar...Logan can't remember a time when Valerie didn't fuel all his hottest fantasies. Now the she-devil is working behind his bar and tempting him every damn night. But no one warned them that sometimes the smallest secrets have the biggest consequences...

Fall in Love with Forever Romance

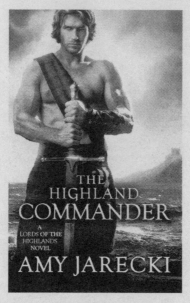

THE HIGHLAND COMMANDER
By Amy Jarecki

As the illegitimate daughter of a Scottish earl, Lady Magdalen Keith is not usually one to partake in lavish masquerade balls. Yet one officer sweeps her off her feet with dashing good looks that cannot be disguised by a mere mask...Navy lieutenant Aiden Murray has spent too many months at sea to be immune to this lovely beauty. But when he discovers Maddie's true identity—and learns that her father is accused of treason—will the brawny Scot risk his life to follow his heart?